THUNDER ON THE MOOR

Andrea Matthews

Inez M. Foster

Thunder on the Moor

This is a work of fiction. All characters and events in this publication,
other than those clearly in the public domain,
are products of the author's imagination or are used fictitiously
and are not to be construed as real. Any resemblance to
real persons, living or dead, is purely coincidental.

Cover designed by Jenny Quinlan, Historical Fiction Book Covers

ISBN 978-1-7333375-0-2

Inez M. Foster
New York

www.andrea-matthews.com

To my sons, who always inspire me

The Armstrongs of Eskdale

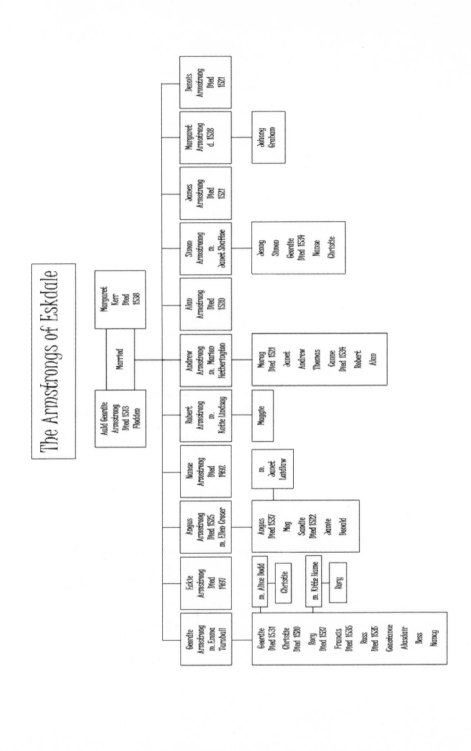

The Fosters of Tyndale

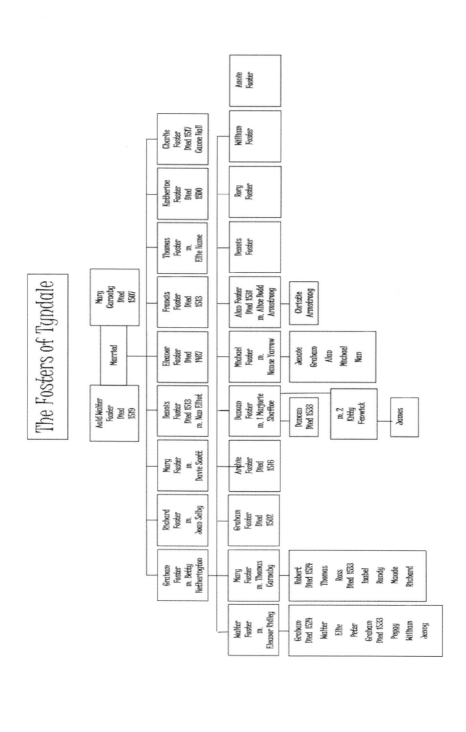

Auld Watter Foster Died 1519 — Married — Mary Gormoleg Died 1507

Children:
- Graham Foster m. Betty Hetherington
- Richard Foster m. Joan Selby
- Mary Foster m. Davie Scott
- Dennis Foster Died 1513 m. Nan Elliot
- Eleanor Foster Died 1487
- Francis Foster Died 1513
- Thomas Foster m. Effie Hume
- Katherine Foster Died 1500
- Charlie Foster Died 1517 Ganne Hall

Next generation:
- William Foster
- Rory Foster
- Dennis Foster
- Alan Foster Died 1531 m. Alice Dodd Armstrong
- Michael Foster m. Nance Yarrow
- Bernard Foster m. 1 Marjorie Sheffiel
- Archie Foster Died 1516
- Graham Foster Died 1502
- Mary Foster m. Thomas Gormoleg
- Watter Foster m. Eleanor Ridley

Children of Alan Foster:
- Christie Armstrong

Children of Michael Foster:
- Jennie Graham
- Alan
- Michael
- Nan

Children of Bernard Foster:
- Duncan Died 1533
- m. 2 Kitty Fenwick
- James

Children of Mary Foster m. Thomas Gormoleg:
- Robert Died 1524
- Thomas
- Ross Died 1533
- Isabel
- Randy
- Maude
- Richard

Children of Watter Foster m. Eleanor Ridley:
- Graham Died 1524
- Watter
- Effie
- Peter
- Graham Died 1533
- Peggy
- William
- Jenny

PROLOGUE

Scottish Border - 1513

Robert Armstrong dug his spurs deep into the sides of his chestnut pony. Twilight was coming on fast, and the thickening mist dampened his azure cap as he reached the crest of the moss-covered fell. It had been a hard ride, but victory was at last within his grasp. There below him, heading for the distant marsh grass, rode the mysterious Englishman who'd been tracking his every move for nigh on to a fortnight.

The hint of a smile crossed Robert's lips, and he turned sharply, making his way down the hill toward the tree line. The Englishman would soon realize he was no longer the hunter, but the quarry. Skirting a small copse of pine trees, Robert wound his way among the shadows, choosing his position wisely.

He'd hunted men before, usually with his kinsmen, but today he rode alone. Until he knew the reason for the Englishman's sudden interest in him, he saw no need to involve his family. Of course, that didn't mean he intended on taking any foolish chances either. If the situation was about to come to a head, he wanted to hold the upper hand. Doing that would require all the stealth his father had taught him.

****

Edward Foster made his way through the trees, casting a quick glance over his shoulder. He was supposed to be following the Scot, not the other way around. When did everything go so wrong?

He cleared the pine grove and started down toward the river below, stopping for a moment to scan the hillside one more time. Where was the sneaky bugger? Disgusted with himself, he spurred his horse forward, but out of nowhere, an arrow shot across his path. It lodged into a tree, well clear of him, but split a branch overhead, causing his mount to spook and stumble.

Edward scrambled from under his fallen steed, all too aware the Scot had turned the tables on him. He rose to his feet, swatting the dirt from his breeches and taking account of the immediate damage. No doubt his entire body would ache the next day, but other than ripping his left sleeve and somehow managing to dislodge one of his spurs, he appeared to be in one piece.

Anxious to be on his way, he reached for his horse, relieved to see it too was none the worse for wear. The animal clearly thought otherwise, for Edward had no sooner taken hold of the reins than the creature bolted and took off in the opposite direction, knocking him from his feet in the process.

"Son of a . . . Bloody nagg." Edward slid down the steep bank, searching in vain for something to grab on to, but instead lost his footing and tumbled headfirst into the thick marshy grass along the burn. He jumped up, his dagger drawn, certain he was about to lose his head, but the Scot was nowhere in sight.

Torn between relief and annoyance, he took a deep breath, wiping the mud from his face before making his way toward the shallow burn. Over the past few weeks, he'd come to know the rugged young man who only moments before had chased him down the heather-strewn knoll, and he felt sure Robert hadn't given up. He lurked out there somewhere, hidden in the rising haze, watching in silence, waiting to make his move.

Edward's heart raced against his leather jack as he looked out across the windswept dale, searching the darkening horizon, but not even a whaup flew from its nest. He had just sheathed his dagger when, without warning, something tickled his ear, and he spun around, plunging himself backwards into the cold water. How fragrant the ivory blossoms smelled, but the mud that clung to his clothes was not so sweet.

Pulling himself back on solid ground, he cursed in frustration and swatted at the air around him. "Damn! I've lost him now for sure. Stinking midges!"

Cold and disheveled, Edward brushed himself off as best he could and climbed back up the slippery bank to a lea just west of where he'd fallen. There, behind the stump of an ancient tree, he uncovered the ragged canvas bag he'd stowed the day before. Dusty and worn, it had seen far better days, but it served its purpose. He pulled out a chunk of salted beef, slumped down against a weathered birch, and gnawing off a good-sized piece, began to chew.

With a weary sigh, he closed his eyes, pressing his fingers against the lids, too tired to concern himself any longer with the whereabouts of one elusive Scot. "Must be out of my bloody mind." He bit off another piece of jerky, still muttering to himself. "Follow him indeed. What was I playing at?" After taking another bite, he wiped his mouth. "Who do I blasted think I am, James Bond?"

Maybe he should go home and forget about the whole excursion. After all, no one would ever believe him without proof, and the way things were going, his chances of that were slim.

After a moment, he opened his eyes, blinking against the last wisps of daylight. The sun sat low on the horizon, and a cool breeze whipped across the moor, causing the evening air to cut through the damp leather of his quilted jack. Instinct prompted him to pull his plaid close around his neck, and he rummaged through his bag for the piece of flint he'd thrown inside. He'd just managed to get a small fire going when a sharp blade slipped menacingly beneath his chin.

"What clan be ye from, man?" the Scot asked with a coldness that rivaled the bog winds. He inched his way around until he stood before Edward, his sword shifting no more than a fraction as he did so.

Edward froze, the auburn-haired Scot's expression brooking nothing less. Though not extremely large, the man was broad, with a strong arm and riveting gaze. Without a doubt, he knew his weapon well, and Edward flinched when the blade came to rest precariously above the blue scarf that covered his neck.

"Speak now, afore ye canna speak at all," the Scot said, his words no more than a hiss.

Edward didn't dare move. He hardly dared breath for fear of causing the sharpened blade to cut into his bare flesh. "The Fosters . . . of Bewcastle."

"Liar!" The word came out in a growl, the Scot's eyes narrowing to catlike slits. "I ought cut yer throat right here and now. D'ye think me a fool?"

"No! Of course not." Edward swallowed hard, knowing at any moment his head might be joining his boots. "All right! I'm not from Bewcastle, 'tis true." The steel edge pressed ever firmer beneath his chin and sweat began to form on his brow. Without even taking another breath, he spat out the words, "But I *am* a Foster."

"Ye're an outlander and noucht more. Perhaps Auld Walt would like to ken who's been claiming his name. Or better still, I'll bring him yer head, so he can see for himself."

"No, wait! I told you, you are right. I am an outlander, from Lancaster, to be exact. I don't know how or when my family moved down there. They just did. Ask the Fosters, if you like. Auld Walt will tell you the same."

"Aye, perhaps so, and that would explain yer daft way of speaking and all." Robert sat down on the moss-covered stump, his head tilted to the side. "Or mayhap ye're noucht more than a spy for yer king."

"I'd make a poor one, then, wouldn't I?"

Robert grunted a half laugh. "Aye, ye would that. All right, then, why have ye been following me these last few days, Foster of Lancaster? Speak true or die this night."

Edward coughed to clear his throat, praying his trembling vocal cords wouldn't betray him. "I swore an oath to a lady, a beautiful one, and I mean to keep it."

"And what has that oath to do with me?"

"'Tis about a box," Edward said, "a jeweled box. May I show you, then?"

Robert lowered his sword, using it to point toward the sack. "Aye, so long as 'tis no' some weapon, for keep in mind ye wouldna even clear the sack afore yer heid hit the ground."

"I wouldn't think of it." Edward forced a smile to his lips and pulled the small chest from the bag. "She said it belonged to an Armstrong lad up this way, and if I would swear to return it . . ." He bit his lip and lifted his shoulder in a shrug. "Well, she promised she would lay with me that night."

"And did she, then?" Robert asked with a roguish grin.

Edward ducked his head, pretending the question embarrassed him. "Indeed she did, but when I woke, she'd already gone, leaving me no indication as to his name. Now I'm bound by my pledge, but I have no knowledge of who the rightful owner is."

Robert scratched his head. "Why d'ye no' just keep it, man? Or are ye afeared the lass will find ye out?"

"I gave my word." Edward straightened up, his chin raised in indignation. "I thought a man's word meant something up here."

"And what would an Englishman ken about honor?" Robert spoke through clenched teeth, his knuckles white as they gripped the hilt of his sword. "The likes of ye dinna even understand the concept. Ach, what more can I expect from an outlander? So tell me, then, why d'ye reckon it belongs to me anyway?"

"You're an Armstrong, are you not?" Edward asked, thinking his reasoning quite sound.

"Aye, that's right enough, but there's many another on the Border, so why come to me?"

Edward leaned back against the birch and sighed, the proverbial albatross reappearing around his neck. He needed to think fast, not an easy task with the blade of a Scottish broad sword less than a foot away, ready to sever his jugular.

"She mentioned he had deep auburn hair," he said at last. "And a quick temper."

Robert swung the tip of his sword back to its original position beneath Edward's chin. "What's that supposed to mean?"

Edward stiffened, his gaze dropping to the polished metal. "Nothing, only please take it so my oath is fulfilled. I just want to be done with it."

"No' so pleased with the lassie now, are we?" Robert relaxed his blade once more, chuckling a bit before glancing over at the miniature chest. "Well, being ye've nae way to ken who the rightful owner is, and seeing I am of the same clan, I guess there'd be nae harm in me taking care of it for a while."

"My thoughts exactly." Edward shoved the intricate chest forward, his heart pounding in anticipation.

"But wait!" Robert turned his head, peering sideways from wary eyes. "Where did ye say ye come by this lass?"

"Where?" Edward hesitated. How should he know? Except for the fact he bore the Foster name, it was all just bollocks. "Um . . . I . . ."

"And why did she no' return it herself?" Robert asked.

"Um . . . well, you see . . ." Edward never planned on having to answer so many questions, and once again his throat tightened and his tongue seemed to have tied itself into a huge knot. The Scot, however, exhibited no patience for such obvious prevarication.

"Ach! I thought as much. Ye're a teller of tales, ye are." Once more, Robert's grip tightened around the hilt of his sword, and his lips hardened into a thin line. Without another word, he drew the blade back up to Edward's neck, pressing the sharp tip into his skin and drawing a tiny trickle of blood.

"Carlisle!" Edward said, his voice coming out in a croak. "I met her in Carlisle."

Robert pulled back but didn't relax his grip or return the sword to its scabbard. "Go on, then. What were ye doing in Carlisle?"

"I had business there." He pulled down on his jack, feigning an air of indignation. "To buy some wool for my father."

Robert looked him over head to foot, his gaze intensifying beneath lowered brows. Once more, Edward held his breath. He could feel his heart racing against his machine-sewn jack, certain the reproduction clothing he wore would never hold up to a close inspection, especially the faux leather boots he'd added at the last minute.

"Hmph!" Robert said at last. "And she? How did she acquire such a braw chest?"

Edward hung his head, stifling a sigh of relief, but he wasn't in the clear yet. "I don't know. Kill me if you must, but 'tis the truth. She stole it, I expect."

Robert made a low guttural sound, then thrust his sword into the ground and leaned on its hilt. He rubbed his chin a moment before speaking, a smile threatening to break out on his ruddy face. "And what was the wench's name, then, or did she slip away afore telling ye that as well?"

"Name?" Edward's mind raced in a desperate search for a viable answer, certain the future state of his anatomy might well hang upon his reply. "'Twas not her name that caught my interest."

Robert burst out in a wholehearted laugh before leaning over and giving Edward a good-natured smack across the back. "Ye're all right for an Englishman, but tell me, was she worth it?"

"Yes, as a matter of fact, she was." Edward gave a tentative shrug to conceal any lack of conviction that may have crossed his face and hoped for the best.

The Scotsman reached down and picked up a piece of jerky, tearing a bit off before resting his hands on his knees. "Well then, 'twas worth a wee bit of trouble, I reckon."

Edward nodded, a smile tugging at the corner of his mouth. This was the chance he'd been waiting for. The Scotsman had at last let down his guard, if only for a minute. Seizing the moment, he thrust forth the jeweled case once more. His hands shook, but he doubted the Scot would ever notice, for he could see Robert's gaze fixed on the box that glistened in the firelight.

****

The peculiar container captivated Robert, but he pondered his acceptance of such an extravagant object. Could it be a trap of some sort? Biting his lip, he surveyed its bejeweled exterior, reviewing the arguments for and against taking it into his possession until, in the end, he could no longer resist. Though still skeptical about its origins, he reached out to touch its glittering surface. In that brief instant, he knew he'd made a mistake. A variety of luminous colored sparks began to fly from beneath its lid, but try as he might, he couldn't unhand it.

"What form of witchcraft be this?" The air began to swirl around his heels, whipping hard against his body and causing his eyes to water as it swept around him in an invisible cocoon.

"Not witchcraft," Foster replied, a huge grin breaking out on his face. "Pure science."

A strong gust of wind nearly knocked Robert off his feet, and he had to duck his head against it. Still, he held firm to his sword, determined to fight whatever creatures he might encounter.

"Curse ye for casting this spell upon me." Robert strained his voice in an effort to make himself heard above the raging storm, but its roar had intensified to the point where his words simply echoed back in his own ears. Try as he might, he couldn't pry his left hand from the chest, and for a fleeting second he considered lobbing it off with his sword. No, he would see this through like a man, whatever it may be.

Squaring his shoulders, he studied the scene before him. Never had he witnessed anything like it, even amidst the wildest squall. His stomach clenched, forcing bile to rise in his throat, his hand so tight on his weapon the knuckles were devoid of any color, but he stood his ground nonetheless.

The sandy-haired Englishman smiled, looking rather like the cat who swallowed the mouse, and not appearing at all bothered by the tempest swirling about them.

Filled with fury, Robert fought once more to lift his sword, but the fierce winds beat hard against it, holding him fast. Then, all at once, a strange calm began to descend upon them, and a radiant glow burst forth from the surrounding area.

Robert stood spellbound, the fragrant scent of Scottish bluebells and meadowsweet permeating his senses. A soft summer mist ruffled his hair, and for a moment, he felt sure he'd found paradise. Could this be a messenger from God, come to take him to his just reward? A sudden wave of fear ran down his spine, but still, he didn't waver. With a solemn reverence, he bent his knee before the Englishman, though he did wonder why the Lord would choose to send him an outlander for an angel.

His heart pounded against his ribs, threatening to burst through the thick leather of his jack, but he wouldn't shame his clan. No matter where he found himself, he would face the situation with all the courage his father had instilled in him. First, however, he needed to determine where that place was.

"Be ye angel or devil coming to claim me?" He took a deep breath, desperate to retain some semblance of composure, for his nerves hung by the thinnest of threads.

"Me?" the Englishman said, his voice filled with amusement. "Neither, I'm afraid. My name is Edward Foster, and I've done no more than bring you four hundred and fifty years into the future."

CHAPTER 1

Lancaster, England - 1988

Robert gazed out across the busy campus, his jaw clenched tight, the muscles in his back and shoulders tense. He needed to let go of the anger, not lash out at his friend of twenty-five years. True, had he been back in his own time, sword in hand, he would have skewered the rogue without a second thought. But this was a more civilized time, and they were noted professors. The thought of the Englishman squirming to avoid being spitted did cause Robert to chuckle, though, and the tightness in his chest began to ease.

He turned from the window to face Edward. "And this amulet, this stone, is the reason I couldna go home afore? Good God, man, ye snatched me from me home, dragged me hundreds of years into the future, and ye're telling me ye had nae idea 'twas the stone's doing."

Though he considered giving the Englishman the kind of old-fashioned tongue-lashing his mother used to give him, the look of utter dismay on his friend's face caused him to relent.

"Ach!" Robert groaned, waving his hand in exasperation. He rubbed the satin finish of the plain green stone Edward had handed him moments before, as if wearing it away could somehow help him make sense out of the whole affair. "I just dinna understand. How could ye no' have kent about it?"

Edward flopped down in the cushioned chair by Robert's desk and leaned forward, his arms on his knees. "It was just an amulet, no different from a hundred others. It never occurred to me it held any power. At least, not until a few days ago."

"And what brought about yer sudden epiphany, then?" Robert asked, the harsh edge returning to his voice. He placed his arms across his chest and cocked his head in a subtle challenge.

"Your daughter, actually."

Robert's eyes narrowed. "What has me Maggie to do with it? She wasna even born twenty-five year back."

Edward looked up and massaged the nape of his neck. "I fancied maybe it was time your daughter knew about you, about your . . . history."

"Ye did, did ye? And when were ye planning to tell me about this sudden revelation? Or am I to have noucht to say on the matter?"

"Now, Rob, don't get your knickers in a twist. I haven't said a word to Maggie. I did decide to look for the jewel-studded chest. I hoped maybe if I dug it out, you might consider explaining your past to her. Let her know that all those stories you've told her over the years are more than fairy tales. That they're part of your life."

Robert made a low guttural sound deep in his throat before turning to look out across the tree-dotted campus once more. His arrival in this century seemed so distant now, as if he were watching it from afar. In time, his initial resentment had faded to a dull ache, rearing its ugly head only at times like this. Yet there was no doubt he'd adjusted to this new world, and it hadn't been all bad.

He drifted away for a moment, memories flooding his senses as he returned to the day he'd met his beautiful Katie.

"Are you okay?" she'd asked. "Your knee is bleeding."

"Ach, 'tis noucht but a wee scrape." Robert's heart pounded beneath his jersey, but it had nothing to do with the exertion he'd expended on the football field.

"Well, I'm glad he got a foul. He didn't need to kick you so hard."

He fought to suppress a smile and used a rag to wipe the sweat from his face. "'Tis the nature of the game, lassie."

"Hmm, well his strategy didn't work, did it? You made the goal anyway. Oh, I almost forgot, can I offer you some Kool-Aid? I've got orange or cherry."

"Ta, lass, orange will be fine." Robert bit his lip, unsure what to say next. "Are ye new here? I dinna recall seeing ye round afore."

Her pretty auburn curls bobbed as she nodded. "Yes, I just arrived from New York last Saturday, Long Island to be exact. My grandmother thought coming to school here would be a good experience for me." She shrugged. "I'm not so sure."

He ran his fingers through his hair, certain the sweat must be dripping from every pore in his body at this point, but he didn't want the conversation to end. "Why's that? D'ye no' care for it here?"

"Oh no, it's great. I just miss home."

A pang of loneliness hit Robert square in the stomach. "I ken how ye feel, lass. I'm from Scotland meself. Would ye like to come to the pictures with me tomorrow night?" he asked. "Two misplaced persons, as it were."

She smiled, and the sun broke through the clouds in spite of the heavy mist. "Sure! I'd love to."

"I'll pick ye up round eight, then, aye?"

"Eight will be perfect. Oh, by the way, I'm Katie Lindsey."

"Nice to meet ye, Katie. I'm Rabbie Armstrong."

"Oh, I know who you are," she added with a twinkle in her eye.

A crack of thunder brought him back to the present. He let out a sigh as he watched another generation of students dart across the campus, donning their umbrellas to get out of the sudden downpour.

No, it hadn't been all bad. He'd married his beautiful Katie, and she'd given him their daughter, Maggie. But there were thunderstorms too, times that left his spirit cold and drenched to the core. A tear trickled down his cheek as he recalled the day his wife died, and he felt anew the painful void her passing had left. Perhaps Edward was right and he should tell Maggie everything.

Or better yet! A wave of excitement shot down his spine, a small seed of hope blossoming in the recesses of his mind. If Edward had worked out the part the amulet played, perhaps he could do more than just tell her. He spun around to face his friend once more.

"Aye, so get on with it, man. Ye went looking for the chest. What has any of it to do with this blasted amulet?"

Edward sat back, folding his hands across his waist. "That's the strange bit, you see. I stumbled across it quite by accident while searching for the bloody box. To be honest, I'd forgotten all about the thing and only put it on for old times' sake. It had been years since I'd seen it."

"Twenty-five year, to be exact." Robert lifted an eyebrow to emphasize the point.

"Twenty-five years, then." Edward grimaced at the not-so-subtle rebuke. "But when the stone got close to the chest, something began to happen. A strong wind came out of nowhere, and I heard an all-too-familiar sound. I could feel the barriers of time crumbling, just like they did all those years ago. Of course, I yanked the amulet away before I could be swept back through the centuries yet again."

"Oh, ye thought to do that now, did ye? And yet twenty-five year back, it never entered yer mind."

"Why would it?" Edward asked. "I spent two years trying to create a time portal. To say I was thrilled when it finally worked would be an understatement."

Robert pulled at his nose and sniffed. "Aye, I reckon I can see yer point there, but what about later, when ye tried to send me home. Why did ye no' use it then?" He ran his hand through his hair. "Good God, man, what were ye thinking?"

"If you recall, I did try." Edward stood and walked to the window. "I'm truly sorry, Rob. More than you'll ever know. If I could go back and change it all, I would, but as it stands, I can't."

A knock at the office door preempted Robert's scathing reply. He swung around just as the door creaked open and a mass of dark wavy hair appeared through the resulting crack.

"Sorry, Professor Armstrong," Dylan Hetherington said. "Should I come back?"

Robert let out a low hiss, cursing beneath his breath. "Nae, Mr. Hetherington. What is it ye want? Class winna be for an hour yet."

"Ah, that's just it, you see, Professor. Something's come up, and I hoped I might be excused."

A frown furrowed Robert's forehead. Dylan's dark hair and blue eyes created an illusion of innocence that never failed to charm the university's female population, but Robert saw through the facade all too well.

"Ye may do as ye like, lad," he replied, "but miss this class and ye'll receive nae recommendation from me."

"But, Professor, you don't understand."

"Ach! I think I do, and I'm sure the lassie winna mind waiting a wee bit when she realizes how devoted ye are to yer studies. Am I right now, Mr. Hetherington?"

Robert could see the heat rising in Dylan's cheeks, but he held the young man's gaze until the student looked away.

"Yes, sir, I'll see you in an hour, then." Dylan straightened his tie and, after giving a curt nod of acknowledgement, closed the door behind him.

Edward slid a hand across his mouth, a huge grin peeking through his fingers, but Robert could only shake his head in disgust.

"He truly is one of me best students," he said. "And he'd make a fine Borderer as well. I've seen him in action at the reenactments here about. 'Tis a shame he allows his passion for the ladies to take precedence ower all else."

"Passion can skew a man's vision of what's important," Edward replied, a hint of regret dimming the sparkle that had been dancing in his eyes just moments before."Aye, it can that, and I'll be the first to admit it, but to get back to what we were discussing afore Mr. Hetherington saw fit to interrupt. I'm finding it hard to understand how ye could realize the stone was the culprit now when ye couldna see it as such all those years back."

Edward chewed on a loose cuticle, hesitating a moment before speaking. "Because I was a bit of an arrogant sod back then." He heaved a great sigh and shook his head. "I devoted a whole semester to assembling the chest, adjusting the gems, measuring the energy each held. When it finally worked, the thought that anything but my own ingenuity lay behind it never crossed my mind. At that point, all I wanted was to go back and capture a piece of history so I'd have proof of what I'd accomplished."

"And I was that piece of history, so nae need worrying about how it all came to be."

Edward opened his mouth to protest, but at first no words came to his lips. With a low groan, he sank back into the desk chair. "Maybe before," he finally said, "but not after. I tried everything I could to send you back; you know that. Everything except putting the bloody amulet back around my neck, that is."

"Aye, I ken ye did." Robert grunted in resignation, his thoughts traveling back to his first few hours in this century.

Still shocked by the Englishman's revelation, Robert had flopped down on a nearby rock, with his elbows perched on his knees, and glared at Edward Foster. He'd remained frozen in that position, his jaw tightly clenched while his abductor explained the details. Robert hadn't been sure he believed any of it, but one thing was certain; he'd wanted to strangle the man before him.

"Just put me back where I belong." He'd lifted his sword, determined to end the scoundrel's life if need be.

"All right, don't get your knickers in a twist. But since you're already here, what harm could it do to spend a few hours taking a look about?"

It would be an adventure of sorts. "Agreed, but after that, ye'll put me back, eh."

Edward had grinned, his eyes sparkling with mischief.

A horn blasted in the distance, dragging Robert back to the 1980s. "Did ye ever really intend to send me back, Eddie?"

"You know I did. How many days did I spend by that stupid, bloody birch, fiddling with gems, opening and closing the accursed box, trying to unlock the portal once more, but not a spark or sputter escaped. I'll admit, at first I considered not even giving it a go, but I'd given my word. Besides, if all went well, I could convince one of my professors to go along the next time."

"Hmm, right noble of ye." And yet, even back then Robert couldn't stay angry at the sandy-haired Englishman whose frantic attempts had carved deep lines in his forehead.

An uncomfortable cough from Edward made Robert ashamed of what he'd implied, and he lowered himself onto the couch. "I've no' forgotten how hard ye tried to send me home, Eddie, nor all ye've done since then. But why on earth did ye have the silly thing round yer neck in the first place if ye didna even suspect the part it played?"

Edward shrugged, pretending to brush some nonexistent crumbs from his sweater. "Because I thought it was an interesting piece, and it just happened to suit the period. I needed to make sure I fit in, didn't I?"

Robert stared at his friend for a moment before rolling his eyes up toward the heavens as if in prayer. "Lord, help us! Good to ken ye apply such tried and true scientific principles to yer experiments, but the real question now is, will the blasted thing still work?"

Edward's head shot up, his eyebrows lifting high on his forehead before lowering over suspicious eyes. "I suppose. It did seem to come to life, but . . . Now wait a minute, Rob. Even if it did, I can't guarantee it would bring us back to the right place, let alone the right time. I never had any control over that."

"Ye what? Dear Lord, I could have ended up anywhere."

"No, not really," Edward said. "At least I don't think so. It worked the first and second time I tried it."

"The first and second time?" Robert raised an eyebrow. "Ye mean I wasna ye first? I'm hurt."

"No, you weren't," Edward replied, the twinkle back in his eyes. "But you can't really count the first time. That was more of an accident. I only intended to send the mouse, but . . . well, I got swept up in it as well. I went back a few weeks, but I didn't even get a chance to look about before I returned. I'm not sure what happened to the mouse."

Robert's eyes widened, but Edward flashed a quick grin and continued. "Anyway, I messed about with the alignment of the stones a bit more and tried again. Only that time I made sure to choose a date a few years before my birth. You know, avoid clashing with my younger self and that sort of thing. I thought it might be the reason the first trip failed. It would explain why I came back and the mouse didn't."

"And how's that?" Robert asked. "Was the wee mousie less than a few week old?"

"Actually, it was, and the result of my second excursion bore out my hypothesis. It went much smoother and didn't spit me out like a piece of sour fruit. So after spending a few hours in 1940, I returned and prepared to head someplace—or some time, I should say—farther back, to a period I really wanted to experience. Since I'd always had a keen interest in the sixteenth-century Borders, I chose 1513, and that's where I ended up."

"So ye did." Robert scratched his chin, deep in thought. "What ye're saying, then, is ye just have to think about the time ye want to go to, and it takes ye there."

"It seems like it, but I can't really be sure."

"And what will it take to make ye sure?"

Edward cast a wary glance in his friend's direction. "You know the answer to that as well as I do."

"I suppose I do." Robert got up and walked back to the window. The rain had stopped, and the sun struggled to break through the remaining clouds. He watched the students shake out their umbrellas and stroll toward one building or another, their day planned out before them, all thinking they knew where they were heading. And yet a stumble, a dropped book, an old friend passing by, could alter their perceived future without them even realizing it.

He heard Edward sigh and, by the tone, guessed the Englishman did not particularly like the turn their conversation had taken. "Just say what's on yer mind, man."

"All right, then. You know you're like a brother to me, Rob . . ."

"Aye, ye've been a good friend to me ower the years. Well, except for bringing me here in the first place, that is." He turned to face his friend once more, and a smile tugged at the corner of his mouth. "There's nae denying it, and I ken ye want to protect me now, but if there truly is a chance this thing will work, then tell me so. Ye owe me that much, Eddie."

Edward rose and joined Robert at the window once more, an unmistakable moan rumbling in his throat. A gentle spring breeze ruffled his hair, revealing the strands of gray that now lay hidden beneath the blond. He was a kind man, with soft green eyes that seemed all the more compassionate in the warm afternoon sun, though now a sadness stirred there as well.

"You want to go back," he said, on the verge of a whisper.

"Aye, I do that," Robert said, his voice firm and steady as he held his friend's gaze. "And I want me daughter with me."

Edward's jaw dropped. "Maggie! But, Rob, she belongs here."

"No, she's me bairn, and she belongs with the clan."

"But she isn't just your daughter. She's Katie's too, and Maggie was born here."

"Actually, she was born on Long Island," Robert countered, undaunted.

"That's not what I meant, and you know it." Edward scrubbed a hand across his face. "She belongs in this century."

"So we're worrying about when a body's born now, are we? It never seemed to bother ye afore." The pained expression on Edward's face stopped him short, and he continued on a softer note. "Katie's passed, and I canna bring her back, or could I?"

"What? No, you can't. I came right back after the first try, remember?" Edward put his hand on Robert's shoulder. "I'm sorry, Rob. I wish I could make it so."

Robert nodded, swallowing the pain. "But Maggie is here with me. She's nineteen now, just the age I was when . . ." He let his voice drift off, and he looked away. Tears welled up in his eyes, clouding his vision, though he quickly blinked to conceal any trace of their existence. "I want her to meet me kin, her kin. She has a right to ken who they are, to see she has more family than just ye and me. From there, she can make the decision for herself whether to stay with them or return to this century."

Edward scratched his head, and Robert could almost hear the cogs turning. "But what about her education? And your career, for that matter. Rob, are you forgetting how hard you studied to get where you are, the work you had to put in? The strings my father had to pull. You're a noted archaeologist. That didn't happen overnight, and now you want to give it all up."

"And what exactly have I been doing? Collecting bits and pieces of me past so I could keep it close and pass it on to me daughter. Twenty-five year of being homesick, Eddie, of hoping against hope I could return someday. Biding me time until the day might come. D'ye ken what that's like?"

Edward swallowed hard, his brows knitted in a frown. "No, I can't imagine, but now you want to do the same to Maggie."

"Nae! I'll no' go unless me Maggie kens the truth of it. It'll be her choice, no' mine. So tell me, Eddie, can I go home? Can I see me kin again afore I die?"

Edward took a deep, frustrated breath, filling his lungs before letting the air escape through his teeth. "I don't know, truly, I don't. I told you, I'm not sure how it all works. If I'm wrong, we could end up anywhere. And then there's the amulet itself. It seems smaller than when I first wore it. Bits of the stone must have melted away with each passage. I'm afraid there might not be enough left to do much of anything."

"Then find another," Robert said.

"Don't you think I've tried?" Edward slammed his hands down on the windowsill. "I sent a bit of the stone down to Cambridge straightaway, as soon as I made the connection between it and the chest. They've no idea what to make of it either."

"And they let it go at that?"

"Well, not exactly. I told them I'd only come across the one sample. When they asked where I found it, I told them up around Lindow Moss. That should keep them busy for a while."

Robert shook his head, a small laugh escaping from his lips. "Ye've got a wicked sense of humor, ye ken."

"Yes, well, maybe they'll find another two thousand-year-old bog body and not start asking questions I can't answer."

"Where did ye get the thing in the first place, then?"

"Let's not even go there." Edward raised his hands in front of him, as if doing so could stop any further inquiry. "Suffice it to say it was a gift from a young lady, a summer fling the year before I entered university, and I have no idea who she was or where she is now."

Barely able to contain himself, Robert struggled to stifle another laugh. "So in a way, ye were actually telling the truth that day we rode across the moor."

"Yes, when you look at it that way, I suppose I was."

Robert nodded thoughtfully before making his decision. "Then we'll go on what we have left. 'Tis as simple as that."

"Did you not hear what I said?" Edward's green eyes flashed with alarm. "I don't know how far it will carry us. It may not even take us back to the same place, that is, if it takes us anywhere at all."

Robert shrugged and plopped down in the swivel chair behind his desk. "We'll find out, then, one way or the other, now won't we?" He picked up the amulet. "There's no' that much of it gone anyway. At least enough to get Maggie and I back, I'd wager. Besides, what d'ye mean *us*?"

"You don't think I'm going to let you go alone, do you?" Edward replied, his tone tinged with indignation. "I took you from your home, and I'll return you to it."

"And if ye canna get back?"

"Then it will be your turn to play host," he said, the shadow of a smile crossing his lips.

"Ye'll do it, then?" Robert held his breath, his heart bursting with hope and expectation.

Edward sighed, then gave a reluctant nod. "I doubt you'll have as easy a time convincing Maggie, though, especially if it means leaving Dylan . . ." He stopped short, biting his lip, but Robert caught the slip.

"If it means leaving who?" He jumped up, his hands flat on the desk. "Ye canna possibly be talking about Dylan Hetherington, that womanizing scoundrel who was just in here? What has that rogue to do with me Maggie?"

Edward rubbed his temples. "Nothing. Honestly, Rob, they're just friends."

"Friends, is it?" Robert could feel his lips turning up into a snarl. "And how long have ye kent about this . . . friendship, then?"

"There's nothing to know, Rob."

"Oh, but I think there is, man. 'Tis all starting to make sense now. The wee rascal's been talking about going on a dig this summer. Wants me to recommend him and all. It wouldna happen to be to the States, now would it?"

"How should I know?" Edward asked.

"Strange how Maggie's developed a sudden yearning to be going home this summer as well. Says she misses the warm Long Island breezes."

"Did she?" Edward's words came out in a croak, and he coughed to clear his throat.

"Ocean breezes, indeed." Robert narrowed his eyes, his teeth barely parted. "Whose side are ye on anyway? This is yer goddaughter we're talking about."

"I'm well aware of that. And I trust her implicitly."

"Oh, aye, and I do as well," Robert said. "'Tis that sniveling reprobate I dinna trust."

"You've got it all wrong." Edward sat on the deep windowsill, his arms crossed over his chest. "There's nothing going on between them. At least, nothing more than a fondness for Long Island. She grew up there, after all, and you haven't been back in more than three years. It's only natural she misses it. The fact is, if you hadn't been offered the job here, you'd still be teaching there. She just wants to go home, the same way you do. What's wrong with that?"

"Not a thing, if it were her only reason for wanting to go back, but there's the little subject of Dylan Hetherington planning to go as well."

"There's a dig there, and I suppose he figures Maggie might have some cute mates. Trust me, there's nothing going on between them. They're just friends."

Robert glared at Edward, but the Englishman didn't budge. "Hmph," he finally said. "Nevertheless, she'll no' be going to Long Island this summer, like it or no'." He realized how harsh his words sounded and softened his tone. "I want her with me, Eddie, in Scotland, my Scotland. Is that so hard to understand? 'Tis all I have to offer."

He reached down into the lower right hand drawer of his desk and pulled out a large book. "Ye're right, ye ken. She thinks they're noucht but stories. I want to show her there's more to them than figments of me imagination."

Edward moaned. "This afternoon, after your class, then. I'll meet you back here, and we'll talk to her together. But I have to tell you, I'm not looking forward to it."

Robert sniffed away the emotion as he flipped through the book, a smile creeping across his lips. He stopped on a page bearing the illustration of a sandy-haired young man in a blue velvet jerkin. "Perhaps if she thinks she'll meet this one here, she'll be racing us all through that portal of yers."

"Who is he?" Edward craned his neck to peer over Robert's shoulder.

"I'm no' sure. He came after ye dragged me away, but I'm thinking he may have been a Foster, one of yer ancestors, perhaps."

"Hmm. Good looks must run in the family."

Robert coughed to stifle a laugh before clearing his throat and continuing his story. "I've been gathering these tales and images together for years. I reckon I planned on telling her everything someday, when she was older, but now I can give her more."

He looked at the portrait again and laughed. "When she was a wean, I'd tell her me stories, and she never doubted a word. She always liked the one I wove about this lad the best. For a long time, when nae more than a bairn, she used to ask which one was me."

"Is there one of you?" Edward had a wicked look in his eye, and Robert slammed the book shut.

"Nae!" he replied. "I'll see ye back here after me class."

Edward ducked his head, clearly suppressing a chuckle. "By the way, if we find that lad when we're back there, and Maggie takes a liking to him, will you let her . . ."

"No' likely," Robert said, his hand still planted on top of the large book. "Now I've got a class, and I believe ye do as well. I'll see ye after, then, aye."

CHAPTER 2

The office door swung open, and Robert smiled as his daughter rushed through, her auburn hair flying out behind her. She flopped down in his office chair with an audible sigh and spun around to face him.

"Finally!" she said. "My last exam of the year, and I think I may have aced it."

"I'm sure ye did, darlin'." Robert turned to gaze out the window. A few young men were playing ball on the grass-covered rugby field, and a lump formed in his throat. Was he being selfish, expecting Maggie to leave her world behind and follow him? Then he remembered a certain graduate student and groaned inwardly. *Dylan Hetherington, of all people!*

"I do still have a few papers to hand in," she added, "but then I can go home and start packing."

Maggie's voice interrupted his reverie, and he turned to face her once more. Though he hesitated a moment, he needed to ask, needed to hear it from her lips. He let out a long breath and cleared his throat. "About that, lass . . . Are ye seeing Dylan Hetherington?"

Maggie's eyebrows crept together, causing the smooth skin between them to wrinkle. "Dylan? What brought that about?"

"Just answer the question, lass."

"No, at least not the way you mean. Now it's your turn. What made you ask?"

"Let's just say ye both seem a wee bit too anxious to get to Long Island this summer, and I canna help but wonder why."

"What!" Maggie's mouth dropped, though a smile sparkled in her eyes. "Between you and Uncle Eddie, it's a miracle I haven't been locked away in a castle keep somewhere."

"Dinna be ridiculous, lass."

"I'm not! Uncle Eddie already lectured me on the perils of falling prey to the charms of Dylan Hetherington. And as I told him, we're just friends—more like siblings, actually." She shook her head and chuckled. "Have no fear, it's not me Dylan's interested in. There's a dig on Long Island, and since I'm going there anyway, he asked if I'd introduce him to some of my friends. That's all it is. So you can relax, Da, I promise."

The door opened, and Edward stuck his head in. "Is it safe yet?" His voice carried a hint of laughter, but Robert knew his words weren't completely in jest. Maggie's temper could build to hurricane force when provoked.

"Uncle Eddie, we were just talking about you." She spun in his direction and flashed an innocent, closed-mouth smile.

Edward rolled his eyes. "You've told her, then."

"Yes, he's told me," Maggie said. "But you promised you wouldn't say anything. Now he's all kinds of worried about Dylan."

"Dylan?" Edward froze for a moment before continuing. "Oh, right. Sorry, love, it slipped out. We were discussing something else and . . ."

Maggie spun back around to face her father, her arms folded across her chest. "There's more to this than Dylan, isn't there?"

Robert sat down on the small couch to the side of his desk. He leaned his elbows on his knees, pinching the bridge of his nose between his fingers, and groaned. "Aye, ye might say that. Ye ken those stories I used to tell ye when ye were a wean?"

Maggie reached for the book on the desk, opening it to the page that held the faded image of a young man, the same one Robert had mentioned to Edward earlier. Though only a miniature copy of the original portrait, his blue-gray eyes twinkled with mischief.

Robert smiled to himself, remembering how she used to climb onto his lap to hear the stories about her special knight.

"When I was a kid, I used to dream about him riding up on his silver steed and carrying me off to his castle. Pretty silly, huh?" The color in her cheeks deepened, and she giggled. "I think I may have even had a crush on him for a while."

"Aye, for a while, I suppose." Robert glanced over at Edward, but his friend just shrugged and nodded in Maggie's direction, so he swallowed hard and continued. "But they're no' simply stories, ye see. They're me life. Well, most of them anyway."

Maggie's whole face lit up. "I know how much you love them. Are you finally planning to write a book? I have to say, it's about time."

"'Tis no' a book I'm talking about, lassie, but me life." He saw her rub her fingertips over the image and felt an inexplicable need for fatherly concern. "And I dinna even ken who the lad is for certain, so put him out of yer head, aye."

"He was English, though, right? I know, I know, *not a braw Scottish lad*." She said the last bit with a deep burr, a good-hearted attempt at Robert's guttural tones. "Still, he is rather cute."

She showed every sign of rambling on, but Robert cut her short. "Maggie!" he said, just this side of a shout. The girl stopped speaking at once, concern written across her face.

"What is it, Da? The last time I saw you look like that you told me we were moving to England. You get this funny little twitch over your left eye when you have something serious to say and you're pretty sure I'm not going to like it."

Without even thinking, Robert reached up and touched his left eyebrow, as if he could command it to stop. A subtle tremor fluttered beneath his fingers, and he frowned to discover Maggie had taken notice.

"Aye, well, in a way, I guess it does concern a bit of a move, but only a wee one."

Maggie cast a wary look at her father before slamming the book shut and leaning back in the chair. "Where now?" she asked.

"That's the thing, ye see, darlin'. 'Tis no' in distance, but in time. To the past . . . me own past."

For a moment, no one spoke. He could almost see the cogs of Maggie's mind working behind her dark honey-brown eyes, trying to process the information he'd given her. It was a lot for anyone to digest, he knew that, but then, to his surprise, a tentative smile began to spread across her lips, the shifting fog of doubt giving way to the prospect of a new adventure.

"Oh! Why didn't you just say so? That's great!" Maggie rose from the chair and sat on his desk, her small feet hanging over the side. Her eyebrows lifted with delight, and it reminded Robert of when she was a child.

"Ye'll no' be bothered, then?" he asked.

"No, of course not. I've always wondered why we've never visited your hometown, especially now, being so close. How could you think I wouldn't want to go?"

Robert massaged his temples, shaking off the ache that was growing in his head and his heart. "Because there's a wee bit more to it than that."

"Oh," she said, her excitement waning. "There's a dig up there, I suppose."

"I dinna think so, no' at the moment anyway, but we won't simply be going to Scotland. We'll be going to *sixteenth-century* Scotland. At least, I hope we will." Once more, Robert turned to Edward to bail him out.

Edward shook his head. "Don't look at me."

Robert scowled in annoyance, then focused his attention back on Maggie. "We're traveling back to me past, darlin' . . . me sixteenth-century past."

Maggie moaned. "It *is* another dig."

Robert walked over to the book on his desk and flipped it to the back cover, removing a faded piece of paper from the dust jacket. Memories flashed through his mind as he stared at the crumpled sheet, and he hesitated for a moment. Then, with a sigh of resignation, he unfolded the page and handed it to Maggie.

"'Tis a portrait me da commissioned just after me nineteenth birthday. Nae more than a copy, I'm afraid, but 'tis me afore Eddie came and snatched me away."

Maggie studied the picture for a minute or so, then glanced up at her father. "He does resemble you a bit, a younger version obviously, but he probably is one of your ancestors."

"'Tis no' one of me ancestors, lass." He frowned, the twitch over his eye returning, and Maggie glanced at the picture again.

"Da, you don't expect me to believe this is you, right?" When he didn't answer, she turned to Edward. "Uncle Eddie, help me out here."

"Rob, why don't you give Maggie and me a minute alone," he said. "We could all use a good hot cup of tea."

Robert grunted his disapproval but conceded, taking no more than a moment to grab his wallet from the desk drawer before heading out the door. Perhaps Edward could convince her to accept the truth. Lord knew he hadn't been able to.

****

Edward stood there, straight as an arrow, waiting for Maggie to speak, which, mercifully, didn't take more than a second after the latch clicked behind her father.

"He needs a vacation," she said. "He's been spending way too much time with his artifacts. How about Disney World? I haven't been there since my twelfth birthday."

"He's not losing his mind, love." Now it was Edward's turn to sit on the couch. "You know how I've always talked about the possibility of time travel."

"Yes," Maggie said, her eyes becoming narrow slits. "String theory, quantum physics, parallel universes . . ."

"Well, it's possible. And your father's my proof. I know, because I'm responsible for him being here. It was an experiment, traveling into the past and returning with a living, breathing specimen." Maggie tutted, and

34

Edward raised his hand. "Let me finish before you start challenging everything I say."

"Fine!" She pursed her lips and crossed her dangling legs. "Go on, then."

"Well, at first everything went according to plan, but when it came time to send him back . . ." Edward rose to his feet and went to sit on the edge of the windowsill. "Something went wrong, and he was stranded here, four hundred and fifty years from his home. No one would ever believe us, of course, and why should they? I couldn't replicate it. The truth is I had no idea how I did it or how to fix it. So there you have it."

Maggie continued to stare at him, a mixture of disbelief and concern causing her forehead to crinkle into delicate lines. He wouldn't be surprised if she suggested they both take an extended holiday, perhaps to a comfortable sanitarium somewhere.

Finally, she twisted her mouth, a suppressed smile deepening the dimple in her right cheek. "So presuming all this is true, Da must have been pretty pissed off."

"To say the least," Edward replied, puzzled by her response. "I thought he was going to behead me right then and there."

"Hmm, and yet you survived. So what did happen?" She slipped down into Robert's desk chair and snuggled back against the soft leather. It reminded Edward of someone settling in for a good story, which he supposed she was.

"As I said, I tried everything I could to send him home, and I guess he realized how desperate I'd become. Eventually, he reconciled himself to a life here, we became friends, and he enrolled in university."

"And of course he fit right in, passed the entrance exam and everything?"

"Your father may be from the sixteenth century," he said, his voice taking on a stern note, "but he wasn't illiterate. He'd studied Latin and French, not to mention geometry and physics, before he even came here. You've been around your father long enough to know there were colleges back then."

Maggie shrugged. "Still, you're asking me to take a huge leap of faith here. Where would he get a high school diploma, a passport—"

Edward cut her off. "We also had my dad pulling every string he could lay his hands on. It's a good thing too, or you wouldn't be here. Rob met your mum at university. After graduation, they married, but Katie's grandmother had grown ill, so they moved back to the States. Your father got a great offer from a local university there, so they stayed."

"Yeah, I'm acquainted with the latter part of the story. It's the earlier bits I'm not quite familiar with. So tell me, this time travel, how does it all work?"

"I'm not sure. I thought I knew, but my theory . . ." Edward threw his hands up in the air. "All I know is it does. Work, that is."

"Really, that's what you're going with? No scientific explanation about the fabric of time or cosmic strings or whatever the heck you call them. It's not very imaginative."

Edward's mind couldn't help but wander for a moment. With her arms folded across her chest and her head tilted to the side, she looked so much like her mother, and yet the spark in her eyes belonged to Robert. Perhaps a bit of Border reiver stirred in her, after all.

"Well?" she added when he failed to speak.

Edward cleared his throat. "I don't have an explanation. If I did, I would have sent your father back a long time ago, and we wouldn't be discussing it now. You need to trust us, Maggie."

"Okay, let's say I do," she said, though her tone made it clear she was just humoring him. Why didn't you write a paper on it? You're a physicist. How could you let anything so monumental go undocumented?"

"It was my original plan, but when I couldn't send your father back, I realized I didn't know how any of it happened. What would I write the paper on? How I thought I had a theory, but it didn't hold up?"

"But if that's the case, what makes you think it will work now? You just said you couldn't explain it."

Edward scrubbed his hand across his face. "I can't, not in scientific terms anyway. This amulet acts as a kind of key, though. Without it, you can go nowhere." He began pacing back and forth, talking more to himself than to her. "It does have to do with four dimensions, I'm sure of it, and perhaps even cosmic strings and negative energy. I didn't realize it then, but—"

"Now there's the Uncle Eddie I know. But slow down; I have a mind for *historical* research, remember? Science and math are not my forte."

He slumped back down on the windowsill. "Unfortunately, I didn't understand how it channeled time until recently, which is why I couldn't send your father back before. The point is Rob's as sane as I am."

"That's what worries me!" Concern was etched into her face, mixed with a touch of annoyance. "Look, I'll go to Scotland. It's not a big deal. There's no need to fabricate some far-fetched tale to get me there. I know you and Da still think of me as a child, but I'm not anymore, so stop pretending you invented some kind of time machine. The only thing you're doing is pissing me off."

Edward rubbed his fingertips across his forehead, hoping to forestall an impending headache. "We're not trying to upset you, love, but it is all true. And if you come, you'll find that out for yourself."

Maggie took a breath, ready to reply, but stopped cold. Her lips curled into a smile, and her eyes narrowed once more. It was as if a light had dawned somewhere in her mind. "Wait a minute. This is all about Dylan, isn't it?"

"Dylan?" Try as he might, Edward couldn't keep from breaking out in a huge grin. "What has Dylan got to do with it?"

"Well, it's not much of a stretch, is it? You tell Da about me and Dylan being friends, and all of a sudden we're going off on an expedition, not just to Scotland, but to the distant past, no less."

Edward didn't know whether to launch a vigorous defense or laugh at the unexpected turn of events. Of all the conclusions Maggie could have come to, this one had never crossed his mind.

"You can't believe we'd concoct such a story just to keep the two of you apart?"

"Can't I?" A glint of mischief sparked in the depths of Maggie's eyes. "All right, then, let's say I believe you. It's not right for me to abandon Dylan on Long Island. After all, I did promise to introduce him to my friends. So how about this?"

Edward almost winced. Once she'd entered the bargaining phase, he didn't stand a chance.

"I'll agree to go along on your so-called expedition to the past, without another moan or groan, on one condition. I get to tell Dylan all about it, including where—and when—we're heading. And if he's interested, I can invite him along."

No doubt about it, she was her father's daughter. Edward combed his fingers through his hair. "You know your father will never agree."

"Why not?" She leaned forward and tapped her fingers on the desk, deep in thought. "I think it's an awesome idea. Da may complain about *Mr. Hetherington*, but I know he considers him one of his best students. Besides, this would be an unprecedented opportunity for Dylan, one he'd never want to miss."

With that, she peeked at her watch and gasped. "Yikes! Is it that late already? I promised to meet my friend Chris. We've got a paper due tomorrow, and it's nowhere near done."

Edward's jaw twitched, and Maggie kissed him on the cheek. "Look, talk to Da about it, okay? I don't believe any of your time travel mumbo jumbo, but even if it is nothing more than a dig, taking part in an expedition with Professor Armstrong would be a great addition to Dylan's resumé."

"And why do you care about him so much?"

"I sort of feel sorry for him. I don't think he has anyone. At least, he never talks about them if he does. And my father—and uncle—always taught me to be kind."

Edward pursed his lips, trying to hold in a smile. "Hmm."

Her brow creased for a moment. "Regardless, it would do us all good to get away." She bent over and gave Edward another quick peck on the cheek, and before he could say another word, she turned and dashed out the door.

CHAPTER 3

When Robert inched the door open a few minutes later, he couldn't hear a sound, but that wasn't necessarily a good sign. He blew out his cheeks, swallowing the lump of apprehension lodged in his throat. Tightening his hand on the knob, he pushed a bit more so he could peek through the crack. Edward sat on the couch, his head in his hands, but Maggie was nowhere to be seen. Robert stood for a moment, scratching his chin as he contemplated what it all meant, until he finally swung the door wide and walked inside.

"What on earth's wrong with ye, man? Ye look as though ye're heading for the gallows."

"That's one way to put it." Edward peered over his fingers before sitting back against the soft leather cushion.

"What happened, then?"

"Maggie agreed to go along. I'm not sure she thinks we're exactly sane, but for the moment anyway, she believes she's figured out the reason behind our sudden trip."

"Did she now? And what's that?"

"She's decided the two of us are plotting to keep her and Dylan apart. So, she has a little . . . *request*, shall we call it."

Robert scrubbed his hand across his face. "Right, then. Give us a minute, eh?" Without another word, he bent down and opened his bottom desk drawer. Taking out a bottle of Scotch, he poured them each a dram. "If I ken me Maggie, we'll both be needing this."

Edward chuckled and grabbed the glass, downing it in one long draught. "You'd better pour another."

"What is it she wants, then?"

The heat rose steadily in Robert's face as Edward recounted his conversation with Maggie. When he was done, Robert downed the second dram, and after taking a few deep breaths, he capped the bottle and put it back in his desk, still not saying a word.

"She wants the wee scoundrel with us, does she?" he said at last. "Just friends, is it?" He spoke to himself as he paced back and forth, his lips pursed and his head nodding in thought. "So be it, then!" He came to a stop and sat in his chair, the decision made. "He's been after me to recommend him for a dig, so I'll oblige the lad. Of course, it winna be the one he's expecting, but that's nae fault of mine."

"You're joking!" Edward's head jerked up. "You can't be serious. The last thing we need is someone else to worry about, not to mention how another body could affect the condition of the stone."

"Ach! Ye dinna really ken what wears it away, now do ye?"

"No, I suppose not. But what if each one of us takes a toll?"

"Aye, ye're right there!" Robert slapped his knees and stood up. "The young cad needs to be told there mayna be a return ticket."

Edward's jaw dropped. "It's not Dylan I'm worried about. Taking him along could mean one less trip for someone else. You do realize he could be the reason one or more of us gets stranded back there."

"I wouldna exactly consider meself stranded," Robert said, "but aye, I do get yer meaning. It makes nae difference, though. 'Tis what me Maggie wants. As long as the lad kens the risk, I'll no' be changing me mind."

"You actually like the idea he might get caught back there," Edward said. "I can't believe it! You of all people know what it's like to be trapped in another century."

"Aye, I do that!" Robert nodded, his jaw set and his eyes focused on distant memories, but after a moment's contemplation, he waved off his friend's allegations. "Ach, 'tis no' what ye think at all."

"Then why take him? And don't tell me it's because Maggie wants it."

"But it is!" Robert said with a wink. "'Twill be the lad's decision to stay or go."

Edward looked as though he might argue the point but stopped short. A sly smile crept its way across his lips, and he nodded in approval.

"So if he won't go along, which is probable considering the implausibility of the entire endeavor, it will be Dylan and not you who disappoints Maggie."

"Something to that effect." Robert leaned against the edge of his desk and broke out in a broad grin. "And while she's thinking about him, she'll have less time to wonder whether or no' we've gone bonkers. Ye ken, the same goes for you as well, Eddie. I will understand if ye choose to stay here."

"Not likely, mate." Edward sighed deeply and gazed out the window, the gathering clouds reflected in his green eyes. "But what about the possibility of Maggie getting stuck there?"

The smile fell from Robert's face. "Aye, I've thought long and hard about that, but I reckon there's enough of the stone for at least one of us to return. Don't take this the wrong way, but if it comes down to it, and me Maggie wants to come back, 'twill be her doing the traveling afore anyone else."

"Understood," Edward said. "I wouldn't have it any other way."

"Right! We'd best get to it, then. The sooner, the better. I'll talk to me daughter tonight, the wee scoundrel. I reckon she'll want to be the one to ask Dylan."

Edward shoved his hands in his pockets and nodded. "I imagine she will."

****

Maggie sat on the park bench, a half-eaten sandwich on her lap all but forgotten. "Dylan, let me finish explaining before you agree to this."

"I don't need to hear anymore. Just taking part in an expedition with Professor Armstrong is a huge opportunity. Traveling to the sixteenth century with him is . . . well, it's incredible."

"You do realize this will be a huge waste of your time," she said. "My dad thinks there's something going on between us, and I suppose this is his way of protecting me. I love him for it, but. . ." Maggie shrugged an apology and leaned back against the bench. "We won't be traveling any farther than present-day Scotland. Maybe there will be a dig there, but I doubt it."

"Maggie, everything your father told you is true." Dylan gulped down the remains of his Dr. Pepper, virtually bubbling over with enthusiasm. "It explains everything. His clothes! His weapons! He's shown them to the class, and they're real. It's always puzzled me because they don't look or feel their age, and yet there is no doubt in my mind they are sixteenth century."

"What do you mean, they don't look their age?"

He stared off into the distance for a moment before speaking, his eyes sparkling. "It's simple, really. If I were to touch the parchment on which Shakespeare wrote his sonnets, it would crumble in my hand. Clothing, weapons, they all possess a similar quality, only not as intense. Your father's things don't *react* the way I would expect four hundred and fifty-year-old materials to react. It's as if they've weathered the centuries without being touched by them."

"And you believe they have?"

"Oh, there's no doubt about it. If they're not from the sixteenth century, they're damn good copies, and I don't know anyone that talented. Not around here anyway."

"Dylan, come on, the sixteenth century! We both know the whole concept's impossible."

"Is it? Think about it, Maggie. Two hundred years ago, no one dared dream a man could walk on the moon, but not twenty years ago they did. They labeled Galileo a heretic because he said the earth revolved around the sun. Leonardo da Vinci was laughed at because he believed man could fly. Today, Einstein's theory says man can travel through time, even if it is the other way round. Don't you see? Yesterday's impossibilities become today's realities."

"But if it's true . . . Dylan, why would you want to go back over four hundred and fifty years? You could be killed."

"Then I'll die happy."

"Dylan!" Maggie crumpled up the old newspaper that held her lunch and tossed it in the nearest waste basket.

"Look, love, every time I cross the street, I take a risk, and I get nothing for it. Well, except to the other side, of course, but you know what I mean. At least with this, I have the chance to touch history, to be part of it."

"And that would make you happy?"

"Yes, it would," he said, his voice filled with conviction. "There's nothing here for me, nothing I really care about. I was a mistake, the result of a hot, torrid evening in the tropics. As soon as I was old enough, it was off to boarding school. No one ever cared about me, not the way your father cares about you, so what have I got to hold me here?"

Maggie thought her heart would break. *So that's why he never mentioned his family.* Feeling a sudden tenderness for the dark-haired grad student, she reached up and touched his face. "I'm sorry. I didn't know."

"You'd best not let your father see you getting so intimate," he said with a twinkle in his eye. "He'll change his mind and not let me go along."

Maggie stood up, shaking her head in exasperation. "All right, but don't blame me when you end up two months in the future with nothing to show for it but windburn. My father's stories are just that—stories! I truly believe this is nothing but an elaborate scheme to keep us apart."

"But it's not. In fact, this expedition almost guarantees we'll be together. If your dad wanted to separate us, why ask me along?"

"Because it's how my father's mind works. He was never crazy about me traveling to Long Island on my own in the first place, but when he found out you were heading there as well, it left him with two options. One, cancel the entire trip and make it look like he doesn't trust me."

"Which he clearly doesn't."

"Oh no, he trusts me. It's you he has a problem with. Anyway, assuming he wants to avoid the whole trust issue, he's left with solution number two."

"Which is to make sure we're together?"

"More like making sure he's wherever we are. Now he can't justify going to Long Island for the entire summer. It's not his field of study. But Scotland's another story. So he tells me we're spending the summer up north but tempers it by allowing you to come along. That way he's not the bad guy in my eyes, and he keeps you where he can watch you. A brilliant idea, really."

Dylan looked like a deer caught in the crosshairs, not sure which way to turn. "Brilliant? It's bloody mad! Does he do this with everyone, or is it just me he hates?"

"He doesn't hate you. It's just he . . ." She hesitated, searching for the right words. "He doesn't think you're right for me. You're already a grad student, and you do have a bit of a reputation."

"You realize it's mostly talk, don't you?"

"Yes, of course." She leaned over and kissed him on the cheek. "But it has to be the reason. No matter what you think, the alternatives are just too weird."

"So why agree to go at all? I know your father can be a bit stern at times, but I can't see him forcing you, not against your will. I imagine you can put on a proper temper tantrum of your own."

Maggie put her hands on her hips. "You do, do you? Would you like to experience one right now?"

"No, thank you." Dylan held his hands up in surrender. "But I still don't understand why you agreed to go."

The question confused her at first, until she remembered Dylan's words about his family. He'd never known what it meant to be loved, or to love, for that matter.

"Because he's my father. No matter what the outcome, I need to be there for him." She put her bag over her shoulder and smiled. "But don't worry, there will be plenty of fireworks when it turns out I'm right."

CHAPTER 4

"So what is Professor Foster's story anyway?" Dylan stretched his back, happy to get out of the cramped car and move about a bit.

They'd stopped along the side of a narrow dirt road, probably medieval in origin, to relieve themselves and get a bite to eat. Hardly more than a path, it rambled through the Cheviot Hills, providing a glorious view of the valley below. Robert and Edward had immediately headed toward a rocky outcrop, but Dylan had chosen to stay below with Maggie. He stood by her side, gazing out over the sweeping hills and windswept dales, a gentle breeze ruffling his hair.

"What do you mean, his story?" Maggie asked. Dylan's breath must have tickled, for she swatted at her ear. "And are you sure you want my dad to see your mouth that close to my neck? He might get the wrong idea."

"What? No, I didn't mean . . ." Dylan stopped short when he saw the twinkle in her eyes but moved back a step or two anyway. "I just wondered, you know, why is he making the trip? How does he know your father? Won't anyone miss him?"

"You do ask a lot of questions." Maggie scratched her head, throwing a glance up the hillside before continuing. "I suppose he's coming along because he's my father's best friend. As far back as I can remember he's always been there. Even when we lived on Long Island, Uncle Eddie visited whenever he could—summer vacation, winter break—almost like he wanted to make sure we were okay."

"Maybe he did. How long have they been friends?"

"I suppose they met in college." She shrugged and bent down to spread a blanket out on the ground. "They've never really said. Although they've both talked about being kids, and it didn't sound like they knew each other then."

"And as for anyone missing him," she went on, "why will it matter? We're not exactly going far, now are we?" A playful smile broke out on Maggie's lips, and she grabbed the basket of food from the backseat of the car. "I can't believe he tried to convince me he brought my father here from the sixteenth century."

It had been close on the ride up, and Dylan pulled at the collar of his leather jack. "Actually, that would explain a lot."

Maggie groaned and headed back toward the blanket.

"Okay, so you don't believe any of it. I get that, but suppose it's true? Isn't there anyone who will miss him?"

For a moment, Maggie said nothing, busying herself instead with unpacking the small picnic case. Dylan thought she hadn't heard him, until at last she handed him a chicken leg and sat back against a broken-down stone wall.

"He's like you, I suppose, except in his case the circumstances were a bit more illicit, like something out of a soap opera. You know, the wealthy noble's son knocks up a local girl, his family disowns both him and his newborn son, the mother dies in childbirth. I'm not sure about all the details. It isn't something he goes around bragging about, though, so I would appreciate it if you never, ever mentioned it again."

"Fine, I get it, but where's his son now? Did he die with his mother?"

"No!" Maggie tucked a piece of hair behind her ear. "Uncle Eddie was the son. His father's name was Charlie."

"Oh, well, where's his father, then?"

Maggie lifted her eyebrows. "Nosy, aren't we?"

"Just curious about the man I'll be traveling through time with." He lifted a shoulder and took a bite of his chicken.

With a roll of her eyes, Maggie continued. "Charlie died a few years back. I always thought he was a pretty nice guy."

"You knew this Charlie, then?"

"Yeah, he was the closest thing I had to a grandfather." She pulled her knees up to her chin, casting another gaze up the hillside, but there was still no sign of either her father or Edward. "I actually did some research after we first moved here to see what had happened."

"So I'm not the only nosy one." Dylan flashed her his smuggest grin and took another bite of his chicken.

Maggie frowned and tossed a bunch of grapes in his direction. "Eddie's my uncle, even if it isn't by blood, and I wanted to know everything I could about him."

"Of course," Dylan said, trying his best to suppress his smile. "Go on, then. What did you find out?"

"Well, it seems Elizabeth Foster, Uncle Eddie's grandmother, wielded all the power and knew how to use it. She demanded her husband, Neville, disown Charlie if the young man didn't deny the whole affair."

"So they wanted Charlie to say Edward wasn't his son."

"Well, Lizzie did anyway, and poor Neville died before he could say otherwise. As a result, the wicked bitch took the reins and presented Charlie with an ultimatum. If he acknowledged *the little bastard*, she'd cut him off then and there."

"But Charlie did? Acknowledge Eddie, I mean?"

"Yes, and he made sure Uncle Eddie got the best education he could afford. The old lady really did cut Charlie off, you see. So he enlisted in the army and applied to be an officer. With his wealthy background and a college degree, he had no problem working his way up to colonel. In fact, when I met him, he was already retired with a pension. He was all the family Uncle Eddie ever knew—except for us, of course. But then, sometimes friends can be closer than relatives."

49

"That's the truth." Dylan's thoughts drifted off to his own father and the ever-increasing abyss he couldn't breach, no matter how hard he tried. He flopped down beside Maggie and gave her a brotherly hug.

"Anyway, I guess we're our own little family now," she said. "And like it or not, you're included." She shot yet another look up the hillside. "Wherever we end up."

Dylan squeezed her shoulder. "I guess we are."

****

After lunch, Dylan made a quick trip up to the rocky outcrop before rejoining the others. Edward was already in the car, but Robert stood on the passenger side, a look of consternation etched across his face.

"Nice of ye to join us, Mr. Hetherington," the Scot said.

"Sorry, Professor. Call of nature and all that." Dylan climbed in the backseat and swallowed hard, jumping as Robert slammed the door behind him. The force knocked him over against Maggie's arm, but she just bit back a laugh and looked out the window.

They drove for about thirty miles, along hillside passes and tree-lined roadways, until at last they turned off onto a winding dirt road, its surface marred by weathered ruts and bone-jarring potholes. More than once Dylan grabbed on to the door handle to keep from landing in Maggie's lap. He could just imagine what her father would say about that. To make matters worse, low-hanging branches and brush scraped along the car's exterior, making it impossible to open the windows. The ride had been stuffy enough with them rolled all the way down. Now it was beyond stifling, and Dylan had never been very good at long, hot car rides to begin with.

After being tortured for another twenty minutes or so, he breathed a sigh of relief when Edward pulled the car up to an old abandoned farmhouse a few miles north of the Border. At least, from the direction they were heading and the time spent getting there, it's where Dylan figured they were. Not that it mattered as long as he could get some air. He opened the door and scrambled outside.

He heard Edward chuckle, but for once Robert didn't seem to be paying him any mind. Instead, he hopped from the car himself, nudging Dylan out of the way so he could talk to Maggie.

"Are ye ready, darlin'?" the Scot asked.

Maggie scooted across the seat toward her father, and he reached out to give her shoulder a little squeeze, his voice tinged with excitement. And something else, something even stronger. Perhaps the joy of returning home after all these years.

"Ye're no' too upset with me, are ye?"

"Of course not." She got out next to Dylan, her brow furrowing as she scanned the countryside. "Where is everybody?" she asked, turning back to her father. "Is this it?"

Edward turned the engine off and stepped out of the car as well. "Yes, and no."

Robert grinned in agreement. "Right place, wrong time."

"Of course," Maggie said. "How foolish of me, thinking we could travel through both time and space in one go. Or here's another theory: this could be nothing more than another dig, and we've just arrived early."

"Time will tell, darlin', but for tonight, we'll be staying here." Robert winked at his daughter, then took a deep breath of the crisp evening air before turning to Dylan.

"Now as for you, Mr. Hetherington," he continued, the softness melting away from his expression, "ye'd do well to remember what I said."

He put a sturdy arm around Dylan's shoulders and led him a few paces away from the car. "So much as look at me Maggie, and I'll hang ye meself. I'm only allowing ye to come along because I promised me daughter, fool that I am, and as ye're one of me best students, I ken ye'll appreciate what ye're about to see. Do we understand each other?"

"Yes, sir, perfectly." Dylan replied with a solemn nod, though he had no intention of paying much attention to that particular edict. Maggie was his friend, the only one he could really talk to, and he had no intention of letting her father's suspicions ruin their relationship. With a casual stretch, he sauntered back to Maggie's side, bending down to pick a clump of bluebells. He waited patiently until her father opened the boot to get some supplies before passing the blossoms behind his back and handing them to her with a wink.

Maggie shook her head but giggled at his antics all the same.

Robert, on the other hand, did not laugh. He came storming from behind the car, grabbed Dylan around the neck, and pressed him up against a nearby tree.

"I warned ye, laddie," he said through gritted teeth.

"Da, stop!" Maggie reached out, touching her father's arm. "He didn't mean anything by it."

"I didn't, Professor, honestly," Dylan said, his voice coming out in an anguished croak. The damp bark pricked his neck, and he writhed around in Robert's grasp, wondering if he was about to breathe his last.

"Have nae fear, laddie, if I'd wanted to kill ye, ye'd be long since gone. Me kin, on the other hand, mightna take so kindly to such as you, so ye'd best be watching yerself." With a hard stare, Robert released his grip and cleared his throat. "Now I see ye've already secured yer own jack, but the rest of what ye'll be needing is in the car. Get yerself dressed, aye. We have some work to do."

Robert strode back to the car as Dylan slumped down along the ancient tree. He leaned back against the weathered trunk, choking and sputtering.

Edward walked over to give him a hand up before continuing to fasten the laces of his jack and checking to make certain his scabbard was secure. "He's right, son. We'll be on Scottish soil, and they may not welcome two Englishmen. You'd best be on your guard, and for God's sake, leave the Scottish lassies alone, or it'll be more than a few bits of bark piercing that throat of yours."

Maggie nudged her uncle out of the way and brushed Dylan off, her cheeks red with annoyance. "I can't believe you two," she said before casting a disapproving glance in her father's direction. But Robert didn't even notice her. He was too busy preparing everything for their departure, right down to the dagger he slipped in his boot.

The stone cottage they entered looked comfortable enough. Edward announced it was an old fishing cabin of his father's, though he hadn't been up there much since the old man died. But he'd stocked it for their departure with everything they'd need on their journey.

Dylan sat down in one of the overstuffed chairs with a bottle of Guinness, but Robert had other ideas.

"Now let's get to it, laddie!" Robert handed him a familiar-looking pole with a long, narrow spike on one end and pointed out the window to the nearby barn. "We'll train in there. If I'm to take ye with me, ye'll learn well to defend yerself afore we go. We'll start with a pike, then, shall we?"

The prospect of sixteenth-century combat made Dylan forget all about a few splinters. He'd been practicing the art of medieval warfare at every reenactment he could find since he'd been sixteen years old, and he felt confident in his level of expertise. True, his usual arsenal didn't contain this particular weapon, but how hard could it be?

"Stand down a bit, lad," Edward said on their way to the barn. "Robbie here's been honing his skills every day for the past twenty-five years. He even managed to turn me into a decent warrior."

"And quite proud of it I am too," Robert said.

"I'm no slouch myself, Professor," Dylan said. Edward and Robert threw each other a skeptical glance, then the former shrugged and moved out of the way.

"Right then, lad," Robert said. "Put yer whole body into it, like it was part of ye. That's it."

Dylan wielded the long spear-like weapon with confidence. *This wasn't so hard.* Not until Maggie walked by with a few bottles of Guinness, and he stopped to wink at her. A moment later, he found himself on the ground with the cold steel of a pike pressed firmly against his throat.

"The first lesson to remember, lad," Robert said with a nod toward his daughter. "Never let a lass come between ye and yer work, nae matter how bonnie she may be. The second lesson concerns me daughter and what I'll do if I see ye looking at her like that again. I thought we'd come to an understanding, Mr. Hetherington."

"Yes, sir!" Dylan said, his voice squeaking out as Robert's pike pricked the damp skin of his neck.

"Now get yerself up and we'll try again, with a sword this time, I think."

And try again they did, over and over until Dylan fell to the ground, every muscle in his body aching.

"Let's go, lad." Robert taunted him with the point of his sword. "Morning will be here afore ye realize."

"I can't," Dylan said in sheer exhaustion. "Just let me rest a minute."

"And d'ye think the Maxwells or the Elliots will be letting ye rest a minute? That's all the time they'll need to finish ye off. Now up with ye, lad, and put some feeling into it. 'Tis more than the playacting ye're used to."

Once more, Dylan raised his sword and, with a battle cry, ran at Robert.

"That's it, lad," the Scotsman shouted as he blocked the blow. "Let yer blood run hot." Dylan lunged again, and Robert parried him once more, shoving him up against the wall. "Come on, lad, I can see the anger in yer eyes. Use it!"

Again and again, Dylan rushed forward, goaded on by Robert's remarks, and time after time Robert thwarted his attacks.

"Is that all ye can do, laddie?" Robert prodded, his words like a bony finger shoved into Dylan's sore side. "Ye spend more time on yer knees than a scullery maid."

Dylan's anger grew with each new thrust until he finally caught the Scotsman off guard, and Robert tumbled to the ground. With the sword pressed against the older man's quilted jack, Dylan stared into his eyes, his breath coming in short, swift bursts.

"Is that good enough, Professor?" He stood over the man, his lips pressed together, heat rising in his cheeks. "Or should I slice your throat while I'm at it?"

"Dylan!" Concern flooded Maggie's expression, but it did nothing to deter either him or his opponent.

"Could ye, lad?" Robert asked. The coldness in his voice would have sent a chill through even the most vicious of enemies. "Could ye rip yer blade across me neck till I gagged on me own blood? And could ye stand there whilst it splattered across yer chest, just to make sure ye cut deep enough? 'Tis a terrible sight, ye ken, a violent death. When ye're done, ye smell it for days. It soaks through yer clothes and permeates yer skin, and ye can see their eyes in yer dreams. 'Tis always the eyes that get to ye. The look of horror that fills them when ye cut through to the jugular."

Robert's remarks produced the intended effect. Dylan pulled back, letting his sword drop to the ground. "Dear God! I could have killed you, Professor."

"Nae, lad." Robert pushed himself up and placed his hand on Dylan's shoulder, his tone considerably softer than it had been. "Ye couldna."

"Yes," Dylan said, his voice strained in protest, "I—"

"Nae, Dylan, ye possess a kind heart, even if ye do give it away too easily. Ye kent when to hold back."

Dylan slid down along the wall and leaned his head against the rough-hewn boards of the barn, still trying to catch his breath. "They'll kill me, won't they?"

"That I canna tell ye, lad, but I've nae doubt ye'll wage them a good fight." Robert clapped him on the shoulder and started to walk away, but Dylan reached out.

"But I couldn't follow through," he said.

"I didna say that, lad. What I said was ye couldna do it now. When the time comes, in the heat of battle, ye'll do what ye must. The time to worry is when the killing comes too easy. Ye're where ye should be, and ye've the makings of a good Borderer. One I'd be proud to have fighting by me side . . . but no' by the side of me daughter," he added, his inflection once more taking on its usual stern tone.

"We really are just friends, Professor."

Robert nodded. "So ye say." He turned to walk away without another word, clearly feeling he'd achieved what he'd set out to do.

A protest died on Dylan's lips, and he dropped his head back down on his arms, his face flushed and sweaty, his knees quivering with fatigue as his arms rested on them. He felt as though every bit of energy had been drained from his body, for Robert had brought him to the physical and emotional threshold of battle. No faux melee with his friends, no matter how invigorating, ever achieved such an intensity, but in doing so, the man had shown him what it meant to be a true border knight. If he hoped to survive the past, these were the emotions he would need to endure and the skills he'd need to master.

"Are you okay?" Maggie knelt by his side and handed him a bottle of Guinness.

"Yes, surprisingly so. Your father knew exactly what he was doing." He glanced over at Robert and nodded, then he gave Maggie a big smile. "He trained me for what's to come. Because of him, I have a better idea of what to expect, and with a bit of practice, I might even survive."

Dylan's couldn't keep the excitement from his voice, and Maggie balled her hands at her side, letting out a scream of exasperation. She stood up, brushing the straw from the seat of her blue woolen overskirt.

"You can't be serious!" she said before she turned and stormed away.

Robert walked over to Dylan's side, the hint of a smile on his weathered lips. "Here, lad, ye'll be needing something stronger to stop the tremors." He handed Dylan a bottle of whisky, then sauntered back across the room, shaking his head and chuckling to himself.

****

The mist was just beginning to lift as they gathered beneath a large birch the next morning. Maggie rubbed the sleep from her eyes and wondered how far they planned on carrying this charade. The change of clothes and faux weapon practice had been bad enough, but now her father insisted they leave their nice comfortable beds at the crack of dawn for no other purpose but to meet beneath a tree. Sooner or later he'd be forced to admit they weren't technically going anywhere . . . or were they?

The thought sent goosebumps down along her arms, and she shivered in the crisp morning air. Determined to ground herself in the twentieth century, she reached up to touch the smooth white bark of the birch. *Just in case Edward really has discovered a way to travel back in time.*

She shook her head, admonishing herself for being so foolish, and looked up at the tall, thin branches that stretched toward the heavens. How she loved the stillness of the morning and the fresh, clean scent it brought with it. She closed her eyes and listened to a thrush as it sang overhead, her momentary insecurity forgotten.

"All right, then." Robert rounded the corner of the stone farmhouse and clapped his hands. "Let's get to it."

With a reluctant sigh, Maggie opened her eyes, hoping they didn't reveal her skepticism, but from the look on Robert's face, they'd given her away once more. In spite of his own enthusiasm, she felt certain her lack of belief troubled him.

"Maggie, darlin'," he said. "I ken ye dinna believe all this talk of time travel and me being wrenched from the sixteenth century, but I swear to ye 'tis all true. Yet as much as I long to return, I'll no' risk causing you a similar heartache. If we're to go, ye must be fully aware of what awaits ye. I love ye, darlin', and would do noucht to hurt ye."

"I know, Da, and I love you for it." She crinkled her nose and smiled as she brushed her fingers against his freshly shaved cheek.

"Then just for a moment, I want ye to pretend 'tis all true."

"Da," Maggie started, but she could see her protests would have little effect and heaved an audible sigh. "All right, suppose I do believe we're about to be transported to the past. What of it?"

"Would ye still agree to go, Maggie? Even if it meant ye mightna be able to return?"

She opened her mouth to answer, but Robert held up his hand, cutting her off. "Think hard about it, and answer as if ye believed it were true. Do this for me, darlin'."

As Maggie looked around the clearing, she came to a sudden realization. Everyone else truly believed this was about to happen. But how could it be possible? Dylan's words echoed in her memory. *Yesterday's impossibilities become today's realities.*

She took a deep breath and touched her father's cheek once more. "Yes, I would. If it's that important to you, then it's important to me as well. My home is wherever you are."

Tears shone in Robert's eyes, and his face beamed with paternal pride. "Thank ye, darlin'," he managed to utter before rubbing a large hand across his mouth and clearing his throat. "Now as to you, Mr. Hetherington, d'ye understand there may be nae coming back? In fact, being an Englishman, ye mightna even be welcome on Scottish soil."

"Yes, Edward has—I mean Professor Foster has made that clear."

"There's nae shame in backing out, lad." Robert's voice had lost its sharp edge and taken on a seriousness not usually present when he spoke to his student.

"And miss out on the chance of a lifetime? Not likely."

"What of yer own kin? Have ye explained it all to them?"

Dylan huffed a sarcastic laugh, the smile on his lips belying the sorrow in his eyes. "No need, sir. They haven't inquired about my whereabouts since I started at uni. They simply deposit the money in my bank account and consider their duty fulfilled."

Robert nodded, shooting an understanding glance in Maggie's direction before rubbing his hands on the bit of breeches visible between his jack and high leather boots. "Well, as I said, let's get on with it, then, eh?"

"Are we ready?" Edward asked. Without waiting for an answer, he bent down and took a small box out of the canvas bag he'd brought with him. He placed it on the ground, reached back into the bag, and produced two amulets. Each one contained a polished sage-colored stone surrounded by a setting of small bronze trinity knots. He gave the first to Robert and hung the other around his own neck.

"I had the stone split and remounted, just in case we get separated."

Robert took the amulet and placed it around Maggie's neck. "Keep it with ye at all times, lass. 'Tis the only way home."

Maggie grabbed on to the pendant, not really knowing why. Was she beginning to doubt her skepticism?

"Are you sure, Rob?" Edward asked one last time. Robert answered with a nod, and for the first time Maggie realized that beyond this point there would be no turning back.

Edward took a long, deep breath and pressed an inconspicuous latch on the side of the chest.

Almost at once, the strange stones began to vibrate and sparks escaped from beneath the lid of the jewel-covered box. A stillness descended upon them, muffling the sounds of nature, and yet Maggie could see its movement all around her, in the shifting of the leaves and the flitting of the birds in the tree above her.

Trying to convince herself it was all in her imagination, she chanced a peek at the farmhouse. Still there. She rubbed her neck, allowing the tension to slip through her fingers, but her relief didn't last long.

A soft haze drifted around the cabin's foundation, rippling and pulsating, like the heat haze hovering above the highway on a hot summer's day. But this one didn't just float above the surface. It crept up the walls and spread out over the surrounding area, completely engulfing it.

Her eyes met Dylan's, and a huge smile crossed his face. Maggie gasped, the full ramifications of what she was seeing dawning on her at last. These were the doors to the past, and within minutes they would all be swept through them.

Seeing it now, unfolding before her, she wondered how it had taken Edward so many years to see the part the amulets played. Thin golden lines bound each to the jeweled chest, shimmering and quivering until they joined as one, then bounced off into the atmosphere. Their movement whipped up hurricane-force winds that swirled beneath their feet, yet at the same time they swaddled them in their embrace.

A distant clap of thunder echoed off the invisible walls, and Maggie jumped, convinced they stood in the eye of some supernatural storm. The hues and pigments of the surrounding area started to meld together as one before bursting forth on their own once more like a giant kaleidoscope of living color. All the while, the golden threads spun around them, cloaking them in an enchanted glow.

Maggie couldn't help but gaze in awe at the spectacular display. Her heart raced within the stiff linen kirtle that bound her ribs, instinct prompting her to reach out and grab her father's hand. But she felt no fear, only strength in Robert's grasp and an overwhelming connection with those around her.

At the same time, she sensed an odd detachment from the world she knew. Though she stood with her feet secure on the ground, she could swear she hovered above it. Cool blasts of air ruffled her hair with a sleepy quality, relaxing her and filling her with euphoric warmth. So much so that a pang of regret surged through her when, little by little, the colors drifted back to their proper places and a soft white aura surrounded them. The wind died down to a gentle breeze, the golden threads fading away and disintegrating before her eyes, and the only sounds she could hear were the song of a thrush and the croak of a distant frog.

Maggie looked at Robert, the gleam in his eyes answering all her questions. There could no longer be any doubt. They'd traversed the threads of time, and at that very moment stood in the midst of another century. Though she couldn't fathom how it was possible, she knew one thing with complete certainty. Her father's tales of border raiders and thunder on the moor consisted of more than fabricated stories. He'd woven them from his memories, and they were all true.

CHAPTER 5

Scottish Border - 1538

Maggie's breath caught as Robert stepped out from amidst the small grove of trees. He closed his eyes for a moment, taking a deep breath before opening them again and reaching over to squeeze her hand.

"Can ye no' smell it, Maggie?" he asked. "The air so clear and fresh. 'Tis as sweet as I remember."

Maggie glanced at her father, studying his expression, and a smile tugged at the corner of her mouth. She couldn't deny a certain crispness hung in the air, filled with the scents of bluebells and pinecones, but an underlying hint of manure pervaded it as well. It reminded her of the summers they'd spent upstate at their cabin on Lake George, yet nothing about it suggested they'd arrived in the sixteenth century.

Something had changed, though, even if she couldn't quite figure out what. She turned toward the broken-down farmhouse, hoping to use it as a reference point, and her heart rose in her throat. Not only was the building gone, but their car and the barn around back had vanished along with it.

Her face must have reflected her astonishment, for the corners of Edward's eyes crinkled. Yet he said nothing to her. Not even one word of explanation. Instead, he knelt to close the chest, tilting his head up toward Robert and directing his comments to him.

"But is it sixteenth-century air?" he said. "We don't really know the date. It could be fifty years ago or four hundred." He stood and returned the ornate container to its small canvas bag. "Worse yet, it could be the same day I handed you this box, which would be four hundred and seventy-five years ago now."

"All the better, then." Her father clapped his hands together. "'Twill be like I never left."

"Perhaps, except you'll be twenty-five years older . . . and they won't."

"Ach well, we'll make the best of it in any case." A smile spread across his face once more, and he squeezed his friend's shoulder.

Edward shook his head and walked a few steps away, but Maggie reached out to grab his arm before he could go very far.

"You mean you don't know how to . . . to . . . drive that thing!"

"In a word, no." Edward shrugged before turning to walk farther away, clearly distracted by something he felt far more urgent.

Maggie pressed her lips together and glared at his retreating form. It wasn't like him to be so abrupt.

"That bloody sod!" With an exasperated groan, Edward moved even farther from the trees. "Where's Dylan?" He spun back around to face her father. "I warned you something like this might happen. It's all just one big adventure to him. He doesn't understand the dangers."

"Reminds ye of yerself when ye were his age, eh?"

"Maybe, yes. And I nearly lost my head, didn't I?"

Her father scratched the back of his neck. "Aye, well, he was here a minute ago. I ken he made it through."

"Oh, he made it through all right. He nearly knocked me over." Edward shook his head. "If anything happens to him, it's my fault. I should never have let you talk me into bringing him along. What are we supposed to do now?"

"We find him, of course." Her father took a few steps in Edward's direction, harebells and thistle brushing haphazardly against his high leather boots. "No doubt he's headed ower yon brae. We'd best go after him afore he gets too far, aye."

Maggie heard a rustling in a wooded area to her right and wandered over toward the trees, scanning the shadows for any sign of her wayward friend. They didn't even know where—no, when—they were, and now to top it all off, Dylan had disappeared. She put her hand to her mouth and began gnawing on her nails. How could any of it be possible?

"Stay close, Maggie," her father called.

With a last look toward the woods, she turned and followed her father. Perhaps it was just a bird or some other woodland creature. Dylan must have enough brains not to be playing hide-and-seek at a time like this. Besides, he wouldn't make her worry.

Her father stepped up next to Edward and slapped him on the back. "Dinna fash yerself. We'll find the lad."

But the three of them had no sooner started toward the distant hill when a thunderous disturbance rumbled over the rise. Clouds of dust billowed up above the heather-covered fell like a wildfire burned beyond, and an air of urgency replaced her father's jovial expression. Edward glared at him, his eyes reflecting similar concern.

"Nae sense running," her father said with a great sigh. "There's noucht we can do but pray they're friendly."

"You could go home," Edward said. "I may not be sure what year this is, but I do know you'll return to our point of departure. And if my calculations are correct, there's enough of the stone left to get you there."

A scowl crossed her father's face, making it clear that wasn't even an option. "No' without the lad!" he said.

Maggie took a deep, calming breath, her eyes glued on the swelling clouds of dust. The reality of the situation came crashing down on her, and she swallowed hard to dislodge the lump in her throat. Yet an undeniable surge of curiosity caused her skin to tingle. Or was it the buckram kirtle pinching her back? She wriggled uncomfortably, but not even the heavy woolen frock, with its stiff linen ruffles, could stifle her growing sense of wonder.

Nor could Edward's abrupt declaration. "Then at least send Maggie back!"

"Oh, no you don't!" She'd inherited a stubborn streak from her father and intended on using it to its full potential. "I'm not leaving the two of you here." To punctuate the statement, she brushed a stray piece of hair from her eyes. "I may not be sure where we are either—or when, for that matter—but I do know you're all I have, and I'm not going to abandon you."

"But Maggie . . ." Edward groaned, his eyes darting between her and the growing cacophony. "Be reasonable."

"If you're staying, then so am I!"

Maggie grabbed on to her father's arm, attempting to adopt a demeanor as firm as his. Perhaps she should have considered her options a bit more carefully, but she was far too impetuous for that. Besides, she had no idea what the approaching danger was; although there could be no denying the grave expression on father's face. Taking a deep, quivering breath, she squeezed his arm all the tighter, her eyes riveted on the grass-covered knoll. A prayer still lingered on her lips when a distant shout caused her anxiety to dissipate, at least for the moment.

"That's Dylan!" She tugged on her father's sleeve. "I'm sure of it."

She would have recognized his voice anywhere, though the content of his diatribe caused her eyes to widen. Aside from a very pronounced Oxbridge accent, every other word out of his mouth consisted of profanity, and in spite of the trembling in her knees, she couldn't help but laugh at the sight that followed.

A group of riders barreled over the brae with Dylan Hetherington thrown sideways across one of their saddles. Though he twisted and turned, writhing against his captor, his efforts didn't appear to faze the men who held him prisoner. In fact, they were riding so hard Maggie closed her eyes, convinced the small band would trample them down where they stood.

Her father yanked her behind him, giving her a spin in the process, and Maggie opened her eyes momentarily to regain her bearings. As she did, she caught a glimpse of someone hiding behind a crumbling stone wall. She blinked to clear her vision, certain she'd seen the man before—in her father's books. For a split second, their eyes locked and her breath caught in her throat. Those dazzling blue-gray eyes! But how could that be? She blinked again, but the figure had disappeared into the woods.

The clatter of approaching hoofbeats brought her back to her senses, and she peeked around her father's arm. Though the men were almost to the foot of the hill, they showed no sign of stopping. Closing her eyes once more, she braced herself for the impact. Dylan's voice continued to ring through the air, and she was contemplating how the last sight she'd ever see was him squirming like a landed fish, when a strong Scottish accent reverberated off the morning mist.

"Haud where ye are, lads!"

It was thicker and gruffer than any burr Maggie had ever encountered. Even her father's harsh guttural sounds weren't that coarse. And yet she wouldn't call it unpleasant at all. In fact, quite the contrary.

Maggie stuck her head around her father's arm once more, his hand still firmly holding her in place. With a mix of apprehension and curiosity, she opened one eye, then the other, until at last she found herself gazing upon the rider behind the voice.

An attractive man of medium build, with light brown hair and broad shoulders, he reminded her of her father. At first, she found it a bit odd, but then it dawned on her. He too must be an Armstrong. Her mouth dropped as the realization washed over her. She'd seen him before as well, in her father's portrait book. Only now he was more than just a legendary figure, for there, standing before her, was a real live Border reiver.

And if he was real . . . She shifted her gaze back to the stone wall, scanning the wooded hill behind it. So was the handsome young man skulking deep within the woods. Her heart skipped a beat. How many times had she stared at his likeness in her father's collection, dreaming of him whisking her off to his home? What did the notation say? *Portrait painted circa 1537, unknown Englishman.*

A new wave of excitement coursed through her body. A Foster, her father had always said, though he couldn't be sure. It didn't really matter. She had to meet this mysterious man whose image had so enchanted her.

Slipping from her father's grasp, she began to inch her way toward the pine trees, but she hadn't taken three steps before Robert's hand clutched her arm and pulled her back to his side. She cast another glance up toward the woody thicket, hoping to catch one more glimpse of the captivating reiver, but just then the horseman spoke again, recapturing her attention.

"Rabbie! Is that you, man?" The rider had brought his horse up short, inches from where they were standing, and now squinted down at them.

"Andy!" her father shouted back, his voice quivering. "Is it really you, lad? Where have ye been?"

"I might ask ye the same."

Robert laughed out loud, slapping his leg with his gloves. "Ma's been searching all ower for ye. Been down to see that Hetherington lass again, have ye?"

At first, the stranger seemed to hesitate. "What are ye talking about, man? Ye've no' been home in . . ." Then he stopped short, a broad grin creeping across his face. "Still the joker, hey brother! See her, Rabbie! I wed her, though I canna say it pleased the warden. Nearly cost me neck."

Robert's eyes twinkled with mischief. "A shame that would have been, leaving such a fine lass as Marion Hetherington a widow afore her time."

"Aye, that it would, no' to mention the fondness I have for me own neck." Andy jumped down and clapped Robert on the shoulder. "But what happened to ye, man? We thought ye long gone from this world."

"Suffice it to say I ended up in Lancashire, no' of me own free will, mind, but . . . well, 'tis a tale for another time, eh?" A sudden thump interrupted their conversation.

"Get your filthy, thieving hands off me." Dylan was on the ground, struggling to stand, much to the amusement of the riders surrounding him. One by one, they took turns shoving their boots in his back and sending him sprawling into the harebell-strewn grass.

Maggie opened her mouth to protest, but the squint of her father's eyes told her it wouldn't be wise. Instead, she pressed her lips together and watched in silence while Andy Armstrong grabbed Dylan by the arm and jerked him up. The reiver glared at the horsemen, his harsh expression daring anyone to challenge him.

"We were just having a bit of fun, Andy," a dark-haired rider said.

"So ye were, lad, but 'tis done now, aye."

Hmm, perhaps not a complete barbarian. Though a moment later, Maggie had cause to question that conclusion when the Scotsman dragged Dylan over to her father with such force the young man could barely keep his footing.

"Look what I caught me, Rabbie," Andy said with a grin. "One of them English scoundrels."

Dylan twisted in the reiver's grasp, his eyes flaring with fire, his jaw set and determined in spite of his bound hands. He tried to brush the dirt from his jack but stopped abruptly when he noticed Robert. Maggie held her breath, praying he wouldn't blurt out something that gave them away.

"So ye have, Andy." Robert nodded and placed his arm across his brother's shoulders. He shot a quick glance at Edward, jerking his head toward the woods before steering Andy around to the other side of the horses, Dylan in tow.

"But ye can deal with him later," he continued. He turned to scold the small group of riders. "As for now, what's the matter with the rest of ye? Are ye no' glad to see yer auld brother, Sim? And is that me cousin Archie bringing up the rear, as usual? Get down here, the lot of ye, and tell me what ye've been up to these last few years."

Almost as one entity, a rush of affection surrounded Robert that Maggie found strangely unexpected. These rough men in their leather armor didn't seem the kind to show any form of emotion whatsoever. But then, her father must be one of these men as well, and she knew how tender he could be.

A flash of movement caught her eye, and she turned to see Edward sidling over toward the stone wall. For the third time that day, she held her breath, searching for her father among the throng of rugged men that pushed and shoved for his attention. Though she couldn't see him, she did spot Dylan staggering in her direction.

"Your father bloody pushed me," he said, rubbing his arm. "And what am I to do now?"

Before she could answer, a blur to the right caused her to jump, though it was only Edward darting across the narrow distance from the wall. He grabbed hold of Dylan's jack and motioned for him to follow, but the young Englishman dug his heels into the ground.

Maggie rolled her eyes and tilted her head in the direction of the wooded hillside behind them.

"Not without you," Dylan said in a voice so low Maggie had to strain to hear.

"Yes, without her." Edward's grip tightened, his expression hardening as he yanked the stubborn man off into the thick pine trees.

Dylan glanced back once or twice, tripping over gnarled roots and fallen branches along the way, but soon both he and Edward had disappeared from her sight.

Maggie tore her eyes away from the fugitives and glanced back at the rowdy swarm surrounding her father. For the moment, he continued to command their attention, but sooner or later they were bound to notice Dylan was missing. She blew out her cheeks and rubbed her sweaty hands on the skirt of her blue woolen gown.

"And who's the bonnie wee lass?" a gruff voice bellowed out in her direction, and she looked up to see Andy Armstrong giving her the once-over. "D'ye no' think she's a bit young for ye, Rabbie?"

"And since when did a lassie's age ever matter to ye?"

"Ye ken better than that, Rabbie Armstrong. 'Tis no' me way, nor yers, I'd wager, but then I reckon ye've been down with them wretched outlanders for so long, who can say what ye've been up to? So is she what's been keeping ye from yer kith and kin, then?"

A hearty laugh burst from her father's lips. "She is me kith and kin, ye daft fool. 'Tis me daughter, Maggie."

He motioned her over, and she went, albeit a little reluctantly. Though she couldn't explain why, instinct prompted her to smile and dip into a slight curtsy.

Her father's eyes sparkled with a pride and excitement that warmed Maggie's heart. She'd never seen him so happy, but then he was with his family again. And he belonged here in this ruggedly beautiful country. Now she finally understood his obsession with the past. All the stories came flooding back, distant images planted in her memory from her early years. Faces began to match names, and the realization filled her with a strange sense of belonging.

"She's a fine lass, Rabbie." The dark-haired man her father called Sim lifted her around the waist, almost tossing her in the air.

"Hey!" she said. The man's thick hands squeezed the air out of her, and for a moment her head spun. Sim, she thought, a younger brother.

"Wait till me ma sees her." He rested Maggie back on the ground, his smile falling away. "She bid us search all ower for ye that night, Rab, ye being her favorite, and all. Ye near broke her heart. 'Twas like ye fell from the earth, and now to find out ye've been holed up in that godforsaken land and not a word to ye kin. What were ye thinking, man?"

Robert turned away, his jaw jutting out as tears glistened in his eyes. "'Tis a long story, and I yearn to get home. As ye say, it's been a while in coming."

Andy put his foot in the stirrup, nodding as he settled into his saddle. "Then mount one of the hobblers there, and we're on our way. Ye can ride with me, darlin'."

He lifted Maggie on his horse and grabbed the reins. "Wait a minute! Where's that English rascal got to? I planned on holding him to ransom. He canna be far."

Andy kicked his heels against his pony's side, but Robert reached out and touched his shoulder. The reiver stopped and jerked his head around, a frown darkening his brow.

"Could we just be getting home, lad?" Robert said. "I've been waiting near twenty-five year. Ye'll have another chance at him, 'tis sure."

Andy stared at his brother for one long moment, then gave a firm nod. "Right then, let's be heading home." And spurring on his horse once more, he led them north along a dirt-covered path.

****

Will Foster crouched behind the crumbling stone wall, watching the Armstrongs approach over the opposite hilltop. They pulled up before what he could only assume was a small foraging party, for the strangers traveled on foot. But where had they come from? Moments before, nothing but harebells and thistle had filled that field. He scratched his head. Perhaps they'd walked from a nearby village. Not too clever with the Armstrongs on the prowl. Then again, maybe they were of the same clan, though he certainly didn't recognize any of them. The Armstrongs, however, he knew all too well, and he thought it best to stay out of their way.

As he peered around the broken wall, one of the strangers turned. An angel amongst a pack of wolves, no doubt. But one of the men tugged her back to his side before Will could determine if she was their hostage. Though he was certain she'd seen him, she didn't cry out, so perhaps she hoped he'd rescue her.

He inched a bit closer, staying low to avoid detection. Though he still couldn't make out much of their conversation, the breeze did manage to catch a few words that caused his ears to perk up. "So, he's a cousin to Archie, is he."

Will scurried amongst the trees, coming to rest behind an ancient pine. He caught sight of the bonnie wee lass once more, standing off to the side this time. Instinct caused him to grasp the hilt of his sword. If he moved quickly, he could run out and rescue her before the Armstrongs realized he was there. Then one of the men spoke again, his words taking Will by surprise.

"'Tis me daughter, Maggie," the stranger said.

"His daughter!" The words had barely hissed past his lips when he noticed two figures stumbling up the slope behind him. He could still grab her, hold her to ransom, but what of the two rogues scrambling through the trees like their breeks were on fire. What were they up to? The band of men gathered before him soon provided a hint to the fugitives' identities.

"Wait a minute!" one of the Armstrongs growled. "Where's that English rascal got to?"

"English! So that's why they've been sneaking about." Will gazed up the hill, then back out at the auburn-haired Scottish beauty. "Another time, perhaps, lass."

With a sigh of regret, he slipped away, circling around to give the pair of rogues a wide berth, for, English or not, they could still be dangerous. When he reached his pony, he led the animal behind a rocky outcrop, where he waited for the fugitives to pass. They took their time, but as they stumbled by, he crept out and placed his sword between the older man's shoulder blades.

"Oh bollocks!" the man said. "Not again."

"State yer name, sir," Will said, "afore ye canna state it at all."

Before the man could answer, Will reached down and yanked the dagger from his boot, pointing it directly at the younger of the two scoundrels. "'Twould be best if ye let go of that hilt, man, elst ye might find me dagger planted in yer chest, no' to mention what me sword will do to yer friend here."

"Leave it be, Dylan." The older man held his head still, barely even moving his lips. "Foster. My name is Foster.

Will's eyes narrowed, his knuckles turning white as he gripped his weapons, though he tried to keep the anger from his voice. "Is it, now? Ye'll be acquainted with me father, then. Strange that, being I've never laid eyes on ye afore."

"Wait! You couldn't be Graham's son, could you?"

For a moment, Will was taken aback, but he recovered straightaway. After all, his parentage wasn't exactly a secret. Anyone on the Borders would be privy to that information.

"Aye," he said, "what of it?"

"I'm an old friend . . . a cousin, actually . . . from Lancashire. Perhaps your da's spoken of me."

Will eased up on his sword, keeping it at the ready as he moved around to face the man. He did remember his father mentioning a distant relative from somewhere outside the Borders. It could have been Lancashire. "Aye, he may have. What did ye say yer Christian name was?"

"You didn't exactly give me a chance to say anything, but it's Eddie. It must be near twenty-five years since I last saw your da. 'Twill be good to see him again."

"I'm sure," Will said. "Ye winna mind coming back to the peel with me, then, will ye?"

"No, of course not, but isn't he here with you?"

Will frowned. "Nae, he'd business ower Hexham way." Perhaps he shouldn't be so honest. "Just me and a few of me brothers this time."

"Your brothers, Walt and Duncan, then. They're sure to remember me. A slip of a lad Duncan was then, but I convinced your father to let him go with us on a foray. I can't say your mother thanked me for it, but the lad was quite pleased."

"That I couldna say, but I'd wager ye're right about me ma." Will relaxed his sword and shoved the dirk back into his boot. "And who's this one, then?" he asked with a tilt of his head. "Another cousin?"

"Yes, as a matter of fact. My sister's son, though she wed a Hetherington. His name's Dylan."

Will sheathed his sword and walked over to retrieve his pony. "Dylan, is it? 'Tis an odd name for these parts, but never mind. We'd best be moving on. The Armstongs looked to be heading north, but ye canna tell with the likes of them. They could be coming ower the hill anytime now."

They walked along in silence for quite a while, Will leading his pony so as not to get too far ahead of his companions. But when his stomach gave an audible grumble, he thought it time they stopped to eat a bite.

He drew a sack from his saddlebag and sat down on a nearby rock. "'Tis nowt much, but 'twill have to do. I wasna expecting to feed anyone but meself." He offered the two outlanders some of his mother's oatcakes, then stuffed the remainder in his own mouth.

Edward took the cold patty and nodded his thanks. "What are you doing this far from home, lad?" he asked when he'd finished the last bite. "It's clear your brothers aren't with you."

Will swallowed his food and heaved a deep sigh. "'Tis a matter of honor between meself and Ian Rutherford. He's been sullying me sister's good name, and I plan to put an end to it."

"What about your family? Surely they'll want to settle it as well."

"Oh aye, they'd like nowt better, but me da wants to spare our Annie having any more grief, so he's been holding back. I reckon I can do what needs be done and nae one will be the wiser."

"All by yourself?" Dylan interjected, his eyebrows raised. "Going to single-handedly take on his entire clan, are you?"

"I'll find him by himself right enough," Will said. He wasn't quite sure he liked this younger one, but his own mother was a Hetherington, so . . . "'Tis simply a matter of learning where to look and putting a few coins in the right hands."

"It's sure to start a feud," Edward said. "What will your da think about that?"

Will took a slug of ale before passing the leather bottle on. "They'll be nae need for me da or anyone else to find out who's to blame. The whores of Hexham and Carlisle might even say I'd spent the night with them in gratitude for being spared his affections. At the very least, they'll thank me, that's sure."

"In that case, I would be honored to offer my sword," Dylan said. "After all, what are cousins for?" A roguish grin crossed his lips, and a naughty twinkle lit his eyes.

"True enough," Will said, a bit wary of the man's enthusiasm. "But we'll see what me da has to say about ye first, aye?"

"Of course, that's quite understood."

Will sat staring at his newfound cousin for a moment, trying to assess his sincerity. "Ye do talk a wee bit daft, lad," he finally said with a shrug, determined to reserve his opinion on the subject until he returned home.

"He hails from down around Oxford," Edward said.

"Aye, well, that explains it, then." Will stood up, brushing the crumbs from his breeks. "Now we'd best be on our way, or we'll no' be home afore dark."

Edward reached out and caught Will's arm. "Aren't you afraid we might turn on you, now that we know you're alone?"

Will rubbed a finger under his nose to conceal a smile. "Me da's quite fond of telling the tale about a certain cousin, ye see. Seems the man incurred me ma's wrath by convincing him to let me brother Duncan go along on a raid. I reckon nae man would willingly pretend to be that cousin, no' if he valued his life."

"She can't still be bothered about it. My God, Duncan must be in his late thirties by now."

"Aye, that'd be about right, but me ma can nurse a grudge to rival any Border feud."

Dylan laughed and Edward threw a scowl in his direction. "Yes, well, I'll deal with Betty when the time comes. Back to this trouble with the Rutherfords, though. If you feel that strongly about it, why did you take the time to help us?"

Will had started to walk away, but that statement stopped him in his tracks. They certainly weren't from the Borders. No doubt about that. He took a deep breath, then turned to face Edward.

"Ye're family, or so ye say, and me da would take the switch to me if I left ye to them Armstrongs. Though if ye dinna pick up the pace soon, it might all be for nowt. They're a tricky lot and on horseback could catch us up in nae time."

"Yes, of course." Edward said, his brow furrowed. "I can't believe Betty's still angry with me."

"Oh, aye. Last time me da mentioned it, she was dressing a chicken for dinner. Put the cleaver right through the table, she did." Without another word, Will veered off the road, a smile touching his lips. He took a narrow, overgrown trail that headed southwest, to England and his home.

CHAPTER 6

Maggie clutched the horse's mane as they galloped along. She didn't appreciate being yanked from the ground and thrust onto the animal, especially by a strange man in a leather vest and thigh-high boots, but she had no desire to fall off and land on her head either.

Seeking some sort of reassurance, she shot a glance in her father's direction. Robert gave a single nod, and, as always, his steady gaze comforted her. With the tension drained from her body, she rested back against her uncle's chest, letting his sturdy arms support her.

So this was her father's family, and by extension, her own. Gazing around at the other men, she tried to match the names and faces with the portraits in her father's book. Andy and Sim she'd already identified. They were her father's brothers, which made them her uncles. And there was the one called Archie. He was a cousin. But what about the others? Could it be they were related in some way too? She shook her head. How she would ever remember them all?

Her father rode close by, but even when they slowed to a trot, she needed to listen carefully to hear what he was saying.

"Did he name his family?" Robert asked his brother Andy. "The Englishman, I mean."

Maggie frowned for a moment, wondering what her father was up to, but then it hit her. His whereabout for the past twenty-five years was going to be hard enough to explain. No sense throwing his acquaintance with two unknown Englishmen into the mix as well.

"No, but I'd never seen him afore," her uncle replied. "A broken man, I'd wager." Andy smiled and slapped her father on the back. "'Tis all right. I ken how ye feel. I didna think ye'd gone soft or anything. Ye havena, have ye?"

Robert did a double take, his eyes narrowing, though a smile touched his lips. "Ye want to test it out here and now, do ye?"

Andy threw his head back, roaring with laughter. "Same auld Rabbie. Would have liked to ken who he was, though."

"Ach, I reckon he run off with the one I met. A Foster, I'm thinking, or near enough."

"Well, that explains it, then. They've been a right bit of trouble lately."

"We feuding with them, are we?"

"I wouldna say feuding exactly, but we've no' been on the best terms for a right bit now."

"What happened to cause the rift?"

"That tale can wait, Brother. There's another more pressing, I'd say."

The muscles in her uncle's arms tightened, and Maggie held her breath, sensing what he was going to ask.

"God's teeth, man! Where have ye been all this time? And nary a word. Lancashire indeed!"

Her father nodded before emitting a deep sigh. "I reckon ye've a right to ask. I'll no' deny ye that, but if ye'd bear with me a wee bit longer, I'm of a mind to wait till we're all together again. 'Tis too painful to recount more than once."

Maggie was sure Andy whispered a curse under his breath, but much to her relief, his arms relaxed once more.

"Aye, I'll grant ye that, but next I ask I'll be expecting an answer."

"I wouldna have it any other way, Brother. Now about our feud with the Fosters . . ."

"Ach, of late 'tis more to do with Ian Rutherford. Seems the lad went sweet on one of their lassies and asked for her hand. Auld Graham gave his blessing right enough, but then two days afore the handfast was to take place, he broke the contract. Accusations were bandied about on both sides, and Ian left without a bride. They'd even gotten permission from the warden to wed."

"Ian Rutherford?" Robert scratched the top of his head, tilting his blue bonnet to the side. "And who might he be that his broken heart is our concern?"

"Hob's son," Sim said, riding up on Robert's other side. "He's quite a strapping young lad. Mayhap our Maggie here can take the poor lad's mind off that Foster wench. What d'ye think, Rabbie?"

Maggie looked over at her father, lifting her right eyebrow in a warning gesture, though it only caused Robert to smile.

"I think me Maggie needs to get settled in a bit afore she has to deal with young Ian."

"Spoken like a true father," Andy said with a boisterous laugh.

They rode at a full gallop for the next mile or so before stopping to water the horses and continuing at a slower pace. Maggie listened intently while her father and his brothers bantered back and forth, the morning sun warm against her face, lulling her into a gentle sleep. When she woke, some hours later by the set of the sun, she found her cheek plastered against her uncle's leather jack and a line of drool running down her chin. She looked around, hoping no one–noticed, before she settled back and took in the scenery.

Rolling hills stretched out before them, cloaked in shades of green and brown, while patches of blue and yellow wildflowers pushed their heads toward the sky in search of the last remnants of sunshine. Off to the right, a silvery river cut its way through the countryside, its gurgling current echoing in Maggie's ears even as it turned off in the opposite direction. They rode along at a steady pace, the buzz of pleasant conversation floating on air thick with midges, until at last they rounded a bend, and Maggie spied a peel tower off in the distance, shrouded in the musty light of the late afternoon haze.

The sight caused a shiver of excitement to run down her spine. What more proof did she need? She could barely believe it, and yet here it was, just the way her father had described it in his stories. Only they weren't simply stories anymore. The dirt road they traveled curved once again, giving her a better view, and she studied the scene before her.

The tower itself stood four stories high, made of gray boulders, with a pitched roof. Each floor contained a few arrow slits, but only one window, and there was a huge door of rough-hewn wood with a narrow wooden staircase leading up to it. A large wall surrounded the area, forming a fair sized barmekin where livestock could easily be sheltered during an attack. At least, that's what her father used to say. The memory of sitting on his lap listening to him weave his stories brought a smile to her lips.

A light mist had begun to fall, enveloping the entire enclosure in a dreamlike cloud and imbuing it with a mystical quality Maggie found enchanting. Familiar portraits from her childhood swam into view, her father's tales ringing in her ears, welcoming her with fond memories. And when Robert clicked his heels and raced across the rugged landscape toward his family, her heart rode with him, for in a way, she too was going home.

They'd barely reached the surrounding wall when an old woman came running toward the group. A kerchief covered her steel-gray hair, her blue eyes shining like beacons, and though she scarcely stood five feet tall, she nevertheless commanded an air of quiet authority.

"What is it, Ma?" Sim's voice was strained as he pulled up on the reins of his pony with a force Maggie thought completely uncalled for.

After shooting a disapproving frown in her uncle's direction, she returned her gaze to the tiny figure now feet away. Maggie's eyes widened, her logical mind thrown into chaos, for there could be no mistaking the woman's identity.

"Ye've brought back me Rabbie," old Maggie Armstrong cried. She stood quietly for a moment, her small, rough hands enclosing a tearstained face, then she stretched out her arms to welcome him, her long-lost son.

Maggie's heart ached, for even after years of separation, the elderly woman had spotted him from a distance, perhaps even known the set of his shoulders as he guided his hobbler up the road. Though filled with tears, Old Maggie's deep blue eyes danced with happiness, and Robert jumped to the ground, rushing forward to greet her.

"Ma," he managed to utter. He blinked furiously, tears glistening on his eyelashes, his breath quivering as the word left his lips. She reached up to touch his cheek, and he turned his head to kiss her hand.

Within moments, the two were gripping each other, Robert lifting the aged woman and squeezing her so tightly Maggie thought he would break her in two. A sob caught in her throat, the scene touching her heart, and for the first time she realized just how much her father had given up. She gazed over at her uncles, surprised to find them similarly affected by the tender reunion. There was even a tear in Sim's eye, though he tried to pretend it was "noucht more than the wind" when he caught Maggie staring at him. But then, another voice, deep and gruff, broke into her contemplation, causing her to jump, and she jerked back around to see who it was.

"Who've ye brought here that takes such liberties with me mother?" The man grabbed Robert by the arm and pulled him around, his face frozen into a hard scowl.

Andy's arms grew tense around Maggie's waist, and she held her breath. For the first time since they'd arrived, she felt truly frightened. Until now, it all seemed like a dream, the men friendly enough, the scenery beautiful; but now, somehow the reality of the situation, the danger it held, became all too clear.

Her mind conducted a frantic search through the pages of her father's book, trying to place the figure who stood before her. He was too young to be her grandfather. Was it Angus or Dennis? There was definitely a Dennis. She glanced around at the others, but no one said a word. Instead, they all sat, watching and waiting, while the heavyset man looked Robert over.

Finally, he spoke once more. "Ye've a bit of explaining to do, laddie."

"Aye, that I have, Geordie," Robert said, the shadow of a smile belying his solemn tone.

Geordie. Of course, she'd heard that name before. Yes, he'd lived back in the sixteenth century—

She stopped short, the realization almost causing her to giggle with relief. This truly was the sixteenth century, and Geordie was none other than her father's eldest brother.

Though a bit heavy around the middle, he was still a sturdy man, of medium stature, with a straggly beard that sported the crumbs of his latest meal. His eyes shone, not quite as bright as Robert's, but they twinkled nonetheless. He reached out, embracing his brother, then he pushed away and stood back for a moment, a tear glistening on his cheek.

"Welcome home, lad!" Geordie ducked his head, chuckling before calling them all into his home.

Robert stood for a moment, a dark veil replacing the sparkle that had so recently filled his eyes. "Your home? Where's me da, then?"

The riders exchanged wary looks, but once again, no one spoke. At last, Geordie took a deep breath and broke the news. "Long dead, lad, but we'll talk more of that later, aye. For now, let's get ye inside and settled down, elst Emma will never forgive me.

"Emma!" A flicker of light returned to Robert's eyes. "Still putting up with ye, is she?"

"Aye, that she is," Geordie said, his shoulders shaking with laughter as he headed back through the barmekin gate.

****

Will Foster groaned as he walked through the barmekin gate, Edward and Dylan following close behind. He knew someone would be on watch, but did it have to be his eldest brother? Walt had the eyes of a hawk and a disposition to match when it came to his younger brothers. The man couldn't seem to accept the fact that Will was no longer a wean, let alone a capable reiver in his own right.

Walt took his time walking over, his hands on his hips, a single eyebrow raised, and Will let out a weary sigh. So much for slipping away to his father without any questions being asked. That wasn't Walt's way.

"And who have ye dragged home now, Bonnie Will?" Walt surveyed the strangers from head to foot, then, spitting out the piece of straw he held between his teeth, turned back to Will. "When ye said ye were heading for Hexham, I thought ye were of a mind to seek out a shapelier leg and a bosom that could smother a man. I'm beginning to worry about yer sight, lad."

"There's nowt wrong with me sight, Walt." Will forced his lips into a mock smile. "And as for the lassies, 'tis no' their bosoms but their kisses they smother me with."

"Dinna let me ma hear ye talking like that." Walt whacked him on the arm and then shifted his attention back to the two strangers. "So who be these two, then?"

Will walked over to the well and plunged his scarf into the bucket, soaking it in the cool water before using it to wash the dirt and grime from his face and the back of his neck. "Cousins, they say. That one there claims to be Eddie Foster."

"Aye," Edward said, taking a step forward. "The last time I came through, you were about Will's age, I expect, courting little Ellie Crosier, if I remember right. But then, I don't suppose you remember me."

"Nae, I canna say that I do." Walt crossed his arms and narrowed his eyes, focusing his cold, hard stare on the elder of the two strangers. "Where did ye say ye come across them, Will?"

"Found them up north of the Tweed, trying to outwit an Armstrong raiding party." The words slipped out of his mouth before he could stop them, and he groaned once more.

Walt's stern gaze snapped back in his direction. "And what would ye be doing up north of the Tweed, Brother? Has the memory of the last thrashing me da gave ye faded as quickly as the blush from a whore's cheeks?"

"I'm no' a wee lad anymore, and 'tis none of yer affair what I was doing there." The muscles in Will's back tightened, the sting of the strap still fresh in his memory, but he refused to react.

Walt relented, a hint of compassion twinkling in his dusky blue eyes. "All right, laddie, keep yer heid. We'll talk more about that later."

"Nae, we winna," Will said, his voice firm, but his brother paid him no mind.

"Now tell me," Walt continued, "what else d'ye ken about these two, then?"

His stare returned to the elder of the two men. Will thought he saw a momentary flash of recognition cross Walt's face, but it disappeared before it took hold.

"Eddie there says he's from Lancashire and visited here once round about twenty-five year back. He says me da would ken him. Said ye might as well."

"Does he now?"

"Aye. Claims he's the one what talked Da into letting our Duncan go on a raid, and him being no more than twelve year old."

"And so he did." A deep voice boomed from not ten feet away, causing both brothers to spin around. Their father strode across the yard, a broad grin on his weathered face. "Dear Lord in heaven, Eddie, I thought sure ye'd be dead by now, hunting that Armstrong lad the way ye were. Did ye ever get him to take back that accursed chest?"

Edward returned Graham Foster's smile as they slapped each other on the back in an awkward kind of bear hug. "Yes and no," Edward replied. He lifted the tattered sack and shrugged.

Graham ducked his head, cackling so hard Will feared he would have an apoplexy, but the man just wrapped his arm around Edward's shoulder and began to walk toward their cottage.

"Well, come on, then," he said to his sons, "and bring Eddie's friend along with ye." Then, turning back to Edward, he continued. "Wait till me Betty sees ye. Ye remember wee Betty Hetherington, now d'ye no' man?"

Will and his brother exchanged a bewildered glance, then shrugged their shoulders. After all, it wasn't the strangest thing that had ever happened. Scratching the back of his neck, Will turned to Dylan.

"Ye'd best come along, then," he said, "afore me ma has to come and drag ye in by the lug."

Walt stood for a moment, a frown wrinkling his forehead, until at last he laughed out loud. "Best we dinna go in the house for a while yet, lads. I just remembered Eddie's last visit, and if I'm right, 'twould be safer riding across the Wastes with a lame hobbler and a pack of broken men on yer tail."

"So 'twas him what talked Da into letting our Duncan go on his first raid, then," Will said.

"Aye, that it is, and there's nae telling how me ma might react."

Dylan turned back toward the cottage, but Walt put an arm around his shoulder. "Never mind, lad. Me da winna let any harm come to him." Then, placing his other arm across Will's back, he gripped the base of his neck. "Now as to ye, laddie, what's this about being north of the Tweed and all by yerself, nae less?"

CHAPTER 7

As the sun rose, Maggie lay awake, trying to sort out the events of the previous twenty-four hours. Her mind raced with the names and faces that only yesterday had been no more than legendary figures in her father's portrait collection. Perhaps if she closed her eyes and went back to sleep. It must be a dream, right?

She stared at the rafted ceiling, attempting to focus her thoughts. Dream or not, she needed to pull herself together, deal with the situation as it presented itself. Not an easy task when that situation bordered on fantasy. Determined to give it a go, she took a deep, cleansing breath and surveyed the room she shared with her three cousins.

Quite cramped by twentieth-century standards, the word *privacy* didn't even appear to exist in their vocabulary. On the bright side, it would be like having sisters, something she'd dreamed about her entire childhood. Adjusting to the furnishings, however, would take a bit more getting used to.

True, they did each have their own bed, but two of them together wouldn't equal the cozy twin she slept in at home. Maggie shrugged and tried to make herself comfortable on the pin cushion masquerading as her mattress. Lumpy and coarse, needles of straw poked every which way through the rough linen sheets. She turned on her side, and a particularly sharp piece dug into her thigh. That was the last straw! Though she sat up with a start, swearing under her breath, she couldn't help but laugh at her clever pun.

With a weary sigh, she squinted down at the floor and considered the possibilities. Not much better. Knotholes dotted the bare, rough-hewn planks. How she missed the pretty blue wall-to-wall carpet that covered her floor at their home on Long Island. Many a summer night she'd fallen asleep there, listening to Twisted Sister or Van Halen, a warm sea breeze caressing her cheeks. She shivered and tugged the coarse blanket over her shoulders. No warm breezes here, at least not at the moment.

Stifling a yawn, Maggie drew her legs up to her chin and wrapped her arms around them in the hopes of generating some heat. Almost at once, the amulet caught her eye, and she reached over to retrieve it from the small stand beside her bed. Though the bronze frame was cool to the touch, the stone itself warmed her palm. She frowned, rubbing her finger across its smooth surface. Such a simple piece of jewelry, and yet it possessed a quality capable of transporting human beings through time. But how?

Even Edward hadn't been able to explain it, and now he and Dylan were out there somewhere, alone and hundreds of years in the past. She took a deep breath to calm her nerves. After all, Edward had been here before. Maybe he'd made friends. Maybe even started a family.

She shook her head. Now she was really letting her imagination run wild. But she couldn't help it. They were her family long before she ever met the Armstrongs, and now they might be in danger, all because of this ordinary stone. Just thinking about it made her brain hurt, so she put the necklace back on the table, hiding it behind the tarnished candlestick, and turned her thoughts elsewhere.

Constance, the eldest of Geordie's three daughters, slept across the way, curled up on her side, the hint of a smile caressing her lips. Dreaming about someone special, no doubt.

Maggie suppressed a giggle and let her gaze wander to the corner just beyond her cousin's bed. There, a hand-carved statue of the Blessed Mother stood on a narrow shelf, three votive candles flickering at its base. Yet even around this small shrine, only the minimum amount of embellishment could be found. Though clearly fashioned by loving hands, the figure's features lacked an artistic touch. And the vigil lights held no carved glass or etched designs. Still, for all its simplicity, the little makeshift chapel filled the room with a quiet beauty and serenity that warmed Maggie's heart despite the brisk morning air.

With renewed excitement, Maggie swung her legs over the side of the bed, determined to make the most of the situation. After all, the company seemed pleasant enough, and being there meant so much to her father. Besides, if nothing else, it would give her a few stories to tell her own children someday.

Stretching to ease the crick in her back, Maggie peered out the open window beside her bed, hoping to get her first real glimpse of the surrounding yard. The enchanted world that met her eyes caused the breath to catch in her throat. It was as if she'd fallen asleep and awoken to find herself lost within one of her father's tales. But then, she supposed she had.

The proverbial tower stood to her right. Tall and gray against the paling night, it cast an ominous shadow over the six or seven thatched cottages scattered around the barmekin yard. A few of these structures, like the one in which Maggie found herself, boasted neatly planted vegetable gardens and small wooden benches outside their doors. Simple amenities in the twentieth century, yet here they identified the attached buildings as homes where Geordie and his servants lived—providing things remained on the quiet side.

A sudden flurry of activity caught Maggie's attention, and she shifted her gaze to the blacksmith shop across the yard. A groom hurried past, leading a pair of horses into the adjacent stables. Off to the left, Geordie's son, Alasdair, helped his father carry supplies from a wagon into the nearby storage shed.

The sound of footsteps hitting wood signaled the approach of yet another reiver. Her Uncle Sim, the one who'd tossed her so far into the air the morning before. Oh yes, she remembered him. He hurried down the steps of the peel and over to the wagon. Once there, he threw a sack over his shoulder and followed her cousin to the shed.

As the men went about their work, a group of boys approached from the opposite direction. Too absorbed in their game to watch where he was going, one towheaded boy plowed right into her Uncle Geordie, nearly knocking him off his feet. Maggie cringed. So did her Uncle Sim. He darted from the shed and grabbed the child by his sleeve, a stern expression on his face. Geordie patted his brother on the arm, then, after growling at the boy in mock indignation, he gave a hearty laugh and tousled the lad's hair.

"Go on then, Simon," Sim said, "but mind where ye're going, aye. Now ask yer uncle's indulgence."

"Sorry, Da." The boy nodded and turned to his uncle. "Begging yer pardon, Uncle. I didna mean to run ye down." Before Geordie could say a word in reply, the child scurried off to rejoin his friends.

"He's a good lad, Sim," Geordie said. "Dinna be so hard on him."

Alasdair and Sim exchanged glances and rolled their eyes.

"I saw that, Brother," Geordie said. "And I catch yer meaning fine, but wee Simon there winna be laird of the clan one day, and Alasdair will. So dinna be filling me lad's heid with yer rebellious thoughts, aye. Ye're still no' too big for me to take the tawse to."

Alasdair attempted to stifle a laugh, but a snort snuck out just the same, drawing his father's attention.

"Or to yer arse either, laddie." Geordie turned away to grab another sack, but Maggie could see his shoulder shaking with amusement as he lifted the bag to it. "Now, back to work, the pair of ye, afore I give ye both a good skelp across the lugs."

Maggie smiled to herself, the picture of Geordie trying to whip his brother's bottom rising unbidden. *I'd like to be a fly on the wall for that.*

With the image still firmly in her mind, she looked away and continued to survey some of the remaining structures. A kitchen of sorts stood off to the side, with a large stone in front of it. She could just imagine what they used that for. Thankful neither appeared to be in use at the moment, she moved on. The tip of a barn stuck out from behind the stables, and if she tilted her head a bit to the right, she could catch a glimpse of the chapel in the far corner of the yard.

In a way, it all seemed rather cozy, tucked in safe and sound on all sides by a protective stone wall. The barmekin, her father called it, used to defend the buildings within. Though it rose no more than fifteen or sixteen feet in height, the crenelated fortification stood three feet deep, with a sentry walk that ran around its entire circumference. But surely it had outlived its original purpose by now, even if it did provide the perfect backdrop for her father's tales of Border feuds and midnight raids.

Maggie rubbed the sleep from her eyes and let her gaze wander through the open gates, beyond the wall, to the moors, woodlands, and purple fells. How rugged they looked, and yet how beautiful. Much like her father himself. The thought made her smile, and she settled herself against the windowsill, content to watch the comings and goings of her newfound relatives.

****

Robert looked out across the vast heath. A stream ran through the far side, and a low stone wall encircled a small rise just to the north.

"Well, what do ye think, Brother?" Andy asked. "'Twas the parcel me da always wanted ye to have. Ma wouldna let us touch it. She said ye'd be needing it one day."

"It takes me breath away. I wish me Katie could have seen it."

Andy kicked at a clump of dirt. "I'll no' ask ye why, Rob. I reckon ye'll give us yer reasons when ye see fit, but I missed ye. 'Twas never quite the same after ye left."

"I missed ye as well, Brother. As much as I loved me Katie, there was a part of me heart still here on the Borders. I wanted me Maggie to experience it as well."

They walked over to the stone wall, and Andy sat down. "Did ye ever give a thought to wee Mary Foster?"

"Aye, every day for a long time, but then I realized I'd no' be back, and there was Katie. Did she take it hard, me disappearing and all?"

"'Course, she did. Her ma said she'd sit staring out the window every night, saying her prayers. After a while, even she kent ye'd no' be coming back. She mourned ye then for a bit, sure ye were lying dead somewhere."

"How is she faring after all these years?"

Andy huffed a laugh. "Were ye of a mind she might be waiting for ye yet?"

Robert shook his head. "Nae, Mary was always a sensible lass. I expect she got on with her life soon enough."

"Aye, she did that. Wed a cousin of Richie Carnaby's, a braw lad with a fair piece of land. They have a passel of weans, last I heard."

"I'm happy for her. She deserved better than me at any rate." He gazed out across the field again, sorrow for what he'd lost and joy for what lay ahead tearing his heart apart.

"Ach, ye would have made her a good husband, Brother. It just wasna meant to be, eh?" Andy took a breath and looked up toward the rise. "So what d'ye think? Ye can build a fine bastle house there."

"Ye'll be helping me, then?" Robert laughed and slapped his brother on the back. "Me Maggie will be well pleased."

"Aye, she will. Them fields ower yon past the trees will make a fine dowry, and being yer only heir, the rest will be hers one day too. Ye should have nae problem making a good union for her."

"'Twill be awhile afore she need fash herself ower such things. She's barely nineteen."

"Need I remind ye, our own mother wasna much older when she wed."

Robert narrowed his eyes, his right eyebrow twitching.

"Ach, dinna lose yer heid. I'm no' making any suggestions. I've me own daughter to be thinking of. Still, 'tis a good feeling to ken ye'll be able to do right by her, eh?"

"Aye, Brother, it is that. Now we'd best be getting back afore Geordie comes looking for us. He can have a wicked temper on him, if I mind right."

****

Dylan grunted as he dumped a sack of oats in the wagon. "Why are we loading food into the wagon?"

"To bring it up to the shielings, of course." Will placed a basket of leeks next to the oats and wiped his forehead with his arm.

"Don't you have servants for this sort of thing?"

Will scoffed. "Having a few servants disna mean ye get to sit on yer arse all day, laddie." A milkmaid walked up carrying two buckets of milk, and he took the heavy pails from her.

Dylan smiled at the girl, causing her cheeks to flush before she turned and hurried off.

"Ye leave wee Effy be, aye," Will said.

"Oh, sorry, I didn't know you and she were an item."

"A what?" Will frowned, still not sure he liked this new cousin.

"Together. You know, your bit of tail."

"I still dinna ken what ye're blethering on about."

Dylan groaned. "I didn't know you were bedding her."

Will slammed the pail down on the wagon bed, some of the milk sloshing over the side. "I'm no'! And neither will ye be if ye ken what's good for ye. She's quite a few brothers and were me da to find out ye'd been plowing her fields, he'd likely let them loose on ye."

"Okay, no need to get yer knickers in a twist."

"I dinna wear . . . knickers."

"Right! Your breeks, then."

Will rolled his eyes and pushed Dylan back toward the storeroom to get more supplies. "Go to the larder and get a bit of dried beef, aye, while I fetch a cask of ale."

That Dylan was a strange one, all right, though he had a sweet tongue on him and looks enough to turn the lassies' heads. Why did his father have to leave the scoundrel in his hands? Surely one of his brothers was better suited to the task. If he didn't keep a close eye on him, he'd likely bed every lass from here to Carlisle and back.

Will lifted a barrel on his shoulder and headed back for the wagon, but he'd no sooner rounded the building than he knew he'd made a mistake. His sister Annie stood by the wagon with some pies, and Dylan was right next to her with his hand on her shoulder.

"What have ye got there, Annie?" Will stepped between his sister and Dylan, giving the latter a good shove.

"Two blackberries, a raspberry, and a gooseberry, and me ma says if she finds out ye've eaten any of them on the way, she'll send ye out to pick enough fruit for a week, and without yer gloves as well."

Dylan didn't seem to take the hint. He reached out, placing his hand on Annie's back. "We won't eat any, love. I give you my oath."

The words had no sooner crossed Dylan's lips than Will hauled off and punched him, causing a stream of blood to gush from his cousin's nose.

"Son of a bitch!" Dylan grabbed Will by his jack, knocking him up against the stone wall of the storeroom. "What was that for?"

"Touch me sister, ye foul-mouthed weasel, and I'll feed ye to the dogs." He shoved Dylan into the wagon, knocking two of the pies to the ground.

"Stop it this instant!" Annie shouted for their mother, but their brother Walt came instead, grabbing both Will and Dylan by the arms.

"Can I no' leave the two of ye alone for a minute without ye getting into a fecht ower something or other? Wait till me ma sees her pies."

Will cursed under his breath. "I warned him to stay away from our Annie."

"Ye what!" Annie's eyes widened, and Will swore smoke was coming out of her ears. She walked over to him, stabbing her finger into his chest. "Last I heard, ye werena me da, so mind to keep yer neb out of me affairs afore ye find it cut off."

Will opened his mouth to speak, but she glared at him, and he thought it best to hold his tongue until they both calmed down.

Annie turned away and handed Dylan her scarf. "Now if ye come with me, lad, I'll fix it so the bleeding stops."

"Thank you, Annie. I don't know what got into Will."

"Oh, dinna mind him. He gets it into his heid he's me da from time to time."

Will was steaming, but he didn't dare follow for fear of saying something he'd regret. Instead, he turned to speak to Walt but found his mother standing by his brother's side, her hands on her hips and a look in her eyes that could make any reiver beg for mercy.

"Tomorrow morn, bright and early, ye and yer cousin there will be going berry picking, and dinna bother bringing yer gloves. Mayhap a few thorns will put some sense into yer thick heids."

"But, Ma . . ."

She gave him a look that would have stopped a wild boar in its tracks, so he just nodded and bent to clean up the ruined pies. He'd have a word with Dylan later, when no one else was around to keep him from knocking some sense into the blaggard.

CHAPTER 8

Maggie spent a pleasant afternoon exploring her new home, and that night she joined her father at a grand feast Geordie held to welcome them home. Friends and family gathered together in the large hall, which made up the first floor of the peel.

Music and laughter filled the room, along with tables laden with food and drink. Plates of veal collops, smoked goose, and wild venison surrounded a platter overflowing with roast leg of mutton. Trenchers burst with leeks from the vegetable gardens and berries from the countryside, as well as homemade cheese and shortbread. And of course, ale and something called aqua vitae flowed freely, but on tasting the latter, Maggie clutched her throat. She coughed and sputtered, discovering too late she'd taken a huge gulp of whisky.

"Are ye all right, Cousin?" Alasdair pounded her on the back, nearly shoving her into a large plate of glazed salmon.

Maggie nodded, flashing him a hesitant smile before wiping the dribble from her chin. "Not very ladylike, I'm afraid."

The boy laughed, a cheerful, sincere laugh, and his hickory brown eyes sparkled with golden flecks. He couldn't have been more than fifteen or sixteen, but already he carried himself like a seasoned reiver. His hands were rough and calloused, his arms hard and firm, and he exuded a certain confidence as he peered down at her. Yet there was a youthfulness in the flush of his cheeks and the turn of his lips that gave him away.

"Nae, 'tis true," he said, "but I'll no' be telling anyone, so ye've noucht to fear."

Maggie gave a quick curtsy, not quite sure how else to reply in this century. "Thank you, Alasdair. I really appreciate it."

He stared for a moment, his smile reaching deep into his eyes. "Ye do talk like an outlander, though I've never encountered another that sounds quite the same."

"Have you ever met anyone from Lancashire before?" she asked, hoping perhaps he hadn't.

"Nae, I canna say I have, though I did meet a lad from Cornwall once, and ye sound noucht like him."

"No, I don't suppose I do." She fumbled with a linen napkin, trying to think of what else she could possibly say.

Alasdair apparently sensed her discomfort. "Would ye like to meet some of our other kin, then? 'Tis sure me uncles will be keeping yer da busy for a good piece yet."

Maggie nodded in relief, and Alasdair took her by the hand, moving amongst a veritable sea of aunts, uncles, and cousins in one form or another. They ate and drank along the way, laughing and conversing with kith and kin, until finally the revelers spilled out into the barmekin yard, dancing and singing old Border tunes. She was definitely captivated, and it wasn't long before all thoughts of a summer vacation on Long Island began to fade.

Armstrongs from Whithaugh and Mangerton flocked through the barmekin gate, along with Rutherfords and Elliotts and other clans whose names she couldn't remember. Maggie was delighted to find so many relatives among the guests. She'd never had much of a family before, save for Robert and Edward, and now that she did, she wanted to meet each and every one of them.

Alasdair had appointed himself her guide for the evening, so when an attractive young man arrived a few hours into the celebration, her cousin gave her arm a nudge and whispered a name in her ear. So that was the infamous Ian Rutherford. Well, he certainly was as handsome as her Uncle Sim had suggested.

He turned his head, and hair the color of burnished copper brushed the top of his broad shoulders, almost blending with the russet tones of his jack. Stopping for a moment, he surveyed the yard before his gaze came to rest on Maggie. A smile touched his lips, then after a moment's pause, he headed in her direction.

"Where are ye manners, Alasdair Armstrong?" he said. "Are ye no' going to introduce me to the lovely lass?"

"Haud yer wheesht, Ian," Alasdair said. "I'm getting to it, am I no'? This is me cousin Maggie, daughter of me Uncle Rabbie, late of Lancashire."

"Lancashire, is it? Well, 'tis an honor to make the acquaintance of such a fair lass, especially seeing ye've traveled so far."

He bowed to kiss her hand, and goosebumps shot up Maggie's arm, her fingers tingling in his touch. A girlish giggle caught in her throat, emerging in the form of a hiccup and causing a warm flush to rise in her cheeks. By the look on her cousin's face, she was sure her face must be a deep shade of pink by now.

Alasdair rolled his eyes, a smile tugging the corner of his mouth. "And this here's Ian Rutherford, a neighbor from across the glen. A word to the wise, though, Coz, he's a smooth tongue, this one, so ye'd best no' take a thing he says to heart."

"Now is that anything to say, ye wee clype?"

"I dinna ken what ye're on about. 'Tis noucht but the truth, or would ye prefer I say what a right bore ye are?" A roguish grin broke out on Alasdair's face, and he leaned back against the rough-hewn stone of the barmekin wall.

For a moment, Ian didn't say a word. Instead, he heaved an impatient sigh and stared out across the yard. Maggie lowered her head, desperate to stifle yet another unladylike snort. Was Alasdair really that naive? Anyone could see Ian was waiting for him to be on his way. Or was her cousin just being a typical sixteen-year-old male and busting his friend's chops? Either way, if something didn't give soon, she'd abandon them both to their own devices.

The thought had no sooner crossed her mind than Ian spoke again, his gaze still fixed on a spot by the base of the peel tower. "Alasdair, is that no' yer cousin Jamie with Rachel Elliott? I thought 'twas ye she fancied."

Alasdair straightened up, his eyes shifting to the source of Ian's attention. "Aye, and so it is! I'd best be taking me leave then afore he beguiles her into thinking 'tis him she wants." He bowed and kissed Maggie on the cheek. "Until later, Cousin," he said before hurrying across the yard.

Well, this was awkward. Maggie flashed Ian a tentative smile, scratching her nose before staring down at the ground. What the heck did one say to a young, handsome, sixteenth-century Border reiver? *Hey, what's happening?* just didn't seem appropriate. Much to her relief, the attractive Scot broke the silence almost at once.

"Would ye do me the honor of taking a step or two with me, mistress?" He nodded toward the large group dancing in the center of the yard.

"Oh, I don't think so. My father tried to teach me, but I'm afraid I'm not very good."

"Nor am I," Ian said. He smiled with a determination in his eyes that made even the most impossible feat seem feasible. "But with you at me side, I'm sure no one will be watching the dancing," he added with a wink.

Maggie smiled. She wondered what it would feel like to be swept up in his arms, but still . . . "I'm sure they'd notice when I began to stomp on their feet."

Ian leaned over, almost putting his lips to her ear, and a pleasant chill ran down her back. "D'ye truly think there's no' a right amount of stomping going on already?"

He chuckled softly, then took her by the hand, beckoning her to join him in a lively reel. Though she hesitated for a moment, the look on Robert's face as she joined the others was all she needed to see. His eyes shone with pride when she took Ian's hands and tried desperately to follow the intricate steps. How did they ever remember what came next? But Ian soon had her moving along as if she were born to it.

Finally, they found a small settle outside one of the cottages, and Maggie sat down, a bit out of breath but somehow feeling quite exhilarated. They sat in silence for a few moments, watching the dancers continue, and Maggie caught sight of her father over by the well. Though he was talking to his brother Andy, his gaze kept drifting in her direction. He'd be giving Ian the third degree before long; if not tonight, then certainly in the morning.

Andy looked over as well and nodded.

Yep, her father was already quizzing her uncle about him. Could his interrogation of Ian be far behind? She smiled to herself.

"Is it the dance or me company that's making ye smile so, Maggie Armstrong?" Ian asked.

"A bit of both, I suppose. I've never seen anything like this before."

"Do they no' dance in Lancashire, then, lass?

Maggie thought of the last time she'd been out dancing and had to keep from rolling her eyes. "Aye, of course they do. It's just not like this. It's easier somehow."

"Will ye show me someday . . . the way ye dance, the way ye sing . . . I want to learn all about ye, lass."

"Maybe someday, but what about you?" Maggie asked. "How are we related?"

"Ach, we're no' kin, lass. We're neighbors is all, though me da's hoping to change that in the near future."

Maggie frowned. Did he mean what she thought he meant? Maybe Ian had a sister who'd been promised to one of the Armstrongs boys.

Ian interrupted her thoughts. "Would ye care to take a walk with me down by the burn, lass? 'Tis a braw night for it."

Maggie hesitated, throwing a glance in her father's direction. He seemed occupied for the time being, so she shrugged off her reservations. After all, if she were at home, she wouldn't have thought twice about it. And Ian wasn't likely to try anything with her family so near. Besides, he was not only handsome and charming, but entertaining as well, so why not enjoy his company?

Ian was right. It was a beautiful sight, so quiet and peaceful. The gurgling water of the burn cut through the meadow, sparkling in the dimming light of dusk. The cry of a curlew filled the air, along with the scent of harebells and gorse bushes.

After spreading his plaid on the ground, Ian invited Maggie to sit beside him and have some of the berries he'd brought along. He pointed out the direction of his home and the various towns that surrounded them and talked of how he would one day be laird of his clan.

She could have gone on listening to him forever, but all too soon the celebration began to wind down, and the moon lit up the darkened sky. He had just finished telling her of how his heart had been broken by Annie Foster when a coarse voice caused them both to jump.

"Maggie! Get yerself back to the peel, lass."

Ian stood at once, but Maggie knew her father sounded far fiercer than he was. "But Da—"

"Now, lassie, and no' another word." He came down the steep slope, his hand on the hilt of his sword.

Maggie scowled at her father. What on earth was the matter with him? Was it possible he could be worse here than in the twentieth century?

Ian bowed. "'Tis me fault, sir. I didna mean any harm, only to show the lass how braw the country here about is."

"Did ye now?" Robert said. "Well, next time ye can show her from the barmekin yard, eh?"

"Aye, sir, of course. May I say good night to her?"

Robert gave a curt nod. "Go right ahead, laddie. Nae one's stopping ye."

Robert stood his ground, his feet firmly planted, his arms folded across his chest. Maggie narrowed her eyes at him, but he just responded with a raised eyebrow. He had no intention of leaving without her. Sensing any argument would be futile, she growled and turned her attention back to Ian.

"I'm so sorry," she said, loud enough for her father to hear, though it had little effect. "Sometimes he forgets I'm not a little girl anymore. I suppose it's just his way of protecting me."

"As it should be, lass. I hope to one day do the same for me own daughters, should God grant me any."

"Thank you for showing me this. It is lovely."

With reluctance, they strolled side by side up to the barmekin gate, Robert following about six feet behind. There within a curtain of mist, Ian bent and kissed her hand.

Maggie's heart stirred as the handsome Scot gazed deep into her eyes. Then, without another word, he melted into the thickening haze, leaving her with nothing more than a dream of what might be.

"Wow," she whispered to herself. "Perhaps this century might not be so bad, after all." Then, with a wistful smile, she turned and walked back across the barmekin yard.

****

The next morning Maggie woke from a pleasant dream and stretched. She pulled the blanket around her shoulders and took a quick look around the room. Her cousins Bess and Nancy were pulling on their shoes, whispering and giggling as young girls are wont to do.

"What are you two up to?" Maggie asked.

"Connie's dreaming about him again, I'd wager," Bess said.

"If me da kent, he'd take the tawse to her," Nancy added.

Maggie tilted her head, curious. "Dreaming about who?"

"Connie would give us a right tongue-lashing if we said." Bess grabbed her little sister by the hand and dragged her over to sit on Maggie's bed. "But we saw them kissing and clapping at the back of the church last month on market day."

"Why doesn't she just tell your da she likes the lad?" Maggie asked.

The girls' eyes widened, and they shook their heads. "Because she kens better," Bess said, "and ye mustna say anything either."

"Of course not." Maggie scratched her head as the two girls scurried out the door and down the stairs. *I wonder who it could be?* Perhaps she should ask

Connie, but they'd just met two days ago. Better to wait until they got to know each other a bit first.

Maggie shrugged the thought off and cuddled deeper into her blanket. She supposed she should be getting up too, but the sun felt so warm on her shoulders she decided to wait a bit. Pulling herself up to the window, she breathed in the fresh, clean air and gazed across the barmekin yard.

Her father was in the barn with Andy, looking over the horses, while Geordie, Sim, and Alasdair unloaded what looked like roofing materials from a wagon. Young Simon ran by with his cousins again—Andy's sons, if she remembered right. It would take a while for her to keep all their names straight.

She giggled as the rambunctious boys headed out through the open gate, laughing and jostling each other, stopping only for a moment to let an older man on horseback pass. A young woman rode behind him, and though the man hadn't even acknowledged the children, the girl waved to them as she passed.

Maggie pursed her lips, deep in thought. She didn't remember the man, but she'd met the girl the night before. What was her name? A quick glance at the silly grin on Alasdair's face, and the information came rushing back. Of course, Rachel Elliott!

She smiled. When it came to young love, men and women acted no different in the sixteenth century than they did in the twentieth. Odd how that simple thought somehow comforted her.

"That wagon winna be unloading itself, lad," Geordie said. "Now I've some business with Christy there, and I'm leaving it in yer hands. See ye keep yer mind on yer chores, aye."

Alasdair cast one more glance in Rachel's direction before shifting his attention back to his father. "I'd be having a word with ye about Rachel, Da," he said, his tone a bit hesitant. "When ye've a moment, I mean."

Geordie nodded. "Hmph! I reckoned ye might be, but now's no' the time to be discussing the matter."

"Aye, Da, but I thought with Christy here and all . . ."

"And I said now's no' the time. Do as ye're told, lad, and tend to yer chores. We'll speak of this after."

A half-smile crossed Sim's lips. Slapping Alasdair on the back, he tossed him a bundle of thatch and led the way to the barn. Meanwhile, Geordie headed across the yard to speak to the man he called Christy.

Hmm, Christy Elliott, no doubt. Poor Alasdair. All he'd talked about last night was Rachel. A bit annoyed at her uncle's abrupt reply, she turned her attention to the landscape beyond the gate.

The gray mist had just begun to lift, engulfing the countryside in a mystical glow, when she spotted Ian Rutherford walking across the barmekin yard, a royal-blue specter rising from the hazy ashes of the previous night. A rush of warmth touched her cheeks, and she leaned farther out the window, hoping to get a better view. That was a mistake! Her elbow grazed the heavy metal candlestick at her side, sending it clattering to the floor with a resounding thud.

Maggie held her breath, praying her clumsiness had gone unnoticed but expecting the inevitable. Sure enough, within seconds her cousin Constance was standing at her side, a huge smile plastered across her face.

"He's a looker all right," she said, "and good in bed as well . . . or so I've heard."

Maggie lifted her eyebrows, shocked by her cousin's candor, yet flattered as well. The young woman would never have spoken so freely if she didn't feel comfortable with her in the first place. It truly was going to be like having a sister.

Maggie returned the smile and lifted a finger to her lips. But though she nodded to the ground below, the gesture came too late. Ian had already heard. With a roguish smirk crossing his lips, he sent a wink in her direction, causing the heat to rise in her cheeks once more.

Geordie shouted across the yard and nodded to the wagon. "If ye're here to help, laddie, then get to it, aye." He feigned a disapproving grunt, which caused Maggie and Constance to jerk back from the window in a fit of girlish laughter.

"So what do you think of him?" Maggie asked.

"About who?" Constance peeked back over Maggie's shoulder, a playful grin tugging at her lips.

Maggie rolled her eyes. "About Ian Rutherford, of course!"

"I'd say ye spent a fair bit of time with him last night, Cousin."

"Yes, I guess I did." Maggie laughed as she too peered out the window once more. Though Ian continued to help unload the wagon, it didn't prevent him from taking a moment to cast another glance in her direction. "So . . . what do you think?" Maggie asked again. "Tell me all about him."

"I wouldna mind having him come to my bed, I'll tell ye that. He's no' got eyes for me, though."

"Oh . . . right!" Maggie's heart sank, and she dropped back on the coarse linen of her bed. "He's taken with the Foster girl, isn't he?"

"Aye, perhaps, but that was afore last night."

"What do you mean?"

Constance nudged Maggie's shoulder. "'Tis ye he likes now, I'd wager, but then 'tis hard to tell with that Ian Rutherford. Any lass in the March would die to be with him."

"Well, he's attractive, I'll grant you that, but die to be with him?" Maggie shook her head.

"Oh, dinna tell me ye're going to be like that Annie Foster, saying there's more to marriage than a good strong husband to care for yer needs. I dinna ken why he ever wanted to marry the English hag in the first place when he could have his pick of fine Scottish lasses."

"I'm not sure, but if he's spoken for . . ."

"Spoken for! By Annie Foster!" Constance scoffed at the idea. "Are ye daft, Cousin? She turned him away right enough, no' two days afore their spousal, nae less."

"What happened?"

"She said he'd broken trust, but how I dinna ken since they were no' yet bound."

"But just two nights before their . . . spousal. I'd be pretty angry too."

Connie shrugged. "Gran says 'tis better if a lad has a bit of experience afore he weds. That way when he does, he'll be less likely to wander."

Maggie couldn't help but smile. "Still, two nights before the spousal?"

"Ach, 'twas all her brother Will's doing; that's for sure. He's the one what made the accusations."

"Well, if this Will thought Ian had been unfaithful to his sister, maybe he wanted to protect her. Wouldn't Alasdair do the same for you?"

Constance lifted her shoulder in a half shrug. "Hmm, I reckon he would. But I'm of a mind 'twas Ian being a Scot that stuck in his craw. Or perhaps 'twas the lass herself who'd been untrue, and they tried to disguise her loose ways by accusing Ian of such. Lord help her if 'twas less than a virgin he'd found on his wedding night."

"He would have turned her away just for that?" The heat in Maggie's cheeks intensified, matching her rising temper. "So what if she'd been with someone before? Ian clearly entertained his share of lovers."

Constance lifted her chin, her eyes glaring with indignation. "Well, of course he has, but a virgin he was promised, and a virgin he should have!"

"Really!" Maggie folded her arms across her chest, a huff of disapproval escaping from her lips. "How archaic."

"What d'ye mean, Cousin? Does a man put no' value on his word where ye come from?"

"His word? Yes, of course, but he wouldn't turn a woman away because she might have been with someone before him."

"Nor would Ian. 'Twould be harder to take, 'tis true, but nae great shame if she put up a fight. Deceiving him the way they did, though, that's quite another story."

Maggie opened her mouth to counter, but somehow her cousin's argument made perfect sense, even to her. After all, a lie was a lie in any century, and yet there must be more to it than that. What did she mean, 'if she put up a fight'?

Constance did hold some strange ideas about love and marriage. Annie Foster seemed much more enlightened, but then Maggie had to remember she wasn't in the twentieth century anymore. People saw things through a different lens here.

A ray of sunlight broke through the morning haze, hitting her in the eye and jarring her from her reverie. "So he's not interested in anyone at the moment, then?"

Constance giggled again, a playful twinkle in her eyes. "Oh aye, I'm of a mind he is, though after last night, 'tis you I'd say."

Maggie lifted her hand to her mouth, trying to conceal the smile she felt creeping across her lips. Without a word, she peeked around the frame of the small window again. He definitely did qualify as handsome.

"Stop yer glaiking, lassies!" Though Geordie shouted, his voice harsh, the upward turn of his lips belied his stern tone. "Time to be tending yer chores."

"Aye, Da," Constance called out before yanking Maggie away from the window. "Come on, then. Get yerself dressed and we can help with the garden. All the better to see him." She dressed in a hurry, lacing her kirtle and pulling on a light blue frock in no time at all. "Are ye no' coming, Cousin?"

Maggie's mouth dropped open. She hadn't even tightened the laces on her kirtle. Besides, she needed a thorough wash before heading downstairs. The day before had been so hectic she hadn't been able to wash at all, so she had no intention of forgoing it again today. When she told Connie, though, her cousin couldn't contain her laughter.

"Have it yer own way, then," she said with a shrug. "But dinna be long about it, aye." Opening the door, she gave one final giggle before walking out and closing the door.

It didn't take long for Maggie to discover why she'd received such a strange response. It may have been mid-June, but the morning air was still quite brisk, and within moments she found herself unable to stop the shivering.

"When in Rome . . ." she said. With tiny goosebumps popping up in clusters all over her body, she donned her clothing as fast as she could. It would be good to get downstairs to the warmth of the blazing fire, even if she was only half-washed.

CHAPTER 9

Maggie hurried down the stairs, looking forward to the warmth of the fire and a hot bowl of porridge . . . and the shawl she'd left on the chair the night before.

"Good morn to ye, darlin'," her aunt Emma said. "Will ye give us a hand with the breakfast?"

An amiable woman of middle age, Emma was still quite attractive and shapely, even after bearing Geordie nine children. Quite a contrast to the rough, ill-tempered man she'd wed. Yet the love in their eyes foretold a bond that defied all outward appearance. Maggie didn't quite understand it, but she knew it existed, just as sure as her father's love would always be there for her.

With a pleasant nod, she lifted some dishes from the shelf in the corner and brought them to the table. Ian Rutherford might be a powerful incentive for working in the garden, but at that particular moment, Maggie found the warmth from the hearth much more appealing.

Constructed of crudely cut stone, it took up almost the entire wall and threw out enough heat to keep the room comfortable. But for how long? Maggie peeked into the blackened pail that stood on the hearthstone and frowned. With no sign of additional fuel, the fire would soon burn itself out.

Beating down a shiver, she grabbed her shawl and threw it over her shoulders. She turned back to the fire just in time to see her Alasdair carting in two heaping buckets of coal. Without a word, he dumped the black nuggets into the empty receptacle, before stooping to gather the few pieces that had fallen over onto the floor.

Alasdair was Geordie's only living son and a handsome boy in his own right. With dark hair and eyes, he looked far more like Emma than he did Geordie, though his build was without a doubt that of a Border reiver.

"Will ye be needing any more on now, Ma?" He stood, wiping his soot-covered hands on a nearby rag.

"Oh, please, just a bit more," Maggie said, the chill still deep in her bones.

"Are ye ill, Maggie?" Emma asked. Concern traced gentle lines along the woman's forehead, and she walked over, putting the back of her hand to Maggie's brow.

"I guess I'm not used to the morning air. It's not quite so cold in Lancaster."

"Take some of that broth, then. 'Twill warm yer insides and chase away the shivers."

Maggie took a small cup, but instead of taking it to the table, she went outside to sit next to the old woman she now called Gran. It would be cold, but she'd never had a grandmother before, and now that she did, she wanted to spend time with her.

The elder Maggie possessed the same blue-gray eyes as her son, filled with kindness, though her face told of the hardships she'd endured over the years.

"'Tis beautiful, is it no', darlin'?" her grandmother said as Maggie sat down next to her. She gazed out across the purple fells, her eyes sparkling with long-ago happiness. The barmekin gate stood open, and it framed the sublime picture in all its majesty. No artist could have duplicated such subtle blues and greens; no photographer could have captured the intensity of the clear crisp air.

"Yes, it is." Maggie sighed, but as she followed her grandmother's line of vision, she realized it wasn't the scenery that stirred the old woman's heart. There, a few feet from the cottage, stood her four surviving sons, together once more.

Maggie listened to her father speak while his brothers hung on every word, like boys enthralled by the tale of an adventurous war hero. And a grand tale it would be if she knew her father.

Her grandmother wouldn't hear a word of their conversation, though. Maggie could tell, for Gran exhibited the signs of hearing loss that so often accompanied advanced age. And yet the woman sat there, a soft smile on her face, not even attempting to move closer or ask her sons to speak louder. Perhaps she didn't want to intrude on what she saw as their moment. Just having them all with her once more seemed to satisfy the old woman.

Maggie didn't possess that kind of patience and scooted forward on the bench. Though a crisp breeze blew across the yard, she simply pulled the heavy plaid a bit tighter around her shoulders and sipped her broth. Cold or not, she planned on hearing every word they said.

"Kidnapped!" Sim cried. "We thought as much."

"Aye, an odd lot they were as well," Robert said. "But then down round Lancashire, wounded and near death, I saw me chance to escape."

"Ma kent ye must be hurt," Sim said with a solemn grunt. "Said she could feel it."

"Aye, and so I was," Robert went on. "I'd all but laid down and closed me eyes when I stumbled upon the Lindsey house. If no' for the vigilant care given me by their daughter, Katie, I wouldna be speaking to ye now."

Maggie crinkled her nose as she listened. *Wounded and near death indeed. You met when Mom brought you a glass of Kool-Aid after a soccer game.* She realized no reiver worth his salt would ever pass up the chance to weave a tale or two, but still. Pinching her nose to stifle a laugh, she helped her grandmother to the bench on the far side of the cottage, which was a bit closer to her father. This was too good to miss.

"And what happened with this Katie, then?" Andy asked.

"I wed her, of course." Robert let out a hearty laugh, but slowly a darkness overcame his face, as if a cloud from the past had burst above, sending its rain down upon his happiness. "I dared no' take her too far from her parents, her being such a frail lass and all. 'Twas a good thing too, for she grew ill and died, with our Maggie still a wee bairn. She took a bit of me heart with her that day."

Tears welled up in Maggie's eyes, her father's words stirring up hazy childhood memories. *All right, at least that bit was true. But as for the rest . . .* She settled back against the bench, listening to her father tell the rest of his tale, certain much of it could be considered no more than that.

"'Tis a sad story, Brother," Geordie said, "but why did ye no' come home then?"

Robert wiped a sleeve across his face and sniffed before continuing on a brighter note. "Katie being an only child, her parents had noucht to cheer them after she passed, save our Maggie. I couldna bear to tear the bairn away from them as well."

"Nae, that wouldna have been right." Andy slapped her father on the back. "Tell me, though, how is it ye return now?"

"The auld couple passed on a few month back, within a fortnight of each other, and so left me free to bring me Maggie home."

"Ye might have written," Geordie said, his tone short.

Maggie bit her bottom lip. Her father was a great storyteller, but this was going to be hard to explain even for him.

"But I did," her father said. "A number of times in the first year or two. Katie's father saw them to the post himself."

"And ye didna find it odd we never answered?" Geordie asked.

"Aye, I did that, but . . ." He shrugged. "In truth, I reckoned me da chose no' to, what with me wedding an outlander and no' even having the decency to bring her home. I never could find the words to explain more than that, ye see, try as I might."

"Never mind," Andy interjected. "Ye're home now, and we're glad to have ye back."

"Aye, especially with Ma being the way she's been of late." Sim glanced over at his mother, his pale blue eyes dimming.

"What d'ye mean, the way she's been?" Robert asked.

The joy melted from her father's features, and a cramp clutched at Maggie's heart. Even if she hadn't heard her uncle's statement, Robert's expression said more than any words could convey. She blinked to stay the tears, not wanting her grandmother to ask what caused them.

"He means noucht by it, Rab." Andy shoved Sim, causing his younger brother to stagger. "He's worse than an auld woman sometimes."

"He's a right to be told," Geordie said. "Ma's no' well. She's no' been for the last year or so."

"She's up in years, Rabbie," Andy said. "'Tis like she's been hanging on, waiting for something."

"Waiting for me," Robert whispered the words, his voice cracking with emotion, but Maggie heard. "Dear Lord, she's been waiting for me."

Their voices lowered, so Maggie needed to strain to hear what the men said. Her father looked over to the house, his eyes filled with concern, and a sense of dread flooded over her. She recognized that look, recalled it from the hours before her mother died. Though very young at the time, the memory had stayed with her, and it sent a cold chill down her spine.

"'Tis me they're speaking of now, lass," her grandmother said. She rested a feeble hand on Maggie's shoulder. "D'ye remember much of yer mother, then?"

"No, not really, except for what my father told me about her."

"D'ye believe she's with ye still?"

"Yes, I do." Maggie nodded, swallowing the sob lodged in her throat, for somehow she already knew where the conversation would lead. She'd heard it before, many years ago, as a younger Robert had knelt to wipe her tearstained face.

"She left ye the locket, then?"

Maggie hadn't realized she was clutching the amulet that hung from her neck. She hated to lie, but it almost seemed as if the old woman wanted to believe she had. And what harm could it do? After all, she couldn't exactly tell the truth.

"Yes, she did, or so my da says."

"'Tis a bonnie trinket. Cherish it and keep it near yer heart, lassie. 'Twill guide ye to the truth, if ye let it."

Maggie looked at the mysterious amulet, rubbing her thumb over the smooth stone. "I will, Gran."

The old woman leaned back against the cottage wall, taking in the fresh morning air. The scent of lilacs and crisp dew-covered grass hung on a gentle breeze, and from the faraway look in her grandmother's eyes, Maggie could tell the sweet aroma brought back fond memories of younger days. But then, without any change in her expression, the woman's slate-blue eyes darkened to the color of a storm-laden sky, and she cupped Maggie's cheek in her hand.

"Oh, darlin', I wish I could be here for ye, protect ye from those who would do ye harm."

"But you will be," Maggie said, though even as the words passed her lips, she could feel the sense of dread overcoming her.

"Ach, me dear wee lassie, I'm an auld woman and have stayed far too long, I fear, buried far too many younger than meself. Ye see ower yon, on that slope beneath the peel, 'tis where me bairns are laid to rest, some with weans of their own lying beside them. Two sons and two daughters came home to sleep beneath their childhood sod. And yet another slumbers in a watery grave, taken too young by an unforgiving river."

"I'm so sorry," Maggie said. She couldn't imagine the pain this small woman must have known. Her eyes reflected that sadness, and yet a contentment born of inner peace overshadowed it.

"Ach, 'tis a long time gone, lassie, and I've still four strong lads to see to me."

Maggie cast a glance across the yard, then flashed a weak smile. She would never have the kind of courage her grandmother possessed.

The old woman must have seen her concern, for she reached over and pushed a loose strand of hair behind Maggie's ear. "Dinna fash yerself so, lass. God has granted me this time to see me Rabbie home and to meet me darlin' granddaughter. Now I can rest in peace. Yer grandda, me dear Geordie, he's been waiting a long time for me to walk beside him again, and truth be told, he wasna always a patient man." She let out a soft laugh, a wistful smile crossing her lips.

Maggie's heart ached. "But it's not fair. We just got here." Overcome by a compelling urge to cry, she blinked rapidly in an effort to stem the tide. For the first time in her life, she had relatives, and the possibility of losing them before she even got to know them left a strange emptiness in her soul.

The old woman took Maggie's hands in her own and cradled them against her breast. "Oh nae, darlin', dinna fash. 'Tis what life's about. One long adventure heading to the most wonderful treasure of all. I'll always be with ye, mind, in here, where it counts, the same as yer ma."

Releasing Maggie's hands, the old woman sat back and reached into her pocket, taking out a tiny ring. "Me name's Maggie too, ye ken." She placed the gold and silver ring upon her pinky, holding it up for Maggie to see.

"It's lovely, Gran." In truth, it consisted of three rings, delicately interwoven to form one band—her wedding band, Maggie suspected.

"It fit once, many years ago, but me fingers are auld and swollen now. 'Tis time for it to find a new home. I'd hoped to pass it on to me daughter, but she died bearing a bairn and lies out there next to her husband."

"That's so sad. What happened to him?" Maggie almost hesitated to ask.

"He rode out to avenge her and paid with his life."

Maggie scrunched up her forehead. "To avenge her, but why? If she died in childbirth, who was there to blame?"

"There were them what bore the burden right enough. Them who brought a fray down upon a farmhouse when they kent full well the lass within had come upon her time. Me lads settled that score soon enough, as did dear Johnnie with his life."

"He must have loved her very much."

"Aye, he did that." She sighed, a single tear touching her weathered cheek. "But now I want ye to take this ring. Ye're me namesake now, darlin'. Someday ye can give it to yer own daughter, and mayhap say a few kind words about an auld woman ye once came upon."

"Gran . . ." Maggie could barely speak a word. She threw her arms around the tiny woman, unable to conceal her emotions any longer. Her grandmother's coarse skin reminded Maggie how hard life on the Borders could be, and she considered whisking the woman away to the twentieth century, where she could receive proper care.

"There, there now, lassie." Her grandmother patted Maggie on the shoulder, her voice soft and comforting. "It winna do to have yer father seeing us like this. Besides, I've no' gone yet."

Maggie sat back on the settle and let her grandmother wipe away the tears, but then the woman's tone changed. She took Maggie's head in her hands once more and stared into her eyes.

"Heed me well in this, though, darlin'. Take care who it is puts this ring upon yer finger, for there are those round these parts think of noucht but what the Armstrong name can do for them. 'Tis no' the name alone what makes ye one of the clan, but the heart that beats within. Be true to that at all costs, Maggie, and ye winna shame yer kin, nae matter what others may think. D'ye ken what it is I'm saying, darlin'?"

"Yes, my father's always taught me that."

"Then God bless ye and keep ye in these woeful times. Now go along and help yer auntie with the breakfast. It winna be long afore there's a horde of hungry men to contend with and weans as well."

The old woman's words confused Maggie, but her grandmother would speak no more about it. How like her son, able to hide her emotions deep within herself, and yet her eyes spoke of an underlying sensitivity none but those closest to her would believe existed. A border trait, no doubt. Maggie finished her broth and went off to help her aunt, the meaning of her grandmother's words still on her mind.

****

"And me Father?" Robert asked, memories assaulting his senses. "What of him, then?"

Andy hesitated, but when no one else seemed inclined to speak, he cleared his throat and answered. "Killed at Flodden Field, about three month after ye left."

"Dear Lord. And Alan? He's gone as well?"

"Aye, he is that. He went off to Hexham one night with his friends. They never returned."

"Who?" Robert fixed his gaze out across the fells and swallowed hard, trying to quell the surge of pain and anger welling up inside. Had he really expected to find everything the same?

"It's been taken care of, Rab," Geordie said, his words coming out stern and sharp. "There's noucht ye can do about it now."

"Nae, ye're right there, but I need to ken all the same. What of our Dennis?"

Andy glanced in Geordie's direction before continuing. "Drowned, about seventeen year back now, just east of the fork in the Leven."

"And who was responsible there?"

"Rabbie!" Geordie scrubbed his hand across his face. "Enough."

Robert glared at his eldest brother, his jaw firm and resolute. "He couldna have been more than sixteen!"

"Fifteen," Geordie responded, his own countenance set in stone, "and we took care of it. Ye werena here."

Robert's chin slackened, the fire in his heart fading to a dull ember. "Ye're right, Brother. I wasna here, and I'm sorry for that. 'Tis just when I think . . ."

"We ken, Rabbie," Sim said. He placed a hand on his brother's shoulder and nodded.

Robert closed his eyes and prayed he could find the courage to go on. "But I need to ken, aye. Now what of Jamie?" he asked, dreading the answer.

"After Dennis, Jamie . . ." Andy said, his throat catching. "We rode out as soon as we heard. Took down quite a few Bells that day, we did . . . but he died on the way home. 'Twas noucht ye could have done, noucht we could do. The arrow went clean through his chest."

Geordie rubbed his bearded chin. "The wee fool should have kent better than to ride against Jock Bell on his own. It nearly killed me ma losing both lads the same day."

A wave of pain pierced Robert's heart anew, but he swallowed hard and continued. "And Maggie?" He dreaded this answer more than any other. "What of her?"

"She married a Graham," Andy said. "And as ye would expect, afore long she was with child. He cared for her well, our Johnnie, but then right afore her time, the Musgraves attacked their place. The lad carried her away, hoping to get her here in time, but the ride took its toll. They couldna stop the bleeding, and she died in Johnnie's arms that very night. In his pain, he swore his vengeance and was slain himself in a raid two days later."

"What of the bairn?"

"Wee Johnnie stays here with us, though he goes to the Grahams three or four times a year. He's growing into a fine lad, almost ten, he is, and every bit of him an Armstrong."

Robert couldn't help but smile in spite of the tragic story. "A right scrapper, then."

Andy nodded, his shoulders shaking in a soft laugh. For a moment, an awkward silence prevailed, the kind that comes when there are no words left to speak, or those that do remain prove too painful to utter. Finally, Robert found the strength.

"There's so many gone," he said. "Angus and Cousin Davie?"

"Hanged in Jedburgh by the warden."

"But what crime—"

"The warden found one right enough," Geordie said, his tone signaling his patience had come to an end. "It's done Rabbie. Let it be."

"They got Johnnie of Gilnockie as well, ye ken," Andy added. "James himself saw him hanged."

"So I've heard," Robert said with a nod. "Some say his own brother betrayed him."

"Some say that, but never ye mind. Ye're back with us now, Rabbie." Andy grinned, smacking his brother on the back. "'Tis all that matters, eh?"

"Ye're right there, lad." Robert took a deep breath of the morning air, putting the pain and sorrow to rest, then he let a broad smile cross his lips. "And if I remember that smell, it means breakfast is on the table."

Without another word, he turned and sprinted toward the small cottage. Though he left his brothers behind for the moment, they had all caught up by the time he reached the door, and the men came in laughing and pushing like children.

Old Mag Armstrong nodded, the hint of a smile tugging the corner of her mouth. Robert stopped and stared at her for a moment. He could almost picture the thoughts that ran through her mind: images of her lads racing into the cottage for dinner, herself scolding them for being so rowdy, their father kissing her cheek as he passed and telling her lads would be lads. A tear tickled the corner of his eye, and he blinked it away before going to her side. With a squeeze of her hand, he bent over and kissed her forehead, thanking God for granting him this time with her, no matter how short it might prove to be.

"It does me heart good to see me lads together again," his mother said. Then she reached up and wiped the tear that escaped down his cheek.

CHAPTER 10

Will cursed under his breath as another thorn dug into his skin. This was all Dylan's fault. If not for him, they wouldn't be out here picking berries in the first place, their gloves confiscated until they returned with two full baskets each.

"Fuck it!" Dylan yelled before putting his finger to his mouth.

Will couldn't help but laugh. "Well, if ye're of a mind to be sarding berry bushes, I guess I've nae worries about ye touching me sister."

"What?" Dylan's eyes flashed for a moment before he let out a huff of laughter. "That's not the way I meant it." Will lifted his eyebrows, and Dylan attempted to elaborate a bit. "It means that of course, but in Lancashire, it's used a few other ways as well."

Will sat down on a rock and popped a berry in his mouth. "So what did ye mean, then?"

Dylan leaned against a nearby tree, cocking his head as if deep in thought. "Something like *God's teeth*, I suppose, only aimed at that wicked blood-drawing bush."

"Hmm, seems a bit silly, though, like ye planned on bedding the bush."

Dylan laughed. "I suppose it does." He took one of the berries and smiled. "They don't taste half-bad, though. Sort of like a woman, all sweet and juicy if they want you to taste their fruits, but prickly as a cactus if they don't."

"I dinna ken what a cactus is, but the rest disna sound very flattering to the lassies." Will frowned, though he took another three or four berries. "Ye're beginning to sound like that Ian Rutherford."

"The bloke that broke Annie's heart?" Dylan stood up straight. "I'm nothing like that bastard."

"He no' a bastard, at least I dinna believe he is. A rogue and a scoundrel, aye, but as far as I ken, his parents were wed when he was born."

Dylan flopped down on the stone wall running along the dirt road. "I really need to be more clear. In Lancashire, a bastard is a scoundrel or knave, not a nice person. It can also mean someone born out of wedlock, but in this case. I meant the former."

"If 'tis what ye meant, then, I stand by me words and call ye a bastard as well."

"You've got a lot of nerve." Dylan threw a handful of berries back in the basket. "You don't even know me."

"I ken ye've no' even been here a week, and ye've already been out behind the chapel with Ellie, the blacksmith's daughter, clapping her bosom and her arse, no' to mention running yer hand up under her skirts."

Dylan jumped up, knocking the basket and its contents across the ground. "And how long did you stand there watching us before you went off behind some bush and spilled your seed across the ground?"

Will flew at Dylan, knocking him on the ground and punching him square in the jaw, but the oaf grabbed a handful of berries, shoving them in Will's face and pushing him off on top of two full baskets.

The contents squished beneath Will as he grabbed one of the shattered baskets and slammed it into his opponent's head. Blood mixed with berry juice as they grappled back and forth on the ground until Will found himself sitting amidst berries, tattered baskets, and trampled grass. Too tired to fight any further, he sat watching curiously as Dylan puked his breakfast up next to the stone wall. His clothes were torn and covered in red and blue stains, some of which Will figured must be blood. He looked down at his own clothing and groaned. His mother was going to kill them both.

"D'ye no' care about the lassie's reputation?" he finally said. "God's teeth, man! Her father works for me da."

"I didn't spoil her," Dylan said, holding the bridge of his nose to stop the blood from flowing. "And I doubt it was her first kiss either, not the way she went at it."

Will shook his head. "Nae, I'm sure ye're right there. She even uses her tongue."

Dylan's eyes narrowed, and Will realized he'd said more than he intended. "I was but thirteen, though I should have kent better."

"So you have had a roll or two in the hay with the local fauna?"

Will picked a berry from his jack. "I'm no' saying I didna, only that ye need make sure the lass kens ye're making her nae promises, even if it turns into more than a bit of kissing and clapping. If she's found with child, and 'tis nae rape involved, she'll be scorned by the rest of the village." He popped the berry in his mouth. "Unless, of course, ye do plan to wed her, which her da could insist upon if he'd so much as an inkling ye were the rogue who deflowered his daughter."

"I get that, and believe it or not, I respect it. I'm just an affectionate sort of bloke."

Will laughed and wiped the squashed berries from his face. "Just dinna hurt me sister, aye, or I might have to run ye through with me sword."

"Is that what you had planned for Ian the day we met?"

"Aye, and he didna even win her maidenhead, so ye can imagine what I'd plan for a rogue who did."

"Your point is well taken, and I give you my word. I will do nothing to hurt your sister. So are we friends, then?"

"Aye, I suppose so. Tell me one thing, though, whilst Ellie was kissing ye, did she shove her hands in yer breeks as well?"

"Aye, she did that," Dylan said, a roguish smile crossing his lips, "and there was no need of anything more. With her skills, I'm surprised she's not already married."

"Oh, she has been. Twice. God rest their souls."

Dylan had stood up and started wiping the berry shells from his jack but stopped short at Will's words. "She didn't . . ."

"Ach, nae!" Will chuckled, standing up as well. "One died of the flux, and the second was killed in a raid."

"Nae wonder she's so . . . skilled." Dylan frowned at his shirt. "I guess this is ruined."

Will nodded. "'Tis me fault. I have a new one me sister made for me last birthday. Ye're welcome to it. Me ma's going to give us a right tongue-lashing, though."

"Because we've ruined our clothes?"

"Nae, because we've broken her baskets and come back without the berries."

Will laughed and started across the field, but Dylan grabbed him by the arm. "What if I really did care for your sister?"

"I told ye, man, just dinna hurt the lass. As for the rest, she's a mind of her own, and I wouldna dare to challenge her on that."

****

Betty stood with her hands on her hips, her lips pressed together in a firm line as Will and Dylan walked through the barmekin gate. Mary had alerted her to their arrival, and she wanted to be ready for them. She could barely keep from laughing, though; the sight of two grown men covered in berry juice a humorous sight, to say the least. But with a house full of lads, she'd learned to control her expression well.

She lifted her chin and pointed to the two of them, then to the ground before her, just in case they had any idea of attempting to slip by her.

"And where are me berries, then?" she asked.

The two young men looked down at their clothes and shrugged, silly smiles breaking out on their faces.

"We had a bit of a tussle with a berry bush," Will said, the tips of his ears turning dark pink, just like his da's when angry or embarrassed.

Betty narrowed her eyes. "Ye watch yer clever tongue with me, Bonnie Will Foster, or I'll give ye a good skelp across the lugs. And who d'ye think will be cleaning them clothes?"

Will and Dylan glanced at each other while Betty continued. "No' to mention mending them."

Will swallowed. "I'll be glad to pay Nan and Kate for their trouble, Ma."

"Oh, 'tis kind of ye, lad, but there's the small cost of the vinegar and such it'll take to get those stains out as well. Who d'ye think will be paying for that?"

Dylan nudged Will. "I've no money yet, except for a few pence Eddie gave me."

"Dinna fash yerself," Will said. "Ye can give it me back when ye get paid, aye."

Betty shook her head. The wee fools thought she couldn't hear them, or perhaps they hoped she would take pity on them. If that was their plan, they were bigger idiots than she'd thought.

"Get yerselves upstairs, the pair of ye." She looked at Dylan and scowled. "The lassies just finished stitching a new shirt and breeks. Ye can pay for them at the end of the week. Ye'll have to wear one of the lad's extra doublets, though, until ye can buy another jack. As for ye, William, I'll be expecting a few new baskets the next time we go to market. And when ye're done upstairs, the two of ye take these old ones and get to work. I'll still be needing those berries."

Neither man said a word, they just hurried up the stairs.

Mary Foster stood over a pot of stew, chuckling to herself. "So yer plan worked then, Ma."

"Of course it did," Betty said. "Give two men something to agree on, and they'll work the rest out for themselves soon enough. I'll put a wee bit extra in Nan's and Kate's pay for their trouble, and yer sister will stop fretting ower Will being the reason Dylan disna pay her any mind."

"I'm no' sure Will's the problem, Ma. Seems to me that Dylan has nae mind for settling down."

"Hmm, ye may be right, but I'm sensing there's more to it than that. He's nae Ian Rutherford, if that's what ye're afeard of."

"He was out behind the chapel with—"

"Ach, that Ellie Smith. Tell me who's no' been out behind the chapel with that one. 'Twould be a far shorter list. Lads are wont to sow a few seeds afore they plant a garden, lass. Nae, I'm of a mind our Annie might be just what that lad needs, and she him. So give it a wee bit of time, eh?"

CHAPTER 11

Within a fortnight, Auld Maggie Armstrong passed from this world in her sleep, a peaceful expression etched on her weathered features. Maggie clung to her father, comforting him as best she could, for while her own heart ached, she could only imagine the deep sense of loss that grew within his.

Once more, the clan came from near and far, friends and family alike, to bid farewell to the old woman they'd grown to love. Maggie thought the ceremony seemed a bit short and rushed, but then again, except for her mother's funeral, which she barely recalled, she didn't have much experience in the matter. Still, considering the clan had spent the better part of two days trying to locate the priest, he could have at least put a bit more effort into it.

Robert must have sensed her annoyance, for he wrapped his arm around her shoulders and gave her a hug. "Death is a way of life here, lassie, and the Father there does his best. 'Tis no' like at home, where every village has a priest or two to tend their needs." He heaved a deep sigh, then continued. "Now off with ye while I join ye uncles, aye."

Maggie peeked around her father's considerable bulk and saw his brothers congregating outside the stables. "Are you going somewhere?"

"Just to the village for a wee dram or two." He bent over to whisper in her ear, giving her a conspiratorial wink. "'Tis how we menfolk deal with our grief, ye ken. Will ye be all right, lass?"

Maggie nodded and looked over at the cottage, where her aunts and some of her cousins had begun to gather. "And the ladies cook." She laughed and kissed her father on the cheek. "I'll be fine, Da."

She walked to the gate and watched the men ride away, but even after they faded from view, she couldn't bring herself to go back to the cottage. In the last few weeks, she'd come to cherish the quiet time spent there with her grandmother, and in spite of all the people milling around inside, it somehow seemed cold and empty. Instead, she decided to walk down in the glen and sit amongst the bell heather and Scottish bluebells that dotted the field.

There, alone in her grief, she pulled the delicate ring from her pocket and placed it on her finger, her grandmother's words echoing through her memory. *Heed me well in this, though, darlin'. Take care who it is puts this ring upon yer finger.* What on earth did she mean by that? Maggie began to sob softly, for she knew she would never again hear the old woman's gentle voice.

Once more, someone she loved had left her alone, and she could do nothing about it. Though she remembered very little about her mother, she couldn't forget how vulnerable her death had made her feel. Never before—or since, for that matter—had she seen her father cry, and the sight had left an indelible mark on her heart. She recalled sitting by his bedroom door, watching her big, strong father sob into his hands, his shoulders shaking in grief. Seeing him that way, she felt so lost and alone, a child adrift in a sea of tears. But she was no longer a child. She knew people lived and died, that life carried on with or without them, that happiness would be found again; and yet, she still couldn't rid herself of the same helpless sensation she'd experienced all those years ago.

A sudden rustling of the grass disturbed her thoughts, and she looked up to find Ian Rutherford standing before her. He knelt by her side, the gentleness in his eyes soothing her aching heart. How she wished he would take her in his arms and comfort her, if only for a moment. She needed that right now.

He took her hand instead, squeezing it within his own. "'Twill be all right, Maggie."

"But I just found her, and now she's gone." She pulled the hankie from her pocket and blew her nose. Not very ladylike, but at that point she didn't much care.

"There's nobody to fight about this, I'm afraid, for if there were, I'd be the first to mount and be on me way."

"You would, wouldn't you, Ian Rutherford?" Maggie let a smile catch the corner of her mouth.

Ian plucked at a few bluebells that sprouted from the ground beside him and tucked them behind her ear. His sea-green eyes stared deep into her own, a hint of mischief sparkling in their depths, and before she could say another word, he leaned over and grazed her lips with a gentle kiss.

A wave of heat rushed into Maggie's cheeks, and she ducked her head, hoping Ian wouldn't notice it.

"I know this mayna be the time," he said, "but I ken yer gran wouldna mind, her caring about ye the way she did and all. I'd like to court ye, Maggie Armstrong."

Maggie's head sprang up. "You want to what?"

"To court ye, darlin'." Ian seemed a bit confused, or maybe rejected. Maggie wasn't quite sure which. "Do the lads no' court the lassies where ye come from?" he asked.

"Yes, of course, in a manner of speaking, but . . . What about the Foster lass? From what I've heard, you were quite taken with her."

"That English wench!" He spit in the grass, then wiped the back of his hand across his mouth. "She was no more than practice."

"Practice for what?" Maggie asked, not sure she liked the anger that flashed across his eyes for a split second. But then again, he must still be smarting a bit from being dumped.

His voice softened, and he took her hand. "For loving ye, darlin'."

Still staring into her eyes, Ian brushed away the curls that fell across her face. He leaned closer to touch his wind-grazed lips against her own. A whispered pledge of love lingered on his lips as he slipped his hand beneath her head, laying her back against the fragrant blossoms and pressing his mouth over hers in a fervent kiss.

Maggie's heart raced against the stiff buckram of her kirtle, convinced it would, at any second, split in two. For one wondrous moment, time stopped, whisking her away to a land she'd only dreamed of. She grasped the long, fiery hair that covered Ian's collar, letting the silken strands run through her fingers like blades of meadow grass. Then, all too soon, he withdrew, his quivering lips dusting her cheek as he spoke again.

"I plan to ask ye family on the morrow."

"Ask my family what?" Maggie sighed, still deep within her dream.

"Why, for ye hand, of course," Ian said, his confusion reflected in his speech. "What else would I be asking for?"

"My what?" The words jarred Maggie from her reverie, and she jolted up with such force she almost knocked Ian on his back. "It was just a kiss. We barely know each other. And why would you be asking my family anyway?"

"'Tis the proper thing to do, lass, and how else am I to see ye if I dinna ask?"

Maggie's head spun. Of course he'd ask her family's permission. Did anyone do anything around here without asking the clan's permission? She blew out a deep, calming breath, reminding herself how different things were in this century. While a man might ask a girl's father for her hand in the 1980s, the gesture played a more symbolic role than it did now. That thought sobered her at once. "Look, Ian, I'd like to see you too, but . . ."

"But what, lassie?" Ian sat back in the tall grass, the sting of Maggie's reservations written all over his face. "I thought ye cared for me."

"I do like you. But everything's happening so fast, and with Gran dying, I suppose I feel a little lost."

"I'll help ye find yer way, then, only dinna spurn me with noucht a hope in sight."

"I'm not. It's just . . ."

"Then what's the trouble, darlin'?"

Maggie opened her mouth to reply, but Ian pressed his lips to hers, and the words caught in her throat, stifled by a pleasant quiver that seemed to culminate in her thighs. The tip of his tongue swirled around her own, titillating her senses, weakening her resolve. She needed to stop this before it went any further. After nineteen years of saving herself for the right man, she had no intention of giving her virginity to the first sixteenth-century hunk that came along, at least not yet.

Then, like a whisper borne on a summer breeze, her father's voice floated across the crisp green field and provided just the distraction she needed. Marveling at her father's perfect timing, she shoved Ian away with a gentle but firm nudge.

"I'm sorry, Ian. I have to go." She stood, smoothing down her skirts, and Ian reached up to take her hand.

"I didna mean to be so bold, darlin'."

Robert called again, and Maggie cast a quick glance over her shoulder before turning her attention back to Ian. "You didn't do anything wrong, but I really do need to go. My father's calling me."

"So ye're done with me, then."

"No, of course not. I would like to spend some time with you, get to know you better, but . . . You do understand?"

"Aye, I do!"

He flashed his usual charming grin, and, satisfied by his answer, Maggie granted him one last kiss before hurrying up the hill to the peel tower. She stumbled over the rise, turning to wave before she passed through the barmekin gate, the memory of his kiss still fresh upon her lips, his proposal all but forgotten.

****

Edward peeked around the door to the cottage, the sweet aroma of raspberries and honey filling the air. Too bad the stink of sour grapes still rose from Betty herself. With a renewed determination, he straightened his jack, clutching the basket of flowers in his hand, and entered the room.

"Now, Betty, I think we've had quite enough of this. I'll admit I was in the wrong, interfering and convincing Graham to take wee Duncan along on that raid, but that was many a year ago, and the lad's none the worse for wear, so . . ."

Edward stopped short and stared at Betty, who was doubled over with laughter. "Lord help us," she said. "I forgave ye for that years back. Now sit down and have a piece of pie, aye."

He stood there for a moment, scratching his head, not quite sure what had just happened. "Then why have ye been treating me like I have the plague? And when you do speak, your words are as sharp as an adder's bite and twice as venomous."

"Because ye didna even think to say good-bye when ye left. Did it no' occur to ye we may have fretted ower ye? And now ye come walking back into our lives, like nowt ever happened, and no' a word from ye in twenty-five year." She let out a frustrated scream and slammed her rolling pin down on the table. "If ye were one of me own, I'd give ye a right skelp across the lugs, ye thoughtless lout."

"I'm sorry, Auntie, it never occurred to me."

"And what did ye imagine I'd think? Ye were like one of me own lads."

"You're right. I was a lout with no thought for anyone but myself." Edward felt a warm flush invade his cheeks—and his heart. "What can I do to make it right between us?"

Betty wiped her hands off on her apron. "Well, ye can start by putting them flowers in yon pitcher of water."

Edward scrambled to do as he was told. He wasn't going to let this attempt at reconciliation slip through his fingers. "Is there anything else?"

"Aye, ye can sit down here and tell me about yer lad out there."

He turned to follow her gaze and saw Dylan and Annie sitting by the well. "Dylan?"

"Aye, I've seen the way ye watch ower him. Ye care about the lad, though 'tis clear ye didna wed his ma."

"No, I mean, yes, I do care about him, but not the way you think. He's my . . . sister's son. When she passed, I took him under my wing. There's nothing more to it."

Betty gave a knowing nod. "Ah, right, and that's what ye told the lad, then."

He stared out at the young couple for a minute and smiled, wondering what Betty would say if she knew the real story. "It's the truth. I never married because I had other obligations."

"Did ye now? And what would they be?" She gasped. "The lass was already wed, then."

"What? No, not at all." Edward took a deep breath. Oh, what the heck did it matter what she thought? It wouldn't affect anything here and now. He sat down on a bench by the table and sighed.

"You can't tell this to anyone. It could only hurt the lass's good memory."

Betty put her rolling pin aside and sat on the opposite bench, all ears. "Of course no', darlin'."

Edward rubbed his chin. *Just tell your father's story. With a few adjustments, it fits perfectly.* "The lass and I did wish to marry, but her parents forbid it. Seems they had another, more suitable lad in mind."

Betty scoffed. "More suitable indeed, but I'm sorry, darlin', go on with yer story."

"Lizzie and I slipped away, and we did indeed wed."

"A clandestine marriage, eh?"

"Yes, we even found a defrocked priest to stand as witness to our vows."

"I'm sorry, lad, I've interrupted ye again. I'll try to keep me thoughts to meself till ye've finished, eh?"

Edward nodded. "Thank you. Anyway, we had but one night of marital bliss before her father caught up with us. He dragged Lizzie home in spite of my protests, and her brothers worked me over well enough that I could barely move, let alone walk, for the next few weeks. By the time I could, they'd already had the marriage annulled."

Betty reached out and took his hand. "I'm so sorry, lad."

"He was a Hetherington, a relative of mine, as it was, but since he was rather well off, they thought the union more appropriate."

"But 'twas yer bairn she carried."

"No one seemed to care much as long as she was wed, and . . . my cousin was happy enough to claim fatherhood, being he could produce no heir of his own."

"And where is the scoundrel now?"

"He died when Dylan was about twelve years old, shortly after Lizzie's parents. Ironically enough, I was his next of kin, barring Dylan, of course."

"So why did ye not marry the lass, then?"

Good Lord these Scots were an inquisitive lot. He thought back to the day Robert had confronted him so many years before. "Lizzie thought it best if we didn't. She feared for her son's reputation, as any mother would, though she did make me his guardian."

"Aye, I can see that, and 'tis clear the lad's fond of ye regardless."

"At times he is." Edward laughed. "Though not always."

"'Tis a parent's lot, darlin'. We need guide them and do what's best for them, regardless of how they despise us for it."

Edward nodded, letting out a sigh of relief. Now all he had to do was let Dylan in on the little story before Betty slipped and said something to him. Then again, he wasn't supposed to be aware of it. Still, better he knew of the tale.

Betty squeezed his hand. "There now, d'ye no' feel better about it?"

"Aye, I do. Thank you for that, but this must remain between us, I beg you, for Dylan's sake, if not mine."

"I gave ye me word, lad, and I'll keep it, though I question the wisdom of it."

Edward nodded and gazed out on Dylan and Annie once more. To think the real truth was even more amazing than any of them knew, Dylan included.

****

Dylan's hands were sweating, and he wiped them on his new breeks. Never before had he felt this way with any woman, but then, he'd never quite met anyone like Annie Foster before. Her hair fell soft over her shoulders, gentle strands of gold and bronze silk, not teased into a rat's nest like some of the girl's he'd dated. He moved a bit closer on the bench, causing her to blush slightly.

Her cheeks were a natural soft pink, and her skin smooth and clear as if it had been kissed by the morning mist. She needed no makeup to enhance her features, for her eyes were a deep blue, the color of the sky just before dusk, and they were rimmed with long dark lashes.

"Would you take a walk with me Annie?" Why did he feel so bashful with her? *Because for the first time in your life, you're afraid a woman might turn you away.* True, but it was more than that. Women had spurned him before, and he just figured it was their loss, but this time . . . this time was different. His heart ached for her, not his dick. Oh, that ached too, but it didn't seem to matter as much.

Annie looked over toward the cottage and giggled. "Aye, for a wee bit, I suppose, but me ma winna be occupied for long. She'll be wanting to start the dinner soon enough and me to help and all."

Dylan scratched the back of his head. "Just what exactly do the servants do around here? It seems to me your family works harder than the lot of them."

"Dinna be daft. Me da says we need set a good example and not grow soft like some of the lords and ladies up in Edinburgh. Having a few servants disna mean we get to sit back on our haunches and watch them scurry about."

Dylan chuckled. That's exactly what his parents had done. "Yes, Will mentioned that. I guess we'd better be on our way, then, while we still can."

Touching her hand, he waited for her to clasp her fingers around his before tightening his grip and guiding her out the barmekin gate. They walked down through the flowered meadow, not saying a word. He marveled at how he could be so happy just walking beside her. Oh, he'd never needed a lot of conversation, there'd always been sex to fill the void. But with Annie, there was no void.

"D'ye no' love it here?" she said. They'd settled beneath a large oak tree that grew beside the river. "Ye see that bend ower yon?"

Dylan followed where she pointed and nodded. "Yes, what about it?"

"Well, sometimes, when the weather's warm, mind ye, and the lads are all off on a raid, the other lassies and I go swimming there."

A chill of excitement shot through Dylan's body. "Just in your shifts?"

Annie laughed. "Nae, ye daft rogue."

"Oh, so you mean . . ."

She giggled and nodded. "Aye, but dinna be getting any ideas in that thick heid of yers. Me brothers would bash it in if they thought ye were sneaking back round to take a keek."

"I would never think of . . ."

"Ach, I'm wise to ye, Dylan Hetherington. Ye're a rogue, to be sure."

Dylan jumped up and walked toward the river, throwing a stone across its tranquil water. Her reproach dug into his heart. "Then why do you even speak to me, Annie?" He turned back toward her, blinking to stay the tears.

She must have seen how hurt he was because she rose and came to stand before him. "Ye're a good man, Dylan, with a kind heart. Ye just havena found a place to settle yet."

"And what if I have now?" He moved closer and touched her cheek.

"Then ye'd best be sowing the last of yer wild seed, I'd say, for a garden such as mine would require all yer attention." She kissed him on the cheek and hurried back up the slope.

Dylan wiped his hands on his breeks again. That was the easy part. Now he'd have to deal with her father and brothers and prove his intentions were honorable.

CHAPTER 12

Ian knew exactly what Maggie meant. She couldn't appear to be too easy to win, not so soon after her grandmother's death. But he could tell by the eagerness of her kiss that she wanted him, and he'd made up his mind to ask for her hand the next afternoon.

No sense approaching Robert, though. After all, the man had been away for years. It would go much better if he asked Geordie. As laird of the clan, his endorsement should hold some influence over Robert and assure him of Ian's suitability, even if the man had forgotten what clan loyalty meant.

Pleased with himself, Ian made his way across the barmekin yard and found Geordie on his way to look over some newly acquired horse flesh.

"What is it ye need, Ian?" Geordie asked. "I've no time to be blethering on about nonsense."

"'Tis no' nonsense I wish to speak to ye of, me laird, but yer niece Maggie."

Geordie stopped checking the hobbler and turned around to face Ian. "Maggie! Go on, then. Say what's on yer mind."

"Only that she's a fine example of Scottish womanhood, and it would be me honor to court her, if ye could see yer way to permitting it."

"And why are ye asking me and no' her father, lad?"

Ian ducked his head, warmth rising in his cheeks. "Because her father kens little of me or what I'm able to offer his lass, so I'm of a mind ye might be speaking to him on me behalf. Surely, with ye being heid of the clan and all, he'd defer to yer judgment and see the benefits such a union could bring to us both."

Geordie folded his arms across his chest. "Hmm, and what benefits would they be, laddie?"

Ian hesitated. He never expected he'd have to enumerate his qualifications for the man. "Well, I am me father's eldest son, and as such I'll inherit a sizeable portion of his lands and become laird of the clan meself one day, much the way Alasdair will."

"No' quite like Alasdair, but I get yer meaning. Nae doubt ye'll provide well for our Maggie, but how does yer future standing benefit the Armstrongs?"

"With Maggie for me wife, me clan will consider it their duty to ride with the Armstrongs against any who would do them harm."

"And wedding our Maggie would guarantee that, would it?" Geordie huffed a laugh and walked to the other side of a hearty chestnut hobbler.

Ian followed, afraid his request might be denied. "Aye, me laird. 'Twould be a matter of honor."

Geordie put his arm on Ian's shoulder, a spark in his eye Ian couldn't quite identify. "And ye think that's the way it works, do ye? Then why are the Hetheringtons no' riding beside us? Me brother Andy wedded one of their lassies, nigh onto eighteen year back now."

Ian tried to control his temper, though he couldn't stop his hands from curling into fists. "Them rogues seen riding with the Fosters ower round Tynedale? I pray ye dinna count us as being of the same ilk as that lot of misbegotten scoundrels."

Geordie let out another laugh. "And I pray ye'll no' be talkin' that way round me brother Andy, elst ye may find a dagger nestling itself in yer gizzard."

"I'll do me best to mind it, me laird."

Geordie nodded. "Right then, I'll take it to mean ye're ower the Foster lass."

"Ach, I am that. I dinna ken what possessed me to profess me love for the wench in the first place." Ian lowered his voice and looked around. "There's talk there may have been witchcraft involved."

"Witchcraft, is it?" Geordie stood from checking the mare's legs and lifted an eyebrow. "I doubt verra much Graham Foster's lass is a witch, though I have heard tell she's a fair enough maiden."

"'Tis just what I've heard some say, me laird."

Geordie swiped a finger under his nose. "There's nae shame in falling for the wiles of a fair lassie. I'm sure ye've had yer share along the way. Me only concern is seeing ye've put it all behind ye and plan on treating our Maggie right. Now ye were saying the Rutherfords would ride with us. Why, may I ask, d'ye think we'd need yer help? On any day, I can put a hundred men and more in the saddle, without so much as breaking a sweat."

"Aye, I ken yer strength well, me laird."

"Seems to me this arrangement's more an advantage to the Rutherfords than to the Armstrongs."

Ian couldn't contradict him there. "I suppose it may be, but I love yer Maggie, and I dinna ken what else I can offer."

Geordie brushed a few pieces of hay from his jack and looked Ian up and down. "Fair enough, lad. There is one wee thing ye might do to prove yer sincerity."

"Anything, me laird, if it means I might win me Maggie's hand."

Geordie pursed his lips, nodding in approval. "Right then. Yer da plans on filing a bill against us at the next Day of Truce—one that could cost us quite a bit of trouble. Of course, if the warden were to find it clear, or better yet, yer da no' bring it up to begin with, well, 'twould go a long way to seeing ye betrothed to me niece."

Ian could breathe again. "Aye, me laird, I'm sure such an issue could be settled right enough when me da comes round to speak of the dowry."

"I expect it could," Geordie said, a smile tugging at the corner of his mouth. "Ye have yer da come see me, then, and I'll speak to me brother."

****

"What d'ye mean promising me Maggie to that Rutherford lad?" Robert asked as dusk settled across the surrounding moor. "Ye didna even have the decency to ask me if I approved of it."

"He's a strong lad, Rabbie," Geordie said, "and he'll make her a good husband."

"She's me daughter, Brother!"

"Aye, and I didna think ye would object to finding her a good home— and helping the clan out in the process."

Robert narrowed his eyes. He should have known Geordie was up to something. "What d'ye mean, helping the clan out?"

"I mean just what I said. There's been some strained feelings with the Rutherfords ever since the incident ower Hobbie Rutherford's cattle. A marriage between Maggie and Ian would put things right and ease the tension."

"Ye're promising me daughter to someone she only just met in place of some cattle?" Robert's voice rose, and his cheeks burned, the heat no doubt turning them a brighter red than usual. "Are ye out of yer mind, man?"

"Nae, but I'm beginning to wonder what those outlanders did to ye."

"Mayhap they gave me some sense down there, and I'm telling ye now, I'll no' allow me daughter to be bartered."

"In truth, ye have little to say about it, Rab. Until I give ye yer portion of the inheritance, ye dinna even own a piece a land. And if Maggie agrees . . ."

"So ye'd hold me land back to get what ye want. I forgot how spiteful ye could be, Geordie Armstrong."

"And I forgot how stubborn ye could be. I am still laird of this clan, and if I feel this union is in its best interest, I would expect ye to agree without hesitation. Me own marriage was arranged, and I've yet to regret one day of it."

"'Tis no' the same, and ye ken that well, Brother. 'Twas yer own father making the match, and he kent ye'd one day be heid of the clan yerself. Why d'ye no' give Ian yer Connie, then?"

"Because young Ian isna interested in her, and a good thing it is, for she's already been promised to another."

"Has she now? And which clan are ye planning to use wee Connie to placate?"

Geordie stood, his fists balled at his side. "That's enough, Rab. I'll have nae more of yer blethering. Ye ken right well 'tis me duty to put the good of the clan afore all else. Me weans understand what's expected of them. There was a time ye did as well."

"I'll no' sacrifice me Maggie's happiness for noucht more than a few kye."

Geordie stood there, glaring at him for the next few minutes, and Robert returned his angry stare. No doubt they must have looked like two bulldogs contemplating the same bone. If not for the gravity of the situation, Robert might have laughed. Instead, he said nothing for fear he might later regret his words. As for Geordie, his expression spoke volumes. There was no talking to him when he got this way, so Robert turned to storm away.

"Wait," Geordie called out, his voice strained in exasperation, "at least see what the lass has to say afore ye make up yer mind, aye."

Robert didn't even turn around to answer. He was so angry the words stuck in his

throat. Rather than risk a verbal response, he paused for a moment and gave a firm nod before continuing on his way. Geordie was right about one thing. Robert had every intention of seeing what Maggie had to say before he lost complete control.

****

"He what!" Maggie jumped up from her bed, pacing back and forth. "What does he think I am . . . his private property?"

"I'll fight him if I have to, darlin'." Robert flopped on Connie's bed, causing the small frame to creak beneath his weight. He rested his arms on his knees and rubbed the bridge of his nose with his fingers.

"Fight who?" She calmed down a bit at the thought of her father locked in mortal combat, for physical confrontation was the way they handled disputes on the border, wasn't it?

"Ian, Geordie, the Rutherfords, the whole Armstrong clan, if need be."

"Da, you can't fight your whole family." Maggie sat beside him, tucking her legs beneath her skirts and resting her head against his arm.

"I'll no' see ye unhappy, lass. Ye mean the world to me, ye ken."

Maggie nodded. "But they're your family too. You just found them again." A loose strand of hair fell across her forehead, and she brushed it aside. "Besides, I don't think I'd be unhappy . . . not altogether. He seems like a nice enough guy, but marriage . . . We just met. I thought he understood. He said he did. And then there's . . ."

"And then there's Dylan Hetherington. Hmph! Perhaps I should let ye wed this Ian."

"Dylan! No, I told you; there's nothing between us." Maggie raised up to give her father a peck on the forehead, then scrunched back down on the bed. "I love you, Da, but you've got it all wrong. We're friends, yes. But he's more like the brother I never had than a boyfriend."

"Perhaps, but more to the point, what does he feel for ye? I've heard what people say about him, darlin'."

"Sometimes people exaggerate or stretch the truth to suit themselves."

"Ye dinna really believe that's the case here, now d'ye, lass?"

"Look, Da, I know he's a bit of a flirt, but most of it is nothing more than an act. He's lonely, and it's his way of dealing with it. His parents haven't been there for him, not the way you have for me. Oh, they send him money and gifts, but that's so he leaves them alone. He's just looking for someone to love him."

"Is that right? Then ye'd best make sure 'tis love ye're feeling for him, lassie, and no' pity."

Maggie took a deep breath, inhaling through her nose and then exhaling through her mouth in a smooth stream, allowing it to release the tension building in her shoulders. "You're the most exasperatingly stubborn man I know." A smile touched her lips, and she reached over to take her father's calloused hands. "I wouldn't lie to you, Da. Any love I feel for Dylan is purely platonic. And I'm nothing more than a sister to him. So stop worrying."

"Now to get back to what I was going to say," she continued. "There's Annie Foster. I'd like to hear what she has to say, make sure it is over between them. I mean, I don't want to be the other woman," she added, the hint of a giggle in her voice.

Robert turned and looked into Maggie's eyes, then nodded, a deep sigh passing his lips. "All right, lass. I believe ye, but what of Ian Rutherford?"

"I don't know. I'm not ready to marry him, but I wouldn't mind dating him. But it's not dating now, is it? If he courts me, does it mean we're engaged—or betrothed? That's what they call it now, right?"

Robert chuckled, his eyes twinkling with silver specks. "Aye, they do, but ye'll be neither. No' if I have anything to say about it."

"Then I guess I wouldn't mind." She bit her lip and shrugged. "Who knows? It may develop into something more one day, but not yet. Love doesn't grow over night, right?"

"I kent I loved yer ma the moment I saw her, but nae, it disna always happen that way. For most, I expect it takes time. And time is one thing ye've plenty of darlin'. 'Tis in yer hands, no' Geordie Armstrong's or Ian Rutherford's, or even mine, for that matter."

"It's all so confusing, but there is one thing I'm sure of. For the first time in my life, I have this huge family, and I don't want to lose them . . . or drive them away."

Robert smiled, patting Maggie on the hand. "Then we'll wait, me wee bairn, and see what happens, aye. Ian can court ye if he likes, but there'll be no betrothal, no' until ye give the word, nae matter what arrangements Geordie makes. And if ye want to call the whole thing off, just say so, eh. I'll handle the lot of them."

"I know you would, and I love you for it, but I want you to be happy too."

"Me?" Robert burst out in a hearty laugh. "I will be, darlin', just as long as ye are. Dinna fash yerself, lass." He got up and kissed her on the top of the head. "I love ye, Maggie, and I always will. Never forget that. No matter what ye decide, I love ye more than life itself."

Maggie watched her father head down the stairs, then she sank back on her bed and stared at the ceiling. Thoughts flitted around her head like butterflies on steroids. At home, people dated, and if things didn't work out, they'd each go their own separate ways, no hard feelings. Well, at least most of the time. Tears might be shed here or there, but in the end, no harm, no foul. But here, the entire affair seemed much more complicated.

In this world, men died for a careless word and took an insult spoken in haste as an affront to their honor. Here, a woman had little to say about who she would wed. Ian had decided he wanted her to be his wife, and that was that. The whole idea made her twentieth-century temper boil, and she scrubbed her hands against her face to cool the fire. What she really needed was to talk to someone else from her own world, someone close to her own age. Someone like Dylan Hetherington.

CHAPTER 13

A light mist dampened her cloak, and Maggie kept her head down, doing her best to move unnoticed among the deepening shadows that engulfed the barmekin yard. Her mind raced, and though she kept her stride steady, she couldn't help shivering when she entered the dark, damp tower, uncertain if it was the thought of what she intended to do or the eerie loneliness of the place that caused her chill. No matter, she was determined to carry out her plan and hurried up the stone steps to an upper floor in search of her cousin.

"Will you take me, Alasdair?" she asked on finding the boy polishing his sword.

"To a Foster stronghold! Are ye off yer heid, Coz? Me da would take the tawse to me, no' to mention the tongue-lashing I'd get from me ma."

"Well, show me which way to go, then," Maggie said.

"What for?" Alasdair brushed back his dark brown waves and shook his head. "Ye're daft as a drunken dog."

"Why? Ian goes down there all the time, and Andy's wife, Marion, is an Englishwoman herself. A Hetherington, I believe."

"Aye, and me uncle came close to dancing 'neath the widdie for that one." He looked out the small window, his gaze traveling across the marsh, and tapped his knee in obvious discomfort.

Maggie sat down by his side. "Please, Alasdair, there's someone I have to see."

"Ye're to be betrothed to Ian Rutherford!" he said, a spark of anger glinting in his eyes.

"Where did you hear that?"

"'Tis nae secret, now is it? Ian's already spoken to me da, and Hob's to come see about yer dowry the morrow."

A wave of fury passed through her body, and Maggie clutched her skirts in an effort to keep her hands from shaking. "Oh, he is, is he? Well, my da might have something to say about that."

Alasdair ducked his head and laughed. "Oh aye, I think he already has, and I'm sure it winna be the last, though I canna say I comprehend why. I thought ye cared for Ian."

Maggie couldn't tell him the truth. He'd never believe a word of it, so she decided to go with her father's suspicions. "Would you have me promise myself to him while an ember of doubt still lingered in my heart?"

"There's someone else, then, down at the Foster peel?" Alasdair spit on his sword and wiped away a speck of dirt. "Ye met him down in Lancashire, I reckon?"

Maggie just nodded, not wanting to say any more than she needed to.

"And ye love this English scoundrel?"

"I'm not sure, but it's why I need to go. I won't betray Ian, not the way Annie did. I've too much respect for him to do such a thing." She almost gagged on the words, but she could think of no other feasible reason for venturing south. At least, no other reason he would believe.

Alasdair's eyes softened a bit, and he reached out to touch her cheek. "All right, then, but we'll have to go by night and keep to the back roads. Ye realize there'll be the devil to pay when we return."

"I know." Maggie smiled, but Alasdair's expression was far more serious, and he rested his hand on her shoulder.

"If we run into any broken men or such, ye let them have their way with ye. 'Tis nae shame in giving in, lass, and me da will pay the ransom soon enough. Better that than what they might do should ye put up a fight."

Maggie tried to swallow the lump in her throat. Could it really be that dangerous? Her father worried about Dylan getting a little fresh while his sixteenth-century counterparts might rape her with no one thinking her the worse for wear.

And what if Dylan never headed south at all? What if he went farther north or to the coast, or worse yet, what if he'd ventured all the way down to London? The thought caused her to shiver, but she shook it off. No, he must be at a nearby Foster peel. After all, she'd seen that boy hiding in the woods—a Foster, her father had said. Edward would have come across him, and being a Foster himself, it would make perfect sense for him to head south to the young man's home. He'd been here before, after all. Maybe he even knew the family. And wherever Uncle Eddie ended up, Dylan was sure to be there with him. Besides, how many Foster peels could there be, right?

Maggie spent the better part of the next day helping her aunt with the baking and then making supper and washing the dishes, but the time still seemed to drag on.

"What I wouldn't give for a dishwasher," she grumbled under her breath as she scrubbed the last of the pots and hung it back over the hearth. The sun was down, yet her uncles still sat around the fire, smoking pipes and laughing about old times. Weren't they ever going to go to bed?

Saying good night, she headed up to her own bed, stopping at the top of the stairs to see if the men showed any sign of stirring. Geordie stretched his feet out to the fire with a contented groan while Sim stuffed more tobacco in his pipe. It was going to be a very long night.

She slid into bed and pulled the covers up around her chin so no one would notice she was still fully clothed, then she closed her eyes and feigned sleep. Sometime later—it felt like hours but was probably only one or two—whispered voices and the creak of wooden steps signaled her father and uncle ascending the stairs. She listened for the heavy breathing that accompanied deep sleep and the familiar snore her father so adamantly denied. At last, his melodious tones reached her ears, and she peered out the window to see Alasdair dashing across the yard to the stables. The moon was high in the sky when she met him, and they slipped away into the night.

****

They'd just crossed the Border when they stopped to water their horses. Maggie flopped down on the bank of a small burn and gave a weary yawn, but Alasdair stood erect, his eyes searching the fading darkness for any unusual movement. He may have only been sixteen years of age, but his demeanor made it clear he was already well aware of the dangers lurking beyond his own walls and had acquired a skill far beyond his years. With a sudden start, he grabbed Maggie's arm, yanking her up sharply.

"We have to go . . . now!" But it was too late. Three slovenly looking men were upon them, their clothes torn and their long hair dirty and disheveled. "Broken men!" Alasdair whispered.

They were outlaws, men who no clan claimed as their own. Vicious men who gave allegiance to no one. Alasdair looked from one to the other, his sword held ready.

"Stand firm, Maggie, and close behind me."

As if she might develop an urge to do anything else.

"Well, what have we here, laddie?" One of the men brushed the tip of his pike along Alasdair's cheek.

"Two fine specimens of Scottish youth, I'd say." The second man snickered, his voice cold and sinister as he came up beside Maggie. "And look, he's set himself to protect his mistress."

"Let's see how fine a treasure he guards, eh." The third one grabbed Maggie and pulled her to himself, causing all three creatures to cackle with laughter.

"No!" Maggie screamed, forgetting everything her cousin had told her. A prisoner of her twentieth-century instincts, she lifted her knee and slammed the scoundrel in the groin, causing the stunned man to double over in pain.

"Run, Maggie!" Alasdair yelled, his hand around her arm, tugging her from the outlaw's grasp.

For once, Maggie did just as she was told, sprinting away from the men. Her cousin followed close behind after slicing one of the villains across the face with his sword. She could hear his breath in the crisp night air, feel the gentle nudge of his hand against her shoulder. Then, all at once, he was gone.

She stopped, frozen in her tracks, listening for any sign of their pursuers. But it all sounded so strange. No fire engines or car horns broke the silence, just the sound of nature . . . predawn's nature.

"Alasdair!" she whispered so low even the hushed tones of the breeze could be heard above her, but no answer came. What would she do? She dared not call out any louder for fear of her cries alerting the outlaws to her whereabouts. And she was no match for such men. Still, she needed to remain calm. It would do neither herself nor Alasdair any good if she panicked. Perhaps if she could make her way to the village. Someone there would be able to help her. Of course, that would mean she'd have to move.

Taking a deep breath, she inched her way forward, walking deeper into the forest, its moonlit path giving way to the blue-gray light of the approaching day. More than once, her heart nearly stopped when a twig snapped beneath her foot or a small creature scurried across the path. Breathless, her knees quivering beneath her linen petticoats, she closed her eyes and rested against the trunk of a large oak. The mist had grown heavy, and she could barely see what lay ahead, but she knew she had to move on, for she was determined to get help for her cousin.

It was all her fault, after all. If she hadn't been so insistent on seeing Dylan, Alasdair would be safe at home, but now . . . She could hear harsh voices whispering off in the distance. What if they'd captured him? They would kill him for sure, just for the sport of it.

Picking up her step, she continued down the moon-drenched path. Misty clouds danced before her, and their shadowy movements confused her senses, making it all the harder to stay on the narrow trail. Something wet crawled up her leg, but she held her breath to keep from screaming, for off in the distance she spied a shadow moving far too quickly to be the fog.

Knowing they might confront her again at any moment, she bent to pick up a stone, her hand trembling with such force she failed twice before securing a rather large one.

"If ye ever be attacked, aim for the temple," her father had instructed her. The memory of his steady voice calmed her enough to quell the nauseous ache in her stomach. She stood, lifting her chin in defiance. With her breath as still as a sleeping babe's, she reached for a low-lying branch, hoping to get a better view. At least, she thought it was a branch until it grabbed her wrist and yanked her to the ground. A scream burst from her lips, and a strong hand covered her mouth, almost smothering her in the process. Squinting in the glow of a small, shuttered lantern, she made out a slender face. Behind him, sprawled unconscious on the soft moss-covered ground, lay Alasdair.

Maggie's eyes filled with fury as the man pressed his knee into her shoulder.

"Be still, lass, elst I'll break it in two," he hissed. "I dinna wish to hurt ye, but I will if need be. I'm going to take me hand away now, aye."

Though against her better judgment, Maggie did what she was told, her cousin's words echoing deep within her consciousness. In truth, there remained little else she could do, given her current position. And at least this one didn't reek of whisky, wet dogs, and urine.

He turned his head to peer through the bushes, the faint light illuminating his features, and she bit her lip to keep from gasping. It was him: the young man in her father's painting, the one she'd seen on the side of the road the day they'd arrived—the Foster lad.

Alasdair groaned, and Foster turned back, holding his sword to her cousin's throat.

"Leave him alone, you thug." Maggie couldn't help herself. The words just seemed to pop out of her mouth.

The young man smiled, the lantern light reflecting off those beautiful slate-blue eyes. "I told ye once, lass. I'm no' of a mind to hurt ye, being ye do as I say. Now haud yer wheesht, would ye, elst ye'll have the lot of them down on us."

Maggie breathed a bit easier. Clearly, Mr. Foster, if indeed that was his name, didn't belong to the band of broken men they'd just run into. And he didn't seem inclined to rape her, though she still wasn't sure about his intentions concerning her cousin.

Alasdair stirred once more, but this time he opened his eyes. Spying the fair-haired young man who knelt over him, he gave a sudden start.

"Calm yerself, Alasdair Armstrong," Foster said. "I've nae intention of harming ye or yer lady, so long as ye speak true of yer reason for being here."

Maggie didn't think it an unreasonable request, but much to her surprise, Alasdair spit in the young man's face. Though the Englishman's hand tightened around the hilt of his sword, he managed to retain his composure.

"But for the lass, I'd run ye through here and now, Alasdair. Ye're on Foster land, and I'd every right to do so."

"Foster land!" Maggie gasped, unable to conceal her excitement.

"Aye, and what of it, lass?"

The words had no sooner left his lips, than his body stiffened. His eyes grew wide, and his breath came in quick, shallow bursts.

At first, Maggie thought he'd taken a seizure of some sort, but when an obscure figure loomed above him, its identity lost in the shifting mist, she knew the young man's reaction could mean only one thing. They'd been discovered.

A combination of fear and dread twisted her stomach into knots. If she could only reach the small knife Alasdair had given her. It might not stop them, but at least she could slow them down a bit, maybe even give her cousin a chance to attack. Too bad it was buried under a multitude of skirts and petticoats. It wouldn't take much to grab it, though. Even a slight diversion would give her the opportunity she needed.

A plan was formulating in her head. *Three of them, three of us. Not bad odds.* With renewed determination, she shot a glance in her cousin's direction, hoping he might be able to reach his sword, but the grin creeping across his lips stopped her short, leaving her more than a bit disconcerted.

Convinced her cousin had knocked himself senseless in the fall, she spun back around. If she was to be their last line of defense, so be it. She'd make her father proud. Plunging her hand beneath her skirts, she grabbed the dagger from her garter, resolved to go down fighting. The heck with this "just let them have their way" bit.

She jumped up, thrusting the small weapon out in front of her, but froze midair when her father emerged from the shifting fog, his own knife pressed against her handsome captor's throat. He stood straight and tall, the hint of a smile tugging at the corner of his mouth, and Maggie dropped back on the leaf-strewn ground, a sigh of relief escaping from her lips.

"Come away easy now, laddie," he said, "and relieve yerself of that blade."

The Englishman dropped his sword and rose to his feet. "Be ye of name, sir?"

"Aye, Armstrong, and these be me kin."

"I beg yer indulgence, sir. I didna recognize ye. As I told the lass, I meant them nae harm, only to help and to inquire of their business here. They were being chased by outlaws. Three of them, down by the Kershope Burn."

"He's telling the truth, Da." Maggie stood and brushed off her skirts. "We were being chased."

"Aye." Alasdair moaned, rubbing his head. "I slipped and fell."

"And what would ye be doing out so late at night, young Foster?"

"Picking berries." The young man sneered in obvious defiance. "Me mother wishes to bake a pie this morn."

Robert pulled the Englishman up, twisting his arm behind his back and whispering over his shoulder. "Does she, now? Ye'd best be heading home, then. And tell wee Betty she owes me a pie for sparing her bairn's life. Now take up yer blade, mount yer hobbler, and be on yer way, lad. And pray I dinna see yer loathsome face on Scottish soil, or I'll skewer ye for sure."

Maggie could hear her uncles in the background and no doubt so could the young Englishman, for he took the reins of his nagg and followed Robert's instructions, even if he did do so with the utmost contempt and unmistakable anger in his eyes.

"'Tis no fear of that, sir," he replied when he was safely astride his mount. "I wouldna dirty me boots on such godforsaken ground." Not foolish enough to push it any further, he clicked his heels against his horse's side and rode off without another word.

"Quickly, Maggie," Robert said as soon as he'd gone. "'Tis but a league to his uncle's peel, and if they decide to ride against us, we'll be doomed for sure."

Alasdair had retrieved her horse, so she mounted at once, far too weary to argue, but she road close to her father. Some questions just couldn't wait.

"The Foster peel you mentioned, that's where Uncle Eddie and Dylan are?"

Robert gave a quick glance around before answering. "I dinna ken which one they're at, but I reckon 'tis one of them."

"But how would they know to go there?"

"Eddie's been here afore, mind, so 'tis no' too much a stretch to think he returned to one of them."

"Right! That boy was a Foster as well, the one from your portrait book, wasn't he? You called his mother Betty. Did you know her?"

A wry smile crossed Robert's lips, a faraway look clouding his eyes. "Aye, I kent wee Betty Hetherington once upon a time, but no' the way ye're thinking, lass. She was a married woman by the time I was old enough to show an interest. 'Twas her son Walt we got friendly with. Yer Uncle Andy married her niece. The three of us used to sneak off with the lassies . . ."

He stopped mid-sentence and cleared his throat, the laughter that had so recently filled his speech gone. "But never mind that—or that lad in the bushes." His eyes darkened, like they always did when he was angry or worried. "Ye're no' back home, lassie, and this was nae carefree excursion to the mall ye undertook. Those men would have thought noucht of beating ye or raping ye, or worse. No' to mention what they would have done to Alasdair. Think on that a piece afore ye go turning this into some sort of romantic adventure, eh?"

Having said his piece, Robert tapped his heels against his horse's side and rode on ahead. Maggie's bottom lip quivered, and she blinked away the tears. He was angry. Rightfully so, she supposed. She pulled a hankie out of her pocket and blew her nose.

Alasdair drew up next to her. "Ye all right, Coz?"

Maggie sniffled, and after one last blow, she tucked the linen cloth back in her pocket. "Yes, my da's a bit irritated with me at the moment, though."

"Aye, mine as well, but ye canna say I didna warn ye."

Geordie shouted for him, and after giving a shrug, he too spurred his horse and rode on ahead.

CHAPTER 14

Will unsaddled his hobbler, giving it some hay and patting its rump before he peeked out across the barmekin yard. The sun sat directly overhead, a sure sign the midday meal would soon be on the table. His stomach grumbled. Why hadn't he thought to bring something besides a few cold oatcakes? The taste of his mother's honey-drizzled scones and buttery shortbread filled his mouth, causing his wame to roar once more, but he couldn't just walk in there without some explanation for his absence, one not involving a visit to Scotland.

He looked toward their cottage and groaned. His eldest brother, Walt, stood by the door, talking to their father, his brows low above his eyes as he glanced toward the gate and shook his head. That couldn't be good. No doubt they were discussing his whereabouts, and he could tell by his father's stance that he wasn't pleased.

Leaning back against the rough stone, Will risked a quick look out the barmekin gate, across the verdant slope sprinkled with shades of blue. He could almost smell the sweet scent of the harebells and forget-me-nots that grew in thick patches between the wall and the wooded ground to the right. A small spring, gurgling along the foot of the incline, sparkled in the early afternoon sun, its waters speaking a promise of trout and salmon.

Perhaps he could say he'd been fishing downstream all morning. But no, the fish were running well this time of year. He'd need to have something to show for his efforts. His father might believe he'd grown impatient and given up, but not Walt. What on earth had brought his brother over at this time of day anyway? He usually took his afternoon meal at home.

It hit Will hard and fast, like the sun bursting forth to hit you in the eye when a tree shifts in the wind. How could he have forgotten? He'd promised to help take stock of the cattle that morning and ride out to check the state of the shielings. In his absence, his father must have sent for Walt instead. *God's teeth!* That was sure to make matters even worse.

He took a deep breath, his cheeks puffing as he let it out again, then stood up straight and adjusted his jack. Might as well get it over with. After all, better to face his father's wrath for shirking his chores than for what he'd truly been about. He'd blatantly disregarded orders by heading for Rutherford land. No doubt if he'd succeeded, his da would have been glad enough to overlook his disobedience. But he hadn't even made it to Scotland, and he'd left his father and brothers shorthanded to boot.

Get your story straight, Will, or there'll be hell to pay. With that sobering thought, he turned the corner and sauntered across the yard. His father and Walt had already gone inside, so he lingered a moment outside the door, reviewing his story one final time. Convinced it sounded believable enough, he pushed down on the latch, but he'd barely crossed the threshold before he regretted the action.

All the lighthearted banter ceased and every eye turned on him, unspoken accusations written on every face. He made a feeble attempt to smile, then went to sit in his usual seat. Perhaps if he ignored them, they would return to their food and leave him in peace.

A spark of hope flared when his brother Rory resumed his meal with nothing more than a snicker, but then Dennis threw a quick look in their eldest brother's direction, and a wave of apprehension snuffed it out. Walt lifted an eyebrow, placed his spoon down, and leaned back against his chair, his arms laced across his chest.

Will muttered another curse. Walt would see right through his feeble story, no matter how plausible it sounded. Being close to twenty-three years older, he always acted more like a surrogate parent than a sibling. Yet in this instance, he seemed happy enough to relinquish the role and let their father handle the situation.

Keeping his head down, Will spooned some beef pottage into his bowl. The way his stomach lurched, though, he feared it would hold little before spewing it back up.

The tension hung heavy in the air as his father finished chewing and wiped his mouth, folding the cloth and setting it neatly on the table.

"Now, laddie," he said, his voice the calm before the storm, "would ye care to tell us where ye've been all morn? And please, I dinna care to hear how ye forgot ye were to be helping me and yer brothers check the shielings. Let's just assume ye did and get on with it, aye."

Will wiped his hands on his breeks, a sudden surge of heat flushing his face. He was twenty years old, for God's sake, a full-grown man, not accountable to his parents. And yet, even if he could convince himself he owed his father no explanation, the man was his laird, head of the family, and as such still demanded respect.

Trying to assume the most innocent expression possible, he cleared his throat. "I rode up to do a bit of hunting with me cousins."

"Did ye now? And which cousins would they be?"

The sound of sleuth hounds echoed in Will's head, warning him to alter his story, but fool that he was, he ignored it, plowing on ahead. He coughed, worried the words might come out in a boyish croak, even though his voice had long since passed that milestone.

"Me Uncle Richie's lads."

His father frowned, then peeked under the table as if looking for something. "Where's yer catch, then, laddie or did ye already give it to yer ma?"

"He gave me nowt," his mother said. She looked in Will's direction, tilting her head in inquiry.

A cold chill slithered down his spine. They knew he was lying. He could sense it, yet how could he change his tale now? Perhaps if he added a few more details. "We didna have much luck. Davie caught a rabbit, I think, but no' much more."

With those words, his mother rose from the settle, smoothed her skirt, and walked around to the washbasin. Will glanced at her bowl. She hadn't touched her food, let alone finished it, nor had anyone spilled anything, so why had she gotten up at all? A flame of dread ignited in his bowels, his body's own beacon being lit to warn him of danger, and he felt the sudden need to add even more details.

"I was for staying on and hunting a bit more, but once Davie got the rabbit, he and Ross were done with it."

A moment later, his mother grabbed his shoulder and spun him around, nearly yanking him off the settle. She glared down at him, holding a bar of soap to his face.

"I ought scrub that lying tongue right out of yer mouth," she said.

The lump in Will's throat crashed to his stomach and exploded into a ball of shame and regret. He opened his mouth to deny the accusation, but the words wouldn't form on his lips. So instead he stared at the floor and pushed the fresh rushes around with his foot, guilt seeping through his pores.

"Never mind the soap!" his father said. "I'll take the tawse to the wee scoundrel and beat the truth out of him."

Will's head shot up, his cheeks burning. He stood and turned to face his father, indignation over being talked to like a child in front of his brothers suppressing the pangs of guilt. "I'm no' a wean to have me mouth washed out with soap or be taken to the shed to have me bare arse whipped."

"Nae, laddie," his da said, his tone still surprisingly calm, "ye're a grown man and should realize the weight yer word carries. Yer very life may depend on it." He walked over to the wall and took the strap from its hook. "Now will ye act yer age and speak true, or are ye still a wean who needs to be taught a lesson?"

Will flopped down on the bench. He needed to own up to what he'd done, even if it earned him a good skelping with the tawse, but before he could answer, his sister Annie stood up with such force she nearly knocked the settle over and her brother Dennis with it.

"I ken what he's been about. He's gone up to confront Ian, hasn't he? And after I told him to leave it be and all."

Will's temper flared all the more. "D'ye no' realize what he's been saying about ye down round Carlisle and Bewcastle, no' to mention ower to Hexham? Nae decent lad will want to court ye after the lies he's told."

"Well, I've nae worry, then, have I? Nae decent lad would be spending any time with Ian Rutherford, let alone taking his word as the Lord's own." Annie straightened as tall as her five feet would allow. "And if they do, I'll no' be wanting them for a husband in any case."

"Ye're daft, lass." Will jumped up once more. This time his brother Rory had to grab the edge of the table to keep from tumbling off his seat. "He had us all fooled for a while, now didn't he? What makes ye think he'll no' be sweet talking others as well?"

"Well, he may, but they'll see the truth soon enough, just as we did. And until they do, I've nae time for them either." She gave a firm nod to her mother and father, then turned her back on Will and stormed up the stairs.

At first, no one said a word. Instead, they turned to face Will, their eyes filled with accusations. He scrubbed his hand across his face, wondering why he'd never chosen to grow a beard, for if the heat in his cheeks was any indication, his face had already turned into a blotchy scarlet mess. If only he could leave the way Annie had, he'd take off for the stream and dunk his head in the cool water, but the set of his father's shoulders warned him he'd do better to put such thoughts aside.

Will sighed and sank back in his seat, waiting for the reprimand that hung unspoken in the air. He chanced a quick peek in Walt's direction, but his brother simply rubbed the back of his neck and shook his head, the spark in his eyes making it clear he had no intention of bailing Will out of this one.

"So is that the way of it, lad?" his father finally said. "Ye decided to take matters into yer own hands. Heid of the family now, are ye?"

Will swallowed hard. He couldn't remember ever being so thirsty. He balled his fist to resist reaching for the tankard of ale that stood inches away. "Nae, sir, 'tis no' what I intended at all."

Walt huffed a laugh. "Then what exactly did ye have in mind, ye wee ideot?"

Walt's words stung, and Will responded, "Protecting me sister's honor, as it appears to be nae concern to anyone else."

Rory's eyes widened. He speared a leek and stuffed it in his mouth, concentrating a bit too much on his bowl of pottage.

"No' that I need to explain me actions to anyone," his father said, slapping the strap against his hand, "least of all me youngest son, but taking yer youth into consideration, I'll do me best. First off, yer sister's right. Any fool who canna see beyond Ian's lies is no' worth her time. Second, when yer sister feels up to it, he'll pay right enough at the Day of Truce. And third, should we no' get satisfaction there, 'tis then I'll consider a raid. I'll no' risk men's lives when there's a chance for redress elsewhere."

"I'm no' a fool," Will said. "I didna plan on having anyone find 'twas me what did him in."

This time Walt let out a full-fledged laugh. "Ye're off yer heid. Did we no' teach ye better than that? The Rutherfords would suspect us straightaway. 'Tis all the proof they'd need to ride against us. And what's more, word has it they're running with the Armstrongs now, so 'twould be a formidable force indeed. Think with the brains the good Lord gave ye, aye."

Walt's words hit with a mighty blow. Will's breath caught in his throat as though he'd been punched in the stomach. "I dinna suppose I was thinking of the consequences so much as the wicked things he says about our Annie. He disna even care if I hear. But I let me temper rule me judgment, and for that I'm sorry. I should've kent better."

"Aye, ye should've," his mother said. "But 'tis no' us ye need be apologizing to. Yer sister longs to put the whole affair behind her, and here ye come stirring it all up again like the wee midges that hover ower the field."

"I didna mean to cause her more grief, Ma. I'll go up straightaway and set it right, eh."

Though facing Annie wouldn't be pleasant, it would save him from his father's wrath, at least for the moment. He stood up, intending to head for his sister's chamber, but his mother put a hand on his shoulder and pushed him back down.

"Eat something first, aye," she said, a twinkle in her eye. "'Twill give her time to calm herself and see ye only acted out of love."

And time for me da to scold me, ye mean. Will groaned inwardly, knowing full well what his mother was about. Best not to argue, though, elst he'd feel the sting of her tongue, and nothing his father could do or say would be as sharp as that.

"So I'm guessing ye didna reach Ian, then," Walt said. "And 'tis certain ye werena with Richie's lads, so what were ye doing all that time?"

"Wait," Will said, his spoon hovering beneath his chin. "How did ye ken I wasna with me cousins?"

A smirk crossed Walt's lips. "D'ye want to enlighten him, Da, or will ye leave that pleasure to me?"

His father hung the strap back on its peg and sat down, the trace of a frown clouding his forehead. "'Tis no' pleasure that fills me heart, nae matter what ye may think." He pursed his lips and glared in Will's direction. "Yer Uncle Richie stopped by early this morn, lad. On his way down to Carlisle, he was, to meet up with young Davie and Ross."

"Oh." The lump of guilt fermenting in Will's gut made him ill, and he dropped the spoon in his bowl even as his stomach growled in protest.

Walt ran a finger under his nose to conceal a grin. "So, lad, I'll ask ye again. What kept ye away so long?"

"Nowt to do with Ian, so keep yer heid. I never even made it across the Kershope Burn. Me pony shied away as we got near, so I ducked into a copse of trees to see what spooked her. I heard them right enough, well afore I saw them—a group of broken men, from out of Liddesdale, nae doubt."

His father nodded. "Aye, me brother's spoken of a band causing havoc of late."

"I thought it best to lay low for a bit, not wanting the likes of them to keep me from crossing ower to Scotland, ye see. But then here comes Geordie Armstrong's lad, out of naewhere mind, and with a bonnie lass, nae less."

"Alasdair?" his father said. "And what was the wee rascal up to, skulking about on Foster land?"

A warmth spread across Will's cheeks once more, and he took a drink of ale to cool himself. "I dinna ken for certain. Him and the lass started to run, and then Alasdair tripped, so I pulled the wee ideot into me hiding hole, and the lass as well. She looked to tell me the reason for them being there, but then . . ." Will squirmed in his seat. Did he really need to tell them the rest?

"Ye didna let the lass get the drop on ye, did ye?" Dennis could barely contain his laughter, but Walt helped him at once with a quick slap to the back of his head.

"Nae!" Will said. "But 'twas an Armstrong snuck up from behind, right enough. I'm of a mind the lass thought him one of them thieving rogues, though, for she pulled a dagger from her skirts and looked as though she were ready to skewer him."

"What d'ye reckon brought them to England, Da?" Walt asked.

"'Tis hard to tell, but best we keep an extra watch tonight, aye. If they meant to attack Richie's place, we may already be too late. Dennis, ye and Rory ride up that way, aye, hiding yerselves well and keeping an eye out. Take a few of the men with ye."

"I dinna fault yer thinking, Da," Walt said. "'Tis best we stay alert, but it may only be Alasdair's found himself a bonnie English lass to love, and his da's sent the clan after him."

"'Twas nae English lass he was with," Will said. "I'd seen her afore when I . . ."

Both Walt and his father tilted their heads. "When ye what?" his brother said.

He had to learn when to keep his gob shut. "The day I met up with Eddie and Dylan. She's a daughter of the one what snuck up on me."

"And which one of them murdering Armstrongs was that, Willie?" Dennis asked.

Will scowled at his brother. He hated being called Willie. "I canna rightly say. I'd never seen him afore, that's certain, and the lass just called him Da, once she realized it wasna the broken men come for us, that is."

Walt scratched his head, rustling the wheat-colored waves. "Could be one of the Langholm or Mangerton bunch, then?"

"I reckon I'd know them as well." Will shook his head and took a bite of the pottage, his appetite slowly returning as the discussion veered away from him and more toward the mysterious Armstrong. "He seemed well acquainted with me ma, though. Said I should tell wee Betty to thank him."

An uncomfortable silence followed, and Will pushed pieces of beef and carrots around his bowl for a bit before finally taking a bite. Once again, he'd said too much, but perhaps no one would expect him to go into any more detail.

"Thank him for what?" his mother asked at last. She picked up her eldest son's bowl and scraped the few remains into a bucket by the washbasin before sitting down beside Will.

"For no' slitting yer bairn's throat, nae doubt," Rory said with a snicker.

"Haud yer wheesht!" his father said, his look enough to wither the sturdiest oak. "How did it come he got the drop on ye, then, lad?"

Will eyed the strap on the wall, thinking a good thrashing might be preferable. "I suppose I let meself get a wee bit distracted, Da, but in me defense I had me hands full between the broken men lurking in the bushes and Alasdair ready to skewer me if he saw the chance, no' to mention the lass herself waving her knife about."

"Her wee toothpick, ye mean," Dennis said.

Will narrowed his eyes and shot a glance in his brother's direction before turning back to his father.

"And yet he let ye go," his da said. "Without even asking a ransom."

"Must have been Andy, then," Walt said. "He's the best of the lot."

"But I'd have known Andy, and it wasna him." Will crumpled his brow. "Did look a lot like him, though."

His da pulled at his beard, his pale blue eyes staring into nothingness. They all knew better then to interrupt him. Finally, he took a deep breath and turned to Dennis.

"Ye and Rory be on yer way, aye. If ye keep up a decent pace, ye should be at yer uncle's well afore 'tis time to fill yer bellies again."

"Aye, Da," Dennis said. "We're off, then." He and Rory grabbed a few extra scones and hurried out the door.

His father reached across the table and took his wife's hand. "Best be sending Marion a missive, darlin', and see what we're up against, eh?"

She stood at once, brushing back Will's hair and kissing him on the top of his head. "Aye, I will that, but whoever he is, I'll be more than glad to give him me thanks."

"He said ye could settle the debt with a pie," Will said, once again forgetting himself as he cut a slice of the fruit-filled pastry.

A broad smile crossed Walt's face. "Rabbie Armstrong!"

Will's parents exchanged glances.

"Ach, 'tis no' possible," his mother said, blessing herself three times in rapid succession. "Rabbie Armstrong's been gone for twenty-five year or more."

"They never did find any sign of him, though," his father noted. "I remember joining the search. Bad business that."

"But what makes ye think it's this Rabbie anyway?" Will asked between bites of flaky crust and thick, juicy fruit.

Walt wiped his knife off on his pants before cutting a piece of the sweet dessert for himself. "Rabbie Armstrong would cross the Wastes in the dead of night, with nowt but his bare hands to save him, if it meant a piece of Ma's pie."

"Aye, that's true enough." Their mother sat back down on the bench, wiping her hands in her apron. "But if he didna die, what could've become of him? Ye ken well he wasna the sort to run off without a word to anyone."

"No' unless someone forced him," Walt said, his smile widening by the minute.

"To what end?" their father asked. "They demanded nae ransom."

Walt shrugged. "Ye both make good points, but I canna think who else it would be that Will didna recognize him."

"True enough," their father said. "Worth looking into at any rate."

Their mother nodded. "I'll get a note off to me niece straightaway. She'll know one way or the other."

"And I'll carry it up there meself." Walt stood, taking one more sip of ale as he did.

"Ye'll do nae such thing," their mother said. "Ye'll ride up toward Billingham, to the Ram's Horn, and let the post take it from there."

Walt looked like he might protest, but his father cut him off.

"Let it be, lad. I ken what ye're thinking, but he'll side with his kin. Ye canna bring back the past. Now saddle yer nagg and be ready to take yer ma's letter."

"But he let Will go unharmed."

"Aye, as I would Alasdair, I reckon, but it still disna mean we're ready to end this. Or have ye forgotten all about yer brother Alan? Now off and do as ye're told, aye. Rabbie or no', we need keep alert."

"Aye, Da." Walt pressed his lips together, effectively stifling any further comment on the subject, then nodded and headed out the door.

Will had a hundred questions, but one burning query stuck in his throat. Who was this Rabbie Armstrong? His father narrowed his eyes, almost daring him to speak, and so he thought better of it.

"Ye've chores to do," his father said, suppressed anger still visible below the surface. "Ye'd best be about them afore I reconsider letting ye off without a good thrashing."

"Aye, Da." Will grabbed a scone and hurried across the barmekin yard. Walt would know the answer just as well, but he'd have to be quick if he meant to catch his brother before he rode off.

CHAPTER 15

Maggie sat by the side of a small stream, her head resting on her knees, and wondered if they would ever reach home again. Images of her uncle's cozy cottage and a nice comfortable bed filled her thoughts. Well, relatively comfortable, she conceded with a smile. Something to eat beside cold bannocks wouldn't go amiss either.

"We're mounting up, Cousin," Alasdair said, his words shattering her reverie. "D'ye need a hand?"

Maggie blinked. "No, thanks. I'm getting pretty good at it."

She pulled herself up into the saddle and sighed. Her bottom throbbed, and the muscles in her thighs ached. Yet, much to her dismay, it didn't appear they were any closer to home than they'd been four hours ago. Granted, she didn't claim to be an expert, but she'd been on many a hiking trip with her father, and either they'd passed by that same copse of trees an hour ago or the Scottish landscape ran on one large repetitive loop.

Uncle Geordie led the way once more, a nasty-looking smirk plastered on his lips. He kept coming up with reasons to stop, no doubt with the deliberate intent of driving her to distraction. First, to eat breakfast, if that's what you could call it. Then to rest the horses, and every so often to question a few neighbors about any broken men they'd seen in the area. She could barely keep her eyes open, and to make matters worse, her father hadn't said more than a few words to her since they'd left England.

Though Maggie doubted they'd ridden more than a few miles, Geordie signaled yet another stop, so she drew up next to her father and let him help her down.

"Da, I really am sorry. I know I screwed up, but are you ever going to talk to me again?"

"Oh, darlin'." He wrapped his arm around her shoulders and gave her a squeeze. "Of course I am. I just need time to think on it a spell."

"Think on what?"

"Yer punishment, of course. Ye canna expect to run off like ye did and no' face the consequences." He leaned over and whispered in her ear. "So I'm of a mind to let ye stew on it a wee bit longer, aye." Then, kissing her on the forehead, he winked and headed off to water his horse.

Maggie debated whether to laugh it off or scream in exasperation. Without a doubt, there would be another, much longer lecture at some point. She recognized the glint in her father's eyes all too well. And that little outburst back by the Kershope Burn represented nothing more than the preamble.

Letting out a weary sigh, she walked to a nice patch of grass and stroked her pony's mane as he chewed the long, slender blades. "Why couldn't Da just finish it there and then? The anticipation is killing me."

The horse whinnied in reply, and she couldn't help but laugh. "But then, that's the whole point, isn't it? Let me stew on it a bit. And it works every time."

****

The late afternoon sun peeked through the gathering clouds, hinting a promise of showers as they rode through the barmekin gate. Maggie stretched her back, attempting to stifle a yawn, before dismounting and dragging herself into the cottage. She finally understood what her father meant by being bone weary. Every inch of her body ached with fatigue, and she could think of nothing but snuggling beneath her blankets for a well-earned rest. Even the smell of her aunt's sweet bread failed to tempt her, though she did manage to snag a piece before heading toward the stairs.

"And where do ye think ye're going, lass?" Geordie asked. He unstrapped his scabbard, laying it and his sword on the table, before sitting in one of the two chairs by the fire, a tankard of ale in one hand and a piece of buttered bread in the other.

She stopped with one foot on the first step and turned, blinking in disbelief. He had to be joking, right? But it wasn't laughter that sparked in her uncle's eyes.

"Just to lay down a bit before tackling my chores," she said.

"Seems to me it ought be the other way round," he said. "Ye can have yer nap when yer chores are done, no' afore."

"But I haven't slept in over thirty-two hours."

"Nor have we, lassie, thanks to your wee trek ower the border. Now get about yer business, aye, and stop yer bellyaching. Yer auntie needs help with the supper."

A flush of heat touched Maggie's cheeks, and she pressed her lips together, stifling a comment about him doing without a bite to eat as well. Instead, she shot a glance in her father's direction, but he simply lifted an eyebrow and nodded toward the washbasin, the hint of a smile playing across his lips. He clearly had every intention of milking this for all it was worth.

"I wouldn't be much help," she said. "I can hardly keep my eyes open."

"Ye dinna need them open to shuck peas or peel an onion," Geordie said. He stretched his feet out toward the fire, rested his arms on his chest, and sighed in contentment.

Her jaw dropped. She stood there for a moment or two, trying to decide what action to take. After all, what could he do if she just ignored him and continued up the stairs? Surely, her father wouldn't let the beast lay a hand on her.

"Maggie!" Robert's sharp tone cut into her deliberations, but then his voice softened. "Go on and help yer auntie, aye. The time will pass quicker if ye keep busy."

She narrowed her eyes and glared over at her uncle, who had dozed off, his head tilted to the side and his mouth open. "It would pass just fine if I was sleeping."

Robert took a deep breath, his nostrils flaring. "That's enough, lass. Consider it part of yer punishment, aye. Now get to it afore I start to see the merit in yer uncle's way of thinking."

Maggie put her hands on her hips with every intention of lodging a protest, but she could see it would do no good. Her father's brows had dropped low over his eyes, and his lips barely moved as he spoke, a sure sign his temper had reached the boiling point.

With an indignant huff, she stomped back across the room and grabbed an apron, though she received even less sympathy there. Her aunt thrust a bowl of peas in her direction, her lips firm as she ordered Maggie to get about shucking them, and her cousin Connie just kept shaking her head and mumbling under her breath.

Maggie took the bowl, but she couldn't help rolling her eyes. *Good grief! You'd think they'd be glad I didn't get kidnapped or something.*

****

Supper proved to be an unusually quiet affair that evening, with "pass the leeks" and Geordie's discussion of the next day's chores comprising the only conversation. Even Bess and Nancy, Geordie's two youngest daughters, seemed to know not to bother their parents with the incessant questions characteristic to young children.

Maggie picked at the flaky piece of trout Emma had put on her plate and struggled to keep awake. She didn't have much of an appetite, and from the way Alasdair poked at his own fish, neither did he.

"Dinna play with yer food, lad," Geordie said. He scooped up some peas with a chunk of bread, then shoved it all in his mouth, never taking his riveting gaze off his son.

"Aye, Da." Alasdair gave a halfhearted nod and picked up a piece of the trout.

Maggie suppressed a groan, sneaking a peek at her father. If she could catch him off guard, she might get a better idea of his real reaction to Geordie's behavior, but as usual Robert was way ahead of her.

"Eat yer vegetables, lass," he said, though a smile tugged at the corner of his mouth.

Not exactly the response she'd expected, but she had to laugh in spite of herself. How many times had he uttered those words over the years, usually to avoid some unwanted discussion. The memory eased the tension, at least for the time being, and she scooped up the peas she'd so diligently shucked.

Her nerves had eased considerably, but she still knew better than to take her leave after dinner. Even though Geordie employed two serving girls, there was always enough work to go around, so Maggie joined her cousins in clearing the table and washing up. Only after she'd put the last trencher on the shelf did she let a yawn escape. Then, saying a quick good night, she headed for the stairs, but once again her uncle's baritone echoed across the room.

"No' yet, lassie. We've some unfinished business, you and I."

Maggie stopped short and turned to her father once more, unsure how to take this latest command, but this time not the flicker of a smile tweaked the corner of Robert's lips. "Crap," she said under her breath. This didn't look good.

Andy and Sim had stopped by after supper, but with Geordie's pronouncement, everyone made themselves scarce, saying a quick good night before tripping over each other to get out the door or up the stairs. The only other time Maggie had seen a room empty out that fast was at Julie Sutton's sleepover, when her brother's mouse escaped and darted across the floor.

She pressed her hand against her stomach to calm her nerves and walked back to the table, her head held high. Geordie Armstrong would not intimidate her.

The room became so quiet the crackling of the fire roared in her ears. Alasdair sat alone on a bench by the table, staring straight ahead, his face devoid of all emotion—except for his eyes. Penned-up tears sparkled beneath his lashes. She sat down next to him and smoothed her skirts. Maybe she should be a bit more nervous.

Geordie confirmed her suspicions moments later with a tongue-lashing that made Robert's lectures seem like a pleasant story time. Maggie could feel her cheeks burn as hot tears trickled over them. Alasdair's face had turned bright crimson, though his eyes remained fixed on a candle off to the side, at least until Geordie began the interrogation phase. A quick smack across the face drew her cousin's attention, and from that moment on he looked at his father.

Maggie jumped at the sound of flesh against flesh. Yet again, she threw a glance in her father's direction, but he just stood there, arms folded across his chest, an angry spark in his eyes. A lump formed in Maggie's throat. She'd never meant to cause so much trouble.

"And ye, lassie, what were ye thinking, wandering off the way ye did, without a thought for yer cousin's life, or yer own, for that matter. I ought skelp ye across the lugs as well, knock some sense into ye, but I'll step aside this time, in deference to yer da." He narrowed his eyes and cocked his head to the side. "One thing I will be demanding an answer to, though, as is me right as laird of this clan: What drew ye to Foster land to begin with, or should I say who?"

Maggie felt her throat constrict, but before she could answer, her father jumped in with his own rendition of the previous night's events, and she breathed a bit easier. Homesick for Lancaster and missing her friends came into the explanation. Thankful he didn't bring Dylan's name into it, she agreed without hesitation, as did Alasdair, though she suspected in his case he just wanted to put the entire affair behind him. Unfortunately for him, that's literally where it would come to its conclusion, for a stern lecture was not to be the end of it.

"Go to bed, Maggie!" Geordie shouted over his shoulder as he took a heavy leather strap down from a peg on the wall. Alasdair swallowed hard and stood to head out the door.

"Da!" Maggie tugged on her father's sleeve, unable to believe what she was seeing.

"Go to bed, Maggie," he said in a voice she knew well not to contest. "'Tis none of yer affair."

"But it is. If not for me—"

Robert whirled around. "To bed, Maggie, or I'll take the strap to ye as well."

Maggie's mouth dropped. Her father had never laid a finger on her. More likely because he feared if he did, he might break her, but that was beside the point.

He must have seen her alarm, for he gently placed his hands on her shoulders, his tone returning to its usual soft tenor. "'Tis their way, Maggie. Ye canna change the code they live by."

"But it's all my fault. I practically forced him to take me."

"He should have kent better, lass. Being Geordie's only remaining son, he's set to be laird of this clan one day, and he canna afford to make such foolish mistakes. Take this as a lesson for yerself as well. Never again put yer kin in such a position. Now to bed with ye, darlin', and think nae more of it. Alasdair winna fault ye for it."

Maggie did as her father bid her, but she watched from her window, tears welling up in her eyes. Geordie led her cousin into the shed across the way, the soft glow of the lantern barely illuminating their path. Tall shadows mingled with the mist, and as Geordie lifted his arm, Maggie tossed herself on the soft straw bed. How she hated him. She closed her eyes and pulled the blanket over her head. Still, she couldn't muffle the awful sound, and she cringed with each new crack of the strap, praying it would be the last. After an agonizing amount of time, the light in the shed went out, and she heard Alasdair slip up the stairs and into his room. How she wanted to go to him and apologize for what she'd done, but doing so would only bring him more grief. All she could do was hope he would forgive her one day.

****

Maggie rose the next morning even more miserable than the night before. She took the small mirror from her bedside and shook her head. Her eyes looked red and puffy, her hair knotted and unkempt.

"Wandering around the woods and not getting any sleep will do that to you."

"Aye, it will that," Constance said. "What on earth were ye thinking?"

Maggie looked up in surprise. She thought she'd spoken to herself, but obviously not.

Her cousin came to sit beside her, lowering her voice. "Ye'd best pray Ian disna hear about ye running off. He might take it the wrong way."

Maggie blinked. "What does my yearning to return home have to do with Ian?" In fact, it had everything to do with him, but her father's story about her being homesick seemed much easier to explain, so she decided to stick with it.

"'Tis all right, Maggie. I canna say I blame ye under the circumstances."

Maggie scratched her head. "Under what circumstances? Where exactly do you think I was heading?"

"Down to confront Annie Foster, of course, and make sure 'twas truly ower between her and Ian. Though he winna be pleased, 'tis sure."

"Really!" Maggie got up and began brushing her hair. "That's just too bad, now isn't it? And why should he care? Unless he has something to hide."

Constance shook her head, clearly confounded by Maggie's reply. "D'ye truly no' see what ye've done, Cousin? Ye didna take his word for it. Ye questioned his honor." Mumbling to herself, she rose from the bed and headed downstairs.

"Good grief!" Maggie sank back down on the mattress. Because of her, Alasdair had gotten a beating, and all for nothing since she didn't even get to see Dylan, let alone talk to him. Her uncle and her father were at odds with each other over Ian's marriage proposal, and now she might have insulted Ian's sense of honor.

"Maggie!" Her father's voice carried up the stairs and through the door, and she groaned. He'd never raised a hand to her, said he'd never had to, but oh, the lectures. Sometimes she just wished he'd put her over his knee and swat her bottom.

She got up and opened the door a crack. "I'll be there in a minute, Da. I'm still getting dressed."

"Be quick about it, lass. I'll be down in the glen."

Yep! It was going to be a lecture.

****

Her father sat throwing pebbles into the stream. He didn't look too angry, but then, he rarely did. Maggie tried sneaking up on him, but as usual he turned around before she had the chance.

"First, never think ye can slip up on a Borderer without him noticing." The hint of a smile caused the dimple in his cheek to deepen, but Maggie knew better than to let down her guard.

She sat beside him and wrapped her arms around her knees. "Tell me something I don't know."

"And yet ye keep trying." He laughed and, shaking his head, threw another pebble across the water.

"My father taught me to be persistent."

"Aye, I did, 'tis one of the reasons I wanted to speak to ye this morn. Ye canna be trying this again, lass. D'ye no' realize the trouble ye could have caused? No' only did ye put yerself and Alasdair at risk, but the rest of the clan as well. The Foster lad mightna have been alone; men could have died, or worse. Ye could've died."

Robert's eyes darkened, storm clouds moving across the dusty blue-gray of a summer sky, and Maggie bit her lip. This was serious.

"I guess I didn't think it through. I just wanted to talk to someone else who'd understand."

Robert reached over and squeezed her hand. "I ken ye did, but ye got off easy this time, darlin'. Mind, ye're no' in the twentieth century anymore. Ye canna stop at the local 7-Eleven and phone me up to come and get ye. All sorts of dangers lurk out there, lass. Things ye ken noucht about."

"That's why I asked Alasdair to take me."

Her father shot up. With his fists balled at his side, he began pacing along the water's edge. "And ye think that makes it all right, do ye? Can ye no' see how afeard his ma was, him taking off without a word? 'Tis their only living son. D'ye no' ken what that means? Emma's had her heart torn out five times afore. And all the while Alasdair was gone, she relived each agonizing moment. Five lads taken from her. And she could have well lost her youngest yesterday."

"Geordie has no problem taking him on raids, though, does he?" Maggie's temper soared as well, causing her father to stop in his tracks.

He sat back down by her side, the flush in his cheeks fading a bit. "Ach, nae, he disna, but that's the way of things here, and ye'll have noucht to do with any of it. But if Alasdair had died yesterday, it would have been yer fault. Could ye forgive yerself for that, lass?"

"But he wouldn't have died. That Foster lad helped us out. In fact, he seemed quite nice once everything calmed down."

Robert picked up a large stone and hurled it across the water. "God's teeth, Maggie. Have ye no' heard a word I've said? Ye ken noucht about him, save he was an image in one of me books. Ye're in another time now, and ye've nae idea what he might have done. Is it yer plan to worry me to death?"

"You always worried, Da, even back home."

A smile caught his lips, and the tightness went out of his face. "Aye, I did that, which is why we had rules. And ye obeyed those rules right enough, did ye no'?"

Trick question, but she was ready for it. "Yes, of course I did, but they made sense."

"Did they, now? For I seem to mind a number of occasions where ye argued against them."

Maggie sighed. Another point for her father. "Okay, I didn't always agree with them . . ."

"But ye did obey them?" Robert lifted an eyebrow.

"Yes . . . usually."

"And when ye didna?"

Maggie groaned. He'd outsmarted her again. "I was punished. Okay, I get it. There are rules now as well."

"I kent I raised a canny lass." Robert smiled and put his arm around her shoulders. "Now give us a hug, and let's be about breaking our fast, eh."

"That's it? Your lectures are usually much longer."

"Aye, well, yer uncle did the job well enough last night."

Maggie returned Robert's smile and nuzzled her head into his shoulder, but she wasn't quite done. "I still don't like Uncle Geordie or what he did to Alasdair."

"Hmm, I reckoned ye'd still be fashing yerself about that, but ye need let it go, lass."

Maggie blinked to hold back the tears welling up in her eyes. She sat back so she could face her father. "He hit him ten times. Ten times, Da, with that strap, or tawse, or whatever you call it. Not just a spanking, but a whipping. I get it! Alasdair should know better, but he's only sixteen."

"Aye, nearly a full-grown man. As ye pointed out, he rides on forays, holds his own in the fray. And if he's caught thieving, he'll be hanged the same as any other. Geordie kens well what the lad will face, and like his methods or no', he's making sure Alasdair's ready to lead when the time comes."

"By beating it into him."

"Aye, if need be.

"But it doesn't need to be. Trust me, one of your lectures would burn it into his memory for all time."

Robert lifted an eyebrow, and Maggie cringed. No words were needed to translate its meaning.

"Sorry, Da. I just meant Uncle Geordie could try talking to Alasdair. I'm sure it would be even more effective."

"Quite a save there, lassie, but this is nae joking matter. Alasdair kent he did wrong, and expected nae less. As for me brother, ye dinna have to like him or agree with him, but ye do have to respect him. He's laird of yer clan, so put what happened to Alasdair behind ye."

Maggie sighed, more of a tut really, and rolled her eyes. "Yes, Da, and I am sorry I got him in trouble. I won't put him in that position again."

Robert chuckled, though his eyes narrowed. "Or anyone else in the clan, lass." He cupped her chin in his hands and looked in her eyes.

She let out an exasperated groan. Her father knew her all too well. "All right, or anyone else in the clan."

"Hmm, I guess it'll have to do, at least for the moment."

Maggie made her smile as sweet as she could, and Robert's eyes narrowed even more.

"Maggie, ye ken I've never so much as spanked ye, but hear me well, lass. Do anything that foolish again, and I'll no' hesitate to put ye ower me knee. These are dangerous times."

The words echoed her grandmother's warning, and she sniffled, pulling her crumpled hankie out and blowing her nose. "I know, Da."

"Just follow yer heart, darlin', the part that tells ye what's right, and ye'll do fine, aye." He wiped her cheek with his thumb and kissed her forehead. "Now I canna speak for a wee lass like yerself, but I'm famished. And if I ken Emma Turnbull, breakfast is just about on the table, so let's get to it, aye."

"When have I ever turned down food?" She got up and ran ahead of him, though by the time they reached the door, the two of them burst into the cottage together, laughing and trying to catch their breath. No matter how much she dreaded her father's lectures, she always felt better afterward.

"I thought ye were going to speak to the lass." Geordie sat at the head of the table, a stern expression on his face.

"Ye handle yer weans the way ye see fit," Robert said, "and I'll do the same."

"Hmph! So long as it's handled."

Robert gave a curt nod, but much to Maggie's surprise, breakfast continued on a more pleasant note. Her father and uncle laughed and joked, shoving one another like young boys. No one mentioned another word about the events of the night before, and as Robert predicted, even Alasdair appeared to have forgotten the entire affair. He teased her over the amount of honey she put on her oatcakes and gave her a playful nudge, the way he always did, although she did notice he sat a bit more gingerly than usual.

Maggie cringed each time he pressed his lips together, sure he must have hit a tender spot. And though she joined in the lighthearted banter, smiling and answering politely whenever her uncle addressed her, it was no more than an act on her part. She could never forgive the brutality he'd administered the night before and vowed never again to have anything to do with him. Of course, avoiding him altogether might not be so easy, given he was the clan's heidsman. Then again, he couldn't stop her from trying.

CHAPTER 16

Robert rubbed the sleep from his eyes as he hurried down the stairs the next morning. The sweet aroma of Emma's scones had shaken him from sleep, and now his belly was demanding satisfaction.

"Good morn to ye, Brother," he said as he took his place at the table.

"And to ye." Geordie wiped some crumbs from his beard and stifled a burp before continuing. "So now ye've had plenty of time to sleep on it, Rabbie, what have ye decided? Have ye come to yer senses, then?"

Robert scratched his head and grabbed a scone, replying as he chewed. "Come to me senses about what, Brother?"

"About Maggie here and young Ian, ye wee fool." Geordie let out a long-suffering sigh, shaking his head before scooping up a spoonful of porridge. "Ye were to think on it a piece afore yer daughter distracted us with her sudden urge to return home and all."

Maggie opened her mouth to speak, but Robert silenced her with one look. So much for a peaceful breakfast. He threw his leg over the bench and sat next to Alasdair, snagging a bowl of the hot cereal for himself.

Geordie grinned. "Ye didna think I'd forget, now did ye?"

"D'ye mind if I have a bite to eat first? 'Tis no' something I want to deal with on an empty wame."

"Hmph, go on, then, but dinna be long about it, aye."

Robert nodded and shoveled a spoonful of warm oatmeal in his mouth. A sense of nostalgia crept over him as he gazed around the table at Geordie's family. The faces had changed or aged, to be sure, but in some ways, nothing had changed at all. Even in their youth, he and Geordie had always been at loggerheads over one thing or another. But this was different. This involved his daughter, and as much as he loved and respected his brother, Maggie's welfare came first. If Geordie would just be reasonable, try to understand, but he was a stubborn man, much like their father before him. If he'd set his mind on a union between Maggie and Ian Rutherford, there would be no talking to him.

Robert groaned in exasperation and threw his spoon on the table. Would Geordie really risk alienating him just to pacify the Rutherfords? Only one way to find out. Might as well get on with it.

"Go help yer auntie, darlin'," he said.

Once more, Maggie opened her mouth, no doubt to put in her two cents, but Robert lifted one eyebrow in his most intimidating stare, and she stomped away. He'd pay for it later, but it couldn't be helped.

"Well, what have ye decided, then?" Geordie leaned back in his chair, his arms folded across his chest.

"Maggie says she's no' appalled by the idea of Ian coming round, but she's no' ready to pledge herself in marriage either." Robert glared at his brother, daring him to say one word in protest, which of course, the old bugger would.

"That's right generous of her, but the pledge has been made, Rabbie. To break it now would surely mean reprisal."

Robert snapped back almost before the words cleared his brother's lips. "Ye should have thought about that afore ye pledged another man's daughter, Geordie Armstrong."

"Ye'd put yer kin in jeopardy just to satisfy the whims of one wee lass?" Geordie shot forward in his seat, his lips pressed so tight together they disappeared beneath his beard. "Perhaps ye should take the strap to her . . . and I to ye besides!"

"I'd give me life for that wee lass, Brother . . . and yers as well."

175

Geordie stood with such force he upended the platter in Connie's hand, surrendering three pieces of smoked haddock to the shaggy-haired dog by his feet. "I've given me word, Rab, and I expect ye to abide by it."

"And if I dinna choose to sacrifice me daughter to ease yer petty quarrels, what then, man?" Robert clutched his tankard with both hands to stop them from shaking, though he couldn't keep his breath from coming in short, steady bursts.

"Ye're under me roof, Rabbie Armstrong. I want ye to stay, but I'll no' start a feud ower it."   Geordie slammed his fist on the table so hard his ale spilled across the wooden surface.

"Away with ye, Samson." Emma waved her cloth at the dog before wiping up the spill, all the while mumbling about thickheaded men who acted like children. When she finished, she stood with her hands on her hips for a moment until Geordie gave a nod of thanks, then she returned to the hearth, still grumbling to herself.

Geordie rubbed his eyes before dropping to his seat once more, a weary sigh escaping from his lips. "Come on, then, lad. We're too old to be bickering like weans."

"Aye, ye're right there," Robert said, "so be a man and admit ye're wrong."

"I'm no' wrong!" Geordie growled the words through clenched teeth. "'Tis ye what has yer loyalties mixed up. Ye let them outlanders get to ye."

"And what d'ye ken about the rest of the world? Ye've burrowed yerself up here in yer own land, taking whatever ye want, living like a common criminal."

"That's enough, Rab. Ye're back on the Borders now, and this is the way of it. Either Maggie weds Ian Rutherford, or ye can be off with ye. Have it yer own way."

"Then I reckon I'd best be taking me leave."

Maggie rushed over to his side, grabbing his arm. "It'll be all right, Da . . ."

"Go back and help yer auntie, lass." Robert placed his hand over his daughter's and nudged her in the right direction. "And dinna say another word. D'ye understand?"

"But, Da? I don't want—"

"No' another word or I'll take ye ower me knee here and now."

Maggie's face crumbled in a disapproving frown. For a moment, Robert feared she might press him on the matter, but after an audible tut, she returned to her aunt's side. With an inward sigh of relief, he shifted his attention back to Geordie, hoping he too would concede, but his brother held his ground.

"Ach, perhaps ye should be on yer way, then," Geordie said. "'Tis sure the lass has been noucht but trouble from the start."

Robert had risen, turning to walk away, but with those words, he spun back around. "And just what d'ye mean by that? The trouble's no' with me daughter, but with this place, and I'll do well to be away from it. The sooner, the better as far as I can see."

"And where are ye talking about going, Brother?" Andy strolled in from the yard and sat on an empty bench, helping himself to one of Emma's oatcakes. "Ye'll no' find a better hostess in all the Borders than Emma Turnbull. Now there's a feat in itself, being married to Geordie Armstrong, the world's most ill-tempered man."

"I've nae quarrel with Emma," Robert said. "She's a fine woman. 'Tis her mule of a husband ye canna reason with."

Andy snickered. "I seem to recall me father arranging for him to marry her when someone accidently ran her brother through with his lance."

"I did nae such thing!" Robert said. "'Twas one of Uncle Camus's lads."

"I never claimed ye did, Rab. But Da expected Geordie here to step up for the good of the clan, and so he did. Now he's asking the same of ye."

"He can marry me off to anyone he likes, but he'll no' be telling me Maggie who she's to wed."

"Ach, there's no talking to him, man." Geordie reached for the platter of smoked haddock, but only one small piece remained. "Emma, see what that serving girl's up to. She's apt to starve us all to death with her dawdling."

"Ye see," Robert said in disgust, "he's nae respect for women at all. They're noucht but property to him." Robert stormed out of the room and headed across the barmekin yard toward the peel tower, but Emma rushed out after him.

"Now wait ye one minute, Rabbie Armstrong. Yer brother's never been anything but loving to me. He talks gruff, but he disna mean a thing by it, and ye of all people should ken that."

Robert sighed and flopped down on the wooden steps of the peel tower. "I'm no' sure about this Ian, Emma. I've kent the Rutherfords afore, and they're a rough lot."

"There are them what says the same about the Armstrongs, ye ken." Her dark eyes reflected the humor in her voice, and the corner of her mouth quivered, though she tried to maintain a solemn expression.

"Well, they're wrong now, are they no'?" Robert let his fists uncoil, and a small smile touched his lips.

"I'm of a mind they are." The quiver gave way to a full-blown grin, Emma's voice holding a softness that seemed odd for this rough Border woman. "Leave it be for a while, aye. Ye may be fighting for noucht at all. From what I can tell, the lass may well be taken with the lad. Time has a way of sorting things out, ye ken. Ye just need be patient."

"Time!" Robert nodded to himself. "Ye may be right, lass. Time is always on our side, after all?"

Emma's eyes narrowed for a moment, but then she shook her head and let out a huff of laughter. "Right, so come in and finish yer breakfast, eh? Afore those brothers of yers eat everything in sight."

****

Robert returned to his place at the table, and Geordie looked up, an oatcake soaked in ale dangling precariously from his fingertips. "Changed yer mind, have ye?"

Andy moaned, his gaze shifting between Robert and their eldest brother, a slice of smoked salmon tantalizingly close to his lips.

Robert shot a withering look in his eldest brother's direction. "I've decided to leave it in me Maggie's hands, at least for the time being." He could see a vein throbbing on the side of Geordie's temple. "And for now, she disna seem to object to Ian's paying her court," he added before retaking his seat.

"And the betrothal?"

"Ye can promise whatever ye want, Brother, but me Maggie will have the final say, just like wee Annie Foster, eh?"

"I'll no' start a feud . . ."

Before he could finish his sentence, Emma sat next to him and slopped another spoon of porridge in his bowl. "Shut yer gob, husband, and see what comes about, eh? Besides, feuds have been fought ower far less."

"But 'tis me word I'm giving, Wife."

"Aye, and Rabbie's daughter, so leave it at that if ye've any hopes of filling that wame of yers with more than dry bannocks, eh?"

Geordie grunted, a terse nod putting an end to the discussion. Though a caustic retort hung on Robert's lips, he pressed them together for fear of Emma turning her sharp tongue in his direction. For now, he'd keep quiet and see what he could discover about this Ian Rutherford.

The clatter of hoofbeats drew his attention to the barmekin yard. Ian led the way, followed by his father, Hob, and his brothers, Sandie and Fergus. Robert leaned on the table, his eyes narrowing as he watched them dismount and head for the cottage.

Andy let out a groan and whispered over his sister-in-law's shoulder. "Brace yerself for the storm, Emma."

The woman shot a glance out the window and rolled her eyes. "Let's leave the men to it, eh, lassies?"

She stood at once and nudged her daughters and nieces toward the door, leaving the serving girls and Andy's wife, Marion, behind to see their guests had food and a good supply of ale.

Robert suppressed a chuckle, certain his sister-in-law's role had more to do with gathering information than serving up the ale. From the glint in Maggie's eyes, she surmised the same, though her expression held none of his humor. The dimple in her cheek had sunk to a dangerous depth, not a good sign when combined with the furrowing of her brow. God, she looked so much like her mother when her temper flared.

The image caught him off guard, though he swallowed the memories it conjured. No time for such things now. Muffling a husky cough, Robert raised an eyebrow in his daughter's direction and nodded toward the door. Maggie's lips tightened, but after a moment's hesitation, she lifted her chin and followed her cousins across the yard. With a prayer of thanks still on his lips, Robert shook his head and turned back to their visitors.

"Good day to ye, Geordie." Hob Rutherford sat at the huge rectangular table and accepted the tankard of ale Andy offered him. "Have ye thought anymore about what I said the other night?"

"That I have," Geordie replied, "and me family's behind ye. We can always use some good cattle, and there's a full moon tonight. The Fosters are as good as any, I'd say."

"As good as any for what?" Robert's heart quickened, telling him full well what his eldest brother meant, though whether it was dread or excitement causing the reaction, he couldn't say.

"The Rutherfords are running low of meat," Andy replied. "And ye ken what that means." He visibly held his breath, no doubt fearing the subject would start his brothers feuding all over again.

"Aye, a raid. But what have the Rutherfords' troubles to do with us?"

Hob puffed out his chest, resembling the sage grouse Robert had once encountered on a hunting trip to Canada. Thin red lines marred his green eyes, and a jagged scar pulled his mouth into a crooked smile, revealing uneven and broken teeth. "Well, now our Ian will be courting yer Maggie—"

"As I said," Robert interrupted, "what have yer troubles to do with us? We've our own quarrel with the Fosters, yet it disna cause us to ride against them. Besides, I can name more than a few Armstrongs with ties to the name. Or are the Rutherfords running this clan now, Geordie?"

His brother shot up from his seat, pounding his hand on the table, the veins in his neck close to popping. "I run this clan, Rab, and ye'd do well to remember that yerself."

"Oh, I'm well aware, me laird. Ye've made nae bones about it. So tell me, then, why are we raiding the Fosters?"

"'Tis nae secret, man," Geordie said. "Ian here's been slighted by that Foster wench, and they want to give it them back."

Robert leaned forward and folded his hands on the table. "And I'll ask ye again, what has that to do with us?"

"As I told ye," Hob said, his tone adamant, "now our Ian's betrothed to yer Maggie—"

"There's been nae handfast as yet." Robert stood, pushing the bench back, and turned on the younger Rutherford. "But tell me, Ian, why are ye fashing so about this Foster lass when ye claim 'tis me Maggie ye love?"

"Oh, I do love her, sir, though I dinna wish her to think me a coward." Ian crumpled the bonnet in his hands. "Them Fosters have made a laughingstock of me. To be turned away by a fair Scottish lass is one thing, but to be maligned by the likes of Annie Foster . . . 'Tis humiliating."

Marion had just carried over another jug of ale, but with Ian's words, she slammed it down on the table and left the room in a huff, her dark eyes shooting daggers in the young man's direction.

Robert covered his mouth to keep from snorting with laughter. Ian hadn't gained himself any points there.

"Thank ye, lass," Andy called after his wife, though a bit of amusement sparkled in his eyes. He turned to Ian and cleared his throat to suppress a snicker. "If ye dinna mind, lad, watch what ye be saying about the English lassies when ye're in this house, aye. Marion's a Hetherington, ye ken, and she's a bit touchy on the subject."

Much to Robert's delight, Ian's face went pale. "I am sorry, sir. I didna mean to bring ye any grief."

"She'll be all right. Just watch yerself in future if ye ken what's good for ye, aye."

A sudden thought struck Robert. "Maggie hails from England as well, lad, so how is it ye profess to care for her?" He tilted his head and lifted an eyebrow in an unspoken challenge.

This time it was Andy who ducked his head and covered his mouth. Geordie didn't appear to find the question quite as humorous, but though he narrowed his eyes, he kept quiet and waited for the young man's response.

"Oh, but that's different, is it no'?" Ian said, his answer perhaps a bit too quick for Robert's taste. "She's well come, of a fine Scottish family."

"And there's nae more to it, then?" Robert searched Ian's expression. Something about the man made him uncomfortable, set off his Spidey-senses, as Maggie would say.

"Nae, sir, I swear on me mother's grave."

"Aye, but will ye swear by God above, and by yer own part of paradise?"

Ian fists tightened at his side, but his expression remained unaltered. "I will, sir, for I speak noucht but the truth."

"So be it, then!" Geordie shot his brothers a hard look, warning them not to say another word. "Tonight we shake the border loose and give them Fosters something to think about."

Though he remained skeptical, Robert agreed to the raid, for he knew well the way of the Borders. Yet he couldn't help but wonder about Ian's motives and had every intention of addressing them further when they returned from the foray.

****

A flurry of activity filled the barmekin yard early that evening, and it appeared everyone

but Maggie knew exactly what was going on. Though she tried to ascertain its meaning, no one would stop long enough to explain until, at last, she spotted her father preparing to mount his horse, and a cold chill ran down her spine.

"Da, what's going on? Connie muttered something about riding to England and the Fosters, but it's not to visit Uncle Eddie, is it?"

She tried to be brave, tried to conceal the tremor in her voice, but she never could hide her feelings from her father. He reached over and squeezed her hand, the hint of a smile reflecting in his eyes, calming her, reassuring her."

"Ye'll always be me wee bairn, ye ken that, lass. Were we home, I'd do me best to shield ye from what's to come. But here . . . here ye're a full-grown woman, and though I'd sooner drive a dagger through me own heart, ye've a right to ken. Tonight we ride, darlin', but it disna mean a friendly visit, nae."

Tears flooded Maggie's eyes. "Ride . . . as in a raid? But why?" She scanned the barmekin yard, searching for some sign of trouble. "No one's attacked us, have they?"

Robert chuckled. "'Tis no' the only reason for a raid, ye ken."

"Wait! It's the Rutherfords, isn't it? They're angry because I wouldn't marry Ian."

"Calm yerself, darlin'. 'Tis noucht to do with ye." He cupped his hand around her cheek and bent to kiss her forehead. "First off, the Rutherfords reside on this side of the Border, aye." He winked and squeezed her hand tighter, causing a lump to lodge in her throat. "And second, 'tis them we'll be riding with. It seems there's a score to settle with the Fosters, no' of our own making, mind ye, but the Rutherfords have asked our aid, and we've pledged the same, so we'll help ourselves to some English cattle and whatever else we can lay our hands on."

"But, Da!"

"Dinna fash yerself, darlin'. 'Tis no' like I've never done this afore."

Maggie's stomach lurched. "I know, but not for long time. You're older now."

"I'm no' quite useless yet, lassie." Robert winked, his blue-gray eyes twinkling.

"I didn't mean it that way, it's just . . . Hold on! The Fosters! That boy the other night, the one you almost beheaded. He was a Foster. Tell me you're not riding against them because I went down there and now Ian's all bent out of shape. He needs to get over himself. And besides, Uncle Eddie could be there . . . and Dylan. We don't know for sure where they ended up."

Robert patted his horse's neck, laughing all the harder. "Slow down, lassie. Ye're making me heid spin. I told ye, darlin', 'tis noucht to do with us. From what I can tell, Ian disna even ken ye went on yer wee trek. And aye, 'tis one place yer Uncle Eddie and Dylan might be, which is what I plan to find out." His tone took on a sober tenor, and a frown created deep lines on his forehead. "I've no' heard a word about either of them, and I dinna mind saying 'tis beginning to trouble me."

"Be careful, Da." Maggie rested a hand on her father's shoulder and kissed his rugged cheek.

"I will, darlin'. We'll be back on the morrow."

Maggie stood back, watching as he mounted and rode away. He cut a fine example of a man in his leather jack and steel bonnet. No wonder her mother fell in love with him, even without his warrior trappings.

Ian galloped by close behind, touching his hand to his burgonet, the hint of a kiss forming on his lips. Her heart pounded a bit harder, and she continued to gaze after him until he crossed the purple moor and faded into the distant trees.

She bit her bottom lip, trying to decipher the rush of emotion initiated by the handsome Scot's presence. No, not quite what her mother felt. Her parents' love had been strong and unburdened by any doubts. Even as a child she could sense the depth of it. But while she did find Ian attractive, their relationship had a long way to go before it could be called love. Perhaps in time, but not yet.

Letting out a sigh, she wrapped her arms around her body and gave a squeeze. The glen seemed strangely eerie that night. The moon's silver glow lit up the distant Esk like a ribbon of pure silver. Tall shadows fell around the peel, and the air hung so heavy it carried the sound of the river across the heather and bluebells.

Maggie stood outside the gate for quite a while. At first, the dancing silhouettes appeared almost peaceful, but then she found herself shivering, not sure if it was the shadows or the cool night air making her tremble so. Regardless of the cause, she pulled her plaid tight around her shoulders and headed back toward the warmth of her uncle's cottage. A dark form brushed against her skirts, and she jumped, letting out a slight squeak before shaking her head and laughing. Geordie's collie, Samson, had come to keep her company.

****

Maggie tossed from one side to the other, unable to get comfortable. Thoughts of her father kept running through her mind. How could he expect her not to worry about him, wonder when he'd return, pray that he would? Anxiety had stretched her nerves to the limit and caused her to bite her nails to the quick. She stretched her hand out beneath a beam of moonlight and wiggled the fingertips, trying to decide what Ian's reaction to the rough, jagged edges might be. Much to her surprise, she experienced a sudden twinge of concern for him as well.

No doubt he'd kindled a spark, even if it hadn't quite reached the three-alarm-fire stage just yet, but would it ever be anything more? Geordie argued it would. He didn't care one way or the other, though, as long as it helped the clan. On the other hand, she didn't want to ignore her heart and spurn Ian just to prove her uncle wrong.

She turned on her back, and unbidden, the image of the young man by the Kershope Burn flashed across her mind. Granted, it had been dark and hard to see his features while hunkered down in the bushes, but something about him warmed her heart. With a contented sigh, she snuggled deeper beneath the covers and let the memory wash over her.

So he was a Foster, just like Uncle Eddie. Could his family's tower be where Dylan and her uncle had taken refuge after arriving in this century?

She bolted up, tears forming in her eyes. But if they were at the Foster peel, they could be forced into the fray, maybe even killed. Aside from her father, Edward was the only family she had, and while she may not be in love with Dylan, she did care for him in a sisterly sort of way.

She pursed her lips and blew out a deep, calming breath. The burning in her stomach eased a bit, and she lay back down, her eyes catching a glint of moonlight as it reflected off her amulet. It all seemed so long ago now, miles away in time and space, and yet, somehow the knowledge eased her fears. After all, they could always return home if things got too dangerous. Uncle Eddie did still have the other locket, and besides, her father would be there to make sure his family didn't run them through.

The air had grown stagnant, and she turned her head to gaze out at the sea of stars. Her mother used to sing a song about three fishermen sailing off to the heavens, though try as she might, she couldn't recall the name of it. She did remember her father watching from the doorway, love for them both shining in his eyes. The memory warmed her heart. They'd put her to bed, then leave the room hand in hand, her mother's head tucked against her father's broad shoulder. She'd always taken their love for granted, but once again she wondered. How had her mother known he was the one? A tear trickled down her cheek, for she would never be able to ask her.

A single star brightened, twinkling for a moment before fading once more, and she put her hand to her mouth, a sob catching in her throat. Perhaps her mother wasn't far away, after all. Blinking back the tears, she rolled on her side, hugging her pillow, a childlike contentment filling her heart.

Patience, darling. The voice floated on a sudden breeze, as real to her as the air itself, and Maggie closed her eyes, savoring the moment. She'd know, the same way her mother had, but she needed to give it a chance, to give Ian a chance.

She drifted off to sleep, the feel of his lips against her own clear in her mind, and all of a sudden she wasn't sure she ever wanted to see the twentieth century again.

CHAPTER 17

Ian rode close to the rear as they crossed the border ready to lay siege—with fire and sword—to a Foster stronghold sitting well within the English Middle March. Other peel towers and bastle houses stood closer to the border, including one belonging to Richie Foster, but Ian had no score to settle with him. No, Graham was the one who needed to pay, and pay he would, him and his wretched family.

Not only had his daughter broken their betrothal, but her clype of a brother compounded the insult by spreading vicious rumors about him on both sides of the border. He'd been able to limit the damage in Scotland, but the brothels in Hexham and Bewcastle no longer welcomed his trade. Ian wiped his palms on his breeks and snickered. Aye, they would all pay right enough.

Then again, maybe they'd done him a favor. After all, Maggie Armstrong represented a much better prize. While both lasses would come to his bed with sizeable dowries and bonnie features, Maggie was much more of a woman than Annie would ever be, and Scottish as well. Granted, the Foster wench might prove easier to control, but oh, the fun he'd have bringing Maggie under his thumb. He liked a mistress with a bit of spunk.

They came to a halt in an oak wood north of the Foster peel. The moon shone full over the barmekin wall and its sleepy inhabitants. Geordie had sent out a scout to determine what sort of force they were up against, and the rider returned with better news than Ian had expected. The timing of their arrival had been impeccable, for few able-bodied men remained to rally in the Fosters' defense. Most still rode themselves, raiding some other unsuspecting family.

For a moment, the thought gave him pause. His own tower would be just as vulnerable. He shifted in his saddle and scanned the horde of men gathered before him. Quite a number of

Rutherford clansman mingled with the Armstrongs, but not as many as there should be.

A smirk crossed his lips. His father hadn't quite committed all the men at his disposal. Leave it to Auld Hob. Geordie probably never even noticed, not that it mattered one way or the other, not at this point. Only a fool would turn his back on such an opportunity. With the Foster men away, they'd all be free to sack and pillage the stronghold at their will, along with anything—or anyone—left within it.

Ian's pony pawed the woodland floor, and he reined the animal in. His gloved hands ached with the effort, but he held his mount back, his father's words still ringing in his ears. *Let the Armstrongs take the lead and bear the brunt of the Fosters' revenge.* Sage words, easier said than done, but he managed to harness his impatience until, at last, Geordie gave the signal and the riders broke from the cover of the trees.

Excitement pounding in his loins, keeping perfect cadence with the beat of his hobbler's hooves, Ian joined his kinsmen. The horde of reivers thundered over the rise, gathering cattle and raiding the various cottages along the way, but he had other sport in mind.

Rallying a few of the men, he battered his way through the poorly guarded gate and into the barmekin yard. It didn't take long to subdue the few able-bodied men left behind. One headed for the tower—to light the beacon, no doubt—but Ian aimed his crossbow and made short work of the rogue.

He turned on his horse, surveying the situation, searching for his prey. Sandie and Fergus rode among the outbuildings, setting them afire, while his father and the Armstrongs gathered what cattle they could find. The full moon provided a fair amount of light, but shadows loomed against walls and lurked in secluded corners. No need to venture into the dark, though. The flames would soon dispel any refuge they provided and expose their cowering inhabitants.

Within moments, the entire scene was pandemonium, and Ian reined up beside the stables to enjoy the spectacle. Women grabbed their children, their homes burning around them, and ran across the barmekin toward the tower or headed for the fields if they found their way blocked. Others stayed to douse the flames or fight their attackers with whatever weapons they could find, only to be knocked to the ground by the heel of a reiver's boot.

A few old men begged on behalf of the children, though the older boys continued to swing their swords in defiance. Andy snatched one up, tightening his grip to keep the child from kicking and screaming, before riding on to help with the cattle. Ian, however, turned his sights to other quarry, and, spying Annie Foster running for the tower's undercroft, he wasted no time in pursuing the young woman.

After pulling off his gloves and storing them in his saddlebag, he jumped from his horse. It was perfect. He couldn't have asked for a more secluded location. At this time of year, the cattle tended to be out grazing, but the cow he sought still lurked inside. Careful to keep his steps muffled, he entered the dimly lit storeroom, pausing to bar the door before continuing across the straw-covered ground. Though the flickering torches provided some light, they cast deep shadows across the barrel-vaulted ceiling and stone walls, and he squinted as he scanned the cavernous room for his former betrothed.

"Annie, darlin', 'tis all right. Nae one saw me come this way."

The shovel came out of nowhere, but he had quick reflexes and managed to duck before it slammed into his face. The girl winced when he wrenched the weathered implement from her fist and threw her up against the rough-hewn stone.

"Ian, nae!" She wriggled beneath his weight, but he held her tight. "Let go of me!"

189

"What are ye blethering about, sweetheart? Are ye no' glad to see yer betrothed?"

The fear in her eyes caused his pulse to quicken. She was a fine-looking wench, with a firm bosom and shapely hips. Why shouldn't he have her? The betrothal had been agreed upon, the contract all but satisfied, until her family reneged on their pledge.

"Me betrothed!" Annie pressed her hands against his jack, shoving him away. "I'd take meself to a nunnery afore I'd have ye as me husband."

Ian clutched his fists, then relaxed them. He reached up to caress her face, brushing his lips along her cheek before leaving a gentle kiss on her lips. "Come now, lass. Mind how it used to be afore yer family spread their lies."

"Stop it, Ian! 'Tis yer own tongue that disna speak true."

This wasn't going as he'd planned. He'd hoped she'd give herself to him freely. No one would fault him for accepting a lassie's affections. After all, he was only human. But she'd be branded as a shameless hussy, her family's condemnation of him seen as wicked lies meant to conceal her wanton behavior. Too bad she didn't want to cooperate.

"Ah, Annie, how could ye say such a thing? Give us a kiss, and I'll prove me love to ye." He bent to touch his lips against hers once more, but she pushed his face away.

"Dinna think ye can charm me to yer bed with empty words, Ian Rutherford. I ken the truth of it."

Empty words, was it? He'd teach her soon enough. If she wouldn't submit to him freely, he'd have to force himself on her. It would just be her word against his, for he had no intention of remaining around to be caught with a red-hand. And it would ruin her reputation either way. Not to mention the fun he'd have taking whatever he wanted. One thing was certain, she'd be no virgin when he finished with her.

Brushing aside Annie's flaxen curls, he made one more attempt to win her over. He pressed his lips against hers, thrusting a hand beneath her skirts to fondle the tender flesh of her thighs. After all her family had done, she should be glad he even took notice of her, but instead the ill-mannered trollop pushed against his chest, shoving him away once more.

An intense sting burned his face, and he pulled back enough to touch his cheek. The shrew had scratched him, narrowly missing his eye.

"Ye vicious English viper!" He seized her chin, pinching it in his viselike grip. "Ye'd best pray yer claws dinna leave a scar."

"Let go, Ian."

He dropped his hand to his side, though he had no intention of stopping. Maybe he could try another path.

"Ye never minded me kissing and clapping ye afore, no' until ye listened to that lying brother of yers." He hung his head and sighed. "Would ye let the wee scoundrel keep us apart?"

Though Annie's voice trembled, it held a spark of defiance. "'Twas more than Will's word that came between us."

"Ye canna believe I'd do the vile things he accused me of." He leaned over to kiss her lips again, but once more she thwarted him, turning her face away.

"Stop it, Ian! Enough of yer lies! I spoke to the lassies ye ravaged, saw the state ye left them in."

"And ye'd take the word of common whores above that of yer betrothed?"

"Aye, I would that, for me brother bore witness against ye as well. And Will wouldna lie about anything so grave."

Ian shrugged. If she wouldn't give him what he wanted, he'd just have to take it. No need for any further pretense. "Of course he did, ye wee slut. He didna tell ye the half of it."

Annie's eyes filled with tears, her lips trembling. "So ye dinna deny yer crimes."

Ian took a deep breath. "Those harlots got nae more than they deserved." He pressed himself against the petite girl, pinning her hands between them.

"I didna want to be rough with ye, darlin', but ye leave me nae choice. I'll have what I was promised, and mayhap a bit more if I have to work for it. So just relax, eh, and let me get on with it."

"Ian, please, dinna do this." She struggled beneath his grasp. "I'll die afore I let ye take me."

He shook his head, letting out a wicked snicker. "And how d'ye reckon to stop me? But dinna fash yerself, I'll no' let ye die this day. I'm always careful to stop afore it goes that far. Though I winna deny, by the time I'm done, ye might be well wishing for it."

The Foster wench wouldn't be as easy to break as he'd expected, but break her he would, even if it took him all night. Grabbing her chin, he ran his thumb over her cheek. Smooth and unblemished, just like he remembered, but he'd fix that soon enough. She turned away and her silken hair fell over his fingers, such a bonnie mix of sun-bleached gold and fresh hay, infused with the scent of wildflowers.

Annie's knee struck him in the groin, sending a bolt of pure agony through him. He doubled over and backed away from the stone wall, gasping for air, sputtering curses and profanities while she pried herself free. The vicious succubus would live to regret that move. She might have damaged him.

Peering through the faint lantern light, he spied the girl struggling to lift the bar on the door. Good thing he remembered to drop it in place before he went hunting for her. *So ye think ye can get away? Well, no' quite yet, me love.* He slid along the wall until he stood within an arm's length, hidden by the shadows. As the pain subsided, his hunger grew, fueled by the panic of her movements: the furtive glances to where he'd pinned her against the wall, the frantic straining against the sturdy wood, the quivering gasps filled with terror. Dear God, he wanted her, and he would have her.

Reaching for her hair, he knotted his fingers in the silken locks and yanked her back to his chest. She let out a shriek, writhing within his embrace. Foolish little slut! No one would hear her screams in this remote corner of the yard, not with the din taking place outside and the doors shut tight besides.

God's teeth, her scent would drive a monk to sard his mother. A few kicks struck his shins, but he swallowed the pain, reinforcing his grip and squeezing all the tighter.

"Hold still, ye wicked little strumpet." He hissed the words in her ear before tossing her on the cold stone floor and straddling her hips.

"I'd been of a mind to mow ye and be on me way, but now I reckon I'll bide a bit longer and see ye pay for yer treachery. See how many lads come courting when I've finished with ye, ye shameless hussy."

CHAPTER 18

Robert reined up next to a cottage across from the peel tower and rubbed the back of his neck. What had happened to drive such a wedge between their two families? When he left, he'd considered this a second home. A whiff of raspberries tickled his nose, and he followed the scent into the thatch-covered dwelling.

It was just as he remembered it, right down to the pies cooling on the table. He'd ride south with his brother Andy to spend a few days fishing or hunting with Walt Foster. But the only real prey they'd been after were Betty Hetherington's pie. Walt's mother made the flakiest crust on either side of the border, and just the scent of her juicy fillings made his mouth water.

The room was empty now, the hearth cooled off and the ashes banked, the large table in the center of the floor scrubbed clean, the dishes stacked ready for another meal. A smile tugged at his cheek. *And no Betty in sight.*

He snagged a plate from the cupboard and slipped over to the table. After all, compared to what his brothers were absconding with, a small piece of pie wouldn't even be noticed. In his youth, such a bold move would have resulted in a good skelping from Betty or the end of the tawse from Graham. The memory made him chuckle. *Well worth the price.*

A lad once again, at least at heart, he checked the room once more before pulling his dagger from its scabbard and cutting into the pie. The sweet aroma filled his nostrils, and he opened his mouth in anticipation, but the savory delight never reached his lips. He froze, his hand on the crust, the cool edge of a sword slipping from behind, its tip coming to rest beneath his chin.

"I canna stop ye from stealing the cattle," a voice said, "but ye'll no' be touching me pies, ye thieving scoundrel."

A warmth spread through his chest at the sound of Betty Hetherington's voice, fond memories causing tears to fill his eyes. He blinked them away before replacing his dagger and holding his empty hands out to the side. The sword moved away—not much, but enough for him to turn around.

"Good day, mistress. Ye wouldna be denying a growing lad a wee bit of pie, now would ye?"

Betty dropped the sword, one hand shooting up to her chest while she grabbed the table to steady herself with the other. "Lovit be God! Is that really you, Rabbie Armstrong? By me soul, I'd heard rumors, but . . ." She lifted her apron and blew her nose.

"'Tis good to see ye again as well, Betty."

Without another word, she reached up and skelped him a good hard one in the lugs. "And where have ye been all these years, with no' even a word to yer dame? First, ye go missing, then no' four month on, yer da goes down at Flodden. She never lost faith, though. Said ye'd come back to her." She wiped her nose again and smoothed out her apron. "Well, I suppose she was right there, though it took ye long enough."

He plopped down on the bench, his heart aching for the pain his mother must have gone through. "She died, ye ken, just a few week after I returned."

"Aye, I'd heard." She sat on the bench beside him and stared into the banked embers. "She wasna alone in her grieving. The lads wouldna stop searching for ye till they didna ken where else ye could be. And our Mary cried herself to sleep for weeks."

"Wee Mary. How is she, then?"

"Oh, she got ower ye right enough, so dinna fash yerself on her account. She's a grown woman now, and wed, with weans of her own. Married Tommy Carnaby."

Robert nodded. "Aye, Andy said. A braw lad, if I recall."

"True enough and good to our Mary." Betty looked in his eyes, her gaze demanding an answer. "But what happened to ye, Rabbie?"

"Aye, well, 'tis a strange tale, but I reckon ye've a right to ken." Robert scrubbed his hand over his face and took a deep breath, hoping he'd keep the story straight. "A band of broken men owertook me in Liddesale, robbing and beating me afore carrying me off to Lancaster. Nae doubt, they planned to hold me to ransom till they found 'twas the Armstrongs they'd be dealing with.

"Two of them wanted to kill me outright, a few others to leave me for dead, but the rest saw a chance to make their fortune, regardless of the risks. While they argued amongst themselves, I managed to make me escape, though I could scarce keep meself upright. A kind family took me in and nursed me back to health. I owe them me life."

"Hmm, forgot how to write then too, did ye?"

Robert let out a groan. "I've nae excuse there, save months had passed afore I could think straight enough to put me thoughts to paper. I did try, but by then . . . Well, let's just leave it there, eh?"

A rider went by and peeked through the open door. "Catching up on things, Brother?" Sim Armstrong asked.

"A bit of privacy, if ye wouldna mind, man," Robert said.

"'Tis just the pie ye're after, ye wily scoundrel." Sim chuckled, tapping his heels against his hobbler's side and riding on.

"I should be out there," Robert said, "trying to stop them."

"Ach, they'll be nae ending it now, no' until the lads come home." She placed her hand on Robert's cheek and sighed. "Have ye forgot the way things are on the Borders?"

"What happened to bring us to such a pass, Betty?" Robert shook his head and shifted on the hard bench.

Betty got up and walked to the cupboard, taking down a plate before returning to the table. "Me son tells me I owe ye a pie for sparing his life. Turn around, then, and sit proper."

Robert swung his legs over the bench and rested his arms on the scrubbed planks before him while Betty cut a piece. "I suspected he might be yers, and a fine-looking lad, to be sure."

A small smirk crossed Betty's lips. "And for that, I'll let ye take one of the gooseberry pies with ye."

Robert laughed, stuffing a piece of the sweet treat in his mouth before speaking again. "Now, what drove this rift between our clans?"

The sound of hoofbeats and a loud crash caused Robert to rise to his feet, but Betty put a hand on his shoulder and pushed him back down. "'Tis nowt but the roof on the shed."

"What if someone was inside?"

"The lads are all off themselves, and the lassies and weans in the tower or hiding in the woods."

"And if one of the blaggards . . ."

"Ach, I've never kent one of yers to harm a lassie, no' without good reason."

"But 'tis no' just Armstrongs riding today. The Rutherfords are with us."

Betty's face went pale, and she sat beside Robert, tears filling her eyes. "I sent the lassies to safety."

Robert nodded, squeezing her hand. "What happened?" he asked again.

Her face took on a sadness that troubled Robert. She seemed to need time to gather her thoughts, so he ate his pie and waited.

"'Twas about seven year back now," she said. "Ye'll no' remember Jenny Dodd, her being nowt more than a bairn when ye went missing. At any rate, she grew into a bonnie lass. The lads gathered round her like bees to the hive. Two in particular captured her heart, one an Armstrong lad, the other a Foster."

Robert swallowed, wiping the raspberries from his lips. "Dinna tell me this feud is ower the unrequited love of some weans."

"I wish 'twas nowt more, but nae, I truly believe the lads loved the sweet lass, and she them. She couldna have them both, though, so she made her choice."

Robert pointed toward the pie, and Betty cut him another piece. "Who did she choose, then?"

"The Armstrong lad won her heart. Of course, it could be said he had more to offer, being next laird of his clan and all."

"Geordie's eldest? But he's passed."

"Aye, and so the feud began. Did yer brother tell ye none of this?"

"He spoke of the lad's death, but noucht the how or the why of it."

A growing sense of trepidation gnawed at Robert's stomach. Had Andy mentioned something about a jealous rival being responsible for the lad's demise? With so many gone, the

causes all blurred together.

Betty frowned, her cheeks dimpling in annoyance for a split second before she huffed a weary sigh and poured them each a tankard of ale. "Well then, I reckon the tale is mine to tell.

"A few month after young Geordie wed the lass, Andy and Sim came across him lying facedown in the Liddel Water, his throat cut. A few of yer more unsavory kinsmen swore they spied some Fosters lurking about, and Geordie, being his usual thickheaded self, drew his own conclusions."

Robert took a long draught of ale, draining the tall mug before setting it down. "He's a stubborn man, I'll give ye that, but even he canna be fool enough to think yer Graham would condone such a vile act."

"I canna say for certain what he thought, but I reckon with all that followed I understand his reasoning, even if I canna agree with it." Betty cut herself a piece of pie and took a bite before returning it to the plate.

"But after all we'd been through together, to ride against ye on the word of . . ." Robert stopped speaking for a moment, searching for the right words before clearing his throat and proceeding with caution. "Ye can vouch for yer menfolk, I'm guessing."

Betty made a tutting sound with her tongue before answering. "For me husband and sons, aye, I would swear afore the good Lord himself, but I canna say the same for all who ride under our protection. 'Tis sure the lass didna help matters either, wedding the Foster lad the way she did, no' three month later."

Robert lifted an eyebrow, and she continued. "And why would she no'? The poor thing was near six month along, with parents poor as church mice and half a dozen weans of their own still at home. Who could blame her for seeking a bit of security?"

Robert frowned. "Would Geordie no' take her under his care?"

"He wanted the bairn, right enough," Betty scoffed, blinking away an errant tear. "But he blamed Jenny for the trouble, called her an English whore."

Robert's fist tightened around his tankard, bile rising in his throat. Doing right by the clan was one thing, but turning the lass away, English or not . . .

"Oh, dinna fash yerself, lad." Betty rested her fingers on his arm, the way none but a mother could. "He said it but once, when he first learned of the lad's death. 'Twas more the grief speaking than his own words. But the lass took it to heart and refused to stay."

"So Geordie lost the bairn, as well as his son, and blamed yer kin for both with noucht a shred of proof." Robert wiped his mouth and threw the cloth back on the table. Somehow the pie had lost its appeal. "Did he even take time to bury the lad afore he attacked?"

"Grief can make a body do strange things, but nae, he didna attack, no' straightaway. A few months later, though, no' long after the lass remarried, some Armstrongs found her new husband in the Liddel Water, his throat sliced, the same as their kinsman." Betty gave her nose a blow and continued. "They brought him home thrown ower the saddle like some common criminal."

"Now a raid is one thing, no' that I'm saying 'twas warranted, but surely ye canna believe us so devoid of honor we'd murder the lad and drag him home to gloat ower it?"

Betty's expression hardened. "Ye or Andy, nae, but some of yer kinsmen dinna have the same scruples." She closed her eyes for a moment, tears leaking out of the corners, before she cleared her throat and opened them again. "In truth, I dinna ken what to think, except I had to bury me Alan afore his time."

"Ach, lass, 'twas no' just a kinsman, then, but one of yer own lads." Robert squeezed Betty's shoulder. "I mind the wean well. Always under Walt's feet, begging us to take him along. I'm sorry for whatever part me clan played in it."

Betty covered his hand with her own, patting it before wiping away any remaining tears and standing up. "At any rate, the feud rages on, though 'tis mostly fought with words these days. There's no' been a raid for three or four year now. Nae, this is the Rutherfords' doing."

Robert grunted, wiping the last crumbs from his beard. "Tell me about this Ian Rutherford. He was once betrothed to yer daughter, if he's to be believed."

Betty's eyes narrowed. "That misbegotten son of a whore. I suppose he told ye me Annie did him wrong."

"Aye, so he says, but I'd have the truth of it, being Geordie's bent on giving him the hand of me only daughter."

A playful dimple formed at the left corner of Betty's mouth. "Will mentioned coming across a wee, bonnie lass. He didna come right out and say it, nae with me anyway, but I could see clear enough the lad was smitten with her himself.

"But as to Ian Rutherford," she continued, her voice taking on a harsh tone, "keep yer bairn as far from his grasp as ye can. He's a lecherous scoundrel and canna be trusted. I'd wager he's the cause behind today's raid."

A flaming arrow flew past the window, missing its target, and Robert stood, nodding. "Aye, ye wouldna lose that bet." He wrapped a cloth around one of the gooseberry pies and bent to kiss his friend on the forehead. "Thank ye, Betty. I pray we can put all this ill-feeling behind us one day."

"Ye're welcome anytime, lad, but I fear 'twill take more than yer return to heal these festering wounds."

Robert's heart ached, but he recognized the truth in her words. And so he smiled, picked up his pie, and headed back outside. While he might not be able to patch the rift between their families, he could make sure Ian Rutherford stayed clear of his daughter. Of course, to do that, he'd need to bring his true character to light.

****

The first streaks of daylight hovered just below the horizon, ready to break forth. No doubt about it, Robert needed to be on his way. The Fosters would be riding through the gates before long, and regardless of Betty's affable greeting, her husband and sons would hardly see him as a welcomed guest.

"Hold, sir!" A young boy of ten or so stood firm, his sword out before him, blocking Robert's way. "If ye've harmed me grannie, I'll slice ye in two." The boy's arm shook despite his stance, and though Robert fought to contain his laughter, he couldn't deny the lad's spunk.

"I wouldna think of harming the lady, me laird. What sort of cad do ye take me for?" The child scratched his head, confusion etched on his face, and Robert took advantage of the situation. "'Twas no' yer gran I sought, but a Foster from Lancashire."

"Uncle Eddie?" The boy's sword dropped a bit, his eyes transforming into mere slits. "What d'ye want with me kinsman?"

"To ask a question, noucht more. About another rogue he's acquainted with, a Dylan Hetherinton by name."

"Dylan's no' a scoundrel," the boy said, his grip tightening on the hilt of his sword. "I'm of a mind 'tis ye what's the knave." With the last word still on his lips, the child's face crumpled, and he bit back the tears, no doubt convinced he'd revealed far more than he should.

After a minute of uncomfortable silence, Robert relented and let the young rascal off the hook. "Ach, 'tis clear ye'll give noucht up about yer kin. Yer da would be proud of ye."

The boy straightened a bit, and Robert could have sworn he grew three inches, but Sim came from behind and swept the lad from the ground, causing the child to drop his sword.

"Now what did ye go and do that for?" Robert asked. "The lad wasna troubling anyone."

"He'll bring a fine ransom." Sim tapped his heels against his horse's flank and took off across the yard, shouting over his shoulder. "He's Walt's son, ye ken."

Robert cursed. He never meant to get his old friend's son kidnapped and held for ransom. Pulling himself into his saddle, he started after his brother but stopped when he noticed Ian Rutherford coming out of the peel's undercroft. Now what had the young knave been about, lurking in the recesses of the tower while his kinsmen raided cattle? It didn't take much to figure it out. That was no sword wound marring his right cheek.

Blood hammered in Robert's ears. After what Betty told him, there was little doubt what Ian had been up to. A cold chill ran up his spine, causing his stomach to clench and strengthening his resolve to make certain the vile pervert stayed clear of his Maggie.

A moment later, Ian rode up beside him, winded, but aside from the scratches and a wet patch on his breeks, nothing seemed out of place.

"What were ye doing in the undercroft, lad?" he asked. He kept his tone even. No sense alerting the man to his suspicions just yet.

"Searching for some cattle, and mayhap a hobbler or two, what else?" Ian grinned.

"A strange place to look this time of year, I'd say."

Ian's smirk fell away. "Aye, I should have kent better. Noucht in there but a wasted auld nagg." With a firm nod, he spurred his horse and headed for the barmekin gate.

Robert had a bad feeling about this, but he could hear the thunder of approaching hoofbeats. The Foster men were returning. Any further discussion would have to wait. That night would be a different story, though, and he had every intention of pinning the lad down as soon as they returned to Scotland.

He turned his horse's head to ride away, but he couldn't shake the nagging uneasiness gnawing at his gut. Turning back around, he surveyed the barmekin yard. A few riders had arrived, but his brothers had the situation well in hand. There still might be time for him to check out the undercroft and see for himself what Ian had been up to. He urged his hobbler into a trot, intent on doing just that, but he hadn't gone two feet before he spotted one of the Fosters riding hard in his direction. Recognizing him as Betty's youngest son, the one who'd saved his Maggie's life a few nights before, Robert stood his ground and risked a glance in the direction of the peel tower, hoping the young man would understand.

The lad reined up short, shifting in the saddle to follow Robert's gaze. No sonner had he caught sight of the undercroft than his head whipped around toward the gate, a curse exploding from his lips. Without a word, he turned back and galloped toward the belly of the tower, his feet hitting the ground before his horse had even come to a halt. Robert hesitated, wanting to see what prompted the reiver's urgent response, and yet he had no desire to cross swords with the lad.

"Let's go, Rabbie," Andy shouted. He too held a squirming child on his lap, this one a bit older than the one Sim carried.

"No' ye as well! What are ye doing with the lad?"

"He's Walt Foster's wean." Andy broke into a grin.

"Another one?" Robert glanced at the child, and a lump caught in his throat, the boy being the image of his father. "We were friends with Walt once."

Andy's brow furrowed, his eyes settling on Betty's cottage. "Spoke to Walt's ma, did ye? Then ye'll ken we nae longer stop by for her pie, eh?" The clash of swords caught his attention. "We'd best be on our way, Brother, for I'm of a mind Graham winna be so welcoming." He bent down and slapped Rob on the shoulder. "But dinna fash so, man. I only mean to hold the lad to ransom. Walt would expect nae less, and I reckon the lads may see it as a way to be part of the fray."

Robert shot another glance toward the undercroft. Young Will had already ducked beneath the lintel, and others would be there soon enough, all better suited to handle whatever trouble they found. An arrow whizzed past his shoulder, and he spurred his horse on, following Andy and his baggage out the gate.

He was halfway down the rise when he spotted another reiver, riding hard and fast, but this one he knew well. Dylan spotted him and pulled so hard on the reins he came near to unseating himself. A groan caught in Robert's throat, emerging as a laugh, but riding lessons weren't on the agenda, not with Graham and Walt barreling across the stream. Instead, he gave no more than a quick nod of recognition before galloping after his brother and heading for the thick pine grove northwest of the peel.

The Fosters wouldn't follow straightaway. They'd see to their families first and assess the damage, maybe even initiate some repairs, but one thing remained certain. Within the next day or so, they would be riding hot trod toward Armstrong land. Robert's stomach lurched. Perhaps Edward had been right, and he should never have brought Maggie back to the sixteenth century. Convincing her to leave now would be difficult at best, but doing so without Edward or Dylan would be nigh unto impossible.

CHAPTER 19

Will jumped from his horse before the creature could come to a halt. He'd caught a brief glimpse of Ian Rutherford by the barmekin gate, and the wicked smile on the scoundrel's lips told him all he needed to know. The misbegotten son of a whore had come from the undercroft. Will could feel it in his bones. There was but one reason for any reiver to be there at this time of year, and the answer made his stomach go into spasms.

That Scotsman feared as much, the one who knew his mother. Rabbie Armstrong, Walt called him. He'd made a point of glancing toward the undercroft, no doubt considering heading there himself to see what Ian had been up to. He hadn't spoken, but no words were needed. The concern etched on his face conveyed his meaning clear enough.

Will paused for a moment on entering the shadowy cellar to let his vision adjust to the darkness and listen for a precious sign of life. His heart hammered against his ribs so hard it hurt. Closing his eyes, he tried to calm himself. How could he help her if he couldn't bring his own emotions under control, couldn't erase the horrid images flashing beneath his lids?

A whimper reached his ears, and his eyes sprang open. Instinct led him to the far-right corner, and there, bathed in the dim torch light, he found his sister, huddled against the wall, a mass of blood and spent tears. Her gaze was distant and filled with pain, and she trembled like a leaf caught on the wind as Will reached out to touch her.

"Oh, Annie!" he cried. "'Tis me, Will. I'll nae hurt ye, lassie."

But she pushed herself farther away, digging her heels into the bloodied straw. Hysterical sobs burst from her lips, and though her terror-filled eyes stared right at him, she didn't recognize him at all.

Bile rose in Will's throat. "What did he do to ye, Annie?" He reached out to touch her battered cheek, but she turned away. Will's breath caught in his chest. He harbored no doubts about what Ian had done to his sister, and one way or the other, he'd make sure the fiend paid.

A rustle of straw caused him to spin around. He stood, drawing his sword, determined to protect his sister from any more pain or humiliation, but it was only Dylan. Will groaned. Although his friend had yet to admit his true feelings for Annie, few questioned his love for her. If Dylan even suspected what had taken place, there would be no stopping him from rushing to her aid, and in her current state, such an onslaught could only upset her more.

Will sprinted to the doorway and pushed his friend outside. "I need ye to find me ma and fetch her here."

A frown creased Dylan's brow, and he craned his neck to search the darkness beyond Will's shoulder. "All right, but what's wrong? I heard you mention Annie."

Will swallowed hard, his mouth as dry as if he'd eaten a wad of wool. Could his friend have spotted Ian emerging from the shadows and come to the same conclusion he had? He needed to clear his head, think rationally, and at all cost, avoid answering Dylan's questions.

"'Tis nowt, but ye need do as I ask, and tell her to be quick about it, aye. Ye'd best be fetching me da as well, I'm afeard."

Dylan's face went white, and he tried to push past Will. "That bastard hurt her, didn't he?"

It took every ounce of strength Will had to hold his friend back. "If ye care for her at all, ye need do as I ask. 'Tis what she'll be wanting now."

"Oh God! What did he do to her?" Dylan asked, his voice trembling. "I saw the filthy pervert coming out, but I couldn't get here."

Will took a calming breath and rubbed a hand across his face. "Dinna fash yerself ower it, aye. She'll be fine, but ye need bid me folks make haste. I'll bide here till they come."

Dylan nodded, his lips pressed together in a single pale line, his nose twitching from the force of his breathing, until at last he turned and ran toward the cottage.

Will steadied himself against the heavy oak door. He swallowed, suppressing the urge to vomit, thoughts of what that villain had done to his innocent sister causing his stomach to turn sour, but he couldn't be sick, not yet, not now.

He returned to Annie's side, bending down before her, but she scrambled back against the stone wall, pushing away from him, her sobs so frantic she was gasping for air. Dear God, where were his parents? Logic told him it had been mere minutes, but the knife piercing his heart made it seem far longer. And yet he could do nothing to calm her fears. In truth, his presence only added to her suffering.

At last, his parents came rushing into the undercroft, leaving Dylan standing by the door, his face drawn and pale, though his eyes flared with fire.

"Sweet Mary!" His mother dropped to her knees, cradling his sister's battered face against her bosom.

"Who did this?" his father asked. His fists were curled so tight at his sides they shook.

"Ian Rutherford," Dylan called from the entrance. "I saw the bastard coming from here . . ." His voice caught, and he paused to clear his throat. "I didn't know Annie . . ." He stopped speaking, stifling a sob, but he needed to say no more.

"We need to mount and ride hot trod after the whoreson." Will started for the door, but his father grabbed his arm.

"Nae, we take care of yer sister first. See to her needs, and to those of the family. When that's done, and only then, we'll consider riding against the Armstrongs. 'Twas Geordie who led the raid, and him that must be held accountable."

"But Ian's the one who attacked Annie," Dylan said. "We should be riding against him."

"Dinna tell me what I should be doing, laddie. Ye've nae notion of how the law works on the Borders."

Will could see his father's ears turning crimson and sort to intercede. "Are ye of a mind ye might find Ian at the Armstrongs then, Da?"

His father took a deep breath and nodded toward the door, neither of them speaking again until they were outside with Dylan in tow.

"Word is Ian's to wed one of theirs. Rabbie's Armstrong's bairn, nae less, if Marion's to be believed. Nae doubt the foul beast will be by her side."

"But Maggie's not to blame," Dylan said. "She can't have any idea what he's done."

Graham's eyebrows lifted. "And how d'ye ken Rabbie Armstrong's lass?"

Dylan turned an odd shade of gray, but Edward came from behind to answer the question. "We met Rab and his daughter down in Lancaster. In fact, we traveled with them until we came across a large band of Armstrongs. That's when Dylan and I decided to excuse ourselves from their company."

Will recalled the sight of the two outlanders scurrying up the hillside, and a sad smile tugged at his cheek. For reasons he couldn't explain, he jumped to the defense of the pretty Scottish lass he'd rescued at the burn. "Ye canna make this Maggie pay for what Ian did here, nae more than Annie should pay for what he did in Hexham."

"Nae, ye're right enough there, lad," Graham said, "but the Armstrongs need mind who they ride with. The Rutherfords are nowt but trouble. If Geordie canna see it himself, I reckon we'd best be about making sure he did. Now go see to the hobblers, aye."

"But, Da . . ."

"Nae one means to harm the lass, William," Betty said. "But yer da's right enough; Geordie should mind the company he keeps. Now do as ye're told and bid our Mary come to the cottage. Annie will need her sister with her . . . and so will I."

Will walked over and grabbed Dylan by the shoulder. "We need leave so me da can get Annie to the house."

"Go on then, lad," Edward said. "You can't do anything to help her here."

Dylan glared at him for a moment, his expression racked with fury, before pulling away from Will and walking off toward the stables.

"He loves her, you know," Edward said. "Even if he doesn't say it."

"He might have done afore this," Will said. "But I'm no' so sure now. And even if he was still of a mind to court her, she winna let him near her." A sob caught in his throat, and he swallowed hard. "I'd best tend to the hobblers and see to Mary."

****

Betty came down the stairs and collapsed in a chair by the fire. Graham and Eddie stood close by, along with all her sons. At first, no one said anything, thank God. She needed time to compose herself, to suppress the sickness churning in her stomach, threatening to rise up her throat. If she could get her hands on Ian Rutherford, she would throttle him to death herself. The wicked son of a whore deserved no better.

The crackling fire relaxed her. She didn't want to take her eyes from it, but a razor-sharp tension filled the room, the anguish over Annie's condition clear in each unspoken word. After a few moments, she took a fortifying breath and answered their silent questions.

"Her body will heal well enough. A broken rib, some cuts and bruises, a bit of swelling. Nowt we've no' patched up on ye lads at one time or another."

"What about a bairn?" Graham asked, unable to keep the pain from his voice.

"Ye ken there's nae way to tell this early on."

"He did rape her, then," Michael said. With a groan of anguish, he flopped down on the bench, putting his head in his hands.

"What else did he do to her?" Dennis asked.

"You ken well enough what the vile buggerer did," Will said, his voice trembling. "Or did ye forget them wee lassies in Hexham and Bewcastle?"

Betty stood, her voice stern, brooking no argument. "There'll be nae more talking of what the whoreson did to yer sister, and if there's a bairn, ye'll all do well to mind 'tis part of our Annie as well. 'Tis her senses I'm worrit about. She winna say a word, as if her wits were a hundred mile away."

Graham came to her side and pressed her against his shoulder. He smelled of wood smoke and horsehair mixed with the underlying scent of pine. A wave of warmth and security swept over her, followed by an intense sadness. Would her daughter ever know the same peace and safety, or had Ian Rutherford robbed her of that as well as her virginity?

"She's a strong lass," Graham said. He kissed her forehead and sighed. "Now, what is it ye're needing us to do?"

She straightened up, brushing down her skirts. "I'm afeard there's little ye can do, save be patient with her. 'Tis best if the lads keep their distance for a bit. There's nowt but Ian's attack in her head, and one young man the same as the next."

Dennis opened his mouth to speak, but she cut him short. "I ken ye're her brothers and want to comfort her, but for the time being, ye'll do nowt but upset her. Now go clean up, the lot of ye. I'll have breakfast on the table when ye return."

"Aye," Graham said. "And after that, we ride. If nowt else, we can seek justice for our Annie."

****

Will entered the stables to find Dylan saddling his horse. "Where d'ye think ye're going?" he asked.

"After Ian Rutherford," Dylan said. He pulled hard on the saddle straps and reached for the reins, but Will grabbed him by the arm.

"Me da says we need bide a bit."

"Right, well I'm not a Foster, so I don't have to listen, now do I?" Dylan lifted his foot to the stirrup, but Will pulled him away, knocking him to the ground.

"Yer clan rides with us, ye daft fool, no' to mention they're under our protection, so ye'll bide till me da says 'tis time to mount." Will glared down at his friend for a moment before shaking his head. "And what did ye hope to accomplish on yer own anyway?"

"Oh, I don't know, maybe putting an end to his miserable life."

"I've seen ye both fight, me friend," Will said, a hint of laughter coloring his tone, "and while ye hold yer own with most, Ian Rutherford would slice ye to bits."

"At least I'd die fighting for her, and maybe, just maybe, I'd manage to take the bugger with me. That's more than any of you are doing."

Will's temper flared. How dare this foul-mouthed outlander question his family's honor? "Ye've a nerve acting all righteous now. When did ye ever bid her more than the time of day?   Ye were always too busy kissing and clapping some buxom wench out behind the stables. Happin if ye'd spared her a moment, she'd no' be lying in her bed, a shadow of the lass she was."

"So it's my fault, is it?" Dylan's fists clenched at his sides, his face turning a putrid shade of red. "I'm not the one who promised her to the bloody scumbag in the first place. So sod off, mate."

Will stood for a moment, not quite sure what Dylan meant, but he understood enough of it to get a pretty good idea. He dragged his friend away from his horse once more and threw him up against the rough planks of the stall.

"Ye scurvy rogue! Ye dinna ken anything about it." He hauled off and punched Dylan in the face, causing his nose to bleed.

Dylan put a hand to his face, then glared at his blood-covered fingers. "Fuck off, you filthy bastard. You know I'm right, and you can't face it. Go on, hit me again. That way you won't feel the need to go after the real villain. You're nothing but a bunch of sniveling cowards."

He lifted his fists and Will followed suit, but a shout from the stable doorway caused them both to halt.

"That's enough, ye dimwitted muckspouts." Walt stood with his fists on his hips, a combination of anger and disgust crossing his face. "How d'ye think our Annie would feel if she heard the two of ye?"

Will opened his mouth to protest, but Walt shut him down before he could utter a word.

"Shut yer gob, ye wee ideot! 'Tis nae more Dylan's fault than mine, and ye're well aware of it."

A smirk crossed Dylan's face, and Will nearly punched him again, but Walt intervened before he could even form a fist.

"And ye, Dylan Hetherington, ye call yerself our kinsman, and yet ye question our honor?"

"I didn't mean that, Walt, it's just . . ."

"Just that ye're worrit about our Annie, and ye're in need of someone to blame, someone close to hand, eh?"

Dylan shrugged. He pulled the blue scarf from his neck and pressed it beneath his bloody nose.

"I'm sorry, man," Will said. "I never meant to say . . . Only why did ye never tell her how ye felt instead of flirting with all the other lassies like ye did? 'Twas plain ye fancied our Annie from the moment ye saw her down by the burn, but now . . ."

"But now what?" Dylan's voice hardened again, and he shoved Will in the shoulder, causing him to take a step back. "Do you think this will change how I feel about her?"

Tears moistened Will's eyes. "'Tis no' what I meant. Me ma says Annie . . . Ian is all she sees. She canna even stand me or Walt near her, let alone any other lad. We're all the same to her."

"Then I'll have to make her see the difference, now won't I?" Dylan headed for the door, but Walt stood in front of him, an eyebrow raised in a not-so-subtle challenge.

"Ye'll be doing nae such thing, laddie. She needs time to heal. Ye barging in there to make her *see the difference* will only cause her more pain. What she'll see is how alike we all are. Now calm yerselves, both of ye. We'll go fill our bellies and see what me da has in mind, aye."

****

"Eddie, can I talk to you a minute?" Dylan said. He scanned the yard, making sure no one stood within hearing distance. What he wanted to say was between the two of them, and he had every intention of making sure it stayed that way.

Edward brushed his hands off and climbed down the ladder. He'd been helping repair some roofs, but the others had gone for more supplies, leaving them quite alone for the moment.

"What can I do for you?"

"You're a scientist, so you must know a bit about health issues." Edward's eyes widened, and Dylan continued. "I mean, you needed to study biology and the likes, right?"

"I'm a physicist, not a physician. They're two different disciplines, but why do you ask?"

"It's Annie. Will she ever recover?"

"I've no idea. Physically, yes, she should heal, but emotionally . . ." Edward shook his head. "No one but Annie can determine that."

"But she can if she wants?"

Edward frowned. "It's not that easy, lad. The brain's a complicated organ, and Annie's suffered a traumatic experience. Women like her guard their virginity; it's personal, intimate. For someone to rob her of it . . . She'll feel violated, probably dirty, maybe even blame herself."

"But it wasn't her fault."

"Of course not. And on one level, she'll realize that, but on another . . . It's hard to explain. Being a man, I'm angry, want revenge, but it's different for a woman, especially one so young. She's not even seventeen years old. All her life, she's been told her virginity is a sort of sacred trust, and now it's been wrenched from her. Logical or not, she may even believe she encouraged him. What she once dreamed of as something beautiful and tender has become filthy and violent."

"But I don't care if she's not a virgin." Dylan ran a hand through his hair. "What can I do to make her understand?"

"There's nothing you can do except try to be patient. Give her mind time to heal, time to realize you're not Ian."

"But they're not even going after him." Dylan's voice shook with frustration. He wanted to act, to do something to help Annie. Patience was not his strong suit.

"Hmm. Graham plans on attacking the Armstrongs."

"Why? Ian Rutherford's the one who should pay."

"But the Armstrongs led the attack. It's them we'll need to ride hot trod against, or it could be condemned as an illegal foray."

"And the Fosters have never broken the law before?"

Edward laughed. "No doubt they have, on numerous occasions, but this is different. Graham wants no questions about the legality of it. Besides, in his eyes, the Armstrongs launched this foray without due cause, and the responsibility for Annie's suffering lies with them."

"But Maggie and the professor are there." Dylan swallowed and looked out across the barmekin yard. "Then again, he didn't think about us being here, did he? He came thundering out of the barmekin gate right behind the rest of them. I had all I could do to stay astride my horse, I was that shocked to see him. Of course, I'm sure the professor thought it quite funny."

"I imagine he did, but you shouldn't take it personally."

Dylan's jaw dropped. "You're joking. He could have killed us."

Edward chuckled. "I doubt that. He spent his time talking to Betty, or so I've been told."

"Betty? But why?"

"In his youth, he spent many an hour at her table, so I can't imagine him being all that keen about raiding his childhood haunt. Talking to Betty kept him out of the frey. Which is what we're going to do when we ride against the Armstrongs. We'll stay on the perimeter, not get in Rob's way. He'll make sure Maggie's safe."

Graham's voice echoed across the yard. "Mount up, lads. We ride within the hour, and tonight we shake the border loose."

Edward grabbed Dylan by the arm. "Remember what I said, son. It's not our place to interfere. Let history play out the way it was meant to."

Dylan huffed and pulled his arm away. "Like it did with Annie, you mean."

Edward stepped in his path. "Don't defy me on this, lad, or I won't think twice about sending you back."

"Let me get this straight. It's all right for me to court Annie, but not to go on a foray because I might accidently wound an Armstrong or a Rutherford?"

"Oh, it's not the Armstrongs or the Rutherfords I'm worried about"

"Well, don't go troubling yourself over me. I've been taking care of myself for years."

At that moment, he was tempted to haul off and punch the older man, but he couldn't bring himself to do it. Over the past few weeks, he'd come to care about Edward, maybe even look up to him. He turned and stormed back toward the stables without saying another word, thoughts of what had happened to Annie causing tears to stream down his cheeks.

CHAPTER 20

Maggie knelt next to her cousin and yawned before yanking another stubborn weed. Though the early morning sun brightened the small vegetable garden, beckoning a new day, she was still bone weary. And why wouldn't she be? After all, she'd spent a good portion of the night tossing and turning, fitful dreams interspersed with restless stretches of wakefulness. She'd curled into a ball, hugging her pillow, unable to suffocate the relentless concerns that sent icy shards of fear through her soul.

Even when she had managed to doze off, some undefined image would jar her awake, leaving her covered in a cold sweat. In the end, she'd resorted to gazing out her window and staring at the blanket of stars until, at last, the pale brush of morning painted them into oblivion.

Now she knelt on the moist, dew-covered ground, a dry bannock sitting in her stomach like her da's lead fishing weights. Quite fitting since her concern for him was responsible for transforming the tasty morsel into a hardened ball of dough in the first place. The sudden clatter of hoofbeats caused her to jump, and she nearly tumbled over. *Son of a . . . Just the lads out exercising their ponies.*

Connie ducked her head, stifling a laugh. "Ye need calm yerself, Cousin, elst ye'll be noucht but a bag of nerves when he returns."

Something about the statement caused Maggie's anger to flare. "I'm worried about my father."

"Aye, I reckoned ye would be, but if he kens ye fash so when he rides, 'twill keep his mind off the business at hand."

"Oh, I thought ye meant . . ."

Constance smirked, her eyes sparkling with mischief. "Oh aye, I meant him as well."

When her cousin stood and walked to the other side of the garden, Maggie bit back a few caustic words of denial and cast another glance out the gate. Not a leaf stirred, so she muttered a short prayer, one her father had taught her years before, and went back to gathering some leeks for dinner.

Moments later, the rumble of galloping hooves echoed out across the glen, and the winsome lowing of cattle reverberated through the air. She leapt to her feet, the basket of vegetables scattering across the ground, and ran across the barmekin yard. It had to be them.

Sure enough, before she could take half a dozen steps, the Armstrongs galloped through the gates, driving at least twenty head of cattle into the barmekin, and with them came her father, laughing and patting his brothers on the back as if he'd never been away. Not far behind, Ian Rutherford slowed his horse to a walk, taking a moment to speak to his father before spurring his pony forward once more.

Relief cascaded through Maggie's body like a soothing river flowing over parched and broken rocks. She took a deep breath and let it out, slow and easy, Connie's words reverberating through her thoughts. *Don't let them see your concern.*

Ian spotted her and jumped from his horse, running over to where she stood. Without a word, he whisked her into his arms, lifting her off the ground and kissing her hard and deep. She should at least pretend to protest, but the warmth of his embrace crumbled her defenses, and she wrapped her arms around his neck. For a long moment, he held her tight against him until, little by little, he released her mouth, leaving soft pecks on her lips as he drew away.

"We'll eat well tonight, lassie." He whirled her around, a broad grin plastered across his face. "And the Fosters dinna even ken what hit them."

"You didn't have to hurt anyone, did you?" Maggie asked. Reality of life on the Borders or not, the whole concept still concerned her.

"Nae, darlin', a few wounded, noucht more . . . But that's no' yer concern, lass." He brushed a few strands of hair back over her shoulder and whispered, "Come down to the glen with me, aye, afore anyone can stop us."

Maggie peeked over Ian's shoulder. Her father stood a few feet away, celebrating with his brothers, pushing and shoving them along, whooping and hollering over the victory. The moment he spotted her, though, he whispered a few words to Andy and moved in her direction.

Geordie caught him around the shoulder and pulled him back. "Leave the weans be, Rabbie, or d'ye no' mind what ye were like at their age?"

"Hmph! 'Tis what I'm afeard of."

"Ach, now, Rab," Andy said. "What can they get into with us all about? Come join us, aye. 'Tis long past due."

"Go on, Da," Maggie said. "My uncle's right. I won't do anything you'd disapprove of, I promise."

He smiled at her but threw a scowl in Ian's direction. 'Tis no' ye I dinna trust, darlin'."

Maggie shook her head. "You're doing it again, Da."

He laughed, and cupping the back of her head in his hand, he kissed her forehead. "All right, lass, but we need speak in the morn, aye. For now, stay in sight of the tower, ye hear." His expression hardened as he focused on Ian. "Ye get me meaning right enough, d'ye no', laddie?"

Ian nodded, a nervous tic causing his cheek to flutter. It seemed to satisfy Robert, for after emitting a guttural grunt, he rejoined his brothers.

"He's not as gruff as he sounds, you know," Maggie said.

Ian chuckled. "Mayhap, but I wouldna want to stand against him during a foray." He kissed her on the nose and tugged her arm, beckoning her to follow.

Maggie offered no resistance. Despite her reservations, she was beginning to like the charismatic reiver, so much so she almost forgot how angry she'd been about their upcoming spousal. After all, her issue was with Geordie, not Ian.

Content in her reasoning, she ran down the grassy brae beside him. The summer air ruffled her hair and caressed her cheeks, and her heart skipped at the prospect of Ian's fingers doing the same.

With the peel tower off in the distance, he pressed her against the trunk of a large oak. "Let's forget about the arrangements me da's making, aye. I'll never hold ye to them. No' unless 'tis what ye want." His lips brushed against her own, a whiff of cinnamon and cloves exciting her senses, before his mouth covered hers in a deep and passionate kiss.

Maggie wrapped her arms around his neck, as if her grasp could hold him there forever. Maybe he did get what she'd been trying to say. But all too soon, he pulled away, desire burning in his eyes.

"So tell me, Maggie Armstrong, will ye have me? I love ye, but I'm asking ye and nae one else, no' yer da or mine, no' even Geordie. Will ye marry me, lass?"

Maggie's breath caught in her throat, causing her to cough. So much for him understanding. For the first time in her life, she didn't have a witty comeback. After all, she did care for Ian, that much had become clear somewhere in the middle of the night, but marriage . . . She wasn't quite ready to plight her troth just yet. Oh, her toes tingled when he kissed her, and a butterfly or two flitted around her stomach, but shouldn't there be something more, something that wouldn't fly away at the first stiff breeze? If she could figure it out herself, maybe she could explain it to him, make him understand.

"I do like you, Ian, and I don't want to lose you, but . . ."

"Ach, darlin', ye're no' going to lose me. I'm a fair fighter and rode on many a foray, so dinna fash yerself on that account. I'll make ye a good husband."

"I'm sure you would, but . . ." She searched for the right words, but they continued to elude her. Not that it mattered, for Ian muffled her response with another kiss.

The sound of a rider galloping hard in their direction put an end to their intimate moment. Maggie muttered a twentieth-century curse. Once again, she'd failed to get her meaning across, and with Ian's attention shifted elsewhere, any further discussion would have to wait.

"They're in hot trod," Fergus Rutherford shouted to his brother, reining his horse in for a split second before riding off again. "Auld Geordie wants everyone in the peel . . . now, Ian!"

Without any further explanation, Ian straightened up and pulled Maggie across the glen, practically dragging her at times.

"Hot trod—that means the Fosters are coming, doesn't it?" She threw a quick glance in the direction of the road and dug in her heels.

Ian stopped, twirling around to face her. Though his countenance remained pleasant enough, the tightness of his jaw belied any tolerance his expression conveyed. "Aye, it does, so let's be about taking refuge in the peel, eh." He tightened his grip, but Maggie wiggled out of it, refusing to move.

"I will, it's just . . . well, I don't hear anyone, let alone see them. Are you sure Fergus isn't mistaken or more likely having a laugh at our expense? I swear I saw him grinning when he rode by."

"Dinna be daft, lass. No' even Fergus would dare risk such a tale. If me brother says they're riding, ye can be sure 'tis true. Now come along." He grabbed her hand once more and continued up the embankment.

"But why attack now while it's still daylight. I mean, don't you usually wait till after dark?"

Maggie stopped once more, yanking hard on Ian's arm and causing him to spin around. His lips were pressed so tight together the line could have been drawn with a pencil, and his cheeks had gone the most unbecoming shade of crimson.

"Enough, lassie! When I give ye a command, I expect ye to obey."

The spark of anger his words ignited in her gut must have manifested itself in her demeanor, for he altered his tack before she could bring him to task. He searched the horizon, the sharpness in his tone shifting from annoyance to concern.

"I didna mean to speak so harsh to ye, darlin', but I'm afeard ye dinna ken what a fray is about, ye being newly come to the Borders and all. Them Fosters are no' much better than broken men. They'll ravage ye for the sport of it, and I canna bear the thought of that."

"I get what you're trying to say, but it still doesn't give you the right—" The distant sound of thundering hoofbeats cut her short. Perhaps Ian's argument did hold some merit. "We'll finish this later, when you've driven the Fosters back over the border."

"As ye say, lass, but let's be on our way now, aye, afore 'tis too late."

Maggie agreed, following Ian through the barmekin gate and toward the tower's wooden forestairs. Her father met them at the foot of the steps and grabbed her arm, pulling her away from Ian and guiding her up the stairs.

"Go on with yer aunties and cousins now, lass."

"But, Da!" She let out a groan, annoyed she might miss some of the action, but he continued to hurry her along with the other women.

"Do as ye're told, lass," he said, a stern edge to his voice.

Maggie rolled her eyes. No sense arguing with that tone. And so, after letting out a loud tut, she followed the others up toward the tower door.

The men took their places, some outside on the barmekin wall, others in the peel itself, either beside arrow slots or up along the roof. Maggie stood at the top of the steps and gazed across the crowded yard. She caught a glimpse of Ian on the wall. With his bow at his side, crouched by one of the crenels, he did present a dashing figure. In spite of the impending danger, she couldn't help but let a smile break through. It was almost as if she'd wandered into her own personal fairy tale, complete with a charming prince ready to defend her against the evil wizard.

The steady rhythm of hooves pounding across the glen soon brought an abrupt end to her reverie. Her cousins were closing the barmekin gate, barring it with a heavy beam. Perhaps it was time she got inside.

221

Hurrying up the turnpike steps, she passed by one of the few decent-sized windows and froze. She could see over the barmekin wall from here, and her eyes fixed on the rugged men who bore down upon them from the southwest. With a flaming spear signaling their lawful approach, the band of angry horseman sallied forth, trumpet blasting and sleuth hounds barking at their heels.

The glint of sunlight hitting a sword caught her attention, and she squinted to see better, cursing herself for not sneaking a pair of binoculars along on the journey. She uttered a quick prayer, hoping it might be Dylan or her uncle, but she couldn't tell, not at this distance.

Biting her lip, she focused on the figure who came closer to the barmekin wall with each stride of his horse. How angry he looked in his plated jack with his pike held high. And yet something about him unleashed an entire flock of butterflies within her stomach and sent shivers down her spine so intense they caused her knees to quiver.

It's him! The late afternoon light illuminated his face, and though she couldn't really distinguish his features enough to identify him, somehow she knew. The heat rose in her cheeks, and she fanned herself, determined to retain her composure. *This is ridiculous! How can you feel anything for this guy? You don't even know him.* Her heart fluttered its reply, and she moaned in exasperation. *Then why can't you stop thinking about him? Besides, it might not even be him.*

The sudden clash of weapons on the thick wooden gate had the effect of a weed-whacker on her butterflies, causing them to scatter into sickening shards of fear. She pulled the cross from beneath her chemise, holding it tight as she scanned the barmekin wall. Ian still crouched beside the crenel, raining arrows down on their attackers. And she recalled her father barreling up the steps for the roof not moments before. A sense of relief washed over her. Maybe it wouldn't be so bad. After all, no one got hurt when they raided the Fosters, right?

A screech from the yard answered her question, sending a wave of nausea up her throat. The sight of Duncan Armstrong clutching his chest and falling limp to the ground shattered all notions of a mystical fantasy.

Rather than a dream of happy ever after, this fairy tale held all the makings of a full-blown nightmare. Even her father's yarns of blood feuds and midnight raids had failed to prepare her for the reality of the situation.

Gripping her stomach, she sank down along the wall and closed her eyes to subdue the queasiness. *Compose yourself, Maggie. You're no good to anyone this way. Now take deep breaths and blow them out, slow and easy. That's it.*

Much to her surprise, the short exercise did help. When she opened her eyes again, a fragile but unmistakable calm enveloped her. She pulled herself up and peered over the windowsill once more before shifting her gaze back across the room.

Most of the women busied themselves readying weapons while others tended the few already wounded or ripped linen strips for those yet to come. Preparing for the next stage of the assault, no doubt. Maggie pressed her hand against her stomach to soothe a lingering batch of nerves, exhaling in one long stream, but while the prospect of what might still come terrified her, the fear no longer controlled her. Brushing off her skirts, she hurried over to ask what she might do to help.

"There's no need to whisper," Constance said. "They canna hear ye . . . no' yet anyway," she added, a hint of concern transforming her features. The sturdy wood of the gate gave way to the battering ram and axe, and she cringed before tilting her head in her brother's direction. "Get some more arrows ower to Alasdair, aye, and Archie needs his wound dressed. By the time ye finish there, ye'll want to grab an axe and ready yerself."

Ready myself for what? Maggie frowned at the heavy weapon. "All right, but I don't know what good it'll do. I doubt I'll be able to lift it."

"Oh, ye'll lift it right enough, Cousin, when one of them is coming down upon ye like a wild boar." Constance pointed toward the barmekin yard, and Maggie craned her neck to see out the narrow window once more. The sight she beheld caused her blood to run cold. A few of the Fosters' clansmen had managed to break through and open the gate. Below, hordes of their kinsman came flooding into the yard, forcing many of the Armstrongs to seek the protection of the peel tower.

Geordie remained in the yard until the last minute, fighting off intruders with one arm while herding his own family toward the tower with the other, until at last he clattered up the outer staircase.

Seeing her uncle in the yard gave Maggie an unexpected sense of admiration for the man. He was no coward. She'd give him that. He'd left some men on the walls, but they appeared to be holding their own while everyone else took up positions from the safety of the tower.

Maggie scanned the barmekin yard, and seeing no one in imminent danger, she released a tentative sigh of relief. A commotion at the top of the turnpike stairs drew her attention, and she turned from the window to see a pale-faced young man talking to Geordie. The boy's voice shook, each word he uttered causing her uncle's face to grow a deeper shade of scarlet.

"I'm sorry, Uncle," the boy said. "It wouldna latch. I'm of a mind it might have been damaged in the last raid."

Geordie reached out, clamping his fist hard around the youth's arm. "And ye never thought to mention it till now?" Her uncle spat the words, his expression matching his tone. "Did ye at least manage to bar the door?"

"I . . . They were coming up the forestair," the boy said, his chin quivering so that Maggie expected him to burst into tears any second. "I thought it best not to waste time with the door, but to secure the gate. But then I couldn't and . . . I . . . I ran for help straightaway. I'll go back, Uncle."

"Nae need, laddie, I'll send someone who can get the job done. That's if it's no' already too late."

The young man's shoulders sagged, his expression etched with shame, but Geordie paid him no mind. Instead, he strode over to Alasdair, and her cousin went bolting down the stone steps.

Maggie scowled at her uncle, but before she could say a word, Constance grabbed her shoulder. "Let it be, Maggie. Donald kent better. 'Twas his job to see the yett secure."

"But he's wounded, and he can't be more than fourteen years old." When Connie didn't answer, Maggie huffed a sigh and tried again. "What did he do anyway?"

"'Tis what he failed to do. He left the yett undone, and worse than that, he hadna even barred the door."

"Oh!" Maggie frowned but forged on. "You're right, he should have taken more care to see it closed."

"Should he now?" Constance said, her eyebrows raised in disbelief.

"Yes, he should have. I'm not a fool. I understand the yett's the last line of defense between us and the Fosters, but Alasdair will take care of it, and all's well, so what's the big deal?"

Connie shook her head and ripped some more linen strips.

A soft growl rumbled in Maggie's throat. "Who is he anyway?" she asked. "I've never seen him before, so I thought he must be a servant, or from one of the other clans, but then I heard him call your da uncle."

"Aye, Donald's our Uncle Angus's lad, but me da's taken him under his wing, his own father coming afoul of the warden last year and all, God rest his soul."

Constance blessed herself, then hurried away to answer her mother's call.

Maggie grabbed a bottle of whisky and a few strips of linen. Someone needed to tend to the young man's wounded arm. A few comforting words wouldn't go amiss either. But before she could reach his side, her Uncle Andy came bounding across the floor.

"'Tis nae good, Geordie. Alasdair did his best to bar the door. He just wasna strong enough to hold them back. By the time we got there . . ." Andy shook his head. "The lads are holding them off for now, but it winna be long afore they're making their way up the turnpike."

"God's teeth, man!" Geordie cursed and spit on the floor, but Andy laid a calming hand on his chest.

"Donald's but a lad, here to learn, and he'll no' do that if ye come at him like a raging bull."

The older man heaved a deep sigh. "Aye, laddie, but perhaps he should be under yer tutelage. I've got me plate full with me own wee scoundrel."

Alasdair had just backed through the turnpike doorway, and Geordie shook his head before taking off in his son's direction. "Have ye noucht better to do than stand there like a scared rabbit, ye wee dolt?"

"I'm no' afeard, Da . . . me laird . . . but waiting for them rascals to stick their filthy heads round the turnpike."

Geordie groaned in exasperation. "D'ye no' see the weans here about?" He gave his son a slap across the ear. "Get yerself down the stair and stop the rogues afore they come this far. And mind the trip steps, aye."

Maggie hated to admit it, but her uncle did have a point. Women and children crowded the large room, along with a few wounded men and her uncle's dog, Samson. She exhaled again, slow and steady, before peering out the window once more.

Her alluring Englishman clamored up the wooden steps of the peel, stopping for a moment to look in her direction and flash a smile.

"Give us a hand here, Will," a voice yelled out, and the rogue gave a slight bow before hastening back down the steps to his comrades below.

Maggie gasped and pulled back just in time to see her Uncle Sim scramble down the steps from the roof.

"What's the trouble?" he asked.

"They've pushed their way in," Maggie said, not wanting to mention Donald's mistake.

He let out a colorful expletive on his way passed but stopped for a moment to give her shoulder a gentle squeeze. "Dinna fash yerself, lassie. We've a surprise waiting for them."

The image of the handsome Englishman flashed through her mind, and she scanned the steps below. For some unknown reason, she whispered a prayer, the lump in her throat disappearing when she spied him back in the yard. Will, someone had called him. She whispered his name and a warmth embraced her like a soft woolen blanket, but a sudden shriek from the outside steps yanked her back to reality. A chill coursed through her veins, causing her to shudder. Sim's surprise, no doubt.

Foster men clambered up the outside steps while Armstrong men tried to down them from the tower wall. Maggie pulled her cousin aside. "You remember the English lad I came across the night Alasdair and I slipped away? Well, he's out there. But I don't think he'll harm us. He never even tried to steal a kiss."

Constance scoffed. "I reckon no', with the woods full of Armstrongs and outlaws on his heels. Ye can thank the Holy Mother yer da came when he did, though. 'Twas Will Foster from what I can gather, and he's sure to have taken ye right then and there if he'd half a chance."

Maggie scowled, but perhaps Connie was right. They had been a bit preoccupied. And yet he'd seemed decent enough at the time. Would he really have killed Alasdair and ravaged her if her father hadn't come along?

A cheer of triumph rose up the stairwell, followed by the blood chilling clang of steel against steel. The Fosters had fought their way to the turnpike steps and would soon be working their way up the floors. In a desperate attempt to help, Maggie ran to the fireplace and shoveled the embers into a nearby bucket. With a bit of effort, she raised it to one of the fourth-story windows and emptied its contents out on those below, cringing when one of the men screamed in anguish and an arrow pierced her bucket.

A strong arm yanked her back against the wall. "Get away from there, Maggie!" Robert's voice echoed off the walls, his forehead creased with concern. "Now go tend to yer cousin's wounds afore a Foster arrow feathers itself in yer breast as well."

Maggie blinked in surprise but headed across the room, too stunned by her close call to protest. Once she tended to Donald's wound, though, she inched her way back to her father's side. His muscular hands launched arrow after arrow into the enemy below, and Maggie watched in awe. When did he learn to do that? Oh, from time to time he'd gone hunting with friends, but he'd never brought anything home. She'd always assumed he wasn't any good, but when one of the Fosters fell, pierced by his shot, she realized how naïve she'd been.

"Maggie!" Her father lifted an eyebrow in her direction.

"Sorry, Da." She kissed him on the forehead, causing the corner of his mouth to twerk.

"Go on and see to Donald, aye."

"But I've already bandaged his arm."

"'Tis the wound to his pride what needs a gentle touch, lass."

A pang of sympathy for the disheartened youth convinced Maggie to move back to his side, but she hadn't been there long when the smell of smoke began to fill the room. Once more, Maggie pulled herself up, this time peeking through the narrow arrow slot beneath Ian's arm.

"Oh my God!" She gasped at the sight she beheld.

The weary reiver stopped for a minute to rest his elbow against the cold stone. "'Twill be all right, Maggie," Ian assured her, but somehow she found it hard to believe.

Smoke was rising from three small outbuildings, their thatched roofs smoldering in the fading light. The scent of seared wood permeated the air, mingled with the tang of sweat and blood. It clung to the men who forced their way through the peel door, wild and full of anger; on the cattle that gathered within the small courtyard, emitting restless bellows; even on the women who helped tend the wounds of their loved ones.

Maggie's heart filled with terror. What if the Fosters succeeded in storming the tower? With her nerves strung as taut as her father's bow, she reached for the axe Constance had given her. They didn't tend to kill the women, or so she'd been told, but were they to endure a fate far worse? The image of clammy English fingers fondling her most private parts nauseated her, and she glanced out the window, hoping to see her kin driving the wretched bastards back. Instead, she caught sight of her uncle's smoldering cottage and clutched her weapon all the tighter, determined to put up a valiant fight.

Not a moment later, the clash of metal echoed off the walls and boots sounded on the turnpike steps. Armstrongs ran from every direction to meet their assailants. Oddly enough, Maggie could think of only one thing. The ring her grandmother had given her was in that smoking cottage . . . and so was the amulet!

CHAPTER 21

Will stopped to stare at the lass in the window. Since that day at the Kershope Burn, he

hadn't been able to get her out of his head. And every time he thought of her, his heart would quicken and his knees grow weak, not to mention what it did to his loins.

"Will!" Walt shouted from the bottom of the staircase, his face pinched in annoyance.

Flashing a smile in the lassie's direction, Will gave a quick bow before hurrying back down the steps to his brother's side.

"Head of the clan now, are ye?" Walt asked. "Or d'ye just think ye ken better than Da?"

"What's wrong with giving the lads a hand?" Will said. Walt grabbed his arm, and he yanked it away. "Ye've nae need to watch ower me like a wean. I'm well aware of what I'm to do, and by the time the Armstrongs run us back into the yard, I'll be on me nagg with me sword and pike at the ready.

"Ye're right, lad," Walt said. "But I've been looking after ye for twenty year now, so dinna be expecting me to change me ways any time soon. Now mount yer pony, aye."

Will climbed on his hobbler and looked down at his brother. "I dinna doubt yer intentions, Brother, but could ye ease up on the reins a bit now and again? Even me da disna hold them as taut as ye."

Walt chuckled. "Nae need. He's got me to do the job for him." He'd no sooner mounted his hobbler than the sound of iron crashing against the stone of the tower reverberated through the barmekin yard. "Keep them occupied a wee bit more, eh, Will? Give Da a good start with the cattle."

Will tightened his grip around the reins and took a firmer hold of his pike. With the yett breached, the Armstrongs and their allies would be driving the fray back into the barmekin yard. When they did, Will would be ready for the confrontation, especially when it came to one scoundrel in particular.

****

Maggie's heart lodged in her throat. No matter what the risk, she needed to get to her uncle's cottage and retrieve the amulet, and her grandmother's ring with it. Without another thought, she sped down the dimly lit staircase. Fierce fighting raged all around her, causing such turmoil she doubted anyone would notice one girl slipping amongst the clashing swords. But someone did notice, and Alasdair whirled her around with such force her head spun.

"Where are ye going, Cousin? Get yerself upstairs; 'tis safest there."

"No, I can't—"

Before she could utter another word, a Foster blade came down upon him, and he had all he could do to block it.

Maggie seized the opportunity and hurried outside. She headed for her uncle's cottage, clusters of burning thatch now lighting its roof in an eerie glow. A filthy arm grabbed her around the waist, but she wiggled out of the scoundrel's grasp, shoving the rogue so hard he landed on his behind. Another tried to take hold of her skirt, but a swift kick in his privates put him in his place. By the time she'd reached the cottage door, three more scoundrels stood nursing various body parts.

That'll teach them to mess with Rabbie Armstrong's daughter. Giving herself a mental pat on the back, she turned toward the flaming roof and groaned. From the look of things, her troubles were just about to begin.

Though the dampened moss sizzled and cracked, the underlying layer of reeds and hazel twigs caught easy enough, and the flames threatened to engulf the entire roof. The heat from it burned her cheeks and made her eyes water. She raised her hand to shield herself from it, but she needed something more. Searching the yard in desperation, she spied the bucket Emma kept by the door. Right away, she recalled her fire-safety training. In one swift movement, she pulled the plaid from her shoulders and plunged it into the lukewarm water, soaking it well before wrapping it tight around her face.

Somehow she found the courage to enter but stopped for a moment to survey the situation. Sparks and patches of burning thatch fell from above, setting parts of the staircase on fire. Here and there, thick wooden support beams buckled while white hazy clouds billowed from the floor above. She swallowed hard, climbing the crumbling steps with care. Her legs trembled, and her heart pounded out a deafening rhythm against the thick linen kirtle, but at last she made her way to the rooms above.

Smoke filled the upper chambers, smoldering embers dropping from every direction like a fiery spring rain. Only the stone and turf of the walls kept the entire structure from going up in a ball of flames, and yet Maggie would not turn back. Her precious items lay on the bedside table, and she had every intention of retrieving them. Using a great deal of caution, she inched her way toward them. The floor below her creaked and sagged until, with a sudden crack, one of the boards gave way. The jagged wood scraped along her leg, and though she couldn't suppress a cry, she managed to pull free and crawl away without falling to the ground below. With bile rising in her throat, she pushed herself the last few feet to the table and ran her fingers along its top, groping for her cherished possessions. "Stay low," she whispered over and over, almost like a mantra, but even so, the dense fog of soot and ash stung her throat. The heat was so intense it penetrated the once-moist cloth, and she began to cough.

A washbasin sat on the table. Would it be too hot? She stuck her finger in. No, warm but tolerable. She poured the contents over her face, dampening the rag once more, and took a tentative breath. Her coughing eased, and she continued searching the tabletop until she felt the smooth gloss of the amulet's stone and the delicate curve of the ring she'd left beside it. Hanging the amulet around her neck, she slipped the ring on her finger and headed back downstairs, careful to dodge the large chunks of fiery debris that fell at her feet.

Her coughing had worsened again, and she tripped over the last three steps, unable to control the movement of her legs any longer. *You're the daughter of Robert Armstrong. Are you going to let a little smoke be the end of you?* With a defiant lunge, she grabbed on to the rickety banister and pulled herself up, shoving her body toward the front door.

Alasdair caught her as she stumbled out into the courtyard and fell to her knees. Fury raged in his eyes, no doubt over her blatant disregard of his warning, but concern flared there as well. With an uncharacteristic gentleness, he wrapped his arm around her shoulders, guiding her away from the heat and into the cool, moist air of twilight.

Maggie followed him into the haze of the darkening courtyard, the wails of the injured echoing in her ears and the scent of blood thick on the evening mist. Her clothes were torn and covered with soot, but the intricate ring was secure on her finger and the priceless amulet safe around her neck. She took a deep gulp of the damp air, and her head began to clear, though she plopped on a nearby bench to rest and get her bearings.

"What were ye thinking, Coz?" Alasdair asked, his brow furrowed into deep ruts. "Lancashire or no', ye should ken better than to run into the midst of a fray, unarmed, nae less." Alasdair shook his head. "'Tis a fair common occurrence here about, so ye'd best learn to stay where ye're told."

A large welt was forming on his cheek, and Maggie reached over to touch it. "Alasdair, you're hurt."

"'Tis noucht." He took a quick survey of the yard and pulled her up from the bench. "Are ye all right?"

"Yes, I'm fine."

"Right then, make yer way to the chapel, aye. 'Tis where the lassies are gathering." Much to her surprise, he lifted her torn skirt to her knee and gazed at the large scrape on her calf. "That'll need tending."

"It's just a scratch." Maggie dipped her plaid into the bucket at her side and washed away the excess blood. "See, it looks much worse than it is."

Alasdair muttered what might have been a curse. "Does it now? Me cousin Gavin died from a scratch nae worse. Now get yerself to the chapel and see to it, aye." He kissed her on the cheek and, giving a quick nod, ran through the gathering mist, back to his battle.

Maggie didn't like to admit it, but Alasdair was right. Her wound did need to be cleansed, but with most of the fighting now outside, she hated to surrender her vantage point for the safety of the chapel. Suppressing a smile, she pulled a small flask from her pocket. A bit of whisky would do the trick. Good thing she'd stashed it there after seeing to Donald's wound. A remnant of her Girl Scout training, no doubt.

She lifted her skirt and inspected the injury once more. This was going to smart, no question about it, but it did need to be done. Gritting her teeth, she poured the amber liquid over the gash and stifled a squeal. *Yow!!!* *And you thought Bactine stung?*

Brushing down her skirt, she shook her leg to stop the sting. "There, that should take care of it," she said, pleased with herself. "Problem solved."

She leaned back against the stable wall and stared in awe at the men who scuffled before her, locked in hand-to-hand combat. Those on horses rode through the crowded yard, swinging their swords and yelling obscenities. Her Uncle Andy yanked one from his lofty perch, and Maggie cringed. From the intensity of the fallen man's scream, his arm must have been torn right out of its socket.

"Are ye lost there, lassie?" A sweaty palm cupped her chin. "Come here and give us a kiss then, eh?"

Maggie grabbed the pail on the bench, swinging it at the scoundrel's head and sending him reeling. Perhaps she should heed Alasdair's suggestion before one of the degenerates decided he'd rather make love than war. Dropping the bucket, she hurried across the yard, but skidded to a halt when she spotted her father.

Though he wielded a sword in one hand and a dagger in the other, his hilted fist appeared to be his weapon of choice for the moment. He slammed it into the jaw of his opponent, a rather scruffy man who looked like he hadn't bathed in months. The crinkle of her father's nose when the rogue collapsed against him told Maggie it might indeed be the case. Odd as it seemed under the circumstances, the thought made her giggle.

Robert shoved the man away, giving him a powerful kick in his groin. As he did, he caught sight of Maggie. His eyes narrowed, and his cheeks flushed deep crimson, the tone of his voice matching his countenance. "Get to the chapel, Maggie. Do as ye're told for once, lass!"

The words still hung on his lips when he cried out, his face convulsing in pain. Maggie stared in horror as her father dropped to the ground. The color drained from his cheeks and blood trickled from the side of his mouth. Ian grabbed his body, bracing his fall, but her father made no effort to rise.

Time froze, every movement around her slowing to a crawl. Maggie's hands trembled, the fear coursing through her body so fierce it hammered in her ears and pounded against her chest, causing her breath to catch in her throat.

She started for his side, screaming his name, but a rider emerged from behind her father's fallen body, blocking her way. She recognized him at once, the young man she'd seen at the stream, Will Foster. He sat there on his hobbler and glared down at her, a smile touching his lips. His penetrating slate-blue eyes pierced through to her very soul, paralyzing her with their strength. Though her instinct told her to run, her legs refused to obey. Her father was dying, and this bastard stood between them.

Without taking his eyes off her, the rogue rode over and ripped the amulet from her neck. He lifted an eyebrow, his gaze daring her to protest, but Maggie bit her tongue and said nothing. Her time in the sixteenth century had taught her well on that count. Instead, she stood stock-still and lifted her chin in defiance.

Undaunted, the young man touched her cheek, running his thumb across her lips. She pulled away, determined not to give him any encouragement. The ploy worked, for he turned and rode away without a word.

Her path cleared once more, she ran to her father's side, tears flooding her cheeks. *No, it can't be true.* Her knees buckled beneath her, and she fell to the ground, unable to stem the river of sorrow that sprang from her heart.

The world closed around her, leaving her oblivious to all but her father. With Ian's help, she pulled him across her lap, brushing back the damp hair at his temples. Blood saturated his jack, and his ruddy complexion, once so vibrant, had turned a sickening gray. In desperation, she ripped off a piece of her petticoat and pressed it against the hole in his back, determined to stem the bleeding.

"Daddy, no!" she said between sobs. "Don't leave me. You promised! We have all the time in the world."

"Maggie, darlin'," Robert said, his breath labored. "Get away from here . . . He'll hurt ye too, lassie."

"Who, Daddy?" Maggie could barely breathe now, let alone speak. "Who will hurt me?"

He reached up and grabbed her shoulder, struggling to form the word, but her question would go unanswered. A final gasp drained the life from her father's countenance and cloaked his soft blue eyes in death's eternal shroud. In one fleeting second, Rabbie Armstrong passed from this earth, leaving a hole in Maggie's heart she feared no one else could fill.

Ian slipped his arm around her waist and bid her rise, but she shoved him away. She would never see her father again, and no one, not the Fosters who escaped through the barmekin gate, not her cousin who stood guard by her side, not even Ian Rutherford who bid her move to safer ground, was going to deny her this moment. Ian opened his mouth to speak, but her glare stilled him. He sighed and, giving a bob of his head, took a step back, his sword drawn.

The tears continued to flow in earnest as Maggie caressed her father's bearded chin, so soft in spite of its bristled appearance. With shaking fingers, she closed his eyelids, sketching a cross on his forehead, lips, and chest. She did the same in the palm of each hand. Though she couldn't administer the sacrament herself, God would understand and take him into heaven.

"It's time, darlin'." A soft voice reached her ears, and she started. It sounded so much like her father that she spun around, her hope renewed, but it was only her uncle Andy. Her spirit crushed once more, she bent and kissed her father's brow, smooth now in death's grip.

His sword lay beside him, cold and discarded, but not for long. Grabbing its basket hilt, Maggie stood, swinging it with both hands.

"I hate you bastards. God forgive me, I hate you all!" She screamed until her voice became harsh and raspy, but it accomplished nothing. Not one Foster remained within the barmekin, let alone within her reach.

Ian grabbed her from behind, hugging her to himself and pressing her arms against her body. "They're gone, lass." He whispered in her ear, soft, comforting words, and kissed her cheek and neck until she released the sword and collapsed to the ground, unable to stop crying. Ian knelt with her. She leaned against him as her uncles carried her father's limp body away, seeking solace in his embrace even when the tears would no longer come.

For the most part, her family left her alone, no doubt figuring Ian would be the best to care for her. She saw her aunts heading for the chapel, but she couldn't bear the thought of what needed to be done and snuggled closer into Ian's embrace. Though he tried more than once to get her to go inside, she didn't want to leave. Instead, she stared at the stars, remembering another sky, hundreds of years away, and the man who would cradle her in his arms and tell her bedtime stories.

With the Fosters gone, her kin began to move about to assess the damage. From time to time, whispered bits of conversation would reach her ears. The Fosters had gotten away with twenty-nine head of cattle and two prisoners, or so Geordie told Sim.

"'Twas Will Foster's dagger in his back," Andy whispered to Marion, though by the look on his face, he had a hard time believing it.

"But Ian saw him do it," Sandy Rutherford hissed in Geordie's ear.

Could any of it be true? Maggie didn't want to believe it, but if Ian and her uncle had seen it with their own eyes . . . She couldn't deal with that now. What did it matter? Her father was dead, and knowing who did it wouldn't bring him back. Perhaps in time she would care, but right now she blamed them all.

Andy wrapped a plaid around her shoulders before continuing his account. The Englishmen left four homes burned and sacked on their way through the glen, not to mention Geordie's cottage and two outbuildings within the walls. Three men lay dead while half a dozen wounded stumbled around the smoldering courtyard. The Armstrongs would seek their revenge, to be sure, and ride hot trod within the week.

Somewhere during the night, she must have fallen asleep, for she woke the next morning in one of the peel tower's chambers. No one else lingered about the room, so she splashed a bit of water on her face, steeling herself for the day ahead. Though still in a daze, she made her way down the spiral staircase to the courtyard, where she found her aunts busy taking toll of the damage.

"Good morning," she said, the gentle light of the early morning sun warming her shoulders.

"Good morn, lass," Emma said. She pulled a few salvageable herbs from her trampled garden and used an apron to wipe the soot from her hands. "Did ye manage a wee bit of sleep?"

"I think so, yes."

"The lads say the cottage should be repaired in a day or two. Till then, we'll sleep in the peel. 'Tis a mite crowded, to be sure, but it canna be helped."

"Me Sim's brought the chests over, if ye'd like to get into a clean gown," her auntie Janet added.

Maggie nodded. "Where did they take my father?" The words caught in her throat, but she managed to get them out.

"To the chapel, of course." Emma stood and blew her nose, once more employing her apron. "Yer aunties and I saw to him last night."

"Thank you, but I'd like to put him in his green doublet. He looks so handsome in it."

Emma's brows rose, and she shot a glance toward the other women before speaking. "He'll no' be needing it, darlin'. We've washed him and placed him in a shroud, even trimmed his hair and beard."

The lump in Maggie's throat swelled, tears welling in her eyes. "Oh . . . I see. It's just, in Lancashire, we dressed our loved ones in their best clothing when they passed, but it's better this way, I suppose."

"A strange custom that," Janet said, "and a waste of good clothes, I daresay."

"Aye, it is, but never mind." Marion took Maggie's hand in her own. "I've kept a bit of his hair for ye. Next time we go to market, we'll buy ye a bonnie locket to keep it in, eh?"

Maggie touched her chest, recalling her stolen amulet. She forced a shaky smile before replying. "I'd like that, but when will they bury my father . . . and the others?"

"No' till week's end at the earliest, darlin'," Emma said, "so the clan can gather and pay their respects. Alasdair's with him in the chapel, if ye'd like to visit."

Before Maggie could answer, Ian came through the barmekin gate driving a wagon loaded with all sorts of food, from sacks of oats to barrels of salted fish and ale. Maggie's temper flared, and she pulled away from her aunt.

"My father's not even gone a day and you're planning a feast?"

A touch of impatience colored Emma's tone. "D'ye no' feed those who come to grieve in Lancashire, lass?"

Maggie dropped her gaze and picked at a thread on her skirt, too ashamed to speak. A long-buried memory surfaced, a peaceful park-like field, flowers strewn across the ground, her father kneeling beside her, the pain in his soul etched on his face. Yet there had been food and drink after her mother's burial, and Eddie's father's too. She swallowed her caustic reply.

"Yes, of course they do. I'm so sorry. I didn't mean . . ." Tears broke forth once more from their tremulous dike. "I just can't believe he's gone."

Ian jumped from the wagon. "Dinna fash yerself, darlin'. I'll avenge yer da. Ye've me word on it, but first we need bury the dead."

Maggie forced another smile, but was revenge really what she wanted? More killing wouldn't bring her father back, wouldn't ease the pain that racked her soul and pierced her heart, leaving her cold and empty and, most of all, helpless. Robert had always been there, with his stories of rugged men and daring adventures. He'd made it all seem so exciting, but now she wished she'd never heard of the Scottish Marches. Now she just wanted to wake from this nightmare and find herself back home, with her father paging through some ancient text and whistling his haunting border tunes.

CHAPTER 22

Maggie stood between her aunts and listened to the priest pray over her father's body. His words echoed off the cold gray stone, the dour tones reflecting the mood of those gathered in the small family chapel. Even the day had turned dark and ominous, and she shivered when a blast of cold air blew through an open window

"We need leave it open," her aunt said, "so yer da's soul can leave this wretched world."

Maggie almost scoffed at Emma's prediction, finding the idea bizarre, to say the least. Did the soul really need an escape route? And if so, would closing it hold the deceased there forever? She loved her father, needed him, but she could never keep him from his heavenly reward. What kind of person would do that?

The raised voice of Father Lindsay, intoning the final prayer, jolted her from her musings.

"Into your hand, Father of mercies, we commend our brother Robert in the sure and certain hope that, together with all who have died in Christ, he will rise with him . . ."

Maggie's chin trembled, and she blinked to stay the tears. It would be good to get out in the fresh air, away from the stench of death and the overwhelming smell of incense, but saying good-bye to her father would take all the courage she could muster.

Alasdair and her uncles lifted the coffin and carried her father's remains through the church door. With a quivering breath, she pulled her plaid closed across her chest and prepared to follow, but her Aunt Marion touched her arm, holding her back.

"The men will go ahead, lass, right behind Alasdair and yer uncles. Truth be told, we shouldn't even go to the grave, but Geordie kens better than to try and keep us from it." She let a soft smile touch her lips and readjusted her bonnet.

Maggie nodded. What good would it do to argue? Though she resented being relegated to the rear, contesting her uncle on the subject could cause him to ban her altogether. And what did it matter? Her father still lived in her heart, not in a cold and dreary grave.

Craning her neck to see past the open doors, she noticed a tall, thin man with a bell who appeared to be heading the procession. As he marched along, he proclaimed Robert's name while Father Lindsay followed, saying a prayer.

"May the angels lead you into paradise, may the martyrs come to welcome you . . ."

"Auntie, the man walking in front of Father Lindsey, what's he doing?"

"He's the bell ringer, darlin', announcing yer da's death to the village. Those who wish to can join the procession as we pass. He did the same on his own yesterday, so the good folk would be ready when we came."

"Oh, how kind. I must remember to thank him."

Marion gave Maggie's arm a loving squeeze. "Geordie paid him to do it, lass. 'Tis the custom, ye see."

"Of course he did. I suppose he paid the villagers too?"

"Maggie! I ken ye're upset with yer uncle, but why would he do such a thing?"

"For appearances, why else? After all, how would it look if no one came to his own brother's funeral?"

A deep frown creased Marion's forehead. "Everyone pays the bell ringer, lassie, and in spite of what ye may think, Geordie loved yer da."

Maggie's cheeks heated with embarrassment. She had to control her twentieth-century responses, now more than ever. "I'm sorry. I didn't mean to say otherwise. I guess I just want to lash out at someone."

Marion released a soft sigh and nodded. "I ken ye do, darlin', but mind, Geordie truly does want to care for ye, the way yer da would."

I doubt it! The thought popped into her head before she could stop it, though she decided to keep it to herself. Instead, she steered the conversation elsewhere. "Do you suppose anyone from the village will want to join us?"

"Oh aye, I'd venture more than a few will be coming along to pay their last respects to Rabbie Armstrong. Yer da didna have much chance to mingle with the villagers of late, but there's many a man who'll remember him from his youth."

Marion's words warmed Maggie's heart. She swallowed hard, trying to keep her frazzled emotions at bay, and followed her kin through the barmekin gate.

The procession wound through the flowered glens and rolling braes of the countryside Robert so loved. Here and there, remnants of the recent attack mingled with signs of hope and endurance, the villagers salvaging whatever they could to make repairs. Yet no matter how busy they were, they stopped their chores and, to a man, joined the procession.

Maggie wept quietly, touched by the sight of so many turning out to mourn her father. A sob caught in her throat, but the resulting hiccup expanded into a full-fledged gasp when she spotted a group of men riding hard over a rise to the northeast. A knot of apprehension formed in her stomach, but her aunt calmed her fears.

"Dinna fash yerself, lass. 'Tis noucht but the Croziers from up near Hawick wanting to pay their respects, and yonder come the Grahams."

Maggie scanned the distant hills, stunned to see other small groups of rugged men thundering down the slopes, only to slow their pace and remove their signature blue bonnets as they approached the procession. A prickling at the back of her neck caused her to look to the south, and there on the crest of a moss-covered fell sat five riders. Her heart pounded out a frantic rhythm. Could it be Edward or Dylan?

Squinting hard, she studied the riders. Though she didn't know the first two, she recognized Edward straightaway, and Dylan's black hair stood out against his fair skin. Part of her wanted to tear up the hill and embrace them both, though another part wanted to scream at them for not being there when her father needed them. In reality, she could do neither, not if she didn't want to be branded a traitor or accused of something equally unpleasant.

Casting both possibilities aside, she considered the next rider. Her stomach lurched as Will Foster stared down at her, sending a surge of desire coursing through her veins. No, she wouldn't allow it. No matter how many butterflies attacked her insides, she would never forgive him. But what about Dylan and Edward? How could they ride alongside him? They must not realize he'd killed her father, for surely her uncle Eddie would run the scoundrel through himself if he even suspected it.

Will Foster's horse bucked a bit, and Maggie took a step back. *Like that will help if he decides to ride down here and carry you off.* Dylan took the reins, though, and the two men seemed to exchange words.

Maggie pointed to the hill where the riders still sat, stern and unflinching. "Isn't that Will Foster, Auntie?"

Marion's lips tightened in a thin line before she spoke. "So it is, the filthy swine, and I see he's brought his kin with him. To think our clans were such friends once, but even I canna forgive them what they've done here." Without another word, she crossed the lea, lifting her skirts to trudge up the gentle incline.

Geordie and a few of the other men drew their swords, but Andy stayed his brother's arm. "They're her kin, aye. Let her have her say. Graham winna harm his wife's niece, nor Walt his cousin."

With a hesitant nod, Geordie signaled to his men, and they all sheathed their swords, though he and Andy moved a few steps closer to the rise, their hands resting on the hilts.

Maggie couldn't take her eyes off their uninvited guests. She didn't recognize the ones Marion spoke to, but they both shook their heads. The younger of the two seemed to do most of the talking until her aunt swung around and faced Will. Whatever she said, the handsome reiver clearly denied it, but when Marion pointed her finger in his direction, his shoulders sagged, and he looked away. The one she'd been talking to first reached over to take her arm, but she yanked it away. They stood for a moment more, her aunt's fists planted on her hips, before the group turned and rode away.

Marion came stomping back down the hill, and though Andy stepped forward to comfort her, she shooed him off.

"We've a man to bury here today," she said, "so let's get back to it, aye."

The procession resumed, and after blowing her nose, Marion took Maggie's arm. "I told the lot of them off. The nerve of them, thinking they could just ride ower here, acting innocent as bairns."

"Perhaps some of them mourned my father too." Maggie's voice croaked, and she coughed to clear it. But when Marion lifted her eyebrows, she thought perhaps she should change the subject. "Who were the others anyway?"

Marion wiped a tear from under her eye and brushed her skirts off. "Ye kent Bonnie Will right enough, the murdering scoundrel. And him sitting there, with the face of an angel, denying it and all. Me auntie Betty ought wash his mouth out with lye for the tales he's been telling." She blew her nose again and continued, her color beginning to fade to its normal shade of pink.

"I didna recognize the dark-haired one, mind ye. Some friend of Will's, I reckon. But lovit be God, if Eddie Foster wasna there. I've no' seen him in ower twenty-five year."

"And who's he?" Maggie asked, hoping her voice didn't crack.

"A distant cousin of me uncle's from the south, if I mind right."

Maggie breathed a sigh of relief. So Eddie had settled in all right, and Dylan with him. "And the others?" she continued, refraining from any further comment.

"Me uncle Graham rode next to Eddie. Will's his youngest lad, and the one on this end was Walt, his eldest."

"You talked to him the most."

"Aye, there was a time I looked up to him. He introduced me to Andy, ye ken, and his sister Mary to yer da . . . Well, 'tis nae matter now. Come along then, lass, elst we fall behind."

Maggie followed, stewing over her aunt's words. They'd all been friends at one time, so what petty disagreement had turned them into such enemies? She clutched her fists, the heat rising in her face. Whatever happened between them, she'd no doubt Geordie Armstrong was behind it.

****

The procession wound its way to the back of the peel tower, and Maggie was shocked to find the barmekin yard so crowded with mourners. They stood on the stairs and along the parapet and overflowed into the surrounding countryside. Yet in spite of their number, not even a whisper could be heard when the priest began to pray over her father's body. Without being asked, the crowds parted, clearing a path so Maggie and her aunts could move forward.

A heavy cloud dimmed her senses as they place her father's lifeless body into the tomb carved into the hillside beneath the peel, and she let her mind drift to a happier time. Wonderful memories flooded her senses, and for a moment he stood beside her, laughing and joking, until Father Lindsay said the words she'd been dreading all day. The words that shattered her reverie and demanded she say good-bye.

"Eternal rest grant unto him, O Lord, and let perpetual light shine upon him."

A wave of nausea overtook her, and she leaned against her uncle for support, praying her knees would not give way beneath her.

"Ye all right, lass?" Andy asked in a whispered tone so as not to disturb the solemnity of the moment.

Maggie gasped for air, the world spinning around her. "I just don't think I can say good-bye."

"What if yer auntie and I walked up with ye, so ye could leave yer flowers, eh? Yer da would like that."

She let out a few calming breaths to steady her nerves and nodded, taking a tight hold of his arm. Though her entire body trembled, she stepped forward to place the small bouquet of rosemary and forget-me-nots at her father's gravesite. Others followed, and one by one they all made their way around to the front of the tower and up into the great hall.

Maggie sat at the dais with her aunts and uncles while kith and kin filled the rest of the large room. Her thoughts kept wandering off to the gathering Geordie held when they'd first arrived. She'd been so eager to take it all in, experience every moment, but now the very smell of it made her nauseous.

"Try to at least eat a wee bit, eh?" Marion said, her soft brown eyes filled with concern.

With a weak smile, Maggie took a piece of bread with a bit of jam on it. Her stomach groaned at the idea, but she forced it down, along with a drink of ale, hoping it would relieve her aunt's concerns. The woman meant well—they all did—and while Maggie didn't want to hurt anyone's feelings, she wished they would all just leave her alone for a while.

The strains of a border reel filled the room, her father's laughter floating on the melody, and a vise clamped tight around Maggie's heart. She'd managed to keep her tears at bay for most of the feast, but on hearing the drone of the pipes, they broke forth once more.

"'Tis noucht but our way of celebrating yer da's life," Andy said, passing her a handkerchief.

Still sniffling, she took the cloth and wiped her face before blowing her nose. "I know. I'm all right." She noticed Ian moving in her direction, and fearing he might ask her to dance, she made a quick excuse to disappear. "If you'll excuse me, though, I'm in need of the garderobe."

"Would ye like me to go with ye, lass?" Marion asked.

Maggie put on her bravest smile. "No, thank you. I'll be fine. It's just the bath . . . the garderobe."

Hurrying from the hall, she headed for the outside stairs. With any luck, they'd realize she needed the time alone and not come searching for her. The tears were flowing in earnest by the time she ran through the barmekin gates and down into the glen, where she collapsed beside the narrow burn, her heart breaking anew.

Though the sun had chased the clouds away, it did little to lighten her mood. She sobbed so hard her entire body shook, but all the pent-up anger and sorrow came flowing out. "It's all my fault. If I'd stayed in the tower, none of this would have happened."

A gentle breeze caressed her shoulders, bringing the subtle scent of Aramis aftershave with it. She sat up with a start, but no one stirred, let alone her father. And yet she could sense him there.

She closed her eyes and let the feeling embrace her. "I'm so sorry, Daddy."

Ach, dinna fash yerself, darlin'. 'Twas no' yer hand what did this. And he'd have ye as well, so take care who ye give yer heart to.

"Maggie, Maggie!" The voice sounded so far away at first that she paid it no mind, but when a hand gripped her shoulder, shaking it hard, she opened her eyes to find the worried countenance of her uncle Andy. At some point, she must have fallen asleep on the sun-drenched grass, for he knelt beside her, hugging her to himself.

"Lovit be God, lass," he said when he finally released his grip. "When ye didna return, we thought ye might be kidnapped. And then we saw ye lying here in the glen . . . God's teeth, lass. We thought ye raped or worse."

Maggie bit her lip. "I'm sorry, Uncle. I needed to be alone for a bit . . . Just me and Da."

Andy ducked his head, a spark of understanding gleaming in his gentle eyes. "And did he put yer mind to peace, then?"

She nodded, sniffling, and Andy came to the rescue with another handkerchief.

He hugged her again and helped her stand before shouting to those waiting at a distance. "All's well. The lass needed some time alone to say her farewells, noucht more."

Maggie gazed across the glen and blinked. The entire clan stood staring back at her. Some grumbled in annoyance, others shrugged their shoulders, and some bowed their heads the way Andy had, as if they understood. Ian waited a few feet away, his face pale and drawn, but he didn't approach.

Her father's words of caution echoed in her memory. *He'd have ye as well, so take care who ye give yer heart to.* Could it have been Ian he spoke of? She frowned, trying to make sense of it all. No, not Ian, but Will Foster. He'd wanted to take her the day he stole her amulet. She could see the desire gleaming in his eyes, but why hadn't he?

Andy stepped back, releasing her from his embrace, and gestured for Ian. "Come ahead, then, lad. 'Tis ye she'll be needing, I reckon."

Ian rushed forward and wrapped his arms around her, the warmth from his body chasing away the chill of the early evening air. He didn't say a word, just held her to himself, running his lips along the top of her head in the whisper of a kiss. His doublet felt soft and warm against her cheek, and his breath smelled of cinnamon bark.

He guided her a little way farther along the burn and sat beneath a gnarled old oak tree, pulling her down beside him. "I'll make the murdering blackguard pay, darlin', him and all his thieving kin. They'll rue the day they took yer da's life."

"You really believe it will help, don't you?" she asked.

Ian shook his head. "I ken it winna bring yer da back, lass, but 'tis noucht else I can think to do. It grieves me to see ye hurting so, and me powerless to ease the pain."

Maggie wiped his dampened cheek, the trail of a tear still present. Robert had never denied his emotions either. *The measure of a man is no' in how he hides his feelings,* he'd once told her, *but in how he owns up to them when they do manage to escape.*

Robert had taught her to be strong too, and she was determined to get on with her life. What other choice did she have? Edward and Dylan could no longer be part of that life. They were Fosters and Hetheringtons, and she couldn't stand the sound of their names. Where were they when Robert needed them, when she needed them? But Ian had been there, comforting her, protecting her, and it would be with him she made her new life. All thoughts of spiting Geordie died along with her father, and with him too, she would bury all thoughts of ever returning home.

CHAPTER 23

Will dismounted and swallowed the ball of dread rising in his throat. They'd pulled up just north of the border, stopping to water their hobblers, but he suspected his father might use the opportunity to lash into him about their recent encounter with Marion. Will heaved a weary sigh. The worst part was waiting for the axe to fall.

Granted, he should have mentioned the loss to his father, but he never suspected a missing dagger could cause so much trouble. It was just another bollock, plain enough except for one distinct feature—the Foster family crest emblazoned on its hilt, complete with the double octofoil that identified it as his alone.

He massaged the back of his neck, groaning as he reached for the flask on his saddle. Surely a dram or two couldn't hurt, given the circumstances. Taking a quick nip, he peered across the clearing to where his father and Edward stood, talking in hushed tones. Though the conversation seemed pleasant enough, deep creases lined his father's forehead, and worse yet, he'd begun to pluck at his beard, a telltale sign his patience had grown thin. When he gave his horse a pat on the neck and shoved the reins in Edward's hand, Will cast a glance in Dylan's direction.

"Don't look at me, mate," Dylan said with an emphatic shake of his head. "I warned you he'd find out."

Before Will could turn back around, his father slapped him hard across his left ear.

"What were ye thinking, ye wee dolt? Rabbie Armstrong stabbed from behind, and yer own dagger lost in the fray. God's teeth, lad! Did ye no' reckon the blame might, just might, mind ye, fall to ye?"

"I didna lose me dagger. I kent well enough where I dropped it."

"Fancy another skelp across the lugs, d'ye?" Walt asked as he came to stand beside their father. He spit out the piece of straw he'd been chewing and wiped his arm across his mouth. "Even our Marion reckons they caught ye with the red-hand."

"She should be listening to her own kin, then," Will said, "and no' taking the word of some scurvy Scot just because he beds her."

Walt's slap landed even harder than his father's.

With the distinctive sound of bells ringing in his ear, Will spun around, but before he could get a word out, his brother cut him off.

"Ye watch yer filthy tongue when ye speak of our Marion," Walt said.

"Aye! She's a good lass," Graham added. "And if she believes ye guilty, ye can wager 'twill be more than a sore lug ye'll be getting if the Armstrongs lay hold of ye."

Will bit his lip to keep from saying anything else in haste. The tips of his father's ears had gone bright red, and that was never a good sign.

"But I didna harm the man, Da. I swear it on me dagger."

"The one ye lost, ye mean," Walt said. "I'm of a mind ye need to be holding it at the time the oath is sworn."

Will drew his new dagger. "Aye, and this one will do fine."

"Enough, the two of ye!" Graham pinched the bridge of his nose. "Now tell us what happened with the knife, lad."

Heat rushed into Will's cheeks, causing his sore ear to throb all the more. "Sandie Rutherford gave me a right skelp across the wrist and knocked it from me hand, no' three feet from where Rabbie Armstrong fell."

"Ye saw who did him in, then?" Walt asked.

Oh cuds! Walt would never let this one go. "No' exactly. I had me hands full with Sandie, ye mind."

His brother huffed a sarcastic laugh. "Ah, right! And ye yanked that amulet from the wee scoundrel's neck, did ye?"

Will barely opened his lips. "Ye ken well enough who it belongs to, ye louse ridden toad, and Rabbie fell afore I even tried to snatch it." He spoke in a whisper, hoping his father would be too preoccupied to remember Marion's accusation about the amulet, but the man mumbled a few incoherent words and massaged his forehead.

"I'm neither blind nor deaf, ye blethering fools, nor am I so auld I dinna mind how a bonnie lass can catch a laddie's eye."

"I'm truly sorry, Da," Will said. "Ye taught me better than to let me heid wander so."

"Yer head, was it?" Laughter lit Walt's face, and Will shot him a warning glance.

"All right, Walter," their father said. "Ye've had yer fun, aye. As to the rest, there's nowt we can do about it now. Geordie will call us on it sooner or later, and we'll deal with it then."

"D'ye reckon they'll ride tonight?" Walt asked.

The glimmer of a smile crossed Graham's lips. "No' if I ken Geordie Armstrong. He'll honor the day, for his brother's memory. But he'll wait no longer than a day or two afore coming at us with all his might, so we'd best be prepared."

"Should I ride for me uncle Richie's, then?" Walt asked.

"Nae, we'll pass by there on the way home. When we get back to the peel, ye can get yerself something to eat and ride on to yer uncle Tom's after. Eddie, would ye mind getting word to the Hetheringtons?"

"I can ride to my own kin," Dylan said.

"Aye," Will added, "and if ye've nowt else for me, I can ride with him."

"I've asked Eddie, but have nae fear, ye'll no' be sitting on yer haunches, either one of ye. There's a roof needs patching, and ye're just the lads to do it."

Will opened his mouth to protest, but his father clamped a hand around the back of his neck.

"No' a word from ye, laddie. I ken right enough what's on yer mind, and I'll no' have ye riding to the Rutherfords on yer own."

"But I could get the scurvy limmer off by himself, force him to tell Geordie the truth of it."

His father tightened his grip, and Will winced. "Last I heard, I'm still laird of this clan, and I'm ordering ye and yer friend to bide where I tell ye. Go against me on this, and I'll take the whip to yer bare backs, same as I would any other who defied me command. Are we clear on this, lad?"

Will pressed his lips together and gave a quick nod. Considering his father's mood, anything more would be beyond foolish.

The man strode back toward his hobbler, but Walt lingered a moment. "I ken ye want to make Ian pay for what he did to our Annie, lad, but now's no' the time to challenge Da."

"Aye, ye taught me well there, Brother."

Walt patted Will on the back and went to join the others.

"Right then," his father said, "mount up, the lot of ye."

"Well, at least he didn't treat us like children," Dylan said. A sarcastic edge clipped his words, but mischief filled his eyes, and he continued on a more pleasant note. "What do ye say we wait a bit, and when they get busy preparing for Geordie, we can slip away and heid north."

"Ye're dafter than a one-eyed cock," Will said.

"Why? You sneak away all the time, and I've never seen you get more than a strap across the behind as you're darting out the door."

"Aye, when I didna heed me da, but this is different. He's made this decree as laird of the clan, no' me father, and given us fair warning to boot, so ye'd best no' go against him. Me brother Dennis tested him on it once, and no' even me ma could stay him from carrying out the sentence. 'Twill be a long time afore our Denny tries it again, I'll tell ye that."

Dylan's eyes widened, but he mounted his hobbler. "So I guess we'll be mending a roof, then."

CHAPTER 24

With their homes repaired and their dead buried, the Armstrongs prepared to ride once more, determined to inflict their vengeance on the Fosters. Maggie stood by the cottage doorway, listening to them make their plans and trying to comprehend why she so readily approved. Robert had taught her to be kind and forgiving, yet she found herself joining the cry for retribution.

Edward's words of caution flooded her senses. Life on the border could be hard, and the people here lived the only way they could to survive. Robert had instilled the same ability to endure deep within Maggie, and now that quality had come to the surface. A shiver ran through her body as she realized how much she was losing touch with her twentieth-century feelings. She tried to grab hold of them, but they seemed to hover just beyond her reach. A tear of regret trickled down her cheek, for she saw her own emotions reflected in Andy's angry expression.

"But why do we no' go tonight," her uncle demanded. "The moon will be full, and we can make a good ride."

"D'ye no' recall what we did this morn?" Geordie said.

"Aye, I mind well. All the more reason to ride hard and bring the fray to them afore they can gather their wits about them."

"Ach, use yer heid, man. D'ye think the scoundrels will no' be expecting us tonight? Nae, we'll wait a day or two, till the moon starts to wane and they think they're safe."

Andy wiped a hand across his face. "But if we dinna go tonight, we'll no' be in hot trod. The warden could take us to task for an illegal foray."

Geordie's features darkened. "And ye're of a mind what them Fosters did was legal, then, are ye?"

"'Tis no' what I'm saying, but there may be them what see it as such, given they rode hot trod against us."

Geordie flew from his chair and pounded on the table before him. "Hot trod or no', we left none of their kin dead."

"Ye're right there," Andy replied, standing to meet his brother eye to eye. "So why no' ride now and leave nae question about our right to do so?"

"For the love of God," Emma said. "Can ye no' see yer niece standing in the doorway, listening to yer every word? Ye buried her da just this morn, and now here ye are like a pack of wolves arguing ower a scrap of meat."

Andy glanced in Maggie's direction before dropping down on the bench. "As ye say, Brother, we'll ride in a day or two and strike when they least expect it."

Ian nodded his assent. "I'm riding with ye. 'Tis Maggie's father, and I canna let his death go unpunished."

"We'll all be riding with ye," Hob Rutherford added. He walked through the open doorway, stopping to put his arm around Maggie and give her a squeeze before continuing into the room.

Andy lifted an eyebrow, and Hob greeted him with a bob of his head. "'Twas our fight to start with," he continued, "and seeing as Maggie's soon to be one of our own, it still is, the way I see it."

"Ye're welcome with us, Hob," Geordie said, "but the contract's yet to be fulfilled. Ye're under nae obligation."

"Ach, nae matter. The weans will meet at the church door soon enough. If no' for this nasty business, the handfast would well be done."

The heck it would. Maggie sniffed her gown, hoping the vile creature's odor would dissipate soon. *Thank God Ian doesn't take after him.*

Geordie grinned and patted the large man across the back. "'Twill be good to have ye with us, Hobbie."

Andy did not seem quite so thrilled and cringed at his brother's words. Hob had no sooner taken a seat at his side than he crinkled his nose and announced he needed some air.

Maggie suppressed a giggle. Andy's reaction seemed a bit insulting, but the notion never appeared to cross Hob's ill-bred mind.

She turned and followed Andy into the crisp evening air. "You don't like him much, do you?"

Her uncle's pale blue eyes sparkled in the yellow glow of the torchlight, and he shook his head reluctantly. "Nae, Maggie, I dinna."

"And what about Ian?" she asked, the words coming almost by instinct.

Andy chuckled. "What d'ye think of him, lass?"

"You're just like my father." She grinned and put her arm through his, leaning on his shoulder. "Always answer a question with a question." From the moment she'd met him, he'd been her favorite uncle, for he reminded her so much of her father.

"Yer da and I were always close, even afore he left. We got on, nae matter what. I've lost a lot of brothers ower the years, and sisters as well, but none has hurt so much as losing yer da."

"You seemed like you wanted to raid the Fosters."

"Oh aye, I do that, but no' for the same reasons the Rutherfords do. I dinna trust them, Maggie. I never have."

"But you said Ian . . ."

"He'll make ye a strong husband, lass, provide well for ye, and the bargain has been struck. I guess I'm just picking up where yer da left off." He grinned, then cupped his hand over hers, and the smile dropped away. "But I want ye to ken ye'll always have a home with us, darlin', in case things dinna work out the way ye hope."

"Why wouldn't they?" Something about Andy's tone worried Maggie, though she couldn't put her finger on what.

"I dinna ken." He squeezed her hand, his countenance taking on an uncharacteristic intensity. "He's a reiver, lass, nae different from me or yer da there, but some are harsher than others, eh? No' many of us die a peaceful death. Some take their loved ones down with them. Things mightna be what ye expect."

"They will, I'm sure of it," she said, though the conviction in her voice didn't quite go beyond her words. "He really does love me."

"Aye, I reckon he does, though I canna help but wonder why wee Annie Foster turned him away so sudden like. Graham's no' the sort to let his bairns go back on their word."

"Connie says Annie lost her virginity, and not to Ian. They figured he'd send her back home when he discovered it and ruin her reputation, so they called off the betrothal, blaming it on his depraved behavior."

Andy released her arm, moving around so he could look her in the eye, his own blue orbs full of mischief. "Ach, well then, if Connie said it, it must be true, eh?"

"Now you're teasing me."

"Aye, I suppose I am, a wee bit anyway, but I'm nae better than yer cousin. 'Tis no' right for me to be judging Ian on one or two members of his family, now is it? Come and give us a hug, darlin'."

Andy wrapped his arms around her, embracing her a moment before stepping back and sighing. "I reckon I'd best be getting back inside."

Maggie shrugged, making no attempt to hide her disappointment. She liked talking to Andy and hated to see him end their conversation so soon.

"Can I move in with you, Uncle?"

"With me! And why would ye want to leave a comfortable cottage steps away from a peel tower to bide in a mere bastle house clear across the valley? No' to mention Geordie would be sorely hurt if ye did."

"Good!" Maggie said with a huff of contempt.

Andy rubbed the back of his neck. "What's caused ye to despise Geordie so, lass?"

Maggie collapsed on a nearby bench, and her uncle followed. "He doesn't care about any of us," she said. "We're nothing but pawns for him to use at will."

"That's no' true, Maggie, and yer da would be the first one to say it."

"My father did nothing but argue with him."

"Ach, 'twas their way, noucht more. I dinna think I've ever come across two more stubborn men, both too thick to admit they were wrong. But it disna mean they cared any less for one another." He leaned forward and stared into the darkening mist. "After yer da went missing, Geordie didna sleep for three days, looking for him. I doubt there's a brae or glen on either side of the border he didna search. Me ma began to fear him lost and all. Only her pleas brought him back, though it broke her heart to do so. Dinna judge him so harshly, Maggie. He does what he thinks best."

"He beat Alasdair." Maggie almost growled the words. "Just because we snuck away one night."

"As would I. Ye could've been killed. Alasdair kent better. A whipping's a small price to pay for yer lives."

"But I left him no choice. I threatened to go by myself if he didn't take me."

"There's always a choice, lassie," Andy said. "By rights, he should've told yer da."

"So Geordie punished him for not betraying me?"

Andy's face grew stern and hard. "Geordie punished him for doing what he kent was wrong. Dinna blame yer uncle for yer own guilt, and never put yer kin in that position again. Alasdair's to lead this clan one day. He must learn to do the right thing, nae matter the outcome, and so must ye."

Maggie had never seen her uncle look so harsh. Did she dare ask her next question? Determined to make her own decision on at least one point, she continued. "Will you take my father's place? At the handfast, I mean."

Andy brushed the hair back over Maggie's shoulder, and his smile returned. "Geordie will be the one for that. 'Tis only right."

"Right! For who? Doesn't a girl get to choose anything around here . . . Bad enough I've been designated a husband, now I'm to be told who I want to stand in for my father too."

"Ach, now calm yerself, darlin' . . . I reckon I'll still be there, eh, so what will it matter?"

"No! I won't do it! Geordie's not like my father at all, and I won't let him take his place! I don't care what you say. I don't care what anybody says."

Maggie raced into the house and up the stairs to her room. Though everyone glanced at her in expectation, she said nothing. If she spoke now, her words might see her behind beaten raw, or worse yet, relegated to the bowels of the peel tower. No, let her uncle explain in whatever fashion he liked, at least for the present.

****

"What's wrong with the lass?" Ian asked, attempting his most concerned expression.

"She misses Rabbie. Noucht more."

"Well, I hope she'll no' be carrying on like this much longer," Geordie said, "or young Ian here might decide he disna want her for his wife, after all."

"Ach, ye've no' fear of that happening, me laird." Ian twisted the blue bonnet he held squashed in his fists. "She holds me heart, ye see. Would it be all right if I went and talked to her a bit?"

"Go to her, lad," Geordie said with a laugh. "Mayhap all she needs is a good strong hand to put her in her place."

Ian headed to the staircase, but Andy stopped him at the foot, blocking his way. "Lay a finger on her, laddie, and they'll find ye floating in Solway Firth."

"I would never hurt her, sir," Ian hoped he sounded sincere, perhaps even a bit hurt by the accusation.

"Of course ye wouldna, lad. Keep it in mind, though, eh?" Andy held Ian's gaze for a moment before he stepped aside to let him pass.

Ian nodded and continued up the stairs, throwing an occasional glance to the floor below. God's teeth! Just how much did Andy know? What if he'd heard about Hexham or Carlisle? Worse yet, what if Rabbie had shared his suspicions?

He reached Maggie's door and breathed a sigh of relief, glad to be clear of the old scoundrel's scrutiny.

Keep yer head, ye daft loon. He'd have brought ye to task afore now if he suspected anything. And what if he does? Ye can put an end to him as surely as ye did his brother, and none would be the wiser.

Ian chuckled. After all, there was always another foray on the horizon, if need be. But for

now, his future uncle posed no threat. His palms still sweating, he knocked on Maggie's door and lifted the latch, but like a true Borderer, he hid his emotions well.

"Good eve, Maggie,," he said with a slight bow before turning to address her cousin. "Could I have a word with me intended alone, lass, if ye wouldna mind?"

"I think I'll go help me mother with the sewing," Constance said. She gave a slight curtsy before slipping past him and descending the stairs.

Maggie nodded, though she continued to sniffle while Ian sat by her side.

"What pains ye so, darlin'? Have I upset ye some way? Overstepped me bounds?"

"No, you've done nothing wrong." Maggie sighed and reached up to touch his cheek. "I just miss my father. Everything's so different here, but he always understood. He let me make my own choices."

Ian stifled a smirk. "Like who ye're to wed, ye mean?" He put his arm around her and kissed her on the forehead. "I told ye afore, darilin', I wouldna hold ye to any plans me da and Geordie made? I meant every word of it. Oh, I'd have ye for me own, there's nae denying it, but noucht unless ye wanted the same."

"Uncle Geordie thinks I could use a good whipping to put me in my place."

Ian couldn't stop himself from laughing. If she only knew what he had planned for her. But no, not yet. She needed to agree to the marriage first, to pledge herself to him at the church door.

"Ye're full of fire, I'll give ye that, but I wouldna change ye one bit, Maggie Armstrong. Any man would be glad to take ye for his wife. I'm surprised some outlander didna snatch ye up afore ye left Lancaster."

"Outlander?" Maggie laughed. "Why some outlander?"

"Ye dinna mean to tell me no' one of them rogues ever asked for yer hand?"

A blush rose in her cheeks. "No, and I'm fairly certain I would've remembered it."

"I ken they're a different breed down there, but are they daft as well?"

"A different breed!" The dimple in Maggie's right cheek deepened. "So that's all I am to you, Ian Rutherford?"

"Oh nae, Maggie, ye've got the Borders in yer blood. Yer da passed it on to ye—his legacy, ye might say—and ye can never lose it."

Maggie leaned against his shoulder, and he squeezed her closer to himself. God, he could take her right here and now, spread her shanks and ravish her right on her own bed, but her uncles would flay him alive for it. Nae, best to wait till she belonged to him.

"Besides, there's more to it than Geordie announcing our betrothal," she said, "which I haven't yet agreed to, by the way."

Stifling a frustrated groan, he suppressed his baser instincts. "Ah, right! Well, ye'll let me ken when ye do then, eh?" Let her think she still had something to say about it. He'd play along for the time being. "So what else is it yer uncles winna let ye have a say in?"

Maggie shrugged, but her forehead crinkled, and a spark ignited her soft brown eyes. "I don't want Geordie to take my father's place at the handfast. I don't even like the stubborn old mule."

Lord, she had a wicked tongue. He'd knock that out of her right enough when she became his to rule. For now, though, he must remain the besotted lover. "Oh . . . I canna contest yer uncle, darlin'. He's laird of the clan and yer eldest uncle, and with yer father gone . . ."

"But he's not the one I want!" Pulling away from his embrace, she jumped up and walked to the other side of the bed, where she stood staring out the window.

"Ye're making something of noucht, lass."

"Well, if it's *noucht*, there shouldn't be a problem letting Andy do it, now should there?"

"But . . . what does Andy say?"

Maggie groaned. "He's a Borderer too! What do you think he said? Isn't there one man here who will stand up to that pompous, domineering, tyrant downstairs?"

Ian ran his fingers through his hair, gathering the long strands together. "I've nae desire to start a feud ower this, lass."

"Oh, heaven forbid," Maggie replied. "Mustn't upset Geordie, laird of the clan."

God's teeth! Did she intend to force his hand even before the spousal? No, he was in charge here. Standing with a grunt, he walked up behind Maggie and wrapped his arms around her, resting his chin on her head.

"Maggie, what is it ye want me to do?"

She continued to stare out the open window, studying the barmekin yard and the countryside beyond, no doubt. He kissed her behind the ear, and her body relaxed in his caress.

"Whatever you want," she said at last. She turned in his embrace and heaved a deep sigh. "I do need some rest, though. Now you'd better go tell my uncles everything's fine, or they'll be up here themselves, ready to break down the door."

Not without a taste of what's to be mine, mistress. Ian kissed her again, his tongue probing deep within her mouth, exploring every crevice with slow, gentle strokes. He pressed her to him, lifting her so he fit into place like a button through its hole.

Maggie moaned, her arms tight around his neck, but he let her down and backed away. "Ye're right there. I'd best be going," he said, "afore I ravish ye here and now. Yer uncles wouldna be pleased, to say the least." He gave her another quick kiss and backed out the door, closing it as he went. For a moment longer, he stood in the hall, quite happy with himself. She would be a challenge, no doubt about it, but he'd tame her soon enough, and have a sizeable dowry to show for it.

****

Maggie sank down on the bed, Ian's kiss leaving her a bit weak in the knees. And yet, for all his bravado, when it came to Geordie, he was as much a wuss as any of them. Only her father had the courage to challenge the edicts of her overbearing uncle, and now he was gone, leaving her in Geordie's care. Why didn't he leave a will or something making Andy her guardian? *Because he thought there would always be time, of course.*

With her chin trembling, she blinked back the tears and gazed through the open gate at the deepening colors of the countryside. The moor shimmered with the blue-gray fog that engulfed it, wrapped tight around each tiny patch of earth like a baby's soft woolen blanket. The sight held an air of seduction, enchanting her and warming her soul, and somehow in that one moment, she understood why her father had been so desperate to return. It was his place, and it shone as brightly as the sparkle that had once filled his eyes. Indeed, the same slate blue filled them both.

But Maggie remembered seeing it in someone else's eyes as well, on the night her father died, brutally murdered by that very person. The pesky butterflies living in her stomach tried to escape again, and she jumped to her feet, slamming the cage shut on their wings.

What was the matter with her, getting all tingly over the murdering scum who had taken her father from her? For the life of her, she couldn't comprehend how she could be so appalled by Will Foster's actions, despising him and his name, and yet at the same time be enchanted by him. Even when Ian had held her to himself, not moments before, his mouth over hers in a passionate kiss, it was Will who flashed through her mind, unbidden and unwanted.

She shook her head, trying to expel him from her thoughts. *Be reasonable, Maggie, he's just a painting in your father's book, and a copy at that. You've never even had a proper conversation with him. It's animal attraction, pure and simple. He killed your father. Ian saw it happen, and he wouldn't lie about something so important. Besides, you saw Will Foster yourself, riding away from your father's fallen body. How could you ever be interested in anyone so cruel and callous?*

Once more, her father's words came rushing back to her. *He'll have ye too, lassie.* Well, she wouldn't let that happen, even if it meant marrying Ian Rutherford. After all, she did find him attractive, and though she wasn't in love with him right now, perhaps her cousin was right. The feeling would grow and blossom over time. Either way, he'd keep her safe from Will Foster.

CHAPTER 25

Maggie rolled out of bed and groaned. She'd spent another restless night, lulled to sleep at last in the small hours of the morning by the light of a waning moon and the low rumble of her uncles planning their next raid. Stifling a yawn, she pulled on her petticoats and struggled with an uncooperative bodice. The blasted thing pinched, but not as much as the heavy linen kirtle needed beneath the unstiffened top of her pale blue dress.

Staying in this century would require some getting used to. Loosening the laces a bit more, she pulled on her skirt and, after splashing some water on her face, hurried downstairs, mulling over her options along the way.

In the light of a new day, the future did look brighter. Her father always said you should sleep on things, but unless she mounted one of those horses and road off to England, managed to locate the right Foster peel, and found Edward, she didn't see how she had any real choices. The amulet was gone, along with her father, and her chances of ever finding Edward again were minimal at best.

A fresh batch of tears flooded her eyes, and she blinked them back. The thought of never seeing Uncle Eddie or Dylan again tugged at the hole in her heart, enlarging it. In truth, she'd lost them as well the day her father died.

She grabbed the newel post at the bottom of the stairs and shook off a wave of self-pity. Instead of dwelling on the impossible, she would make the best of her circumstances. After all, if she understood correctly, the handfast was a kind of trial marriage that either party could break at the end of a year. And in the meantime, she'd stay alert for any opportunities that might present themselves, unlikely though they might be.

Once again, her father's words echoed in her ears.

Mind St. Francis, darlin', and accept the things ye can do noucht about, change things if ye're able, and ask God for the sense to see the difference, eh?

Maggie smiled. He never did get the quote right, but the meaning always came through. "I'm trying, Da," she said, taking a deep breath to steel herself for whatever lay ahead.

The barmekin yard buzzed with activity. Her uncles hurried about, sharpening their weapons and donning what armor they owned while her aunts made sure they had food enough to sustain them through the long night. Maggie grinned when she spied Marion sticking an extra scone or two in her husband's saddlebag.

"Can I help with anything?" she asked Emma.

The woman brushed the flour from her nose and looked up, smiling. "Aye, ye can run down to the glen and fill those baskets with berries. I'm of a mind to make a few pies for the lads afore they ride. When ye've finished there, see what vegetables ye can find in the garden. Most have been trampled under, but ye might find a few yet. Lucky I'd already hung some up to dry."

Maggie smiled and picked up two baskets, but her aunt turned, wiping her brow with the back of her hand.

"Oh, and when ye've finished there, lass, would ye mind filling those flasks ower yon with some aqua vitae? No' too much, mind ye, or the lot of them will be tippled afore they even reach the border."

Maggie grabbed the bottle of golden liquid and took a sniff to double check. Yep, whisky! Her aunt was wise to advise pouring it with an easy hand. A few shots in each leather flask should be more than enough. She gazed across the table and sighed. There must be over a hundred of them. One bottle wasn't going to do it.

As if in answer to her thoughts, her aunt tapped her on the shoulder. "There'll be more in yon undercroft. When ye're ready, have Alasdair carry out what ye need, but mind the wee rogue disna take a nip or two on the way, aye." She chuckled to herself and returned to her dough.

Maggie scratched her head. If she didn't know better, she'd swear they were all preparing to go on a picnic or road trip, albeit one that could result in fatal consequences. She took another whiff of the whisky and headed off to pick some berries.

****

Her cousin Bess came to help and listening to the young girl's gossip made the day go quickly. Maggie had to laugh, recalling what she was like at thirteen. Some things just didn't change no matter what century you were in.

"Can I tell ye a secret?" Bess finally said.

"Yes, of course."

"I ken they're saying Will Foster killed yer da and all, and I'm sorry for that, but I canna help it. I wouldna mind him coming to pay me court."

Maggie's eyes widened. "And what would your da say about that?"

The girl snorted. "Ach, he'd send me to a nnnery for sure, but dinna fash yerself ower it. 'Tis nae more likely to happen than Connie wedding her Rory."

"Rory? I didn't realize she was betrothed to anyone."

Bess grabbed Maggie's arm and whispered, "Oh aye, but no' to Rory. Me da would go mad if he learned of it. 'Tis Archie she's to wed, as soon as he's able to build a good size house."

"Does Connie know about this?"

"'Course she does, and she kens well what she has to do, nae matter how that rascal Rory tries to convince her otherwise."

Maggie bit her tongue. "Hmm. Well, maybe your da will demand Will Foster marry you in reparation for killing my father. That seems to be the way it's done, isn't it?"

"Aye, sometimes, but I dinna see me da agreeing to such an arrangement. We've been feuding with them since I was a wean. And besides, even if Will were to consent to the terms, I dinna reckon 'twould be me he'd be choosing."

A cold chill caused Maggie to pull the shawl tight around her shoulders. "For heaven's sake, why not?"

"Ach, d'ye no' ken how bonnie ye are? And I'm but a wee lass with nae curves or bosom to speak of."

Maggie smiled. "A few more years and you'll have your pick of lads, Bess."

She shrugged. "Aye, 'tis what me ma says, but I dinna see it." She squished up her face and giggled. "I hope me da does find me a braw lad, though, and one who treats me as kind as he treats Ma."

Maggie refrained from saying what she was actually thinking. "I'm sure he will when the time comes." *One who'll be of some benefit to the clan anyway.*

****

By midafternoon, Maggie was back at the cottage diligently filling the empty flasks with whisky. The fumes almost made her giddy, but before long her cousin Connie interrupted. "Me ma needs help carrying supper ower to the peel."

"Is it that time already?" she asked, instinct prompting her to glance at her wrist for the time. A pang of homesickness struck her heart. So many little things gone forever.

And so many people. *Breathe, Maggie, in and out, slow and easy.* If she could only speak to Eddie. He'd know what to do, but how to get to him? Perhaps she could dress like a lad and sneak along on a foray. She remembered reading about women who'd done it in different wars. No, that would never work. With her build, they'd say she was just a lad and too young to go along.

Of course, she could always try flinging herself in Will Foster's path the next time his family attacked, but that could get her raped in the process . . .

or killed. She heaved a deep sigh. And for what? Edward would just want to send her back to the twentieth century.

She looked out the door into the barmekin yard and bit her lip to stifle a sob. In truth, did she really want to return home at all? There may not be running water or flush toilets here, but this was her family, her father's family. Who would she have in the twentieth century? Dylan wouldn't want to leave such an adventure, and Edward wouldn't abandon Dylan alone in another century.

What would her father do? Once more the prayer of St. Francis came to mind. *Hmph, easier said then done, Da.*

"Are ye all right?" Connie asked.

Maggie nodded and finished filling the last two flasks. "Right as rain."

Her cousin's brows furrowed for a second before she shook her head. "I suppose ye mean to say ye're fine, then." She pointed at a large cauldron of pottage sitting by the cottage door. "Alasdair can give ye a hand getting up the steps."

Maggie's mouth dropped. The cauldron had to weigh twenty pounds on its own, not to mention full of stew, yet her cousin lifted the one next to it with no trouble at all. Of course she did. Maggie took hold of the handle and, grunting, managed to get it into the yard before stopping a moment to stretch her back. If she intended to stay in this century, she'd need to work on building up her biceps.

After catching her breath, she began to shimmy her way across the yard and had made it halfway when Ian came up from behind and grabbed the massive pot.

"Give it here," he said, a slight scowl crossing his face. "What are ye doing, lass, lugging heavy kettles across the yard? Geordie has scullery maids for such chores."

Maggie wiped her sore palms on her skirt. "Only a few, and they've got their own chores to tend to. Besides, my aunts and cousins all pitch in, so why shouldn't I?"

"Aye, well, yer uncle needs to take a firmer hand with his help and no' be expecting his womenfolk to haul cooking cauldrons out to the peel."

Maggie stopped in her tracks, her fists clutched at her sides. "But it's all right for those poor girls to do it?"

Ian turned to face her, his forehead crinkled. "'Tis what they're hired for, darlin', and I'll tell ye straightaway, when we're wed, I'll no' tolerate me household help shirking their duties. Ye're to be me wife, no' a kitchen wench."

She kissed Ian on the cheek, and they headed toward the peel tower. "That's sweet, but just what would my duties be?"

"Ye'll be me wife, of course, and bear me bairns. And I'll expect ye to see me guests are made welcome. Ye'll be the lady of the house, after all."

Maggie stopped short once more, and Ian nearly tumbled over her, pot and all. "And that's it? My sole purpose in life would be to satisfy your needs and bear your children, a trophy to parade in front of your friends, but never an equal partner. Just your property."

Confusion filled Ian's green eyes. "I'm no' sure what I said wrong, lass. D'ye no' want to bear me weans?"

Maggie sighed. *Remember where you are, girl. No women's lib here.* "That's not what I meant. I just want someone who'll love me and respect me as much as I do them."

Ian shrugged one shoulder and stared down at the cauldron full of meat and vegetables, one side of his mouth hitching up in a smile. "Ach, darlin', I ken there's many a man who takes a woman for noucht but his own pleasure, to be at his beck and call, but I wouldna have ye think such of me. I mean to have ye for me wife, to love and care for ye, no' to make ye me servant."

"I know, and whether you believe it or not, my uncles are good to my aunts, even Geordie. They don't expect their wives to wait on them hand and foot, but when help is needed, my auntie's pitch in, not because their husbands demand it, but because they love each other."

Ian put the cauldron down and wiped the sweat from his brow with his sleeve. "I ken that, darlin'. Ach, I've made a right mess of things. Noucht came out the way I intended." He hung his head like a little boy with his fingers caught in a gumball machine.

Maggie giggled. "Don't worry. I understand, but if you don't get this pottage to the hall soon, my uncle may come up with his own ideas about what's keeping it."

Ian's lip curled and his eyes sparked with mischief, but a stern voice from behind cut off his response.

"On yer way, Ian Rutherford," Emma said. "I've seen that twinkle in a laddie's eye afore, and if ye've any thought to siring a bairn one day, 'twould be best if ye saw to the pottage and noucht more."

Ian bowed and, without another word, grabbed the kettle and hurried off to the peel tower, casting a look over his shoulder from time to time.

"Auntie!" Maggie tried to sound upset, but she couldn't help laughing.

"Ach, dinna fash yerself, lass. Ye need to put the fear of the Lord in them from time to time. Now let's get to the hall, or there'll be no' a morsel left for us to eat."

****

Much to Maggie's surprise, the atmosphere in the hall was relaxed and jovial. Little talk revolved around the upcoming raid, and her uncles bantered back and forth as if it were nothing more than another day's work. Then again, for them it probably was.

They ate a hearty meal, but before long Geordie stood and beckoned the men to follow him. With their bellies full and the sun sinking low in the sky, they bid farewell to their loved ones and mounted their hobblers, riding off in a rush of braying horses and barking dogs. Maggie touched her lips, the imprint of Ian's kiss still firm upon her mouth, but though the setting sun warmed her face, a shiver ran through her body.

She drew her plaid close around her shoulders, recalling all too vividly the last time they'd ventured out. Her father had ridden with them then, eager to join his brothers, robust and handsome in his leather jack and burgonet. How happy he'd been, so filled with life. A tear ran down her cheek, and she wiped it with the back of her hand.

Connie walked across the barmekin yard and stopped beside her. "Ye all right, Coz?"

Maggie shrugged, forcing a smile to her lips before sinking down on the small settle nestled against her uncle's cottage. "I'm just a bit tired."

After all, what else could be wrong? I mean, aside from the fact that my father's dead, I'll never see my home again, my hand's been promised to a man I hardly know, and the prospective groom has just ridden off to get himself killed. Yep, everything's peachy keen.

"Ye've nae need worrying about yer Ian, ye ken," her cousin said. "He's been on many a foray and come back unscathed."

Maggie's eyebrows shot up. She didn't think she'd spoken out loud, but then maybe Connie could read her mind. With all that had happened in the past few weeks, it wouldn't surprise her. She rubbed her eyes, trying to shake the cobwebs from her brain.

"I'm sure you're right."

"Of course I am." Connie breathed deep of the crisp evening air and, after squeezing Maggie's shoulder, bid her good night.

Maggie watched her cousin go inside, waiting for the door to close before leaning back against the cottage, welcoming the moment of solitude. With a sigh of relief, she pulled her feet up on the bench, rested her chin on her knees, and gazed out the barmekin gate.

Though the moon had started to wane, it still lit up the glen and the village beyond, giving it an almost preternatural glow. A gentle breeze carried the sweet song of a thrush, and the distant lowing of cattle echoed off the hillside. She closed her eyes, and if she listened hard, she could almost hear the rushing river tumbling over centuries-old rocks. A barn owl screeched from somewhere deep within the woods, injecting a bit of eeriness into the otherwise soothing scene.

Her mind drifted away, imagining what it would be like to ride on a foray, to feel the damp evening air whip through her hair and color her cheeks. At first, the idea made her laugh, but then the cold, hard truth crashed over her like storm waves against the shore. Riding to England wouldn't fill the emptiness in her heart, so what purpose would it serve?

True, Edward and Dylan would be there, but what comfort could they offer now? A home with the Fosters, the very people responsible for taking her father's life? The idea sickened her. She could go home, of course, provided Edward still had his amulet, but did she even want to anymore? Without her father, nothing would be the same.

None of it mattered anyway. A woman riding along on a foray was unheard of. Her uncles would never allow it. Few among them would permit such a deviation from tradition. Women were meant to cook and clean and keep a husband happy, no matter what Ian claimed, but to wield a sword and ride a foray across the border . . . Not a chance! And even if, by some miracle, she could convince the others, Geordie would still never concede, especially since her welfare had so recently become his concern.

Maggie opened her eyes. The prospect of being Geordie's ward caused her to shiver once more, though judging by the goosebumps on her arms, she suspected this time it had more to do with the late hour. The air had grown thick and damp. Even the heavy shawl no longer kept its icy grip at bay. And the mist crept around her feet, creating the otherworldly sensation of floating on a mystic island. She was so absorbed in her reverie she nearly fell off the settle when a sudden voice off to the side whispered in her ear.

"Up to bed with ye, lass, afore the bogie man reaches up and pulls ye under." Emma smiled. "Sleep has a way of pushing the time along."

Maggie clutched the shawl to her chest. "Oh, Auntie, it's only you."

"And who else did ye suppose it would be, with the menfolk away and the weans all to bed?"

"Um . . . well . . . not the bogie man, but . . ." The words seemed to stick in her throat. Her aunt would think her insane. Then again, they were a superstitious lot, or so her father used to say. Before she could continue, her aunt spoke.

"And if he did come, d'ye reckon he would do ye any harm, lass?"

A tear trickled down Maggie's cheek, and she shook her head.

"Then why would ye be afeared of him? He lived a good life, Rabbie Armstrong, and if ye can be good in this wicked world, how could ye be anything else in the next? They're all around us, ye ken, watching ower us, so why shake with fright if we catch a glimpse of them on an eerie summer's night?"

Maggie leaned into her aunt's shoulder and cried—a deep, cleansing cry—and the woman let her. Emma said nothing, but Maggie welcomed her warm and comforting presence. She hadn't felt so safe, so loved, since her father left this world, and for that she was grateful. Finally, she sniffled, pulling a handkerchief from her sleeve and wiping her nose.

"Tears cleanse the soul," Emma said, her voice soft and lilting. "'Tis what me ma always told me. Now to bed with ye, or ye'll be useless when the lads come home."

CHAPTER 26

As the first wisps of daylight broke through the morning haze, Maggie searched the horizon for any sign of the clan's return. In the distance, a curlew squawked, and she tilted her head, listening for the steady drum of hoofbeats. With a sigh, she flopped back down on her bed, for she heard nothing save the muffled moan of grazing cattle.

Taking a deep breath of the crisp morning air, she flung her legs over the edge of the bed and scrubbed a hand across her face. She glanced over at her Connie and shook her head. How could she sleep at a time like this?

A cool breeze blew through the window, chilling her bones, and she pulled on her green woolen dress. Lord, how she missed waking up covered in a thin layer of sweat with her sheets tangled around her feet. She'd throw on a bathing suit and head for the beach to cool off in the ocean.

Of course, it had all changed when they moved to England, but even there the heat would kick in if it got too cold. One thing her father had demanded when they arrived in Lancaster was a house with central heating. And the estate agent had located one.

Maggie sighed as she recalled what it felt like to be comfortably warm all the time. She'd hoped the mornings would be warmer in August, and she supposed they were. Still . . . On that optimistic note, she hurried downstairs to help her aunt with breakfast.

"Good morning, darlin'," Emma said. "Breakfast will be ready in a wee bit. Would ye go and wake yer cousins for us? I swear they'd sleep through a horde of reivers riding hot trod into the barmekin yard if I let them."

Maggie rolled her eyes. She found it odd that anyone could sleep at all under the circumstances, but her aunt had already returned to ordering the serving girls about, so she kept it to herself. Stifling a sigh, she bit her lip and climbed upstairs to rouse her cousins.

She ran in and pulled the blankets off their slumbering forms. "Time to get up," she said with a giggle before hurrying back down to the warmth of the hearth and a hot bowl of porridge.

After breakfast, Emma and Connie went about their morning tasks, chatting about nothing more serious than Alasdair's recent infatuation with Rachel Elliot. If they were worried about their men, they didn't show it. Could they really be so devoid of emotion?

Maggie helped one of the serving girls churn some butter, and after watering what was left of the garden, she wandered down along the river, sitting on its banks in hopes the gentle motion would inspire serenity. On the contrary, it only reminded her of her father and how much she longed to be near him, to once more feel his gentle caress. Overwhelmed by the sense of loss, she slipped around to the side of the peel, to the enclosed graveyard behind the chapel, and began to read the names engraved on the stone tomb, where her father had been laid to rest.

Nanse Armstrong - died of fever - b. 1491 d. 1492

Eckie Armstrong - fell from tree - b. 1488 d. 1497

Christie Armstrong - died of fever - b. 1511 d. 1520

Denis Armstrong - slain by the Bells - b. 1506 d. 1521

Jamie Armstrong - cut down in his youth - b. 1502 d. 1521

Morag Armstrong - died of fever - b. 1521 d. 1521

Sandie Armstrong - died of fever - b. 1520 d. 1521

Maggie Armstrong - w/o John Graham - died in childbirth - b. 1504 d. 1528

Geordie Armstrong - s/o Geordie Jr.- found murdered in Liddel Water - b. 1510 d. 1531

Geordie Armstrong - s/o Sim - drowned in river - b. 1532 d. 1534

Ross Armstrong - slain in battle - b. 1518 d. 1535

Maggie Elliott w/o Geordie Armstrong - Beloved Mother - b. 1464 d. 1538

Robert Armstrong - slain in cold blood - b. 1493 d. 1538

Maggie couldn't read any more. Most hadn't even reached adulthood. No wonder her grandmother had viewed death with such a sense of peace. She was going home to her children.

"They're no' all here, ye ken." Connie slid down the gentle embankment and sat next to Maggie.

"No, I suppose some are buried beneath the smaller gravestones."

"Aye, but that's nae what I meant."

"What do you mean then?"

"Me Grandda, he died in the war, and quite a few of me uncles are buried elsewhere, as well as me brothers Francie and Rory."

"Where are they?" Maggie asked.

"Grandda's somewhere ower the Border, I reckon, by Flodden Field, and me uncle Alan, he rode for Hexham one day with his friends and none ever returned."

"And the others . . . I heard my father speak of Angus and Davie."

"Oh, they're up by Carlanrig."

"They live there?" Maggie asked, wondering if she'd overheard wrong.

"Nae, Cousin, they died there." Connie stifled a laugh.

Maggie's cheeks burned. How naïve could she be? "Oh, that's what I thought my da said, but how did they die?"

"Hanged, they were. I'm no' sure why. I'm no' sure anyone is."

"Don't you care?" Maggie blinked, taken aback by her cousin's casual attitude. She could never be so nonchalant about death, especially when it concerned those she loved.

"I was but a wean when it happened," Connie said. "I mind a big stir ower it, but me ma dragged us all out of the room afore it got going. I found her crying once, though she pretended 'twas something in her eye. She worrit about me da, though, I ken that plain enough."

"Did they have families?"

"I'm no' sure about Davie, but me Uncle Angus did. In fact, ye met our Jamie the night of the Gathering, and ye tended Donald's wound during the last fray, though their brother Angus followed his da to the gibbet no' a year past. He couldna have been much older than us and married just under a year."

"And they hanged him?"

"'Course they did. Caught him with a red-hand, the wee fool."

"But surely the punishment wouldn't have been so harsh if he was younger, say Alasdair's age?"

Connie's brows furrowed. "What's age to do with it? The lads are born to the saddle, and as soon as they can rightly lift a blade, they join in the fray."

"Andy seems to think it matters . . . age, I mean. Those boys they captured in the last raid. He said they were just lads."

"Some hearts are larger than others, eh? I ken 'tis hard for ye, Maggie, to understand the way we live. Cordial enemies, I reckon ye'd call us. We hate the English, and yet we marry them. We rob from them, and still we celebrate with them. We're different from the rest of Scotland here. In truth, the English just beyond the border are closer to our own kin than those Scots living in the Highlands. 'Tis much the same on the English side, I expect."

"Outlanders, Ian calls them."

"Aye, I guess they are. And they welcome us as little as we do them. So ye see, though we may fight with those of the English Marches, we can never truly forsake them, for we're of one spirit . . . kin, ye might say, in more ways than one."

"I'm trying to understand, but it's not easy. What about your brothers though? I didn't realize you had so many."

"Oh aye, four of them, no' counting Alasdair, and another sister besides."

"What happened to them?"

"Me sister Christie, the fever took her, like it says, when I was noucht more than a bairn. And Geordie, he got himself murdered one night while riding home to his new bride. To this day, we're no' sure who did it. Me da's of a mind 'twas the Fosters' doing, for one of their own wed the lass no' long after."

"So that's what started this feud?"

Connie shrugged. "In part, I'd wager, but I canna rightly say, being nae more than twelve or so at the time. I expect there's more to it, though. Noucht is ever as simple as it seems."

Maggie stood in silence for a moment, staring at the worn gray stones before leaning over to brush some dirt from the top of the nearest one. "What happened to the others, then?" she asked. "You said there were four."

"Aye, Francie, he died during a feud with the Johnstones, as did Ross, though they never did find Francie's body. And the warden hanged Rory the same day as me cousin Angus." Connie sniffled and wiped a stray tear from her cheek.

A wave of relief washed over Maggie's heart. At last, her cousin showed a bit of emotion. "Did he have a family too?

"Oh aye! Kitte birthed his bairn almost the verra same moment, they say. I mind the day well. 'Tis the only time I've ever seen me da cry. He hid it well, mind ye, taking off by himself to walk along the river, but even I could see the worry on his face. It left him but one son to carry on as laird of the clan, ye see."

"It would be all your father cared about," Maggie said

"That's no' fair, Maggie. With yer da gone, leaving nae male heir, and Andy's bairns so young . . ." Connie groaned, her exasperation showing. "He had to think of who would lead the clan should something happen to him and me uncles. 'Twas no' his own welfare weighing on him, but ours. Ye just dinna understand, Maggie."

"I suppose not," she said, not quite ready to let her uncle off the hook. She opened her mouth to argue further, but a blast of damp morning air brushed across her shoulders, causing her to shiver.

"Me ma says that's the lost ones coming home," Connie whispered, a twinkle lighting her hazel eyes. "What d'ye reckon?"

"I don't believe in ghosts." Maggie forced herself to laugh, though in truth she did wonder, particularly when the hair on her neck began to tingle.

"Come on, then, the washing needs doing."

Maggie smiled and made her way back to the cottage to help Connie and her mother with the laundry. Thank heavens the servants had taken the clothes out of the bucking tubs and run them through a few rinses already. The pungent stench of urine and lye made her eyes water. No wonder they kept the washtubs close to the barmekin wall. All they had to do now was rinse them in water a time or two and spread them out to dry beneath the warm afternoon sun.

Connie passed her a bar of lavender-scented soap, and she took a sniff. Much better than her uncles' pee. She grimaced and threw a linen shirt in the washtub. At least Geordie spent a few dollars on decent soap, but come to think of it, Emma did get pretty much whatever she wanted from him. Of course, her aunt never asked for much either. A smile crossed Maggie's lips. They really did love each other, and yet her aunt didn't show the slightest signs of concern about the danger he faced.

Grabbing another shirt, Maggie plunged it into the washtub and scrubbed. Why did her nose always itch at the most inopportune times? Not wanting to get dirty water and soap all over her face, she looked up to wipe it with her sleeve. As she did, she caught a hint of anxiety flicker across her aunt's eyes.

Emma smiled, clearing her throat and brushing off her skirts before she lifted the large wicker basket and headed for the barmekin gate, but Maggie touched her arm, stopping her.

"Don't you feel anything? Your husband may be dead, and you're afraid to show even a slightest bit of worry."

Emma put down the basket with a sigh and shoved back a few stray strands of hair.

"Oh, darlin', d'ye think me heart so hard? Of course I fret about him. Every time they ride out, I wonder if he'll come home, but I canna stop me life. What of the weans? 'Tis the way of things here, and ye learn to live with it, or it will destroy ye. It disna mean I feel noucht, only that I go on and treasure whatever time we may have."

"Will they be back?" Maggie glanced across the glen and clutched the small cross she wore around her neck.

"Some will always return, staggering in, wounded and dying, though they may be. That's the worst time, ye see. When they ride through the gate, and ye strain to see yer loved ones, praying they've made it back, afeard they've been taken, or worse. 'Tis then, darlin', ye ken ye have a heart, for it'll nearly push itself right through yer breast."

Smiling once more, she touched Maggie's cheek before bending to pick up her basket. "Ye've nae need to worry about that Ian, though. He's a cunning one, and I'd wager me best silver he'll come back . . . even if others dinna," she added, a cold edge to her voice as she continued toward the gate to lay out the washed clothing.

Maggie started to ask her aunt what she meant, but the woman had stopped in her tracks. Something had drawn her attention, and Maggie spun around, following her gaze, listening for the sound she'd grown so accustomed to. At last, she heard it, the distant thunder of hoofbeats. She dropped the shirt she was rinsing out, using her apron to dry her hands, and said a quick prayer. "St. Michael the Archangel . . ."

Within moments, the riders came into view, shouting and driving about twelve head of cattle through the barmekin gate, along with two blond-haired boys a good deal younger than Alasdair.

"Look what the Fosters send to protect their homes." Geordie threw one of the young men to the ground and laughed. "What d'ye reckon, will he bring any ransom at all?"

"It'll bring the wrath of me family upon ye, Geordie Armstrong," the boy shouted in defiance, but a kick from Ian's boot silenced him at once.

"Send word of the ransom," Geordie said. He lifted the boy from the ground and dusted him off. "But dinna make it too sweet, or we'll never be rid of these two fine specimens of English manhood."

"Curse ye." The fallen lad pulled away from Geordie. "Me grandsire will pay whatever ye ask, right afore he slits yer throat."

"So he will, laddie." Geordie chuckled and nodded for Andy to take them to the peel tower.

Maggie tried to join the frivolity, reminding herself what their family had done to her father. She stared at them in defiance, but as the boys passed, she could see the hate and fear written in their own expressions. A sudden wave of guilt shook her. With her resolve wavering, she turned to Ian and frowned, not sure she liked the smirk curling his lips, but he didn't even notice.

Without a moment's hesitation, he strode over and put his arms around her waist, lifting her and pressing his lips against hers in full view of kith and kin.

Though he took her breath away, she managed to squirm free. "Ian!" she said, surprised by the sharpness of her own voice.

"What?" He rested her back on the ground and laughed. "Does a brave soldier no' deserve a kiss from his betrothed?"

"It's not that, Ian . . . Did you need to kick him so hard? He's only a child."

Ian's grin dropped away. "He's a Foster, mistress! I'd have thought ye'd be the last to defend him."

"I'm not defending him. I just don't see any need to be so cruel."

"Then perhaps ye dinna belong here on the Borders. Mayhap ye should go back to yer own people."

Ian's tone had grown cold and hard, and it startled Maggie. She'd never heard such anger in his voice, at least not when he was speaking to her. Sheer indignation must have shown on her face, for in the very next breath his demeanor softened, and he brushed his fingers across her forehead.

"I'm sorry, lass. I'd nae call to speak to ye thus. 'Tis just when I think of Rabbie . . . How much it hurts ye . . . I canna even stand to gaze upon them. Do ye forgive me, lass?"

Maggie nodded, for she couldn't deny the anger she too continued to harbor deep within her heart. The memory of her father's death caused streams of tears to burst forth, and she buried her face against the coarse leather of Ian's jack. He held her close, combing his fingers through her hair and kissing the top of her head.

Though she responded to his touch, snuggling closer in his embrace, the effort was halfhearted at best. She missed her father, and all of Ian's tender gestures did little more than provide a temporary shelter from the memory of his death.

****

They had a late supper that night, but Maggie picked at her food, shoving it from one side of her trencher to the other. She didn't know what to think or feel anymore. Ian came over and put his arm around her shoulders, and she sighed. Couldn't he leave her alone with her thoughts, just for a little bit?

"Will ye walk with me, Maggie?" Ian's breath brushed her ear, and she rested against him, surrendering to the inevitable. The warmth of his body provided a haven against the cool air, and yet something uncomfortable lingered in his caress. Something hard and detached.

"What's troubling ye, darlin'?" he asked as they walked down to the river. "No' me hasty words, I pray. 'Twas the fire of the fray still burning within me, noucht more."

"It's not you, Ian . . . It's these . . . English boys . . ." She blew out a steadying breath. How could she explain the tangle of emotions tumbling around in her head and her heart? She didn't understand it herself; what made her think Ian would, especially the way he felt about the Fosters? Her father would have known what to say, how to clarify everything for himself as well as everyone else, but Ian would just presume she'd lost her mind . . . or worse.

"The prisoners! The wee scoundrels would plunge their daggers in yer gut as soon as look at ye. Ach, darlin', ye let yer emotions rule too much of yer life, and I fear 'twill bring ye to harm one day."

Maggie pressed her lips together, her hands balling into fists. What did Ian know! Her father had always told her to follow her heart, and if she did, she couldn't go wrong. She blinked to stay the tears and let her fingers unfurl. And what did it get him but a cold grave? Perhaps Ian was right, and yet . . . Could she be happy not allowing her heart to show her the way? She pulled from Ian's embrace and sat on a rock beside the river.

"Ye're no' saying much tonight, lass." Ian threw a pebble into the river and turned to face her. "I did ask yer forgiveness for me harsh words. Is this to be me punishment, then? No' to hear yer sweet voice speak to me ever again."

"No, of course not." Maggie forced herself to smile. "I'm concerned, that's all."

"About what, lass? The lads will be home again in a day or two at most. Graham's sure to pay the ransom for his grandsons."

"It's not the boys I'm worried about. It's me. I'm angry and lost, and my da's not here to guide me."

He cupped her cheek in his hand. "I'm here for ye, darlin'. All ye need do is ask."

A cold breeze blew off the river, and Maggie cast a glance out over the water. Hmm. That came out of nowhere.

"Maggie! Did ye hear me?"

Maggie blinked and turned back to Ian. "What? Oh yes, I know, and I will, but right now what I need more than anything is a good night's sleep."

Ian kissed her again. "Come on, then, we'd best be getting back." He took her hand and they walked back toward the peel tower. "If we were already wed, I could take ye to me bed and chase away the bad dreams." He wrapped his arm around her and squeezed her to himself. "But never mind, we're to meet afore the church door in a fortnight."

"A fortnight? But my father just died."

"Aye, all the more reason to get on with it. Ye'll be needing someone to care for ye."

"I thought Geordie was supposed to be doing that." She pulled away from Ian and walked through the barmekin gate, but Ian reached out and grabbed her arm, squeezing it tight.

"D'ye no' want to wed me, then?" The nearby torches highlighted the tears in his eyes, touching Maggie's heart.

"I'm sorry, Ian. I don't mean to hurt you, but the only thing I know for sure right now is that I need some time to grieve. Why can't anyone understand what I'm going through?"

"I understand it, lass, and I'm sorry we didna get Bonnie Will for ye. That auld fox Graham lay in wait for us. We'd all we could do to grab a few scrawny kye and be on our way. If Walt's lads hadna crept out to take a keek, we wouldna have them either. Of course, Alasdair will be sore for a few days, but he'll survive."

"What do you mean, he'll survive?"

"One of the lads drew his sword when we took hold of him and slashed Alasdair in the thigh. Caught more breek than flesh, but his ma will need to tend it."

"I'd better see if I can help."

"He'll be fine, darlin'. Me brothers have given me far worse with a tournay sword. But go, then, and get some rest, eh? Grieve for yer da, and when ye're ready, perhaps I'll be waiting for ye." He kissed her on the forehead. "Or mayhap no'." With those final words, he turned, fading into the rising mist.

CHAPTER 27

Ian was furious and rode his pony hard all the way back to his father's peel tower. He shoved the animal at his groom when he arrived. "See to the creature, ye worthless lout!"

"Aye, me laird," the scrawny boy said.

The fifteen-year-old looked incapable of taking care of himself, let alone the animal, but they couldn't afford anyone better at the moment. God's nails! This marriage to the Armstrong whore was important. His family needed the alliance, and he needed her land if he intended to wield any sort of authority in this godforsaken territory. Granted, she wasn't hard on the eyes, and she had a good, slim figure with shapely hips sure to bear him a litter of strong sons, but she could be headstrong and obstinate as well. Not to mention her misguided idea about a woman having the right to her opinion.

He snickered. Aye, he'd beat that out of her soon enough. Once they were married, she'd be his to do with as he pleased, and her kin would have nothing to say about it. Let them try and come between the business of a man and his wife.

He sat on the bench beside their peel and stretched out his legs, imagining what she might be like in bed. Her kiss held promise. She let him put his tongue all the way in and didn't recoil from it like auld Davie Milburne's scullery maid. He'd had to slap that wench into submission. No,

Maggie didn't seem repulsed by his touch at all. She'd prove quite satisfactory in bed and keep him entertained, for a while at least.

But this incessant hesitation about coming together outside the church door worried him. What if her uncle found someone who could bring more to the clan? Or worse yet, what if his dalliance with Annie Foster came to Geordie's attention?

He took a deep, calming breath and smirked. No, the dagger he'd plunged into Rabbie Armstrong's back ended any danger of that. And by placing the blame on Bonnie Will, he'd ensured the feud between the two families would continue.

Odd how fate worked sometimes. His father had started the feud, quite by accident, years before when he'd robbed and murdered young Geordie Armstrong. Alan Foster marrying the widow within months of her husband's death had raised more than a few eyebrows and the promise of retribution from his family. When Alan turned up dead a few months later, murdered in a similar fashion, the Fosters had no doubt who they should blame. And now Graham Foster's bairn had dropped his dagger right at Rabbie Armstrong's feet. What more could Ian ask?

He shook his head, a quiet chuckle rumbling in his throat. No, his secret would remain safe . . . unless—a new possibility struck him, and he frowned.

Andy's wife, Marion, could be a definite problem. She was a Hetherington, and those rogues rarely swayed in their loyalty to auld Graham Foster. If she decided to speak in Will's defense . . .

A hand touched his shoulder, and he jumped.

"Ye all right, Brother?" Sandie Rutherford asked. He sat beside Ian and spit in the dirt.

"It's me betrothed. She seems to balk every time I mention the handfast. I'm afeard word of me wee tryst with Annie Foster might have reached her ears."

"Ach, and what if it did? After Rabbie's death, I doubt the Armstrongs will be putting much store in anything the Fosters say. And mind, me da gave that dagger of Will's to Geordie, with Rabbie's blood still on it."

"It might have been anyone's blood, ye ken. D'ye reckon the Armstrongs winna consider that?"

"Aye, but I made sure Andy saw it sticking out of his brother's back." Sandie grinned and spit again.

Ian shrugged. "True enough, but it disna mean Bonnie Will put it there, now does it?"

"Look, Brother, the Armstrongs and Fosters have been at each other's throats for nigh on to eight year now. With Geordie holding Bonnie Will's bloody knife in his hand, and Andy seeing it for himself in Rabbie's back, they're no' about to question who's to blame, especially with the two of us saying we saw the rogue do it. And if they need more convincing, there's always Da's threat to file a bill against them if the betrothal isna honored. So ease yer mind, man. Geordie winna be backing out of the arrangement on the word of some Foster."

"Ye ken Da's bill against Geordie will never haud up. 'Twas no' even our cattle."

"But Geordie will never find out, now will he, ye daft fool. No' unless the complaint is filed, so ye've noucht to fash yerself ower."

"Aye, I suppose ye're right there. But Maggie could still turn her uncles against me, Andy in particular. I'm afeard he already has his suspicions."

Sandie chuckled. "I imagine he might, but even he's no' going to put much store in the word of one wee lass, now is he, or the vile scoundrel what murdered his brother? 'Twas a canny move on yer part, Brother. Besides, if Rabbie's lass is so much trouble, why d'ye no' take another in her place? Geordie's a fine daughter of his own, ripe for the picking."

"Aye, he does, and she's been all but promised to Archie Elliot, ye blethering swine."

"Ach, nae matter. Arch could meet with a wee bit of trouble himself, a bucking hobbler say, leaving him with a crushed skull."

"Ye truly are a wee ideot! Too many accidents and auld Geordie's sure to look deeper. I canna chance another incident."

"Then ye'd best control yer pisle, brother. Even if ye do meet the lass afore the church doors, 'tis but the handfast. Ye'll need to keep yerself in check for another year, elst her uncles will end the union."

"True enough, but 'twill be nae problem taking me pleasure with the wee strumpet for a year or so. I'll see her plump with a child in nae time, and when the nuptials are done and she's mine by law, I'll do as I like. After all, she brings a hefty dowry and the promise of an alliance with the Armstrongs."

"Ye reckon her uncles will rally to yer call when they learn she's noucht more than another of yer whores? They mayna be able to take her from ye by law after the wedding, but they dinna owe ye any allegiance either."

Ian waved off his brother's concerns. "She'll be well on her way to birthing a bairn by then, and if she thinks to open her wee gob, I'll thrash her a time or two and keep the wean from her. She'll come round soon enough, and the Armstrongs will have nae notion of how I'm treating their niece."

Sandie smirked and patted Ian on the back. "So ye've noucht to fash yerself ower, man. 'Tis but a fortnight to the spousal, and after Red Rabbie's death, Geordie will be anxious to get the lass off his hands. Just keep yer pisle in yer breeks for a wee spell, aye, unless 'tis with the lass herself, of course."

Ian let a smile cross his face, the concern lifting from his shoulders. "Aye, she's bonnie enough to hold me attention for a year or so, and I've been promised a virgin, so her towdy should be good and tight." He took the flask from over his shoulder and lifted it to his lips, drinking deep of the potent elixir. "Here's to us then, eh, Brother?"

****

Maggie watched the sky grow darker, but she loathed the idea of heading up to bed. She could go in to see how Alasdair was doing, but then again, maybe she'd better not. From what Ian said, the wound was in a delicate spot, and her cousin might not appreciate her walking in on him with his private areas all but exposed. Instead, she slumped down on the bench outside the cottage door and waited.

She had just settled down when Alasdair came out and sat beside her, his forehead crinkled.

"I dinna ken why me ma made such a fuss ower me wanting to show Rachel me wound. After all, if she's to be me wife, she should be aware I'm no' without battle scars."

Maggie suppressed a giggle, clearing her throat before speaking. "I imagine she's more concerned about Rachel seeing other things before you wed. It may be on your thigh, but it is rather close to your . . . um . . ."

Alasdair laughed. "Ach, she's already seen me . . ." His face went white. "I meant to say . . . Ye winna tell me ma, will ye? We've no' done anything yet. Just a wee touch here and there. I ken she needs to be a virgin and all, though I dinna see why when I'm the one she's to wed anyway."

"But what if you're not? If I recall, your da hasn't finalized any agreement with Rachel's father."

Alasdair folded his arms across his chest and scrunched down on the bench, his frown deepening. "Nae, he says I've a lot to offer a lass, being in line as laird of the clan and all, and he wants to make sure I take a wife who can bring an equal portion to the marriage."

"But the Elliots are a strong riding name, or so I've heard, so why wouldn't he want the alliance?"

"Oh, he likes the alliance right enough, but Rachel's the second daughter, ye see, and well . . . Tis no' the alliance what troubles him so much as the dowry."

"So she won't bring what her older sister might."

"Aye, Kate, to be exact, but I dinna love her. She's a fair enough lass, I suppose, but she's five years older than me."

"An old hag, then." Maggie lifted her eyebrows, a smile tugging at the corner of her mouth.

"Oh nae! She's a fair lass, but . . . Ach, Cousin, I meant ye nae disrespect, and her age wouldna matter, ye see, excepting I dinna care for her the way I do Rachel. I need do what's best for the clan, though."

Maggie growled. "Why? You deserve to be happy, Alasdair, both you and Rachel, and her sister too. Can't your father understand that?"

"He understands his duty to the clan. Da never planned on wedding me ma, ye ken. But me grandsires struck the bargain, and so they did."

"Your parents do love one another, though. I can see it in their eyes and the way they act toward one another."

"Aye, they do, so mayhap I shouldna be so quick to complain. Kate's a bonnie lass and pleasant enough."

"What? No! Just don't give up on Rachel yet, all right?"

Alasdair cracked a tentative smile. "I dinna plan on it. And I will be showing her me scar." He gave a conspiratorial wink and headed toward the peel.

She leaned back against the cottage wall and snuggled into her shawl. The air was cool, but not unbearable, and it helped to clear her mind. Her aunt had already called her in twice, though, and when Geordie appeared at the cottage door, she decided to comply with the request rather than face the "wrath of Khan." She giggled at the Star Trek reference and curtsied before slipping past his ample girth.

Convinced she was destined to spend another restless night, despite the weary yawn she'd let out not moments before, she threw herself on the soft mattress. The next thing she knew, a bright shard of sunlight hit her in the eye, and she blinked to clear her vision. She'd slept through the night. Sitting up, she stretched her arms and scratched the back of her head. All the anger and worry had taken more of a toll than she'd thought.

Judging by the empty room, her aunt must have let her sleep in, so she threw some water on her face, smoothed out her crinkled dress, and hurried downstairs.

"I'm sorry I slept so late, Auntie. Why didn't you wake me?"

"Ye needed yer sleep, darlin'. The last few days have been hard on ye. Sit yerself down and eat something, eh?"

"You mean I didn't miss breakfast?"

Her aunt laughed, a deep, warm chuckle. "Of course no', lass. Weary or no', there's chores to be done. It's no' yet gone seven."

"Where is everyone? It seems so quiet."

"Yer uncles are about, tending cattle and preparing the tower for another attack from the Fosters."

Anger swelled in Maggie's gut once more. "You don't mean they'd have the nerve to come back here after what they did?"

Emma sat by her side and poured them both a cup of ale. "Oh, Maggie, I dinna ken if ye'll ever understand life on the Borders. We rode against them, stole their cattle, injured a man or two, and kidnapped two of Walt Foster's lads. They'll feel the need to give it us back, the same as we did them."

"But one of them stabbed my father in the back, not in battle or by accident, but on purpose."

"Now, lass, ye dinna ken that for sure. Mayhap yer da turned at the last minute, or Will might have been aiming for someone else and yer da stepped in the way."

"Why are you defending him?" Maggie stood to walk out, but Emma touched her arm and bid her sit back down. Though she did so, she pushed the mug of ale aside, the smell sickening her.

"I'm no' defending him, but it was during a fray, lass. whether ye want to believe it or no'. Things happen in the heat of battle, and we canna always tell the reason for it. I've kent Bonnie Will for a long time, since he was a bairn, and the whole notion of him doing such a thing troubles me. I never took him for the type to come at a man from behind."

"People change," Maggie said, almost spitting the words. "Besides, Ian saw him do it."

"Aye, so he says. Perhaps Ian didna quite see what he thought."

"So Ian's a liar, but Will couldn't possibly be a backstabbing bastard."

Emma's eyes widened. "I can assure ye, William Foster's nae bastard."

"What?" Maggie groaned and took a drink of the warm, pungent ale. She needed to watch her choice of words. "I didn't mean illegitimate. In Lancaster, calling someone a bastard means something else."

Emma crossed her arms, her head tilted to the side. "Oh aye, and what does it mean there?"

Maggie searched her memory for the right word. "It means a scoundrel, a villain."

Emma nodded and took a drink of her own ale. "Ah, right, well that's fair enough, I reckon, but 'twill all be settled at the Day of Truce. Yer uncle plans to file a bill against the Fosters for the murder of yer da."

"That's like a court, right?"

"Aye, the two wardens will come together to hear cases, most likely at Kershopefoot. Yer uncle's complaint will be one of those heard."

"And if they find Will guilty?"

"Let's no' think on it now, eh? Connie's taken the weans berry-picking, and I'll be needing ye to bring some oatcakes to yer Uncle Andy. He's guarding them Foster boys ower in the tower, and the poor wee lads must be close to starving by now, no' to mention yer uncle."

"They're so young. Do they really need to be guarded?"

Emma chuckled again. "I expect he's keeping them company more than guarding them. If he had his way, they'd be sleeping upstairs with Alasdair, but Geordie disna want them going back to their grandsire telling him how welcome we made them feel."

Maggie hated to admit it, but she could see Geordie's point. "Maybe they should be left alone in the undercroft. It might put the fear of God in them so they wouldn't grow up like their Uncle Will."

"As ye said, lass, they're only wee lads, and Walt's their father. He's a good man. Now are ye taking breakfast to them or no'?"

"I'll be happy to." Maggie curtsied and took the basket, carrying it across the courtyard. Here and there, the servants went about their respective tasks, but Maggie had a singular purpose of her own. Were these prisoners her uncle guarded or welcomed guests? She meant to find out.

A few feet from the peel tower, a small boy crossed her path. "D'ye want to play some football, Maggie?" Andy's son Tom asked, his face lit up with excitement. "I promise I winna knock the wind out of ye this time."

Maggie laughed, remembering the day she almost tumbled down the grassy slope. "Not this morning, laddie. I've these cakes to fetch to your da.

Maybe later, though." She ruffled the boy's chestnut hair and continued on her way, though she stopped for a moment before entering the peel.

Those boys were no older than Tommy, and she would hate to see him sitting all alone in a cold, dark undercroft. In a few years, they'd all be reivers, though, capable of stealing and thieving, and yes, murdering, just like Will Foster.

Taking a reinforcing breath, she opened the peel door and entered the tower. Dark and dreary, its few windows had been barred with heavy wooden shutters in an attempt to keep the morning chill at bay. A useless endeavor since the dampness cut so deep it caused Maggie's bones to ache. To make matters worse, the odor forced her gag reflex into overdrive. The stench of rotting moss grass and birch twigs strewn across the floor made it smell like a sewer. The servants were generally conscientious about changing the rushes, mixing rosemary and heather in to sweeten the smell, but they'd been otherwise occupied for the last few days. As a result, the room reeked with the lingering scent of mildew and decaying grass.

Maggie hurried across the hall to find Alasdair sitting beside an open trap door, a torch burning over his shoulder. How he could stand it in there, she had no idea, but he seemed engrossed in the crumpled parchment he held on his lap.

"Wouldn't you see better outside?" She gazed over the edge of the trapdoor and down into the darkened dungeon-like room.

Alasdair glanced up, a crooked smile on his lips. "I'm to keep watch with me uncle Andy."

Maggie gave a slight nod and peeked back over the edge of the shadowy pit. Filled with snakes and hairy rodents, no doubt. Suppressing a shiver, she offered Alasdair an oatcake.

"Well, I've brought you some breakfast."

"Thank ye, Cousin." Alasdair must have noticed her reluctance to descend into what she perceived as nothing less than the bowels of hell and put his parchment aside. "D'ye want me to bring it down for ye?"

"No, I can do it!" She flashed her sweetest smile and began to descend into the blackened abyss, regretting her words almost at once. The harsh air burnt her nose, worse than that of the tower, and she could scarcely see the ladder's crude wooden steps. With no natural light, the only illumination came from a small lantern hanging from a hook on the vaulted ceiling. At least the tower retained a few uncovered arrow slots here and there, and large, flickering torches.

Maggie held her breath, her foot searching for the earthen floor, but an ungodly squeal told her she'd found something else, and she yanked it back up. She clung to the wooden rungs, dropping the basket of oatcakes in the process.

"I suppose that was me breakfast." Andy stood at the bottom of the ladder, a broad grin on his face, and motioned her up the steps. He followed and made himself comfortable on the moss-covered floor next to Alasdair.

Maggie stood beside him, unwilling to dirty her skirts by sinking down on the rotting grass. "I'm sorry about the oatcakes, but please tell me I didn't step on a—"

"A rat," he said, a spark of humor twinkling in his pale blue eyes. "Aye, I'm afeard ye did, lass, but dinna fash ower it. They'll eat well this morn anyway."

"I'll get you some more right away and try not to step on another . . ." Maggie swallowed, cringing at the image of the hairy little rodent squirming beneath her foot.

"Why d'ye no' let Alasdair fetch it? He's doing noucht but scriving love poems."

"They're no' love poems," Alasdair said, his voice raised in protest. "This one's about Uncle Rab."

Maggie blinked away a tear, but not before it reached her heart. "Really, could I hear it?"

"I'm no' finished with it yet," Alasdair said with an awkward shrug, "but 'twill be about the day he died."

"Oh." The memory of her father's life slipping through her fingers, his loving eyes dimming to a cloudy blue haze, caused Maggie's voice to waver. "I'd still like to hear it when you're done. I'm sure it will be a fine tribute."

She turned to walk away, but a giggle from below reminded her what had brought her to the peel in the first place. Stopping beside the open trapdoor, she peered over the edge once more.

"What's been going on down there, Uncle? It sounds more like a festival than a prison."

"Ach, the lads and I were just playing a wee bit of cards. I've been letting them win, ye see."

"No, I don't see." Maggie's tone turned bitter. "They're Fosters. They murdered my father. How can you play games with them?"

"They didna murder anyone. They're weans, Maggie. Would ye prefer me shackle them to the wall and take the whip to their wee backs?"

"No, but . . ."

"Those two lads were no' even here, darlin'. They're nae more than twelve, or so they say, though I reckon the one's barely ten."

"They can ride, so what makes you so sure they weren't here?"

"Mayhap they were, then, though I canna see Walt putting his sons in the saddle so young, or his wife letting him. But even if he did, lass, they didna kill yer da. Their clan rode, and they rode with them. And the clan will pay for it."

"My father's dead. I don't care about money or cattle."

"I ken that, lass, but they were in hot trod. 'Tis all we can ask, and 'twill give ye a good dowry."

Maggie opened her mouth, but Andy raised his hand, so she satisfied herself with a loud sigh.

"Now all that aside," Andy said, "will mistreating those two weans make yer father rest any easier?" Though he stood up, brushing off the seat of his breeks, he bent over a bit so he could look in her eyes.

"No, but . . ." Maggie hung her head, regretting her words. Once again, her sixteenth-century emotions had risen to the fore, and she hated herself for it. "You're right. I don't know what's gotten into me lately."

"Ye're grieving, lass, noucht more. Now get on and bring us some oatcakes, aye, afore the rats grow stronger than the lot of us."

Maggie gave a quick curtsy and hurried back to the cottage, where she found her aunt waiting at the door, a fresh batch of oatcakes in hand.

"This time let Alasdair take them down, aye." A frown covered her brow, making her appear stern, but the hint of laughter in her voice gave her away.

"I'm sorry, Auntie. I'll make some more when I get back.

"There's nae need, darlin'."

"But how did you . . . ?"

"Ye're no' the first, ye ken. I once dropped a whole pitcher of ale. Ye should have heard the ruckus that caused."

Emma broke into a large grin, and Maggie returned the gesture, trying hard not to snort with amusement at the picture her aunt painted. This time, though, she planned on letting Alasdair do the honors. After all, if her aunt reacted the same way, she was in good company.

CHAPTER 28

By late afternoon, Maggie had finished most of her chores and decided to take a walk along the river. Her mind kept replaying the events of the past few weeks, trying to sort out her conflicting emotions. She needed someone to share her feelings with. Someone she could trust with her secrets. At home, she'd run things by her girlfriend Chris or one of her other friends. If it was really serious, she'd talked to her father or Uncle Eddie. And there was always Dylan, of course. But here, despite all the relatives surrounding her, she was more alone than she'd ever been. For her own sanity, she needed to find someone she could confide in, but who?

Dylan and Edward couldn't help, not all the way from England. And she could never ask her uncles to take her there, especially when Edward lived with the very family responsible for her father's death. Going there on her own would never work either. Aside from never finding her way, sneaking off again would no doubt see her locked in the undercroft with the Foster boys, Andy, and the rats. A shiver ran through her at the thought of the hairy little rodents, but the image gave her another idea.

Andy would be the perfect choice. He was so much like her father, right down to the little tic over his eyebrow. Confiding in him would be like having her father back again. And since he watched over her as if she were his own daughter, he'd probably believe her. Maggie groaned and sat down on the bank. But he'd also feel obliged to send her back home at once, even if it meant risking his life to get the amulet back.

Pulling her knees up under her chin, she wrapped the shawl tighter around her shoulders and gazed out over the hills and valleys surrounding the peel. So who could she bare her soul to?

Emma or Marion might believe her, but their first loyalties were to their husbands, so that would never do. What about Alasdair? No, he might feel he needed to tell his father, and she never wanted to put him in that position again. She did care for Ian, of course, but he'd most likely want to protect her and send her back too. She snorted. No, he'd think he could keep her safe all by himself. But did she want him to? Something about him still bothered her, a nagging doubt she couldn't dismiss.

A ray of sunlight broke through the trees, hitting her in the eyes and causing her to blink. Did she even want to go back? Certainly not without Edward and Dylan, but even then, life in the twentieth century without her father seemed a lonely prospect. And yet it held so many memories of him.

Connie's voice echoed across the glen, nudging Maggie from her contemplation. Of course, her cousin would be the perfect choice. They'd spent many a night whispering secrets by the light of the moon, huddled under their blankets. Besides, Connie believed in things like ghosts and selkies, so Maggie's tale shouldn't seem too far-fetched.

"Maggie!" Connie said, her sweet face marred by a frown. "Did ye no' hear me calling ye? Supper's ready, and me ma wants to get to it afore me da starts his grumbling."

"Sorry, I'm coming." Maggie got up and brushed off her skirts.

"He's in a right mood already. Says ye should ken better than to be outside the peel alone with a feud raging and all."

Maggie sighed, struggling to keep her thoughts on the matter to herself. *Just curtsy to the old blowhard and say you're sorry.* He'd still grumble, but so would his stomach, so a little apology would keep him from launching into a lecture—or worse.

With a nod, Maggie hurried back up the hill, her decision made. That night, after they went to bed, she would share her secret adventure with her cousin.

****

The soft blue light of the moon filtered in through the windows, casting deep shadows across the room. Maggie listened to the midnight symphony outside her window. The whinnying of the ponies blended in perfect harmony with the lowing of cattle and the occasional hoot of a lone owl until a discordant note shattered the melody. She tried to suppress a giggle, but an unladylike snort escaped instead. Her uncle's snores reverberated through the house, drowning out the peaceful chorus of animals.

It was now or never. Trying not to arouse her younger cousins, she tiptoed over to where Connie slept and gave her a gentle shake. Her cousin started, but Maggie shushed her before she could raise the alarm.

"I just need to talk to you." Maggie took a deep breath and began her incredible tale.

Connie stared, her amazement growing as Maggie related each aspect of her adventure. "The twentieth . . ."

"Yes," Maggie said. "Things are so different there. I don't know how to handle all of this anymore."

"You dinna ken how to handle it!" Connie said, her eyes wide.

Yet in spite of her initial shock, her cousin seemed to accept the concept far better than Maggie had hoped. Perhaps the remains of ancient superstitions did make Connie more open to such things. Quelling the last vestiges of uncertainty, Maggie finished her tale and waited for her cousin's response.

"Maggie, I've never been farther than Jedburgh, and there but once. Tell me more about it. What were the lads like? Did ye have one of yer own back then . . . or would it be up then or ahead then?"

Maggie laughed. "I'm not sure, but the lads weren't much different than they are now. And yes, I liked a few, but no one special."

Maggie decided against mentioning anything about Dylan. No sense throwing their relationship into the pot, not for a while anyway. For now, Connie had enough questions to keep her occupied.

"A few!" Her cousin sat clutching the thin linen sheet to her chest, hanging on Maggie's every word. "And yer da had no' arranged for ye to marry one of them?"

"No, he wouldn't think of it," Maggie said.

"But having granted his approval for them to court ye, did he no' expect ye to choose one?"

Maggie groaned, expelling a steady stream of air. How could she explain twentieth-century dating practices? "I didn't need my father's permission to date someone."

"What d'ye mean *to date* someone?" Constance rested her arms on her knees, her brow furrowed.

"Kind of like courting, I guess, except without the expectation of marriage."

"And the lads didna mind if ye'd been with others?"

"No, why would they?" But the horrified look on her cousin's face answered the question, and she attempted to clarify her statement before she was deemed the village harlot. "Yes . . . I mean . . . you didn't go to bed with everyone you dated."

"So there were some, then?" Connie gasped, but her eyes glistened with a naughty fascination.

"No, are you insane? My father would have flipped."

"Flipped?" Constance scratched her head. "And what does that mean?"

"It means he would have gotten very, very angry," Maggie replied.

Constance frowned once more. "Then I dinna understand the difference, whether yer world or mine?"

"The difference is I could have, if I wanted to, with whomever I pleased." Maggie bit her bottom lip. "And if I didn't like them, I could say good-bye, no harm done."

"A bit like a handfast, but with nae pledge to bind ye."

"Yes, I suppose so, only I would be the one to choose, not my father."

"But with all those lads, how would ye ken?" Constance asked. "Who to wed, I mean?"

"By listening to my heart. I may not know right away, but if I listen, my heart will lead me to the right person. The way it led you to Rory."

"Oh aye, but it can never be. Me da winna have it."

Maggie wanted to scream, but her cousin would only defend her father's decree, so she didn't press the issue. "Well, that's how you know, but where I come from, it would be your decision."

"And ye'd marry against yer father's will?" Connie asked, though this time sadness tinged her voice, and Maggie could tell her cousin's thoughts had turned to Robert.

"No, of course not." Maggie blinked away the tears. "But it would be because I cared for my father and valued his opinion, not because he commanded it."

"I'm to wed Archie Elliot this winter." Connie sighed. "Me da says 'tis a strong riding name, and 'twill be a good union."

Though her cousin tried to sound excited, Maggie could hear the disappointment in her voice, and she wanted to throttle Geordie on the spot. Her father never would have put the clan ahead of her happiness.

"For who?" Maggie asked. "You or your father?"

"Ye dinna understand, Cousin. I must do what I can. Da's no' commanding me either, no' the way ye think, but he expects me to do me part."

"No, you're right; I don't understand. You don't love Archie. How could that be good for the clan?"

"But I can learn . . ."

"You shouldn't have to learn to love someone. It comes from inside, and you can't fight it, no matter how hard you try. It just keeps coming back. You need to be with them, day and night. You want to give them everything. It's like a fire, and no one else can put it out. You can't teach yourself to feel that kind of emotion, and once it's there, you can't deny it."

"What do ye want from me, Maggie? To say yer world's a wonderful place? I love me world too. To tell ye no' to marry Ian? Ye've already been promised to him, and though the pledge has no' yet been sworn, 'tis all but understood. Besides, I thought ye did care for him, so why should ye mind being wed to him?"

"It's not the point."

"Seems to me 'tis the only point. If ye love Ian, what does it matter who arranges the marriage?"

"But I'm not sure I do. And truth be told, after the other night, I'm not sure he loves me either. He hinted he might not be waiting when I sorted things out."

"Of course he did. With all the fuss ye've been making ower the betrothal, ye canna blame him if he gets a wee bit frustrated now and again."

"I suppose not, and I do like him well enough. But I don't think I love him, not yet anyway."

"What do ye mean, ye dinna think?" Constance huffed in disapproval. "One way or the other, ye need make up yer mind."

"I know." Maggie hesitated a moment. How much should she tell Connie? Oh, what the heck, in for a penny . . . With a determined sigh, she continued. "It's this lad I met. In a way, he frightens me, but at the same time I'm drawn to him, as if I've loved him all my life."

"Who is he, then, and why d'ye fear him?"

"He's a Foster, and everyone says he killed my father."

"What!" Constance threw her sheets aside and sat on the edge of the bed. "Are ye daft, lass? Have ye nae respect for yer da? Nae loyalty to the clan?"

"Yes . . . I do. And I despise him for what he did, but I can't stop the tingling that runs down my spine every time I think about him, standing there, gazing through me."

"Ye saw him kill yer da, Cousin. 'Tis no' love ye're feeling, but hate."

"Maybe it is, but how can I be sure? I didn't really see him do it. In fact, Ian's the only one who actually did."

"Well, there ye are, then." Constance narrowed her eyes. "Dinna tell me ye doubt his word?"

"No, of course not. It's just . . . maybe he only thought he saw Will do it."

"Ach, and d'ye reckon our uncle only thinks he saw Will's knife there in yer da's back as well?"

"No, I suppose you're right, but that's why I needed someone to talk to. I have so many conflicting emotions; sometimes it seems they're at war with each other. Yesterday, when Ian kicked the Foster boy, I was angry, but I wanted to cheer as well. My two worlds are colliding, and I don't know what to do about it."

"I reckon ye need to let go of the one and take the other as yer own. Which ye choose has to be yer decision alone." Connie shrugged and lay back down. "Ye'd best get some sleep, aye. We can talk more on the morrow if ye like."

Maggie nodded and tiptoed back to her bed, snuggling under the blankets. What her cousin said made sense, but it wouldn't be an easy decision. At times, she loved the sixteenth century and forgot the world she grew up in. Ian could sometimes make her forget, so could the purple mist that covered the moor at night. Her father's death made her forget too, and she let her anger guide her emotions.

But there were times when she remembered, and the memories left her lost and confused. She missed TV and video games, her hair dryer and telephone, but most of all she missed her father being there. And she missed dating! What gave Geordie the right to tell her who to marry? It was her life and her decision. At least, it would be in the future, but therein lay the problem.

Her twentieth-century worldview had come head to head with a sixteenth-century world. To resolve her dilemma, she needed to let one or the other take the lead—not an easy decision in any time period. One would put her at odds with the world in which she found herself, and the other would put her at odds with her heart.

The first faint tinge of daylight was beginning to color the horizon, and though Connie had dozed off once more, Maggie still couldn't fall asleep. After tossing and turning for a while, she threw her plaid around her shoulders and headed for the glen just outside the barmekin wall. She stopped for a moment at the gate, gazing across the field of meadowsweet and blossoming bluebells to the hills and wooded thickets beyond. Every feature brought back a memory of her father, and she closed her eyes to savor it. If she listened hard enough, she could even hear his voice in the rushing river, and a warmth and contentment overcame her.

Though reluctant to break the spell, she reopened her eyes, hesitating for a moment longer at the gate. Geordie had already scolded her once for wandering away from the safety of the tower, but what danger could befall her so close to the barmekin wall? She'd just go down the slope a bit. After all, she'd hear them coming, and if anything did happen, she'd always have plenty of time to run for cover.

CHAPTER 29

Maggie lounged back amongst the fragrant blossoms, the soft sunlight no more than a golden glow along the horizon. Though the air remained damp, the promise of warmth comforted her, and she closed her eyes, letting its delicate cocoon engulf her weary body. A few yards away, a thrush welcomed the coming day, tweeting its morning song in perfect harmony with the steady bass of a croaking frog. The sweet melody soothed her cluttered mind and lulled her into a light sleep.

Images of beaches and warm summer days at the shore filled her dreams. Memories of sandcastles and dabbling her toes in the ocean sent her senses reeling. She could almost smell the salt air, hear the surf crashing against the shore. But wait—those were no breaking waves she heard, but something else, something far more menacing.

With a sudden jolt, she woke, the predawn tranquility shattered by a distant rumble. Maggie sprang up, her eyes widening as she recognized the thunderous beat of hooves rising from beyond the ridge. Behind her, about five hundred yards away, pressed against the graying sky, stood her uncle's tower. He'd warned her about venturing from the safety of its walls, but she'd been too stubborn to take his words to heart. Perhaps she should have put her dislike of the man aside just this once.

Frantic visions of vengeful reivers sprang to mind, and she rose, determined to make a sprint for the distant peel tower. With the creak of leather armor already echoing in her ears, she struggled to gain purchase on the dew-covered ground, but she slipped and fell into the tall grass of the gentle slope.

Pushing herself up, she chanced a glance over her shoulder and froze. He was nearly upon her, his steel-blue eyes reflecting the mood of the moor. A wave of terror washed over her, for somehow she knew this time Will Foster wouldn't turn and ride away.

She slumped back on her elbows, unable to move, the world around her fading into obscurity. Riders rode by on their way to the tower, their images blurred and distorted, for nothing could pry her attention from Will or the amulet he wore around his neck. He paused a few feet from where she'd fallen, tugging hard on the reins, hunger burning in his gaze.

Maggie swallowed hard, anger and fear lodged in her breast. She tried to embrace the former, but it was tempered by a sudden desire that caused her thighs to quiver and her mouth to long for the touch of the striking young reiver before her.

Will nudged his horse closer, the fire in his eyes intensifying, and this time fear surged to the fore, jarring Maggie back to her senses. No matter how handsome he may appear, he remained at heart a murdering barbarian, his intentions all too clear. Digging her heels into the soft earth, she pushed herself into an upright position and started running for the tower.

The jangle of spurs and the smell of horseflesh told her he was in pursuit, but she still let out a squeal when he grabbed her around the waist and scooped her up in one fell swoop. Her feet were wrenched from the ground, the air forced from her lungs. Though the maneuver left her winded, she fought to resist, writhing in his grip and clawing at the heavy linen of his shirt sleeves, but it did little good.

Will hissed a curse. "God's teeth, lass! If ye dinna stop wriggling so, ye're bound to land on yer heid, and I'll no' be taking the blame for that."

"Then . . . put me . . . down," she said between gasps, "and you won't . . . . need to worry . . . about it."

"Now what would be the profit there?" Yanking her across his saddle, he locked his arms around her ribs before turning his horse and heading back across the moor toward the nearest hill.

Will clutched her so tight black dots began to cloud her vision. Only the crisp, cool breeze blowing across her face kept her from passing out. She rested against his shoulder, inhaling the brisk morning air, trying to quell the urge to faint, but the steady beat of Will's breath upon her neck was making her ill. Determined to remove the cause of her distress, she reached up and shoved his face to the side, digging her nails deep into his rugged skin and leaving a nasty scratch across his cheek.

A gasp caught in her throat. What was she thinking? Though not bulging or herculean, the muscles in his arms and chest were hard and flexed with strength every time he moved. He could snap her neck without a second thought, and she'd just prodded the beast. Not for the first time, her cousin's words echoed through her head.

If ye get taken, dinna try and resist. 'Tis nae shame in letting them have their way with ye.

No, her father had taught her to be brave, to value courage. With renewed resolve, she pressed her lips together and lifted her chin in defiance.

For a moment, Will continued to stare at the road before them, his jaw clenched so tight the muscle twitched. Maggie bit her lip, waiting for him to react. At last, he pulled up on the reins. Grabbing her hand, he bent over to whisper in her ear, his breath so hot it almost burned.

"That wasna very kind of ye, lass, but I'm a forgiving sort. Now calm yerself and I'll ease me grip a bit, aye."

"Not while there's a spark of fight left within me, you murdering swine."

"Then perhaps I'll have to squeeze the fight out of ye, wench."

Will made good on his threat, squeezing all the tighter and making her position even more uncomfortable. She'd heard stories of rape and violence, of hefty ransoms and forced marriages. Her own uncle had come by his wife that way, though in their case she suspected the abduction had been arranged by the lovers themselves well in advance. Maggie scoffed to herself. She had no intention of submitting to such an arrangement. Her uncles were certain to come for her before anything so drastic could happen.

With a sudden surge of hope, she thought of Edward. He must be there, somewhere amidst the galloping horde thundering around her. She began to twist and turn once more, focusing on each rugged profile, but not even one familiar face passed by. In desperation, she leaned back farther and farther until she almost fell from her perch in front of Will.

Clearly fed up with her wrestling, Will made a low grumbling sound before tugging on the reins once more. He didn't say a word, but grabbed a bunch of her hair, jerking her head back and muffling her screams with a kiss.

Maggie tried to push him away, squirming and pounding her fists on his chest, but the blows had little effect. Bile rose in her throat, making her gag, and yet, deep down, a secret part of her longed to respond to his kiss, to embrace his broad shoulders and pull him closer. The thought frightened her even more than the threat of physical harm and left her weak and flustered when he pulled back.

Will's gaze never left her, even when his pony began to paw the ground, eager to be on its way. His jaw softened, though, and for the first time since he'd carried her off, there seemed to be tenderness in his expression.

"Now sit up, and throw yer leg ower the saddle, aye. 'Twill be far more comfortable than being tossed ower it like a sack of oats. And less likely to see ye fall off and break yer neck to boot."

Maggie wanted to refuse, but in truth her back ached and her legs had gone numb.

"Fine!" She hissed the word, loath to admit the suggestion held any merit, but she wasted no time in adjusting her position.

He slid his arms back around her waist and, taking hold of the reins with both hands, gave them a snap. "There, now stay still, lass, or I'll . . . I'll take ye right here on this rise."

Maggie shifted uncomfortably. From the hard lump pressing against her spine, not only was he capable of it, but it wouldn't take him very long either.

****

The morning mist shifted and swirled around the horses' hooves as they rode through a stretch of birch trees. Though heavily shaded, the sun peaked through the branches here and there, helping to burn off the last remnants of early morning fog. Maggie stifled a yawn and pulled her plaid tighter across her breast. Judging by the nip in the air, it must still be early, around eight or so, if she read the angle of the sun's rays right. Which meant they couldn't have been riding more than three or four hours.

With a weary sigh, she rested against Will's hard leather jack. Having his chest for support did prove to be more agreeable than being tossed over his arm, but she wouldn't call it comfortable. Her back was still stiff, her thighs chafed, and she could no longer feel her behind, which was just as well since it also meant she couldn't tell the current state of his arousal.

As if on cue, Will pulled on the reins, and his fingers brushed against her breast. She swatted his hand away, prompting him to mutter a hissed expletive, and though he didn't say a word aloud, the scent of fresh mint and sage reached her nose once more. She'd been so busy fighting off the urge to vomit she hadn't noticed it before. At least he'd taken a moment to clean his teeth before kidnapping her. Maybe he did possess one or two redeeming qualities, after all. At any rate, the brush of his breath against her neck no longer made her ill, and he'd loosened his hold quite a bit, so the stiffened kirtle no longer dug into her side.

Trying not to consider what would happen if her uncles didn't pay the ransom, Maggie scanned the countryside in case the opportunity for escape should present itself. Leaving the trees behind, they crossed over a narrow burn, and after rounding a bend, Maggie spied a two-story structure made of stone. There were no windows on the bottom floor, only two barn-like doors, and an outside staircase led to an entry door on the second floor, just like her uncle Andy's bastle house. Could this be Will's home, then?

"Where are we?" she asked.

Riding around to the side of the building, Will reined up his horse beside a stone barn and jumped off. "England, mistress."

Not only a villain but a smart-ass too. Maggie made another quick survey of the countryside. Did she dare hope? Scotland and refuge at one of its peel towers couldn't be too far away, an hour, maybe two, by her calculations. A viselike grip tightened around her waist, reminding her of the bigger obstacle. First, she'd need to figure out how to get away from the bastard holding her prisoner.

"Let me go, you brute!"

Will chuckled and lifted her down, pausing only long enough to flash a charming smile. "Brute, is it? Would ye prefer I left ye sitting astride the beast for the rest of the day?"

With his hands still tight around her waist, he gave a squeeze and stood her on the moss-covered ground, stepping back to look her over. A spark of lust flashed in his eyes, his smile reduced to a quiver tugging at the corner of his mouth.

"Ye'll be worth a hefty ransom, that's sure."

Maggie stamped on his foot, shoving him away, but he only laughed harder, making her all the angrier. "You'll rot in hell for this, you pox-ridden pervert!"

A frown crossed Will's brow, the desire in his gaze transforming into something more akin to hatred. Grabbing her by the shoulders, he put his face so close to hers she could smell the fresh mint once more. "I may well do so, wench, but I'll see yer Ian there first."

Though common sense suggested she back away, she stood her ground. "Let me go, you filthy savage. You may take what you will, but I'll never be yours."

"Ye flatter yerself, mistress." The hatred faded away as fast as it had come. "But I will take another kiss for me trouble."

Maggie squirmed, but Will's lips engulfed her own once more, causing an unwanted surge of desire to settle in her groin. The sensation dissipated almost at once when he pulled away, winking at an old reiver who'd come to stand beside him.

"'Tis a prickly blossom ye try to pick there, Bonnie Will." The man grinned, giving her captor a friendly slap on the back.

"Ah, but the fruit itself is as sweet as any, Uncle." Will wrapped his arm around the old man's shoulders, greeting him with an affectionate hug. "'Tis good to see ye again, Richie."

"Aye, and yerself as well. Odd, though, I was of a mind I'd no' seen ye by this way for a wee bit, but to hear yer da tell it, ye were round these parts hunting with me lads no' so long ago."

Much to Maggie's surprise, Will's cheeks flushed a rosy pink. "I'm sorry, Uncle. I didna mean to . . ."

The older man broke into a full-fledged laugh. "Ye ought to ken better, lad. Yer da's worse than a sleuth hound when it comes to sniffing out the truth."

Maggie half listened to their conversation, her attention drifting elsewhere. Instead of concentrating on their words, she glanced around her new surroundings, hoping to see a familiar face or landmark.

The bastle house they'd stopped at was large and, according to Will, situated on the English side of the border. The inhabitants did seem amiable enough and welcomed the raiders with food and drink. Relatives, perhaps? Didn't Will call the old man Uncle?

"Let's go, lassie. Ye'll be coming with me." Will grabbed her by the wrist and tugged her toward the building's outer staircase, where two disheveled looking reivers blocked the way. Their toothless grins made her skin crawl, and their stench rivaled any twentieth-century cesspool.

Maggie covered her nose with her free hand. "I'd prefer to wait over by the horses and get some fresh air, if you wouldn't mind."

"Would ye now, m'lady?" Will glanced at the men and let out a grunt of amusement. "Aye, well, I'd prefer to go inside and fill me wame with some nice hot oatcakes, and I've nae intention of letting ye out of me sight."

"We'll take care of the lass for ye, Willie, me lad," one of the men said, drool running down his chin.

"Move aside, ye filthy louts, elst I'll make sure me auntie puts a good dose of physic in yer oatcakes."

"Ach, nae need to be like that, Bonnie Will," the man said. He grabbed his companion by the sleeve, and both men scurried off toward the barn.

Will gave a subtle bow, indicating Maggie should precede him up the narrow wooden steps. No use refusing. The brute would just put her over his shoulder and carry her if she didn't comply, and then no doubt make her pay for his trouble with her body. She swallowed a new wave of bile and concentrated on the steps before her.

The room they entered looked so much like her uncle Andy's main hall she found she needed to stop and blink to stay the tears. A long table with wooden settles and one ornate chair sat before a wall-length stone hearth. To her right, a makeshift sleeping area held a few rolled-up blankets, discarded for the moment, while on her left, a wooden partition separated another chamber or two, no doubt with additional sleeping space above. She'd put her younger cousins to bed in just such a loft a little over a week ago. A twinge of homesickness pinched her heart, and she swallowed a sob. Would she ever see her family again?

Will broke into her reverie with his usual finesse when he shoved her down on one of the wooden settles. A dirty-faced girl plopped a bowl in front of her, the broth it contained slopping over the rim. The brat took great care in serving Will though and broke into a shy smile before placing his dish on the table. Without missing a beat, he returned her grin, winking and causing the child to giggle and run off.

Maggie flashed him the most disgusted look she could muster, causing him to frown.

"She's nowt but a wee bairn," he said. "What do ye take me for?"

"A baseborn rogue who's of the opinion every woman should swoon in his presence, no matter their age. It's why they call you Bonnie Will, isn't it?" Maggie could see the snicker simmering below the surface, but Will twisted his lips to conceal it.

313

"Ach, ye dinna ken what ye speak of, lass. Me da's laird of the clan, so I'm far from baseborn. And ye can blame me brothers for the name. I'm the youngest lad, ye see, and they claimed neither me ma nor me sister could see the light for me, so . . ."

Will grabbed an oatcake and dunked it in his soup. "I do tend to turn the lassies' heads from time to time, but I reckon there's more than a few lads who've fawned ower yerself."

"A few," Maggie said, still not inclined to see him in a better light, "but none referred to as weans."

This time he did laugh. "Bessie there fancies me, to be sure, but I've nae intention of acting on it, and she'll forget me soon enough when the lads start coming round."

"So why encourage her if you don't mean anything by it?"

"It makes her feel good about herself. Her sister's a beauty and has the lads flocking round her like midges on a hot summer day. Nae one notices wee Bessie, except her ma and da, of course, but they dinna count, now do they? I ken what it's like, so I give her a wink and make her feel like the bonnie lassie she is."

"Oh!" Maggie peeked at the little girl. "I suppose I understand. It might help if she washed her face, though."

"Aye, well, I suspect she'd rather be climbing trees." Will grinned, lifting his bowl and slurping down some of the soup.

Maggie rolled her eyes and scanned the room, anything to quell the flutter of desire erupting in her stomach. The reivers had all settled in to eat, a motley-looking crew indeed. Some stood against the wall or sat at the table while others squatted on the floor, but they all talked of their recent conquest on Scottish soil, laughing and joking about their exploits. Maggie's blood boiled at the thought of her father lying cold in his grave. How she wanted to plunge a knife into Will Foster's back, but she didn't see it happening. They hadn't even given her a spoon, let alone a knife.

Will offered her an oatcake, but she tossed it on the table, scowling at him before she turned away. He heaved a sigh and, leaning over, draped his arm across her shoulders.

"Ye canna fight if ye dinna eat."

His fingers brushed against her cheek, sending a pleasant chill along her spine, but she fought the urge to give in, even though her stomach protested. When she didn't respond, Will hissed a curse. He took hold of her chin, his grip firm but gentle as he coaxed her around to face him once again. Much to Maggie's dismay, her knees morphed into silly putty.

His wheat-colored hair fell over his forehead, framing those dazzling silver-blue eyes. For one fleeting second, she saw no cruelty there, but a roaring laugh from across the room broke the spell. He'd murdered her father. Clenching her fists, she glared at him in defiance.

"Have it yer own way, then, lassie." Shaking his head, he returned to his dish and shoved a broth-soaked oatcake in his mouth.

Maggie continued her surveillance of the room, and a sudden realization hit her. These men were no different from her uncles and cousins. They'd all been so excited after raiding the Fosters. The truth be told, Ian had been almost giddy. Did any of the women here mourn someone who'd been killed in that raid?

Maggie jumped when Will nudged her. "Come on, then, lass. I've eaten me fill and plan to get a bit of rest afore we ride again."

Maggie's mouth went dry. Ride again? "What do you mean, before we ride again? Where are we going?"

"'Tis nowt for ye to fash yerself about. Now come along afore I need drag ye." His voice had grown harsh and stern once more, his touch no longer gentle. A knot formed in her stomach when he led her over to the corner and threw her down on his plaid. Did he plan on taking her right here in front of everyone? He lay next to her, turning on his side and locking his powerful arm around her body.

"And dinna even think of running, lass," he said, "elst ye'll find me arrow feathering itself in yer back."

Maggie rolled on her side, a sob catching in her throat. His hot breath, tinted with honey this time, caressed her cheek, and the nausea came back with a vengeance. She yanked as far away from him as his grasp would permit, placing one arm under her head and closing her eyes. She wouldn't sleep, but maybe he would, and when he did, she'd make her move. Though she had to admit, at the moment she had no idea exactly what that move might be.

CHAPTER 30

Maggie concentrated on the nearby sounds, hoping to glean some tidbit of information that might facilitate her escape. Though small groups of men whispered here and there around the room, they kept their voices low and proved to be of little logistical help. And the few women present were too busy with kitchen chores to let anything of value slip.

With a weary sigh, she shifted under the weight of Will's restrictive hold. The man to his left snorted in his sleep, another against the wall hacked up a hair ball, and a third, at the table, slurped some broth. Such a fine assortment of English masculinity; she had to wonder if kidnapping was their go-to method of courtship. Will murmured something in his sleep and snuggled closer. She pushed against his arm, but it only caused him to tighten his steel-like grip.

Suppressing a low growl, Maggie adjusted the position of her legs. If she angled them right, she might manage to give him a good, quick kick in the shin. But before she could put her plan in action, Will threw one of his booted calves over hers.

"D'ye no' ken by now, lassie, a Borderer never allows himself to be taken off guard, sleep or no'." He snickered and planted a big, wet kiss on her cheek before pulling her closer and settling back on the heavy woolen blanket.

Maggie let out a low growl and tried to at least put some space between them, but Will squeezed all the harder. She wanted to kick the bastard all right, but his nuts would be a more appropriate target. Too bad he kept them nice and safe, pressed against her butt, no less. In an attempt to calm her nerves, she closed her eyes, but the sound of Bessie's giggling drew her attention, and she opened them again.

The small girl hurried down the outside steps. A bunch of children were playing in the yard, a game of tag from the sound of it, and their presence gave Maggie an idea.

She couldn't be more than a few steps from the door. If she could break free of him, she could make a run for it and zigzag among the kids. They might even think it a game and hamper Will's pursuit.

Starting with a soft cough, she increased the frequency and volume until she pretended to be gasping for air. Will, not being a complete barbarian, reacted just as she'd hoped.

"Are ye all right, lass?" He sprang up and leaned over, brushing back her hair.

She pushed herself into a sitting position and leaned against the wall. "Something to drink," she said, wheezing and coughing between the words.

Will's blue-gray eyes reflected sincere concern. For one fleeting moment, Maggie believed her plan might work, but instead of fetching the drink himself, the blaggard motioned to one of the women standing by the hearth.

"Some ale here, Auntie Joan, if ye wouldna mind."

The woman who came to kneel by Maggie's side bore an uncanny resemblance to her aunt Marion, albeit an older version, perhaps a cousin or aunt? And yet she answered Will's beck and call without question. And why wouldn't she? The woman was English, after all, and married to Will's uncle no doubt.

Maggie tried to cover her groan with a cough. She tended to forget her aunt was English born and continued to hold a soft spot for her relatives south of the border. But her marriage to Andy commanded her main loyalty now. Marion had made that point all too clear during the funeral when she'd lashed into Will and his family.

Maggie cleared her throat to hide a huff of satisfaction. Well done, Auntie! It would be a long time before Marion forgave her English kin this latest escapade.

"Nae more than a sip or so at first, lass," Will's aunt said, "elst 'twill make ye cough all the more."

After taking a drink or two, Maggie pretended to be breathing easier. The woman smiled and, passing the cup to Will, hurried off to tend her cooking.

"Ye'd best lie back and rest a wee bit now, eh, lassie?" No longer harsh or taunting, Will's voice could have charmed an angel.

He'd foiled Maggie's plans, though, and he could take his smooth talk and stick it. Clenching her fists, she squealed in frustration, knocking the small vessel from the reiver's hand. It skidded across the floor, spilling ale everywhere and causing the entire room to break into a fit of laughter.

Will chuckled as well. "Ye didna suppose I meant to go and get it meself, now did ye? And here I reckoned ye to be a right canny lass."

Maggie shoved him away, causing the reiver to fall back on his behind. The room erupted in laughter once more, but this time, Will didn't find it amusing. He pushed himself back up and grabbed her by the wrists.

"The next time ye try anything so foolish, I'll bring ye to the barn and take the tawse to yer bare arse, just like me da would any misbehaved whelp."

"Will!" A rugged but refined-looking man beckoned him from across the room. "I need speak with ye, lad."

****

Will frowned in annoyance. Walking away now would give Maggie the very opportunity she'd been waiting for. Didn't his father realize that? Or did he want the lass to run off? He released a disgruntled sigh. No matter, he didn't dare refuse his laird's request, not in front of the entire clan.

"Aye, Da!" He stood to straighten his jack but knelt back by Maggie's side for a moment. "Mind what I said, lassie," he warned before rising again and crossing the room.

He opened his mouth to protest, but his father lifted a hand, cutting him off at once.

"Haud yer wheesht, laddie," he said. "If the lassie's inclined to bolt, best let her do it and be done with it, eh? Either way, she'll no' get far. Now come ower here and bide with me a bit."

Will nodded, swallowing his objections and joining his father at the table. As he did, his uncle Richie got up, giving him a sympathetic squeeze of the shoulder before leaving them alone.

His aunt placed two tankards of ale on the table. "Dinna be forgetting ye were a lad yerself once, Graham Foster."

She gave Will a peck on the forehead and returned to the hearthside without another word, though the look she bestowed on his father would have caused Atlas to cower.

Will bit his lip to keep from laughing. He did love his auntie Joan. But though he gave her a tentative smile, his gaze remained on the auburn-haired vixen he'd left in the corner.

"What's troubling ye, Da?"

"Bind her if ye feel the need, laddie, but if 'tis me ye're speaking to, turn round here and do it, aye."

Will knew that tone all too well and shifted his focus to his father at once. "I didna mean ye any disrespect, Da."

The older man grunted and took a long draught of ale, slamming the tankard on the table when he finished. "Right then! I need to ken what ye're about with this lassie, William."

Will cast a quick glance in Maggie's direction. "I mean to hold her to ransom, nowt more. Being Geordie Armstrong's niece, she's bound to bring a right sum."

His father sat back and crossed his arms over his chest. "Ah, right! So I've nae need to fash about ye claiming her for yer wife or any such foolishness?"

"I've sense enough no' to be trysting with a Scot, let alone one bearing the Armstrong name."

The half-lie caught in Will's throat. In truth, the lass did cause his heart to quicken and his loins to ache with desire, but nothing would ever come of it. After all, the wench made it quite clear she bore no love for him. He suppressed a sigh. Besides, there was more to it anyway.

His father pursed his lips, tipping his head to the side. "Revenge against Ian Rutherford, then, for what he did to yer sister?" He nodded in Walt's direction. "Yer brother used to ride with Rabbie Armstrong when they were lads, ye ken, so ye might want to tread lightly when it comes to his daughter."

And there it was, his half-lie about to be made whole. "I'll bear it in mind, Da, but I've scant use for the lass excepting for the ransom she commands." A wave of shame caused the heat to rise in his face.

"Ye're a poor liar, lad, and I suppose I should be glad of it, but I taught ye to speak true. If ye were still a wean I'd take the tawse to ye for telling such a tale."

The disappointment in his father's voice stung in a way no strap ever could. Will picked at a crumb on the table, too embarrassed to look his da in the eyes. He must be a fool to imagine his father wouldn't see right through him. What had his uncle said earlier? *Yer da's worse than a sleuth hound when it comes to sniffing out the truth.*

Will chanced a peek at his father, and the man lifted an eyebrow. *Lord, he's waiting for me answer, the real one.*

"I'm no' sure why I took her, Da. I came ower the brae and spied her sitting on the heath, her hair mussed and blowing in the breeze, and I . . . I thought to save the wee lass from that sarding blaggard Geordie would see her betrothed to."

"Ye did, now did ye? Right noble of ye, laddie." His father rubbed a finger along the side of his nose and sniffed. "So I take it ye feel nowt for the lass yerself, then?"

His father was a wily old fox. Will considered choosing the tawse and having it over with. He shifted on the settle, weighing his options. He might walk away with a sore arse, but at least his emotional dignity would escape unscathed.

"Mayhap a wee bit. I reckoned if I could just get her away from them lying Armstrong tongues, I might stand a chance. She'd sooner skewer me than bestow her favor on me, though, so I might be wagging a wand in the water."

His father laughed. "Aye, ye well might be." The man cupped his hand around the back of Will's neck, his tone becoming stern once again. "Just think well on the consequences of yer actions, lad, for there will be some, one way or the other. The question ye need ask yerself is whether or no' she's worth it."

Before Will could answer, a commotion erupted over in the corner, and he turned to see what was going on. "Ach, God's teeth, lass!" He took off toward the door, shouting over his shoulder, "I'm no' sure she is, Da, but I mean to find out."

****

Will's threats stuck like a ball of raw dough in Maggie's stomach, making her ill, but this might be her best chance to escape. Lifting her skirts so she could run faster, she darted down the steps and across the yard, her heart pounding against the heavy quilting of her kirtle.

Someone called Will's name, no doubt alerting him to her attempted escape. Judging by the clan's reaction, he must be close on her heels, for a cheer went up, followed by the gleeful screams of children. She didn't need to outrun him for long. Once she made it to the woods, she could use them for cover, delaying him enough for her to make it to the burn midway through. If she remembered right, Scotland sat just beyond it, and she'd be able to seek refuge at one of the towers she'd spied on the way there. Maybe the bastard wouldn't even follow her onto Scottish soil.

A few more steps and she could duck amongst the trees. Her side ached and her legs trembled with a combination of fear and exertion, but she wouldn't give in. Reaching for the nearest tree, her palm barely grazed the bark before two strong arms jerked her back and spun her around.

Will Foster seized her by the elbow, blue-gray storm clouds brewing in his eyes. "Happin there is something to ye, after all," he said before throwing her across his shoulder and carrying her into the nearby barn.

Maggie scratched and clawed, trying to free herself, but Will held her fast until he tossed her on the straw-covered ground like a sack of flour. Frightened tears dampened her lashes, but she blinked to keep them at bay, letting the hate and anger rise to the fore. *He wouldn't dare.*

Kicking out, she hit him hard in the shin, and though he emitted a muffled grunt, he didn't budge. Instead, he turned to retrieve the strap that hung on the wall.

Maggie pulled herself up, brushing the coarse straw from her shirts. "What do you think you're doing?"

"I warned ye, wench," he said with a coldness that reached all the way to his eyes and sent a shiver of terror along her spine. He grabbed her by the wrist and yanked her toward a workbench that sat against the far wall.

"Let go! You're hurting me." Maggie remembered his words of caution all too well, could still feel his breath against her cheek as he spoke them. *Stay still, lass, or I'll take ye right here on this rise.* Determined not to let it happen, she twisted her arm, trying to pry it from his grasp, but it only caused him to tighten his hold.

"God's teeth, wench! Stop yer writhing and let me get on with it, eh? 'Twill be nowt to what yer Ian's bound to do when he gets a bit of drink in him."

Before she could stop herself, she slapped him hard across the face.

"Ye foul whore!" Releasing her arm, he wiped the thin trickle of blood from under his nose.

Maggie took advantage of the opportunity and turned to run, but she slipped on a wet patch of straw. Much to her dismay, Will was on her heels. He caught her by the elbow and spun her around to face him.

God, the bastard was fast, but she wasn't about to give up that easily. Without a second thought, she thrust her fist into his Adam's apple, determined to distract him from whatever deviant sexual behavior he had in mind.

A red flush had crept over his countenance and spread to the tips of his ears. Coughing and sputtering, he tightened his grip and pulled her to himself. He didn't say a word, or maybe he couldn't, but if his expression could be translated, it would no doubt include some hardcore curses and a serious warning. A cold chill ran through Maggie's body, but after taking a few gasps of air, Will eased his hold a bit and whispered in her ear.

"I wonder if Ian has any notion of the wild vixen he's to take as his wife. Now calm yerself, eh. 'Twill go easier if ye dinna try to resist."

Maggie pounded against his jack, trying to push him away, but his arms were locked around her waist. Their eyes met, and much to her dismay, a butterfly took flight in her stomach. Will leaned closer until his lips touched hers, soft and gentle, the taste of honey still fresh on his breath. Instinct caused her to raise her hand to his head and run her fingers through his hair. It was far softer than she imagined and not at all greasy.

Good Lord! What was she thinking? *Bonnie and braw he may be, but this bastard killed your father.* She yanked his hair, and he pulled back, his brows furrowed. He'd pushed her up against the stone wall and even now stood only an inch or two away, rubbing his head.

"So that's how ye want it, eh? Let's get to it, then." He yanked her from the wall and threw her face down across the workbench. As he did, here chemise caught on a nail and ripped, but he didn't even seem to notice.

Dear God! He really was going to rape her. Without warning, a sob escaped from her lips, and she couldn't quell the tears running down her cheeks. How could she ever feel even the slightest affection for this animal?

"Dinna fash so, lass. I'll try to be quick about it so it shouldna sting more than a minute or so. Lift yer skirts up, then, and let's get on with it."

Maggie pushed herself up and spun around with such force she nearly knocked Will over. This might be her last chance. Taking advantage of his momentary loss of balance, she shoved him hard against the wall and darted toward the door. His shoulder slammed into the cold stone, and she cringed at the sound. Serve him right if he broke something. She hadn't saved herself all these years to have her virginity wrenched from her grasp by a murdering lowlife like Bonnie Will Foster. The third time was the charm. He wouldn't get his clammy hands on her again.

Before she'd even finished the thought, his strong fingers clamped like a vise around the top of her arm, and he tugged her across the straw-covered floor.

"That's going to leave a mark." He rubbed his shoulder with his free hand and tossed her back toward the workbench. "Now lift yer skirts and stop being such a wee bairn about it. Me sisters never made such a ruckus."

Maggie sprung up again, but this time she just stared at him, her eyes wide. "Your what! You disgusting piece of shit! You raped your own sisters?"

Will's mouth dropped open for a second before he spoke, his own stormy blue eyes wide with what appeared to be shock. "What are ye blethering on about, lass? I never laid a hand on me sisters."

"Then how do you know they didn't make a ruckus?"

"I kent when they'd done something wrong and me da would take them to the barn. They'd be a bit put out, to be sure, but aside from a whine or two, they went quiet enough."

Maggie thought she was going to throw up right then and there. "Your father raped them?"

"What!" Will shook his head, and though he tried to speak, he could do no more than stutter a few incomprehensible sounds. After a moment, he took a deep breath. "God's teeth, lass, me mother would have taken the axe to him if he even thought such a thing. Is that what ye think I mean to do?"

She huffed and rolled her eyes. "Oh, let's see, you kissed me, hoping I'd just give myself to you, but when I wouldn't, you threw me over that bench and told me to lift my skirts. Use your imagination."

Will blessed himself. "Ye canna be serious. First off, Walt would see me pisle quartered if I even thought of it, no' to mention what me ma and da would do. And second, I didna force that wee kiss upon ye, nor did ye resist it if I recall."

"Oh, yanking your hair and pushing you away wasn't a no?"

"Aye, but pressing yer lips against mine and running yer hand through me hair wasna. And I'm of a mind I stopped when ye near tore it from me head."

"Oh, don't be so dramatic. It was just a little tug."

"Was it now? And all I wanted to do was give ye a wee tap or two with the tawse."

"Oh . . ." Maggie was taken aback, but only for a moment until she recalled what exactly that meant. Her temper flared again. "And you thought I was just going to stand there and let you smack my behind with that leather strap. My father never even hit me."

"Aye, that's clear enough. Mayhap he should have."

Just then, Walt squinted into the barn. "What are ye doing there, Will?"

"'Tis none of yer affair, Brother."

Walt folded his arms across his chest. "Aye, well if 'tis what I fear, I'll be making it me business soon enough. Now gather yerselves together, aye. Da's about ready to ride."

****

Will scrubbed a hand across his face. Did everyone think he'd dragged the wee lass into the barn to sard her? He looked back at the girl, her fiery hair tousled and filled with straw. If he had to be honest, the thought of laying with her had crossed his mind on more than one occasion, but not that way. Unlike Ian Rutherford, abusing women was not part of his nature.

He reached out to lift her torn chemise, tucking it beneath the kirtle on her shoulder. Lovit be God! She smelled of heather, bluebells, and the fresh morning dew that covered the summer grass. His senses reeled, and he had all he could do to keep his pisle from rising to the occasion. If she would only forsake Ian, he would fall on his knees before her and declare his love, but never would he force himself upon her, even if it tore his own heart to pieces.

Of course, if she offered . . . He shook his head to clear away the thought, sure his mother would give him a good skelp across the lugs for even thinking it. Exhaling a long stream of air, he wiped the back of his hand across his mouth and glanced out at the gathering mist.

"Get yerself together, lass. We leave forthwith."

Maggie nodded, but tears had started to stream down her cheeks. Will drew his fingers through his hair and groaned. What was he supposed to do now? Pulling the scarf from around his neck, he handed her the blue linen material.

"God's nails, mistress. Stop yer greeting. I'm no' yer Ian, and I winna take what's no' freely given."

Maggie sniffled and blew her nose. "Ian's always been a gentleman with me. I've never been afraid he was about to rape me, and he certainly never raised a hand to me. You should be ashamed of yourself."

Will pressed his lips together, his hands curled into fists at his side. As angry as he was, her reprimand stung, and he wasn't about to let her paint him in the same ilk as Ian Rutherford. With an exaggerated sigh, he took a step back, taking care to keep his expression serious, lest she doubted his motives.

"I beg yer forgiveness, lass, for taking such liberties without yer leave." *Though what they were, I canna rightly say.* "Nae matter how righteous the reason, I regret me actions. And so, to show me sincerity and beg yer pardon, I'll grant ye two blows. Though make them yer best, for I'll no' allow ye a free hand to take more than that."

Maggie narrowed her eyes and cocked her head to the side. "I'm not sure I understand," she said with a sniffle. "You want me to hit you?"

"Aye, or scratch me or kick me, or whatever else ye deem fitting."

She barked out a laugh and started for the doorway, but he touched her shoulder and she turned around.

"I meant what I said. Now be about it, aye. Or did that kiss mean more than ye'd have me believe?"

Sparks of gold flashed in her deep honey eyes, and she shrugged. "We wouldn't want you to get the wrong impression, now would we? But just for the record, it meant nothing." Then, grabbing him by the shoulders, she drove her knee into his groin, causing a searing pain to rip through his private parts.

Suppressing a grunt, he bent over, gasping for air and gripping a nearby stall for support. After a minute or two, he managed to straighten up, though he would have preferred to curl into a ball and nurse his wounded pride. He blew out a long, steady breath and blinked away the tears, praying his voice didn't come out two octaves higher.

"Get on with it, then," he said, worried his pisle would break under another blow.

Maggie looked him over, no doubt deciding where she could inflict the most revenge. He felt the sting of her hand almost before he saw it. God in heaven for a wee slip of a lass she packed a powerful blow. Blood filled his mouth, so he ran his tongue over his lip, feeling the deep slit. At least she hadn't knocked out a tooth.

Once again, Will retained his composure, taking a moment to wipe away the blood that had dripped down his chin before seizing Maggie by the wrist and yanking her toward the barn doors. "Now let's be about it, lass, or we'll be left to travel on our own, and with twilight approaching and everything from broken men to yer accursed family lurking round every wall and gorse bush, I've no intention of doing that."

"Excuse me?" Maggie said. "You think we're even now?"

Will spun around, a frown creasing his forehead. "Even? For all ye did to me, wench, I'd say 'tis me who landed on the wrong end of the pike."

"What!" Maggie's cheeks flushed a deep crimson. "You scum-sucking sack of shit."

Will scratched the back of his head. "Ye do have a way with words, lass. I canna say I've ever been accused of such afore, but nae matter. The fact remains ye've barely a mark on ye, ye're still able to sit on yer arse without wincing, and yer maidenhead's intact. I, on the other hand, am covered with scratches and bruises. No' to mention I may be ruined for life. Bear it in mind, if I feel the urge to *steal* another kiss or two, eh."

****

With a firm tug, Will dragged Maggie through door. Though she almost fell once or twice when she stumbled through a thick clump of straw, Will seemed oblivious to her discomfort. He never even hesitated, but continued on his way, hauling her along behind him. Once or twice he let out a muffled groan, and Maggie smiled, glad to see her blow had left a lingering impression.

How she wanted to hate him. No matter what his rationale, nothing gave him the right to kidnap her, let alone to raise a hand to her. And yet he did have a point, small though it may be. He hadn't attempted to rape her. As much as she hated to admit it, he hadn't even stolen that last kiss. Even the ones he'd snatched on the road were no more than boyish pecks. And he never did get around to spanking her. In fact, he'd even apologized for upsetting her and given her the chance to take her anger out on him. Which she'd done with great relish.

She shook her head. Her brain spun a web of muddled thoughts and emotions, but what did any of it matter? Even if he hadn't raped her, he'd still kidnapped her, and worse yet, he'd taken her father's life. For that one act alone, she would never, could never, forgive him.

CHAPTER 31

The soft glow of twilight cast a surreal atmosphere over the surrounding landscape, and Maggie squinted to see better as Will dragged her out into the fading light. She scanned the mist-covered courtyard, hoping to spot Edward lurking about. He must be there somewhere, unless . . . Could he be dead too? A rock twisted her ankle, almost causing her to stumble, but a bearded reiver caught her around the waist.

"Best watch yer quarry there, Bonnie Will," the man said. "Geordie Armstrong winna be paying a ransom for damaged merchandise."

"She's no' damaged, Walt," Will said, "so haud yer wheesht."

A cool breeze blew against Maggie's moist cheeks, causing her to shiver, and the man handed her a plaid. "Ye left this behind, mistress," Walt said, "in yer haste to escape me brother's affections." With a quick wink in Will's direction, the older man sauntered off toward his hobbler and mounted the sturdy animal.

So that was Walt. Aunt Marion had pointed him out the day of the funeral, said he'd been close to her father once. Maggie gave a dismissive huff. What kind of man stood by and let his friend's daughter be treated so roughly? One who put family loyalties above all else, she supposed.

Will tugged on her sleeve and tilted his head toward his waiting horse. "If ye wouldna mind, m'lady."

Maggie yanked her arm away, sneering at him before storming over to his hobbler. Most of the clan had already mounted and sat milling around, talking to one another, but all she saw was a barbarian horde who would be more than glad to ravish her in turn if given half the chance.

"So, Will," Richie Foster said as his nephew hoisted Maggie on his pony, "have ye had yer way with the wench?"

"And a fine one she is," a third voice added. A vulgar-looking Englishman stroked her leg, and Maggie cringed, almost tipping over to clutch Will's shoulder. Though she would prefer to box his ears, he did seem a far more desirable alternative than his rougher associate.

"Keep yer hands to yerself, Johnnie o' Dell." Will shoved the rogue away, a cross between anger and disgust coloring his tone.

"So ye've thoughts of keeping her for yer wife, then, Will?" Richie asked. He scratched under his nose in a failed attempt to hide the trace of a smile.

"The notion never even crossed me mind. But I'll no' see her mauled by the likes of him either. She's my prize, and I'll do with her as I like."

"For now, but what about when Geordie disna come for her?" Johnnie smoothed down the front of his crinkled jack. "Me coin's good as any other. Ye'll need make a decision soon enough, Bonnie Will Foster, and when ye do, I'll be waiting."

Johnnie grinned, and Maggie marveled at his resemblance to a hyena. He mounted and rode away snickering to himself, but Richie walked alongside Will.

"I kent ye'd never go through with it, Will, angry though ye were, and justified too."

Will stopped short. "Why does everyone think I was about bedding the lass?"

Richie chuckled and slapped him on the back. "Are ye saying ye wouldna like to?"

Will cast a glance up at Maggie, and she lifted an eyebrow. He narrowed his eyes and pressed his lips together before speaking. Clearly, he wasn't going to answer that, not in front of her anyway. *Wise move, Foster!*

"And you would have, Uncle?" he asked, the coarseness fading from his voice once more.

"Me!" The man gave a hearty laugh. "Nae, I prefer a lady who enjoys the adventure as much as I, but she's a fair catch, and in time . . ."

"I'll hold her to ransom and nowt more. When I wed, I want to be sure the lass winna take a knife to me in the wee hours of the morn."

"And I would too!" Maggie growled, her teeth clenched so tight they hurt.

"She's a fair maid, lad, and a feisty one too." Richie looked her over with an appraising gaze. "Are ye sure ye're no' of a mind to make her yer own? With the proper incentive, she's sure to agree. A whipping or two can drive the contempt from any lassie's heart."

"Hmph!" Maggie let out a loud snicker, and she could see Will clench his fists.

He turned and looked up, studying her like a prize turkey, his jaw firm as he surveyed her body with his cold steel blue eyes. "I'm sure. Ian can keep her—if he's willing to pay the price."

"And if he's no', lad?"

"He will!" Maggie snapped, anger seething in her bowels. "And he'll see you all hanged!"

"Then Johnnie Hetherington can have her." A smirk crossed Will's lips before he mounted behind her. "To do with as he pleases." He hissed the words in her ear.

Richie nodded, a softness transforming his rough expression. "Ye'd best pray yer Ian comes for ye, then, lass."

A wave of nausea flooded Maggie's stomach, and she swallowed to keep it from surging up her throat.

"For me own part, lad," Richie continued, his attention turning to Will, "I reckon ye did the right thing. I love our Annie too, but violating this wee lass winna bring her back to us. 'Tis Ian's crime, and him what should pay for it."

Richie patted Will's horse on the rump and, after bidding them on their way, strolled off toward his house.

Will tightened his grip, both on her and the reins, but though his pony pawed the ground, he held it in check. After a short time, a gray-haired man raised his hand, giving a signal of sorts.

"That's your father, isn't it?" Maggie said. "I saw you talking to him before."

"Just afore ye run off, ye mean." Will pressed his knees against his mount and followed his kinsmen out of the courtyard. For all she could have given him another good kick in the balls, he really was quite a good horseman.

"Before I tried to escape my captivity," she said.

Will snorted. "Aye, he's me da and laird of the clan."

"And which one wanted to speak to you?"

"Both, I reckon." He leaned over, resting his chin on her shoulder while he spoke. "But if ye're of a mind he was telling me to release ye, ye'd best be thinking again. He's the one told me where the tawse was."

A shiver ran through Maggie, but was it from fear or something else? Rather than debate the issue, she gazed around the darkening countryside, hoping and praying her family would come for her.

Oddly enough, Will didn't seem in the least bit concerned about the possibility. "They'll no' be coming tonight, lass. Me kin's made sure of that."

"What did you do to them?" Maggie's heart sank.

"Let's just say they'll be otherwise occupied," Will said, a chuckle in his voice.

"How many more have you killed, you . . . you . . ." *What words would they use?* "You foul-smelling wretch."

Will sniffed a time or two before clearing his throat to speak. "If they've any brains in those thick Scottish heids of theirs, there'll be nae more dead."

"And if not?" Maggie asked, almost fearing the answer.

"Me kin lie in wait and will do what need be, but nae Armstrong will clear the Border this night."

Maggie bit her lip, trying to quell a sob. What if they were ambushed? Not only would she be left in Foster hands, but the people she loved could very well be lying dead. She needed to know, and yet the words stuck in her throat. They'd been riding quite a while before she summoned the courage to speak again.

"What do you think they'll do?" she asked.

Will hesitated a bit before answering, but when he did, his voice was softer and not so angry. "I told ye, lass. They'll attack if they're forced to."

"No, I mean my kin. Will they turn back?"

Will drew in a breath and sighed deeply. "I dinna ken. Geordie's a fair heid on his shoulders, and he may choose to wait a day or two afore he follows. He's sure to ken 'twas us did the deed, so there's nae real need to call out the dogs."

"He will come though . . . won't he?"

Will brushed his lips against Maggie's hair, sniffing in the scent and causing her stomach to lurch again.

"Aye, lass, that's certain."

"And if he doesn't, will you really give me to Johnnie Hetherington?"

"He'll come!" Will replied, his tone abrupt. "Leave it at that."

Maggie, however, wanted to know more and continued to press the issue, though she could hear the annoyance in Will's tone. "What did your uncle mean about me praying Ian comes? What would Johnnie Hetherington do?"

Will muttered under his breath, another curse no doubt, or maybe a prayer for patience, but after a moment or two, he relented. This time his tone was cold and without any emotion.

"Ye might say Johnnie's a wee bit hard on his women, especially when they come from yer side of the border. By last count, they say he's already taken five wives, all Scots. That little tryst we had in the barn would feel like nowt more than a pleasant romp in the hay when Johnnie got through with ye. 'Course he'd wed ye first to make it all nice and legal. Short of murder, ye'd be his to use anyway he liked."

Will's words stung, and Maggie clutched the chemise to her chest, the whole terrifying incident replaying in her mind.

"I'm sorry for treating ye in such a crude manner, lass. His breath brushed against her ear, warm and tantalizing, and he tightened his grasp around her waist.

"You don't need to squeeze so hard." She winced, wiggling in his grip as they cantered along the rolling hills.

"I do if ye insist on no' holding on."

They jumped over a fallen tree, and Maggie jolted forward. Only Will's strength kept her from tumbling to the ground, and instinct forced her to grab at his sleeve.

"It'll be yer own fault if ye land on yer heid." Though an edge of laughter colored his tone, he eased his embrace a bit.

Reluctant, but seeing his point, Maggie clasped onto his arm, hugging it to herself, and for a split second she trembled with delight. She turned a bit, and he leaned over so she could see him better.

"Ye forgive me, then?" He tilted a bit to the side and smiled.

A few wisps of his sandy-blond hair brushed against her cheek and tickled her ear. Though his clean-shaven face revealed his youth, his smoke-blue eyes foretold a strength and experience far beyond his years. Yet there was a harshness about him Maggie couldn't understand, a bitterness that transcended any tenderness she might have for him.

She spun back around. "Not likely!" Deciding not to stir that can of worms, she returned to the previous subject. "So what happened to his wives?"

Will straightened up again. "Whose wives?"

"Johnnie Hetherington's!" She hissed the words through gritted teeth, not liking the touch of triumph in his voice.

"Oh, them. Well, I'm no' sure about the first two. Some say they run off after he'd taken the whip to them. At any rate, we've no' seen hide nor hair of them since."

"And what of the other three?"

"Well, they found Eleanor in Liddel Water, though how she got there no one can tell. Miriam died in childbirth. Fell down a flight of stairs right afore her time."

"He has a child?"

"Aye! 'Tis a frightful thought, eh?" Will sighed, almost letting a tenderness come through in his voice, and Maggie let herself snuggle closer, relaxing a little as the cool evening breeze blew against her torn kirtle.

"And his last wife?"

Will wrapped the plaid around her shoulders, his touch gentle against her skin. "He beat her to death, that's sure!"

"And no one did anything? They just let him get away with it?"

"He'd witnesses enough . . ."

"Witnesses enough for what? To say he didn't do it?"

"No, to say she took a cleaver to him. He claimed he was defending himself."

"You don't really believe that, do you?"

"That she took a cleaver to him? Aye, I've nae doubt she did. But that he needed to beat her so to get it off her . . . Nae, Maggie, I dinna believe it, no' for one minute."

For the first time since he'd swept her away, he called her by her given name, and she couldn't stop a momentary fondness from stirring her heart anew. After all, he wasn't exactly repulsive. Quite the opposite. He presented a rather handsome figure. Had the situation been different, she would have no trouble falling in love with him. Even now, knowing what she did, a warmth deep in her soul prevented her from despising him.

She clenched her jaw. No, he'd killed her father. She could never pardon him for that. For now, though, she was stuck practically sitting on his lap, so she cleared her throat and continued their conversation.

"He murdered her," she said, "and no one did anything?"

"Well, no' exactly. It started a kind of feud with the Milburnes, though nowt came of it. The Hetheringtons are no' much of a riding clan, ye see."

"Then why is Johnnie with you?"

"Oh, they'll ride with us from time to time, but on their own they only ride for blackmail."

"Blackmail?" Maggie said almost to herself. *The Borders . . . 'Tis where it all began.* Her father had mentioned it to her one night when she'd enlisted his help on an assignment for school. She couldn't recall the class, though, or even the grade, and in a way it bothered her. The thought of forgetting her father, even the smallest bit, pierced her heart more than any dagger ever could.

The sound of Will's voice reminded her of that loss, and her back stiffened against his jack. Will must have mistaken it for confusion, for he continued right away.

"Aye, lass, protection for the smaller clans in return for money." Will chuckled like she had no sense at all. "Do they no' tell their womenfolk anything in Scotland?"

The heat rose in her face. She'd straighten him out. "I was born in Lancashire, so I wouldn't be aware of all your quaint customs."

"Lancashire! Well, that explains the odd way ye speak, then. But I thought ye were Rabbie Armstrong's bairn?"

Maggie could hear the hair rustling and pictured him scratching his head. Panic set in for a moment until she recalled the tale her father had told his brothers.

"I am. A band of broken men kidnapped him and left him for dead down in Lancashire. My mother found him and nursed him back to health."

"So it explains why he decided to stay on, I reckon, but no' why he returned."

"My grandparents died, and I suppose it made him wonder about his own kin."

"And what of yer ma?" Will asked. "How did she feel about moving to the Borders?"

"My mother died when I was a child, and before you ask, he didn't return then because I was all my grandparents had left."

"Aye, so ye're an outlander of sorts." Will snickered. "And Ian Rutherford wants to wed ye? Does he even ken about any of it?"

"Of course he does, but why should it matter?" Maggie said, making sure the annoyance came through in her tone. "I'm an Armstrong and a Borderer, just as sure as you, Will Foster, and I'll be proud to be the wife of such a fine and honorable man."

"Honorable!" Will almost spat the word. "Is that what an outlander considers honorable? Nae wonder they follow fat King Harry and his heresy."

"I'm not a heretic!" Maggie said. "I'm a Catholic!"

"Are ye? And why have ye no' betrayed yer faith like the rest of them, then?"

"Not everyone agrees with what the crown does. Besides, I'm a Scot, remember?"

"Ah, right! Well, ye're better off on the Borders, then, lass."

"Am I? Oh, much better, for here men beat their wives to death and nothing at all is done about it."

"They found nae proof to say he wasna defending himself." Will readjusted the plaid on Maggie's shoulders. "Whether I believe it or no', the witnesses bore him out."

"You're barbarians!" Maggie shook her head, disgusted by Will's nonchalant attitude.

"Well, we may be, lass, but some are worse than others, so ye'd best watch yer tongue. Such a sharp instrument could get ye a beating, or worse, especially with the likes of Johnnie Hetherington. Mind, he loves sweet young things from north of the Tweed."

"And if my family doesn't pay the ransom, he might." The words caused her stomach to ache, but they had to be said.

"Ye didna suppose I'd just give ye back, did ye? Johnnie was right about one thing. His coin's as good as any other."

CHAPTER 32

Maggie's stomach churned at the idea of being sold off to Johnnie Hetherington. Just the thought of his grimy mitts touching her caused her to gag. Taking a deep breath, she tried to suppress the urge to vomit, though it would serve Will right if she threw up all over his nice, clean linen shirt. Not that the wretched bastard would care. No doubt he'd dump her on the ground and wipe her face in it without thinking twice.

The damp evening air filled her lungs, helping to quell the nausea, but its icy fingers chilled her to the bone. Though she despised the idea of showing any sign of distress, the heat of Will's body beckoned her, offering a welcome haven. Oh, what the heck. He wouldn't even notice, and if he tried anything, she'd puke on him. With a satisfied sigh, she leaned against his chest and let him wrap his cloak around her shoulders.

Things remained quiet for the next few miles. The gentle swaying of the horse and the warmth of Will's embrace induced a desire to sleep, and her lids began to droop.

"'Twas you that night down by the burn, aye?" Will said. "What were ye doing so far from home?"

Maggie's eyes sprang open. "I sought to get home to Lancashire." She cleared her throat, managing to keep her tone curt.

"Did ye now, and with nae more than one day's rations?" Will scoffed. "D'ye expect me to believe Alasdair Armstrong has nae brain at all?"

"You can believe what you like; it's the truth," Maggie replied with a huff. "And what about you, picking berries indeed! Would you really have hurt us?"

"Ye'd nowt to fear from me that night," Will said in all seriousness. "Yer only concern was the broken men after yer hides. If I'd no' gotten ye off the trail, ye'd have both been lost to them for sure. Alasdair's a canny lad, but young yet."

"Oh, and you're so much older and wiser."

"Aye, enough to ken better than to be keeping to the trail, alone, in the dead of night. I'm no' saying the lad winna learn. He does need a bit more experience, to be sure, if he's a mind to keep a lassie safe."

"I guess I should be grateful, then, but it still doesn't tell me why you were there in the first place."

"Fair enough, I'll tell ye the truth, if ye'll do the same."

A lightheartedness seemed to enter his voice at the prospect, and Maggie didn't see what harm it could do. After all, she wouldn't exactly be lying. "Swear it," she said.

"Ye're in nae position to be demanding any conditions, lassie." He went quiet, but after a minute he reconsidered. "All right, I swear it. Now tell us, lass. What brought ye to the Kershope Burn?"

"I grew up in Lancashire, and before we came to Scotland, I met a sweet lad, an Englishman. He came from the Borders, but I loved him anyway." She heard Will let out a sarcastic tut but continued with her tale. "At least, I thought I did. I heard he'd moved back this way, and I needed to know if I harbored any lingering feelings for him before I pledged myself to Ian."

Will laughed so hard he almost fell off the horse. "So in reality, ye ran out on yer precious Ian."

"No! But I didn't want any doubts either. Is that so awful?"

"I reckon 'tis fair enough." Will's cough betrayed the snicker he fought to restrain. "And were there any lingering doubts about this mysterious Englishman, then?"

"None whatsoever," Maggie said, though the conviction in her voice didn't quite reach her heart. "Now what about you?"

"Haud up now a bit, lassie. Ye didna say who ye came to see."

"No, and I'm not going to," Maggie said. "I promised to tell you the reason for me being there, and so I did. Now you keep your part of the bargain, or are you Englishman oath breakers as well as murderers?"

Will's body stiffened, and his voice became cold and harsh once again. "I was on me way to take revenge against yer betrothed."

"Revenge for what, not marrying your sister?" Maggie sneered in disbelief. "She's the one who called it off."

"Aye, she did, after discovering he'd broken faith with her." Will's fist tightened around the reins. "Laid with another, two nights afore their betrothal."

"You're lying." Maggie tried to turn and face him, but he pushed her back around. "She just did it to shame him," she added.

"Believe what ye will, but I saw it for meself. I ken the kind of man he is, and rest assured, being with another's nowt but the half of it."

"Ian was right." Maggie fought to keep her temper in check. "You have no honor."

Will snorted. "That's a strange word coming from such as Ian Rutherford." He cracked his reins, spurring his horse over the next rise, and Maggie ducked for fear of being knocked off by a low-lying branch.

They rode well into the night, not saying another word, until at last Maggie saw a tall gray tower emerging in the moonlight. It looked stark and bare, set amongst the shadows, and sent a shiver of dread through her entire body. Once again, Will wrapped both his arms around her, perhaps hoping to offer some comfort. Yet the move carried no emotion and seemed almost like a reflex action. She pressed her lips together to stifle a latent sob and swallowed hard, tears welling in her eyes. How she wished her father was alive.

****

Will held tight to the reins as they approached his home. Maggie shivered, and by instinct he drew her closer, trying to afford some warmth against the crisp morning air. At one point along the trail, he'd draped his cloak around her. After all, she'd been forced to leave hers behind when he whisked her away, and now he'd torn her kirtle too, thanks to his hunger for revenge.

Suppressing a sigh, he spurred his horse into a gallop, unable to dismiss the passion that continued to rage through his veins each time he touched her. Revenge had nothing to do with it, though he wasn't about to admit any such thing to Maggie—or to himself, it would seem.

He wiped a sweaty palm on his breeks. God, how he longed to feel her bare flesh against his, to hear her moan in ecstasy as he released himself within her. It felt unlike anything he'd ever experienced, and it puzzled him.

Ye've been with women afore, ye wee dolt. He'd even fancied himself in love a time or two, though as the sun rose, he'd been on his way, his passion dissipating along with the morning dew. But it had been different with Maggie. His loins stirred at the very thought of her.

Ye just need a bit of sport to spend yerself.

Maggie snuggled into his shoulder, and he groaned. In truth, he could sard his way across the whole of England and not satisfy the burning desire that throbbed in his groin and caused his heart to pound like a tabor. As hopeless as the situation might be, he'd fallen in love with the fair Scottish maid who'd claw his eyes out if given half the chance. But she'd been promised to Ian Rutherford, and worse yet, she loved him, or at least she said she did.

Will, on the other hand, despised the foul creature. He rubbed his eyelids, trying to dispel the sight of Annie crouched in the corner, bruised and battered. She'd shuddered in terror when he went to comfort her. In fact, even now the touch of another caused her to cringe, and she clung to her sanity by the thinnest of threads. He hungered for revenge; he craved it. Even so, he couldn't exact it from Maggie, though he was well within his right to do so.

He pulled up on the reins and came to a stop. Blessed be God, they'd arrived at his father's peel tower. Perhaps now his pisle could get a rest, right after he found a quiet corner to relieve his yearnings. Jumping from the silver pony, he grabbed Maggie around the waist and lifted her to the dampened earth.

"So, William, what's this I hear, ye've taken yerself a bride?" His eldest sister, Mary, greeted him, a tinkle of laughter in her voice.

"If I fancied a wife," Will said, "I'd no' go to Scotland to find her."

He shoved Maggie toward his sister as if he'd bagged her on a hunting trip. His brothers had taught him well how to guard his emotions, keeping them hidden beneath the surface. Mary could see through him, he reckoned, but he avoided her taunting with harsh words and actions.

"Watch her well, Mary. She'll bring a fine price from the Armstrongs . . . and the Rutherfords." He hissed the name.

The woman smiled and took Maggie's wrists, binding them with a leather strap. "If ye're of a mind to hover about, William, perhaps ye'd rather do it yerself?"

Will stepped back. "I wanted to make sure ye didna tie them too tight, what with us asking for a ranson and all."

"Ah, right," Mary said. "Who is she, then?"

"Her name's Armstrong, but she's to be claimed by Ian Rutherford, and a fine pair they'll make—a defiler of women and a lady, or so she says she is."

"And so I am!" Maggie shrieked, her eyes narrowed into catlike slits.

"'Course ye are." He ran a finger beneath her chin. Though he attempted to appear smug and carefree, the knot of emotion forming in his stomach threatened to betray him, so after a moment's gloating, he turned and hurried away.

"Will," Mary shouted after him, on the verge of laughter.

"Just see to her," he called over his shoulder, not even daring to look back.

******

"Come this way, darlin'." Mary led her through the maze that cluttered the large barmekin. It was full of women and children welcoming their men home, horses being led to feed, and stolen gear spread across the torchlit ground.

"Where are you taking me?" Maggie asked. Though she tried to remain calm, she couldn't deny the pall of apprehension descending upon her like the heavy morning mist.

"To the pend, lass. Ye winna be any trouble down there, and ye'll be safe as well."

"Safe . . . safe from what?"

Mary bent to lift the rough wooden hatch, a sad smile touching her lips. "Will's kind and good, and whatever he did to ye, be assured others would do far worse. Dinna get me wrong. Most are good, decent men, but there's always a few, especially after they've been on a raid. Their blood's boiling and their hearts' racing. They think nowt of what they do, only what they desire."

Maggie peeked down into the pitch-black pit and gasped. Though similar to her uncle's ground floor, it differed in that the first section had been penned off as a kind of dungeon, complete with a locked door. The cold, damp walls and sound of rats squeaking in the background reminded her of something out of a horror movie, and she shivered. An image of the two young English boys she'd seen in her uncle's tower caused her stomach to churn anew, and she swallowed hard.

"Go on, then," Mary motioned. "Ye'll be safe enough there till yer family sees fit to pay the ransom."

Seeing no other alternative, Maggie descended the wooden ladder, her bound hands clutching each narrow rung. The sickly sweet smell of manure wafted up from below, almost gagging her, but with Mary watching, she could do nothing to escape its unmistakable scent. Her nose burned, and her stomach mimicked a volcano nearing eruption.

I hope I barf all over everything. She gazed into the darkness and heard the outer door slam shut. *Oh crap! I bet they didn't take the shit with them, though.* Only a few slot holes, high in the wall, provided any light, and she squinted to make sure she didn't land in a huge load of cow dung.

Maggie grimaced and prepared to sit in what she hoped was a shit-free spot of hay when Will's voice echoed from above.

"No' down there."

Though she doubted he intended to show it, Maggie could once more detect a certain kindness in his voice, a tenderness he couldn't deny.

"Word's already been sent to the Armstrongs," he said, "and they're bound to come forthwith. Keep her here in the hall. Get her a plaid to lie on, if ye would, and some food and drink."

"Are ye sure 'tis ransom ye're wanting, Willie Foster?" Mary beckoned Maggie back up the ladder, a grin crossing her pleasant face.

"Aye, I'm sure," Will said, his tone turning harsh again. "Ye mind her well, Mary, and nae matter how she cries, keep her well bound, elst she'll bolt the first chance she gets. And if she tries, whip her good and throw her to the rats. See if Ian Rutherford pays the price for what's left."

"If it comes to that, ye'll be doing the deed yerself, wee William." A momentary frown creased Mary's brow before she shook out a blanket and spread it on the floor.

She smoothed the woolen cloth and nodded for Maggie to sit. "Dinna mind him," she said with a smile. "He always gets a bit crabbit when ye catch him out."

CHAPTER 33

Maggie sat huddled in a corner, the cold tower wall pressing hard against her shoulders. Her legs and backside ached from the long ride, so she shifted position to get more comfortable. In doing so, her skirt lifted to reveal a bit of calf. At first, she didn't think anything of it, but when a rowdy youth passed by, coming to an abrupt halt at the sight of her stockings, she realized her mistake.

The horse-faced young man grinned from ear to ear, bending down to slip his hand beneath her skirts. Maggie clenched her fists. She may not be able to keep Will from feeling her up, but she could certainly handle this little pip-squeak. She swung her bound wrists, hitting the boy in the right temple and sending him sprawling across the rush-covered floor.

A few men seated at a nearby table snickered. "She's too much woman for ye anyway, laddie."

The boy drew his dagger, a scarlet flush creeping across his cheeks like a red tide. Bile surged up Maggie's throat, and she swallowed to keep it down, but before he could act, Walt Foster grabbed him by the neck,

"Now, laddie, use the brains the good Lord gave ye, aye, few though they may be. 'Tis Bonnie Will's prize. How d'ye reckon he'll take to ye damaging his goods afore he's even had a go at her himself?"

The boy's eyes flitted across the room, and Maggie followed his gaze. Will stood with a hand on his sword hilt, his fingers flexing on the cold steel.

The young ruffian replaced his dagger and inspected the rush-covered floor, poking at it with his foot. "Just having a wee bit of fun, Cousin. I meant nae harm."

"Ah, right! Ye'd best be on yer way, then, afore Bonnie Will thinks otherwise, eh?"

The teenager scrambled away, giving Will a wide birth. Walt nodded to Will, and the latter relaxed his fists and returned to his meal.

"I ken ye mayna see it now," the man before her said, "but ye could do nae better than our Will. I'm of a mind yer da would approve were he here."

"We'll never know now, will we? Your brother saw to that."

The man grunted, rubbing a grubby mitt across his face. "Ach, ye're Rabbie's bairn, all right. There's nae talking to ye once ye've set yer heid to something—for right or for wrong." Walt gave a curt bow before hurrying across the room to a comely looking woman, who threw her arms around him in a passionate embrace.

Maggie was doomed. Will and his brother couldn't protect her forever, even if they were inclined to. A painful shiver racked her body, and she tugged Will's cloak tight around her. What if Ian fell before he could come for her? Johnnie Hetherington would claim her for sure, and that could well be a fate to rival death itself.

Tears flooded her eyes once more, a sob hovering on the brink of despair, when a spark of hope emerged from the distant stairwell in the form of Edward. Though she almost cried out to him, she hesitated at the last minute, realizing it might be hard for either of them to explain their familiarity.

How could he be so relaxed at a time like this, laughing and joking with the bastards? She'd give him an earful when she got him alone. At least, she intended to, but when he veered in the opposite direction, she panicked.

The volcano in her stomach sent a new batch of bile into her throat. If he walked away now, she might never see him again. A sudden idea, borne of desperation, began to form.

While she might not be able to account for their acquaintance, she could explain a fear of mice. No doubt she'd draw the scorn and mockery of many around her, but if she screeched loud enough, Edward would be sure to notice. Then again, so would Will. He sat quiet enough for now, at a table across the room, but his attention never strayed very far, and she worried she might arouse the anger and whatever else it was churning just beneath the surface.

"Take her, lad," she heard a tall gray-haired man exclaim. "She's yer prize, and ye've a right to her." The man came over and yanked her to her feet. "She's a fine bosom and hips broad enough to bear ye some fine bairns."

"And what of love, Uncle?" Will inquired. "Am I to put it aside?"

"She's a fair lass," the man said. "What more d'ye need? A good night filled with lust can be as fulfilling as any touched with love, and no' as binding, I might add."

"She belongs to Ian Rutherford." Will's lips curled in disgust.

"More the reason to seize her for yerself," the man countered.

"I'll no' force her to me bed," Will said, doubtless irritated by the older man's suggestion.

"Then ye're a fool, Nephew, and she the more for no' going willingly."

"And what have we here?" a third voice interjected. Edward came up behind Will, placing a hand on his shoulder.

"Me uncle reckons I should drag the lass screaming to me bed, for nowt but to save her from the clutches of Ian Rutherford." Will's voice shook, his tone dripping with sarcasm.

"Ian Rutherford!" Edward said. "Perhaps Tom's right. 'Twould be a pity to see such a fair young thing wed to that savage."

Maggie couldn't believe her ears. Didn't Edward recognize her? How could he even suggest such a thing? Raw anger boiled in her veins.

"He killed my father." She clenched her hands, shouting in defiance. "Drag me to his bed he may, but never a touch of tenderness shall I show him. I'll scratch his eyes out before he's a chance to wet my lips."

"Will ye, wench?" Will leapt to his feet and sprinted across the few feet between them, causing Maggie to jump. He shoved her against the wall, cupping her chin in his palm, his face inches away from hers.

A crowd had gathered, and she could sense the warmth of their bodies closing in around her, causing a wave of panic to rise in her chest. She'd done it now, challenged him in front of his kin, defied him to steal a kiss, and now he'd do as he pleased. The lump in her throat felt as if it were about to choke her.

Will leaned over to whisper in her ear, his breath soft against her neck. "Perhaps I will steal one of those kisses now, lass.'Twill go a long way to making us even, eh?"

Caressing her cheek, he pressed his mouth over hers. She stood stock-still, clutching her skirt, determined not to give him any encouragement. And oh, it would be so easy to. His tongue snuck passed her lips, and her heart raced. If only he hadn't killed her father.

The memory brought tears to her eyes, and she released her skirt, pushing against his jack, praying he would back away. Nothing seemed real; even the voices in the background had become muffled and somehow distant until one voice broke through the fog, and Will jerked away on hearing his name.

"Is this what you want, lad?" Edward asked. "Will this lessen our Annie's pain or wipe away her shame?"

Will shook his head, his breath coming in short, deep gasps. Without uttering a word, he wiped his mouth and darted across the hall toward the outer stairs.

The crowd dispersed, and Maggie sank against the wall. Relieved to see a familiar face, she reached for Edward, who knelt beside her and pretended to check her restraints.

"I can't unbind you, Maggie," Edward said. "Will's folks trust me all right, but there are those who don't."

"Like Johnnie Hetherington?" she asked, throwing a glance in the pervert's direction.

"True, but then I don't trust him either." He chuckled a bit and continued. "Now how did you end up here, honey?"

"Why don't you ask him?" Maggie scowled, her line of vision burning a path through the stone doorway Will had just vacated. "He killed my father!" The words escaped on a sob, a flood of emotions threatening to overrun what little composure she had left after the day's events. "He came at Da from behind and . . ."

"Yes, I heard about Rob." Edward sighed, a solemn frown crossing his brow. "I'm so sorry, darlin'. I should have been there by his side, but . . ." He shook his head. "I wish we'd never come."

A pang of guilt tore at Maggie's insides. She'd been angry at Edward for not being there, but he wasn't to blame. "You couldn't have done anything. Andy was there close by, and Ian too, but neither of them could prevent Will from killing my father."

Edward's brow creased. "You know how I felt about your da, sweetheart, but Will? I can't believe he'd knife a man in the back. Did you see him do it?"

"Well, no, but who else could it have been? Da fell right at his feet, but Will didn't even stop. He rode toward me, calm as you please, and stole my amulet."

"Ah yes, the amulet," Edward said, nodding in confirmation. "He prizes it. Whether he cares to admit it or not, he's in love with you."

"In love with me?" Maggie shouted the words but lowered her voice when a few heads turned in their direction. "He has a strange way of showing it. He kidnapped me. Then he dragged me out to a barn and took that strap thing off the wall. Do you see this?" She scowled, pointing to her torn chemise. "I didn't know whether he was going to rape me or beat me to death."

Edward bit his lip. "Yes, Walt mentioned something about the incident, and I'm not excusing Will's behavior, but—"

"But!" Maggie glared at him. "Were you even there?"

"Lower your voice, Maggie, or I won't be able to stay. I told Graham I knew you and Rob from Lancashire, but still. Others will wonder what's going on. Unless you call me a filthy old reprobate, of course. Now calm yourself while I get you something to eat. And no, I wasn't there."

Maggie did as Edward instructed and let the tension flow from her body. Just seeing him again soothed her frazzled nerves and even brought a bit of her appetite back.

Edward handed her some bread and cheese with a small pile of raspberries and sat beside her while she ate, pretending to polish his sword.

"You know I thought I loved him once," she said.

Edward's brows lifted. "Will? He made a trip to the future, then, did he?"

"Well, sort of. I recognized him right away. He was the guy in Da's portrait book. The young knight I used to picture riding up on his silver steed to rescue me."

"Well, in a way he did, and he does ride a gray hobbler."

Maggie narrowed her eyes. "Not the way it played out in my mind."

Edward bowed his head and chuckled. "I know you don't see it right now, but Will was actually acting quite chivalrous." She let out a disgruntled moan and Edward lifted a hand, signaling she should be quiet and listen. "Maybe not by our standards, but believe it or not, it took a lot of courage for him to walk away just now."

"Courage!" Maggie strained hard to keep from raising her voice again.

"Yes, love, courage. People here take what they want. It's how they survive. The only way they know."

Maggie huffed. "Then how come Da didn't . . ."

Edward cleared his throat, to stifle another laugh, no doubt. "Your father lived in the twentieth century quite a while before you came along. He . . . mellowed out, shall we say."

"No, Da never behaved—"

"Yes, he did. I had a right time keeping him out of trouble the first year or so." Edward let a soft smile touch the corner of his mouth, and he squeezed Maggie's hand. "And if the truth be told, Will did me a favor.

351

With Rob gone, I planned on coming to get you myself. I couldn't leave you there all alone. I promised Rob I'd watch over you."

Maggie couldn't refrain from emitting an abbreviated snort. "Did you? Because I'm pretty sure Geordie thinks it's his job."

"Hmph! He would, the old bastard. Well, he'd be wrong, now wouldn't he? Besides, you're not going to be in Scotland. You're going to take my amulet and go home. You don't belong here."

"Go home to what? Anyone I ever loved is here." Maggie blinked the tears away. "Unless I could come back, before Da . . ."

"No, it's not possible," Edward said, his demeanor brooking no argument.

"Why not? I could go home and return again before my father's death, make sure he stayed away from the battle."

"Because it won't work."

"Of course it will. I'm a genius when it comes to misdirecting his attention." Maggie giggled for the first time in what seemed like forever, but the sadness clouding Edward's face checked her enthusiasm.

"I've no doubt you are, but convincing Robert won't be the problem."

"Then what will?"

"You're already here, love," Edward said. "You can't be in two places at once."

"But I wouldn't be, not really."

"I'm afraid you would be."

"How can you be so sure?" Maggie argued the point, not ready to concede defeat. "Isn't it worth a try?"

"We did try, or I should say Dylan did, and he couldn't reappear until after he'd left."

"Dylan went back? Why?"

"For Will's sister Annie." A gentle, faraway look brightened his countenance. "He's in love with her. Oh, he won't admit it, not yet, not to himself or anyone else, but when he discovered what Ian Rutherford had done to her . . ." Edward's expression hardened again, his gaze sending a chill through Maggie's heart. "I can't believe Robbie agreed to let you marry that butcher. He was far too cunning not to have picked up on Ian's deviant behavior."

But Maggie could no longer hear Edward. Instead, she heard her father's dying words. *Maggie, darlin', get away from here. He'll hurt ye too, lassie.* "No, it couldn't be. Not Ian." She whispered the words, hoping they couldn't be true if she didn't say them aloud, and yet there could be no mistaking the suspicion in Edward's eyes.

"What is it, Maggie?" he asked in concern. "Rob found out, didn't he?"

"No . . . I mean, maybe. The afternoon they got back from the raid, he tried to talk to me, but his brothers kept drawing him away, and Ian asked me to go for a walk with him. Da made me promise to stay where he could see us. He said we'd discuss it later. But we never got the chance." She sniffled, and Edward offered her a hankie.

"A warning about Ian, no doubt."

"But Da let me go off with him. Surely if he suspected Ian of anything horrible, he would have insisted I stay in the barmekin." Maggie swallowed twice in quick succession, trying to dislodge the sob materializing in her throat.

"Or maybe he chose not to tip his hand until he'd spoken to you. But there's more, isn't there?"

Maggie shrugged. "It's just something my father said before he died. A warning about someone hurting me. But before he could tell me who, he . . . he . . ." She bit her bottom lip to stop it from quivering, and Edward wiped the single tear that ran down her cheek.

"Ian Rutherford . . ."

"No!" Maggie protested. "He's a good man, and he loves me. More likely Da meant the one who stole my amulet—and his life: Will Foster. No wonder he told me to leave right away."

"But Will had ridden off. He posed no more threat."

"Not then, no, but I guess Da figured he'd be back, along with the rest of his thieving family."

"It's possible, I suppose, but why assume Will would hurt you? He'd never even met the lad."

"He did once."

"At the Kershope Burn. Yes, I heard about Will's little encounter, but Rob let him go."

"True, and look what he got for it."

"You're assuming Will's guilty, but I don't see it. Dylan doesn't buy it either. They both talk a good game—you know what Dylan's like—but neither of them would ever hurt anyone, not without due cause."

"True enough of Dylan, but I can't say the same for Will, and neither can you."

"I'd wager I know him better than you do Ian, but I understand how you feel. To you, Will acted badly. But this isn't 1988. And when all is said and done, a bruised ego is the extent of your injuries."

Maggie opened her mouth to protest, but Edward wagged his finger, cutting her short. "You're his prisoner, sweetheart. He could have thrown you in the dungeon with a piece of moldy bread, but he didn't."

"I'll be sure to thank him, then, right before I watch him hang."

Edward groaned and tugged at his ear. "Okay, let's say you're right and Will did murder your father. Fair enough. Do you expect me to believe you wouldn't throttle the nearest Foster in retribution if given half the chance?"

"Of course I would, but that's different."

"Is it? Annie is Will's sister, his younger sister. From what I hear, he appointed himself her guardian the moment she was born, and despite his pledge, he couldn't save her from Ian's attack."

"What attack?"

Edward hissed something incoherent before answering. "You mean you don't know?"

"I know she basically broke their engagement two nights before their wedding, or handfast, which is apparently an even a bigger deal here than it would be at home. But of course, the Fosters blame him, saying he betrayed her."

Edward downed a long draught of ale and massaged his temples. "Let me tell you about Ian, darlin'. Annie broke the betrothal, true enough, but she did it because he raped and nearly beat a whore to death down in Carlisle. Will found out about it just in time."

"So they just took Will's word for it?"

"Graham went down to talk to the ladies, and they supported Will's account."

Maggie rolled her eyes. "Will probably paid them to say it."

Edward shook his head. "You really are as stubborn as your father. Regardless of what happened in Carlisle, Ian's crimes didn't end there. He may deny ever touching Annie, but what he did to that innocent girl was brutal, savage, something Will would never lower himself to, no matter what the reason.

"Ian raped and beat the poor child near to death, but he didn't end it there." Edward swallowed hard, taking a shaky breath before continuing. "He sodomized her, Maggie. He took that sweet little angel and . . ." He sniffed and rubbed a finger under his nose, but he pressed on. "These people may be wild and uncivilized by our standards, but there's still a code of honor, and Ian Rutherford broke every rule of that code."

A gasp caught in Maggie's throat. "But it's just Will's word, right? No one saw it happen. Maybe Annie got involved with someone else, but when she got caught, she blamed it all on Ian, to save face. Some girls do that, don't they?"

"Annie's almost catatonic, Maggie. Will found her bloodied, bruised, and half-naked, staring into nothingness. When he tried to touch her, to comfort her, she pulled away, her sweet face filled with terror."

"I'm so sorry. That's horrible, but then how did she accuse Ian?"

"Will and Dylan saw Ian heading for the gate, a huge grin on his face. Rob saw him too."

"No, Da would have told me if he expected anything so wicked."

"He probably didn't know exactly what Ian had done, only that he was up to something. In all honesty, Rob may have just thought the rogue had gone for a roll in the hay."

Maggie shook her head, not sure what to believe anymore. She needed time to sort it all out, but how could she tell who was lying and who was telling the truth? Ian had always been kind and gentle with her. Will, on the other hand, had stolen her away from her family. She'd been wrong about him planning to rape her, though. Could she be wrong about this as well?

"So why did Will take me in the first place if he's such a saint? And don't tell me it's because he loves me."

"All right, I won't, even if it is the case. The reason he's giving is that you're to be Ian's wife, his property. He takes you, he hurts Ian."

"But I'm not Ian's, not yet."

"Thank God for that, though word is it's all but done."

"No, not officially anyway. I never agreed to marriage, no matter what Geordie says. Da told him Ian could court me, nothing more, but now Da's gone . . ." Maggie shook her head again. "I just can't believe Ian would do such a thing. He loves me, Uncle Eddie. He's a decent man, and he'll care for me."

"Don't you understand, Maggie? He's not. You'd be far better off with Will."

She glanced across the room and shivered. "You're joking, right? Last I heard, he was contemplating giving me to Johnnie Hetherington if Ian didn't pay the ransom."

A shadow transformed Edward's countenance. "You can't believe he'd give you to that creature?"

Maggie shrugged. "I don't know what to believe anymore. I only know I've heard him state on several occasions he has no desire to make me his wife. As for Ian, he's been nothing but kind to me. You say he attacked Annie, but you really only have Will's word for it. No one saw Ian do it, and unless Annie can tell us herself . . . Will hates Ian. He'd say anything to disgrace him. More than likely he didn't like the idea of his sister marrying a Scot, so he spread those rumors. And now he's killed my father."

"Maggie, I love you, but you're wrong. I've heard the talk about Ian myself. That girl down in Carlisle wasn't his first. I believe Robbie discovered the truth about Ian, or at least suspected it, and it's what got him killed."

"What do you mean?"

"Think, lass. Where was Ian when Rob died?" Edward gazed into her eyes and nodded, bidding her to recall the fatal day.

"With him, of course." Maggie blew her nose on the cloth Edward had given her earlier. "They were fighting together, side by side, the way they were supposed to be."

"And you're sure it was Will's dagger they found in your father's back?"

"Yes, Ian saw it," Maggie said, trying to recall, though her memories of the day were hazy and muddled. "It had his crest or something on it. Uncle Andy recognized it too."

"Hmm. Well, it may have been Will's knife, but his hand didn't plunge it into your father's back. Sandie Rutherford knocked it from his fist during a scuffle. Maybe Ian or one of his brothers retrieved it and used it to frame Will."

"And maybe Will never dropped it at all. I love you too, Uncle Eddie, but I can't imagine Ian stabbing my father, of all people. I mean, he had no reason."

"Didn't he? Think about it. If what I've told you is true, Ian had more than enough reason to see Rob dead."

Maggie couldn't bear to eat another bite and pushed the trencher aside. Her stomach ached again, and she longed to lie down and try to get some sleep. "But I saw Will riding out from behind Da, and all he cared about was taking my amulet. Not in helping him or comforting me. I don't know what's true and what's not, but I can't stay here. The Armstrongs were Da's family, and now they're mine. They'll pay the ransom, and when they do, I'll go home."

"We can go home together, love, back to the twentieth century, you and I."

"And what of Dylan?"

"He won't leave Annie. It's not in the stars. And this is where he truly wants to be."

"And you'll just leave Dylan here, all by himself?"

Edward didn't answer. He didn't have to. They both knew the answer.

"You have friends at home. They'll take care of you, watch over you."

"But I won't have you or Da, or any family, not from this century or the twentieth. You'll all be four hundred and fifty years I the past. Look, I know this sounds ridiculous, but Da is here, in Scotland, and somehow I feel close to him here."

Edward huffed a sad sort of laugh. "I know, sweetheart. Take this with you, then, just in case." He grabbed her hand, pressing the amulet into her palm.

Maggie drew her arm away to wipe her dampened lashes. "No, if I can't use it to help my father, it's no use to me. Besides, you might want it one day, or Dylan might change his mind."

"There's nothing for us there anymore either, so take it, please. I can't do anything else to protect you. I'll see the chest is delivered . . . as a wedding gift."

"No, not now anyway. If I need to get in touch with you, I can always ask Marion to send word."

Before Edward could protest, Walt Foster came up and grabbed him by the shoulder.

"We need be going, Eddie. The Armstrong's are no' pleased about the ransom, and me da reckons they might strike just afore dayset instead."

Edward watched him run toward the turnpike steps. "Let me get you over to the Hetheringtons, Maggie. You'll be safer there."

"How is Dylan, anyway?" The thought of seeing him again brought back happy memories and lifted her spirits. It also reminded her of a time when Edward and her father were her only family. She'd always trusted him then. Was she wrong to question his judgment now?

"He's fine, love, becoming a right borderer. He'd be glad to see you, though. Since we lost Robbie, it's been all I can do to dissuade him from running up there after you."

"Nice try, Uncle Eddie, but I'm no fool. He'll be on his way here, won't he, ready to fight for the Fosters? That's if he's not already here. No, I'm not leaving. But don't worry. I'll speak to Uncle Andy about Ian when I get home. He'll get to the bottom of it."

Edward ran his fingers through his hair. "God, Maggie! They're not even willing to pay your ransom."

"I'm sure there's a reason," she said, though her voice shook as she spoke the words.

"Are ye comin', Eddie?" a voice called out. "Or mayhap ye're considering claiming the lass as yer own."

"Now that might be a thought, Walt, but I fear I'd be obliged to fight your Will for her."

"Then leave this one to him, aye, and let's get on with it."

Edward turned back to Maggie and cupped her cheek. "If you ever need me . . ."

She forced herself to smile despite the ache in her heart. "I know, and I'll always love you, Uncle Eddie."

"Consider what I've told you. Please, Maggie, do that for me."

"I will, I promise." Maggie watched him follow in Walt's steps, the hole in her heart growing deeper. Once again, her worlds were colliding. Her twentieth-century uncle condemned Ian and sang Will's praises, while her Uncle Andy confirmed Will's guilt.

She slumped against the wall, alone and abandoned, and wiped at the stray tears with Eddie's hankie. How could they refuse to pay the price? Her father would have surrendered a king's ransom for her. Perhaps she should reconsider Edward's words. Could everything he said be true? Had Ian murdered her father after he violated Annie? The very idea made her ill, and she dismissed it before it could take hold. As she did, Will knelt before her and fastened his cloak around her neck.

"'Tis time to go," he said. "We've spotted yer kin on the rise. It winna be long afore they're here." His voice seemed cold and distant, his expression as unemotional as ever, yet in his gestures Maggie sensed a warmth he could no longer hide, try as he might.

"Don't you ever feel anything . . . not for one minute?" she asked.

He gazed at her for a moment with those piercing steel-blue eyes before giving a solemn nod. "Aye, lass, whenever I touch yer lips, but what does it get me? Nowt except yer scorn."

An inexplicable urge to defend herself caught Maggie off guard. "Perhaps if you tried asking."

"And ye'd agree if I did?" Will asked, the catch in his voice revealing a vulnerability he tried to hide.

"No, but you've no right—"

"I've every right, wench! Me sister's near dead, and yer Ian's the cause." Will started to turn away but stopped himself, his jaw set so tight the muscle twitched. "Will ye do me the honor, then, lass?"

"You killed my father!" Maggie said in disbelief.

"Nae, lass! I've done many a wicked thing in me life, but coming at a man from behind's no' one of them. And to what end? He'd done me nae wrong. I truly am sorry for yer loss, Maggie, but Ian Rutherford's the murdering swine what took yer da from ye."

"You're worse than a coward, Will Foster, for you'd condemn another man to save yourself, and all for a meaningless kiss."

"Keep yer kiss, wench, for if those lips long for such a knave, they're no' worthy of mine." He lifted Maggie and carried her up the long, winding stairway.

She held tight, for fear of being dropped down the dark stairwell, but before they got very far, word came. The Armstrongs were at the gate. Will hurried across the floor and sat her against the corner wall. He bent beside her, pulling his cloak tight across her chest.

"Ye'll be safe here." Touching her cheek, he stared at her, as if he were trying to memorize her face. "Should I no' return, I ask nowt but yer forgiveness and a few prayers for me wretched soul."

She swallowed a rather inappropriate response, thankful Will didn't seem to expect an answer. He'd already risen and grabbed one of the heavy wooden tables. Tipping it over in front of her, he lifted a small child and sat her behind the makeshift barrier as well.

"Ye watch her well now, Peggy."

The small girl cuddled close to the soft woolen cloak Maggie still wore. Though the child seemed to be dressed warm enough, her tiny body trembled, and Maggie placed an arm around her shoulders.

For the first time since she'd met him, Will's mouth softened into a tender smile. Without saying a word, he leaned over the makeshift barrier and gave Maggie a kiss on the forehead.

Once more their eyes met, but this time no anger hung between them, and when Will drew near again, Maggie let her lips part to receive his. There, for one brief moment, they were neither Armstrong nor Foster, neither Scot nor Englishman, but one enamored entity locked in a fiery bond of passion. All too soon, however, reality beckoned, and Will tore himself away, a tear glistening on his cheek as he turned and left the tower.

"God be with you, Will Foster," Maggie whispered, and much to her surprise, she found she meant them.

CHAPTER 34

Will could see about eighty of them lined across the rise, but there would be more bringing up the rear. He stood next to his father, not saying a word, and waited while a party of ten came riding down to within shouting distance of the peel.

"Good day to ye, Geordie," Graham Foster bellowed across the windswept vale. "Come to pay the ransom, then, have ye?"

"Ye're off yer heid, ye thieving son of a whore." Geordie's horse stomped and snorted in its position outside the barmekin wall. "Bad enough yer murdering whelp killed the lassie's da. Now just give us our Maggie, and I might see me way clear to leaving it at that."

"Well now, it's right kind of ye, Geordie, but me lad didna take yer brother's life, and when he carried the lass off, we were in hot trod. So be reasonable, man, and pay the ransom. Happin I'll consider letting it go as well."

"I'll no' pay a shilling to claim what's mine. 'Tis us what's in hot trod now. Bonnie Will took our Rabbie from behind. We only want what's due us."

Graham turned to Will, his voice loud enough for Geordie to hear. "Tell me true, lad. Did ye take Rabbie Armstrong's life?"

"Nae, sir, I didna," Will replied.

"D'ye swear on yer life, William, and on God above ye?"

"On me life, I swear, and on God above me, I didna harm the man."

"Ye heard him, Geordie. Me lad swears he didna do such a thing."

"Then he's a lying scoundrel as well as a murderer!"

Geordie roared the words, and Will could see the color flushing the man's face even from this distance.

"I didna raise me lads to tell tales," his father said, his knuckles white against the parapet, though he cast a warning glance in Will's direction.

Will swallowed hard, recalling all the petty lies he'd been telling of late. But he hadn't sworn to them. Surely his father would see the difference and believe his oath now.

"I swear by heaven above me, by me part of paradise, I didna kill the man, Da."

His father grunted, the hint of a smile touching his lips. "Aye, but let this be a lesson, eh?"

Will nodded, leaning against the crenel to let the evening air cool his heated cheeks, but he cursed under his breath when he heard a voice from below.

"Ach! I've no' doubt ye tried to teach the pup, Graham, but I've proof here says he paid ye nae mind." Geordie pulled a dagger from his jack and held it up for all to see. "Ask the lad how his weapon came to be in our Rabbie's back."

"I've nae need. The answer's plain enough. One of yer men knocked it from his hand during the fray. A Rutherford, I believe."

"So that's the yarn he's spinning. A wee bit too convenient for me taste. Mayhap 'tis why he rode off with our Maggie, eh? To keep his lie from coming to light. Ask her who did it, then. Or are ye afeard she might show yer lad for the brazen limmer he is?"

"Bring the lass to me, William," his father instructed.

Will's heart sank. "But Da, she's bound to—"

His father grabbed him by the shoulder, his eyebrows rising. "Now, William! Or I may be forced to question yer reluctance."

"Aye, Da. I'm on me way." Will gave a nod and hurried toward the peel, though he feared whether he brought her or not, he was doomed.

****

Will came running from the turnpike steps and, without a word, seized Maggie by the hand, dragging her across the barmekin and up to the battlement. She had no idea what was going on, but it was cold and windy, and she wished she could go back inside. The sight of the Armstrongs lined across the horizon, however, warmed her blood, and a sudden wave of strength and defiance bolstered her spirit.

"Did ye see me lad murder yer father, lass?" Graham asked.

Maggie longed to exclaim a resounding yes, but her father's words lingered in her mind. *Always speak the truth, darlin'.* She puffed a breath and rolled her eyes, for she hadn't really seen Will do anything.

"Well, lass?" Graham barked, clearly not in the mood for any theatrics.

"Not exactly," she said.

"What d'ye mean, no' exactly? Either ye did or ye didna."

"I mean, it couldn't have been anyone else." Maggie lifted her chin, no longer sure if she was trying to convince Will's father or herself.

"But did ye see him, lass?" Graham pressed the issue, his ears now such a deep red they were almost purple.

Maggie hung her head, hating to say what she knew she must. "No, I didn't! Are you satisfied?"

"Well now, it depends. D'ye speak the truth, lassie, or are ye saying what ye reckon I want to hear?"

Tears caught on her lashes, blurring her vision. "I wish it were a lie, because then I'd know the truth. But the whole day's such a blur; I can scarce remember seeing my father fall, let alone who stabbed him."

Graham gave a solemn nod. "Aye, lassie. Yer da was a good man." Clearing his throat, he turned and bellowed over the battlement once more. "Geordie, we have yer lassie here, and she says she didna see our Will slay yer brother, so that's an end to it, then."

"No' likely, Graham," the Scot countered, "for I have a lad here swears he did."

"Ian Rutherford?" Graham said. "Ye're off yer heid, man. He'd like nowt better than to see Will dancing 'neath the widdie."

Geordie glanced over at Ian. What passed between them Maggie couldn't say, but after a brief discussion, he held his ground. "Ian has cause to wish yer lad ill, I'll give ye that. But he seeks me niece's hand in marriage now, and the lad's no' fool enough to risk it all for a wee bit of revenge."

"And nae lad of mine is guilty of swearing falsely." The veins in Graham's neck stood out in the deepening shadows of the early evening light. "For if he dared, I'd hang him meself."

"Enough of this bickering like weans!" Geordie said. "'Twas during a fray, so we're willing to let it go. Now give us our Maggie, and a few head of cattle to keep her, and we'll be on our way."

"Right kind of ye, Geordie, but there's still a small matter of the ransom."

"God's teeth, man! After killing the lassie's father? I think we're being right generous, letting yer lad off so easy."

"'Twould be indeed, excepting me lad's done nowt wrong. Mayhap 'tis the scoundrel ye're riding with should be paying retribution to us for what he did to our Annie."

"Ach! I've heard that tale well enough," Geordie growled, the grumble in his voice clear even on the parapet. "And there's nae more truth to it than Will's innocence."

"So be it, then. If ye want the lass, ye'll have to take her."

****

Maggie's jaw dropped. She'd never seen so many angry Armstrongs in one place. Worse yet, she didn't even recognize most of them. Will stood by her side, so she turned to him.

"Where did they all come from? I mean, I've never seen half of them before."

A smile pulled at the corners of Will's mouth, and he ran a finger under his nose to conceal it. "They're yer kin, lass, one way or the other, or those who owe allegiance to them. Rutherfords, Elliots, and Crosers, from the looks of it. Just like the Hetheringtons and Selbys will be fighting for us."

"And you give them protection in return," Maggie said, a cross between disgust and disbelief flavoring her tone.

"Aye." Will frowned. "If need be. But there's more to it. There's loyalties and honor—"

Before he could say another word, his father called his name.

"Take the lass to safety, and then make sure the beacons are burning. We'll be wanting all the help we can get against a force this size."

"Aye, Da."

Will yanked Maggie down the steps with such agility she had to fight to keep from stumbling. They hurried across the enclosure toward the peel, but before they could reach the safety of its massive walls, an arrow cleared the barmekin and pierced Will's shoulder. Though he moaned slightly, he didn't stop until they were inside, where he paused only long enough to break off the projectile's narrow shaft.

Maggie gasped. "Will, you're hurt!"

"And what's it to ye? Ye'd see me hanged, remember? Or happin ye're afeard I might die here and deny ye the pleasure."

"You're an uncaring, lecherous lout, Will Foster, and I'll be well rid of you!" But nothing could be farther from the truth. Maggie had an overwhelming urge to cradle him in her arms and care for his wound, wrapping it in the crisp linen of her petticoats while she stroked the thick blond hair that fell across his rugged cheeks. God help her! A few hours ago, the thought would have disgusted her, but she was finding it increasingly difficult to summon those sentiments. It didn't help to see the pain on Will's face when he lifted her and placed her back behind the table.

Without another word, he headed for the roof to check on the beacon calling all with any loyalty to the Fosters to rally against the Armstrongs. Though he'd instructed Maggie not to leave the safety of the table, she paid him no mind, following him up the narrow turnpike to the roof.

"God's bones, wench!" He hissed a few more expletives before addressing her again. "Get yerself below."

The sickening sound of splitting wood and agonized screams echoed in her ears. She peered over the crenelated roof to see the heavy Jedburgh axes slashing their way through the thick barmekin gate, and she froze.

Will cursed again but hurried off to stoke the beacon fires. When he'd finished, he grabbed Maggie by the arm again, nearly tossing her down the narrow steps.

"When I tell ye to bide somewhere, wench, I mean ye to do it." His cheeks had gone scarlet, and she could swear sparks of silver flashed in his eyes.

"You don't get to tell me what to do. I'm not your wife."

"Lovit be God for that." He shoved her behind the table once more. "Now bide here whilst I join me kin, and if ye so much as point a foot outside this barrier, I'll take the tawse to ye."

"You and who else?"

Will opened his mouth to reply but stopped to grip the table instead. Rich crimson blood soaked through his linen shirt and saturated the smooth leather of his jack. A light layer of sweat covered his forehead, darkening the wisps of hair that clung to it, and pain clouded his expression.

Setting his jaw firm against it, he'd no sooner turned away than his legs collapsed beneath him, leaving him unconscious a few feet from where Maggie sat. Enemy or not, the sight caused her breath to catch in her throat and a wave of fear to wash over her. Though a tug-of-war continued to muddle her feelings for the handsome young rogue, she had no intention of standing by and watching him bleed to death.

As if she'd been doing it all her life, she tore two pieces of cloth from her petticoat, taking a minute to soak one in a clean basin of water before she ran to his side. Will's sister Mary already knelt beside him, and though she was trying to help, three wailing children made it almost impossible.

Maggie's heart ached for them. An adult might grow used to it, take it as a part of their life, but it must be terrifying to a small child. Maggie placed her hand on Mary's and smiled. "Let me."

At first, Mary appeared skeptical, but after a moment she moved aside, her countenance lightening. She seemed both amused and puzzled by

Maggie's offer, though she didn't hesitate in voicing her suspicions. "So when did ye realize ye loved him?"

"What? No! That's ridiculous! I just don't want him to die some hero's death. There's a hangman's noose waiting for him, and I'll not be denied the pleasure of seeing him swing from it."

Repeating Will's words made Maggie shudder. With any luck, she'd managed to hide her emotions as well as he concealed his, for in truth she didn't even believe them herself.

"A hangman's noose indeed." Mary flashed a roguish grin before running off to rescue one of her children from its older sibling.

Maggie considered denying the implication but decided not to bother. Instead, she went to work, pulling away Will's bloodstained jack and linen shirt to reveal the tip of an Armstrong arrow. She pursed her lips and blew out a stream of air to calm her nerves. First things first. She'd need to remove the bolt. There was no other way to staunch the bleeding.

With a sudden jolt, Will sprang up, knocking Maggie on her behind. She emitted a squeal of surprise before brushing herself off and scrambling back to her knees.

"Lie down and keep quiet, or you'll make it worse."

"The aqua vitae," Mary shouted as she hurried to her brother's side. She placed Will's head on her lap, caressing his tawny blond hair with sisterly affection.

"Leave it be," he said, trying to suppress a groan.

Maggie ignored him. Pushing the shirt aside, she began to wipe away some of the blood around his wound. "And let you bleed to death? Not likely."

"Oh aye! Be a waste of a good rope, then, would it no'?"

"Yes, it would!" Maggie poured Mary's amber liquid over Will's shoulder, causing him to grit his teeth. "Aqua vitae indeed," she mumbled to herself. "This is pure whisky."

The astringent washed over Will's open wound, and he bit down on his lip. "Ye must be enjoying this."

"A little. Now give me your knife."

"Oh aye, and should I bear me breast as well so ye can plunge it through me heart? Though I have to say, Maggie Armstrong, it wouldna be the first time ye've pierced it."

Maggie hesitated, wondering what he meant, before turning her attention back to his injury. The tip of the arrowhead peeked out of his flesh, but it was sharp and slick with blood. To make matters worse, he'd broken the shaft off so close to the entry site it would take more than a shove to push the bolt through. She'd have to widen the incision first to help it along.

"Give her yer dagger, Will," Mary said, "afore ye bleed to death, ye wee fool. She disna wish to see ye die."

"No' here anyway." He groaned with the effort as he unsheathed the weapon and held it out to Maggie.

She took it by the hilt, giving a yank to pry it from his grip, and set the blade into the small fire that continued to burn in the hearth. While they waited in silence for its cold steel to become white-hot, Maggie stared at the flames, hoping they might help calm her nerves. How could she go through with this? Her stomach lurched, and the smell of blood gagged her. Removing a splinter made her queasy; how would she ever be able to pry the bolt from Will's shoulder?

"Get to it, lass." Mary held Will against her bosom. "Elsbet!" she called to a rather large girl across the room. "Come here and hold his legs, now will ye?"

Though Maggie had never tended anything more serious than a few scrapes, she could imagine what was about to happen, and she braced herself for the inevitable. Even the strongest couldn't resist thrashing around under such circumstances. Will would be no different.

Subduing the growing unease in her chest, Maggie drew the glowing blade from the flame. "He should drink some of the . . . aqua vitae," she suggested, a glimmer of sympathy tugging at her heart.

"Nae! Yer family's at the gate, and I'll need all me wits about me." He pushed the flask away, his words coming in short, deep gasps. "Now either get on with it, if ye've the stomach for it, or leave it be." He bit into a piece of leather Mary had given him and clutched her skirt with his fist.

Maggie willed herself to stop shaking. *Do it right the first time, for God's sake.* She took a deep breath to calm her nerves and, after wiping her sweaty palms on her skirt, cut into Will's injured flesh, causing him to muffle a scream in his sister's shoulder. His hair had turned dark with sweat, and the women fought hard to hold him still.

"I can't," Maggie said, the sight of the crimson blood covering her hands causing her to swallow a new wave of nausea.

"Ye can!" Mary shouted. The poor woman was straining against Will's strength, and Maggie could see the urgency of the situation.

Reaching around to Will's back, she coated what remained of the shaft with honey and began to push. Little by little, the arrow emerged from his flesh. She tried grabbing the tip, hoping to pull it free, but the blood and sweat kept making it slip from her fingers. A bit more and she would have it. With a final tug, the tip came free, and the shaft followed much easier.

Maggie looked up and wiped an arm cross her forehead, using the opportunity to check on Will's condition. Though he breathed much easier now, all the color had drained from his face and his eyelids flickered. Yet he only flinched a bit when she checked the wounds for any splintered pieces and cleansed the lesions once more.

Mary's kirtle was saturated with Will's sweat, but she kept him cradled against her bosom. "Now finish it," she said, indicating the hearth with a tip of her head.

Maggie understood what the woman meant and returned the dagger to the fire while Will grasped his sister's skirt all the tighter. This must be a regular occurrence to him, just another part of life, but that didn't mean it would hurt any less.

On Mary's signal, Maggie retrieved the weapon and laid it flush against Will's open wounds. He came close to kicking Elsbet across the floor as the smoldering blade seared the jagged skin, but she managed to pinion his legs. At last, it was over, and he fell limp on Mary's lap.

"Can ye wrap it while I hold him?" Mary asked.

Black spots clouded Maggie's sight, and although she fought to remain conscious, she nodded, coating the incisions with honey before taking a clean piece of linen to bandage the injured shoulder. When she'd finished, she leaned against the wall for a moment, trying to fight off the sickening heat rising in her throat.

In the meantime, Mary rested Will against the overturned table and gave him some hot broth. How vulnerable he looked. His face was still pale and drawn, and the fury in his eyes seemed extinguished, at least for the time being.

"You should drink it, you know," she said. "You'll need your strength."

Will managed a halfhearted smile, and he took a sip, though Maggie doubted he had much interest in eating or drinking anything.

"I'll be fine," he said. "'Tis no' the first arrow I've taken, nor the last, I'll wager." He gazed around the chamber and curled his hands into fists, as if commanding them to stop trembling.

"I'm sure it's not, so you know what you have to do."

"Aye, I do." He released a long, slow breath and reached for his discarded latch-bow.

"Have you lost your mind?" Maggie said.

Will huffed a laugh. "Mayhap, along with me heart, but I've no intention of sitting here and doing nowt while yer kin storms me home, so I reckon I'm still right enough in the heid."

The Armstrongs had broken through the gate and were now working on the tower door. And though many of the Fosters had taken positions within the security of the tower walls, they continued to mount a courageous defense against their attackers. With a reassuring wink, Will stood and steadied himself against the wall, his bow held in his uninjured right arm.

"No, Will, please. You're not strong enough. They'll kill you."

"Aye, ye may well be right. Either way, they mean to see me dead. But tell me, lass, if I should survive here, will ye deliver me to the hangman yerself?"

"If I've the chance." Her answer came out firm and determined, but she suspected he didn't believe the words she said any more than she did.

371

"Since I'm to die, then, I'll add the theft of a kiss to me crimes." He grabbed her with his left hand, wincing as he pressed his lips against hers, but Maggie offered only a feeble resistance before returning his affection.

Will sat on a bench a while longer, claiming her kiss had drained him of his strength. But after closing his eyes and releasing a deep sigh, he stood and flashed her a defiant smile before rejoining his brothers.

Maggie watched him walk away, a knot forming in her stomach. He'd already ripped off the sling she'd fashioned to immobilize his left arm. His shoulder must be throbbing, and yet he showed little sign of injury. Apart from leaning against the wall once or twice to expel a few short puffs of air, he never wavered. One after the other, he sent his bolts down on her kinsman, his aim as confident and true as ever.

The fool hasn't got the brains to know he needs to rest. Maggie gazed over at Will's sister, the woman's expression reflecting Maggie's own anxiety, but Mary just shrugged, for they both knew better than to argue with a border knight.

Slipping behind the table, Maggie embraced the little girl, who sat cuddled up with her rag doll, her lower lip trembling on the verge of a sob.

"Your uncle will be fine," Maggie said. "He's way too stubborn to die."

"Will you wed him, then, and be me auntie?" Peggy asked.

"What? Why would you think that?"

"Because you're looking after him the same way me ma looks after me da."

Maggie held the child all the tighter, fighting the idea she could ever love a lying, murdering bastard like Will Foster. But what if Edward was right? A single tear escaped and slid down her cheek. *Dear God, keep him safe . . . at least until the court finds him guilty.*

CHAPTER 35

From his station by the arrow slit, Will could hear the echo of footsteps and the cold sound of crowbars and axes thumping against the heavy oak door that protected the tower. The Armstrongs had managed to breach the barmekin wall and were now clambering up the foresters stairs.

Will hurried to the roof and continued hurling arrow after arrow down upon the invaders, stopping only occasionally to rest his shoulder. The wound had reopened and bled anew upon the linen wrap, but he wasn't about to give in, not with a vicious pack of Scottish dogs snapping at his heels.

A hand touched his shoulder, and he spun around.

"Calm yerself, lad," Graham said. "The scoundrels are fetching straw from the barn."

"They'll be scumfishing then?"

"Aye, 'tis me best guess. We'll need quit the tower afore the smoke gets so dense we canna see the way."

Will nodded and laid his latch aside to draw his sword, but his father stayed his arm. "Get that shoulder tended to first, aye. It will take a bit afore they get a fire going."

"'Tis fine, Da. A wee bit sore is all."

"Right, then, we'd best get to it. No sense in letting them ruin a perfectly good door."

"Ye mean to surrender, Da?"

His father barked out a laugh. "No' likely, laddie. We'll drive the scoundrels back out to the yard and mount a defense from there. Ye and Walt gather some of the lads and wait on the turnpike steps, eh? Some of them wily rogues are sure to slip past us. and I want a warm welcome for them."

"What of the women and bairns?"

"With ye and yer brothers blocking the way, they should be safe enough. They'll no' fire the door if we're already out there. Mary's lad, Tom, will keep watch. When ye've driven the last of the scurvy lot back into the yard, he'll bar the door behind ye and secure the yett." A smile broke out on his father's face. "Dinna fash yerself, laddie, yer lass will be held safe and secure."

Will could feel the heat rising in his face. "She no' me lass."

His father laughed again and patted him on his good shoulder. "As ye say, lad. Now get to it, eh?"

Will waited on the turnpike, just above the second floor. Only the clank of steel and the sound of clashing swords alerted him to the arrival of the Armstrongs. His father had opened the door. The die was cast. Instinctively, his fingers tightened on the hilt of his sword.

"Ye all right, lad?" Walt asked.

"Are ye?" he replied, causing his brother to laugh.

"*Si fractis fortis*, eh, Brother?"

With a firm nod, Will bolted down the steps, determined to stop the invaders. Walt joined him just below the second floor as Fergus Rutherford and Andy Armstrong came charging up the turnpike.

"What have ye done with her, lad?" Andy's eyes blazed with fire, but even so, he held out his arm to restrain Fergus.

"I'll die afore I turn her ower to such as Ian Rutherford," Will shouted.

"Then die ye shall." Andy lunged forward, narrowly missing Will's side. He cursed and drew his dagger but stopped short, his eyes fixed on the steps above.

Will frowned, surprised the Scot allowed his attention to be so diverted during a skirmish. He turned to follow Andy's gaze and groaned in exasperation. Maggie had just come around the curve in the staircase and stood gaping down at them.

"Uncle!" Though she cried out to the man, she made no attempt to run to him. Instead, she came up behind Will, placing a hand on his shoulder. "Please, we can sort this out, if everyone would just put their weapons away."

"Maggie!" Andy's arm dropped, and for one fleeting moment, Will considered doing the same. He placed his left hand over hers for a moment, a thrill of hope surging through his heart.

"Come here, wench!" Fergus Rutherford stepped forward, his weapon raised, his tone more of an order than a request. "Shove the dog-faced scum toward me, and I'll end his worthless life."

Will tightened his grip on the hilt of his sword once more. Maggie's pleas might have worked on Andy, but Fergus was another matter. Nothing she said would stop the bloodshed. There was honor at stake here, and it involved more than one slip of a girl.

"Maggie," Will whispered, "get back upstairs till ye're called for. Do as I say, lass . . . please."

Will looked deeply into her eyes, and for a split second he saw some tenderness there, but another shout from below broke the spell. Rounding the stairwell, Dylan Hetherington rushed to his aid, blade in hand.

"Dylan!" Maggie's mouth dropped, her eyes wide as the man came running up the steps to join the others. Before she could say another word, Fergus Rutherford whirled around and knocked the dark-haired Englishman across the face with the hilt of his sword.

Maggie darted to the floor below, shoving the others out of her way and taking Dylan in her arms. Fergus went to grab her, but she pulled away. "You weasel," she said, spitting the words. "Touch me again and I'll claw your eyes out."

Will shot a glance in Walt's direction before returning his attention to Maggie. He knew she and Dylan were acquainted. Still, why would a fair young Scottish maiden put herself at such risk for that one particular Englishman? Andy's and Walt's expressions told him they must be wondering the same thing. But the fate of his friend concerned him far more than Maggie's curious reaction.

Will had become as close to the strange-talking Englishman as he was to any of his brothers and was troubled by the blow he had taken. Giving Fergus a hard jab in the stomach, he made his way down the curving turnpike to where Dylan lay motionless and knelt by Maggie's side.

"He should be all right," she muttered. "He's just a bit dazed."

Will frowned, still a bit confused by the extent of Maggie's concern for his friend, but there was no time for explanations. The Armstrongs were scumfishing in spite of his father's efforts, and the fires they had set below soon sent thick billows of smoke up into the tower. He had to clear the path so his nephew Tom could lead the womenfolk and bairns to the safety of the moors. By instinct, he lifted Dylan and, with Walt's help, carried him outside. He shouted for Maggie to follow, but either she didn't hear or chose not to, for when they emerged into the cool, clear air, she was nowhere to be found.

Will spun around, searching the barmekin yard for a glimpse of the auburn-haired lass he'd lost his heart to, but the smoke from the burning straw that surrounded the peel temporarily clouded his vision. When he finally spotted her, she was being mounted on Andy Armstrong's horse, though whether or not it was of her own free will he couldn't be sure. Either way, he wasn't about to abandon her to the depravity of Ian Rutherford. In a frantic bid to rescue her, he ran toward the silver stallion, but before he could raise his sword, he was knocked off his feet by one swift blow.

Stunned by the impact, his sword thrown halfway across the yard, Will groped for a discarded pike and managed to thwart Andy's thrust just in time. He pushed the rugged Scotsman aside and jumped to his feet, lunging forward, though he missed Andy and drove his weapon into the tower wall. The impact split the narrow shaft in two, causing him to stumble against the hard gray stone and once more leaving him weaponless.

Andy raised his blade again, but Will lifted his foot and sent his assailant crashing into the nearby vegetable garden. Without a moment's hesitation, he raced across the yard to reclaim his sword, reaching it just in time to stop Fergus Rutherford from running him through. But when Sandy Rutherford and Andy Armstrong joined in the fight as well, Will could see it might not end well for him. He scanned the yard for his kinsmen, but they all had their hands full. He was on his own.

With his pike broken and his sword once more yanked from his hand, the only defense he had left was the small dagger tucked in the cuff of his boot. Its sharp edge was little use against the three swords aimed at his heart, but Will was not about to give up. His eyes darted back and forth between the three Scots, trying to determine which one he was going to take with him.

That chance never came, for Alasdair Armstrong slipped up from behind and now held his own dagger to Will's neck.

"Drop it, Will, or I'll cut yer throat here and now. 'Twill make nae difference to me."

"Do as he says, lad." Andy pressed his sword against Will's sore shoulder. "'Twill be best for all concerned."

Will looked to Maggie, but she turned away, ignoring his unspoken plea, and so he threw his dagger to the ground. Once again, her dart had pierced his heart, but still, he would not waver.

"Beat our Maggie, will ye," Fergus scowled. "We'll see how brave ye are when the odds are against ye." The Scot took the hilt of his sword and jammed it into Will's stomach, causing him to fall to his knees. "That's for our Rabbie, ye murdering scoundrel."

****

Maggie felt a cold chill pierce her heart. For a short time, she had actually felt something for Will. How could she have forgotten what he'd done? But if Edward was right, Will hadn't been the one responsible for taking her father's life. A wave of nausea clutched her stomach. She needed to be sure, but how?

She watched in silence as Sandy Rutherford stepped forward, knocking Will across the face with his axe handle. She gasped and tightened her fingers around the reins. *There was no need for that.* Will fell prone at Sandy's feet, dazed by the blow, but still she held her tongue. What if Andy was right and Will had killed her father? Her uncle had said as much, hadn't he?

The fighting continued all around them, and for a moment she almost hoped someone would come to Will's aid, but as she cast her gaze from one scuffle to the next, she realized they were all otherwise occupied. A pang of regret jabbed at her heart, but then the vision of Will riding away from her dying father stifled it almost before it had formed.

Andy mounted behind her, clutching his arms around her waist and shouting something to Fergus. Without wasting any time, Ian's brother bound Will's hands and feet and threw him over Sandy's horse.

"Wait!" Maggie said, turning in the saddle to see her uncle better. "What if he's innocent? You didn't actually see him do it, did you?"

"Nae, lass, but Ian did." He took the reins, but Maggie grabbed his arm.

"What if Ian is lying? Everyone knows how much he hates Will."

Andy smiled, his eyes full of sadness. "Ach, Bonnie Will's a sweet-talking rogue, to be sure. I dinna ken what he's been telling ye, darlin', but did ye forget I saw his dagger in yer da's back, plain as day?"

"But anyone could have put it there. I mean, even Ian."

"Now, lass, I ken Bonnie Will's a braw lad and catches many a lassie's eye, but ye canna trust a thing he says, no' in this. 'Tis his life at risk, ye ken. Besides, the warden will sort it all out on the Day of Truce."

"So he will have a fair trial, then?" The tension in her stomach eased a bit. If he wasn't to blame, they'd find him innocent. In fact, this was best for him as well, providing he was telling the truth. And if not, he deserved whatever he got.

"Aye, we'll hold him to ransom and demand he appear. Graham's an honest man. If he gives his word to it, the lad will be there, whether he pays the ransom or no'. Now turn round, aye, or 'twill be us they're holding to ransom."

With a flick of the reins he followed his kinsmen and headed for Scotland, leaving the Fosters and their allies to take account of their losses.

*****

Dylan groaned as he pulled himself up against the cold stone wall of the peel. His head throbbed, and he was sure the left side of his face had been smashed in beyond all recognition; at least, it felt like it had. He stumbled across the crowded yard, staring in awe at the burning buildings and utter confusion that surrounded him. Smoldering embers fell at his feet, and all around people were dashing back and forth, yelling, shouting, bandaging wounds, or rushing with buckets of water to douse yet another flaming cottage.

Edward Foster lay dead against the far wall, and Dylan fell down beside him. His heart ached as he closed the kind man's eyes and gently removed the amulet from around his neck. How they'd argued over that stupid stone, over what it meant to be able to travel through the centuries.

To Dylan, it was an adventure, something to be experienced to its fullest, but to Edward it had become a sacred trust. He had almost forbidden Dylan to take part in a foray, warning him that anything he did could change history. But what did it matter now? Edward was gone just the same, and years from now that's all anyone would remember. Right or wrong, each man must make his own course, and history would unfold around it.

Dylan knew now what his path must be. Edward's life had meant something, and he was going to make sure the Armstrongs paid. But what of Maggie? With Edward and Robert gone, he was her only hope. Panic flooded his senses as he began to search the courtyard, hoping to catch a glimpse of her deep auburn hair, but his eyes came to rest instead on Will's sister, Annie.

She was sitting right in the middle of the barmekin yard, oblivious to the turmoil that had taken place around her. Had one of those beasts dragged her out there? Dear God, no! Not again.

Without a thought for his own welfare, Dylan made his way to her side. "You shouldn't be sitting out here this way, Annie. Come over against the peel." He reached out hesitantly, expecting her to cringe at his touch, but she brushed her hand against his battered cheek.

"If we can find a pitcher of water that's no' been overturned, I'll clean that wound for ye," she said with a tender smile.

Dylan was stunned, as well as heartened, by Annie's reaction. Yet at the same time, he was reluctant to hug her for fear of breaking the spell, so he simply returned her smile as best he could. "Thank you, lass. Is it as bad as I fear?"

"Ye men are all alike." She laughed the way she used to before Ian ravaged her. "Ye'll be run clear through with a pike and say 'tis nowt, but a wee smack about the face and ye swear ye're dying. Come on, then, and mind where ye walk."

They found some water, and Annie gently patted Dylan's cheek. "'Tis a nasty bruise, I'll give ye that, but ye'll live to be as bonnie as ye were afore, I'm afraid. Then ye'll no' spare a glance for such as me, I'll wager."

"And why would you think that, Annie Foster?" Dylan asked. "There's none prettier than you in all of England."

Annie's face grew stern, and Dylan feared he'd uttered the wrong words. "Ian Rutherford's had me, ye ken."

"And what of it?" He took a chance and placed his hand on her arm, hoping not to lose her again. "What he took, he stole, for 'tis well-known you put up a valiant fight. You couldn't have kept him from what he wanted, any more than I could have kept Fergus from smashing my face."

"D'ye truly believe that, Dylan Hetherington, or are ye just saying it to be kind?"

"Oh, Annie, of course, I believe it. Will saw that coward slinking out of the barn, and he'll pay for what he did to you."

"Will!" Anxiety transformed Annie's pretty face, and she grabbed Dylan's arm. "They carried him off."

"What do you mean?" A jolt of fear struck Dylan in the gut. "Who carried him off?"

"Fergus Rutherford, I think it was, though the lot of them attacked me brother, him wounded and all. And that Maggie Armstrong, just sitting there and letting them do it, like she had nae feeling for Will at all."

"She doesn't, I'm afraid, Annie," Dylan said. "The Armstrongs say Will murdered her da. She most likely wishes him dead."

"Dinna be daft," Annie said, her sweet lips dimpling into a shy smile. "She loves him just as sure as I love . . ." She ducked her head, her cheeks blushing a pale pink. "Are ye hurt anywhere else?"

"Annie." Dylan whispered her name, not wanting to upset the girl lest she withdraw back into herself. "I have to go after Will, but I don't want to leave unless . . ."

"I ken what ye're thinking, Dylan Hetherington, but I'm all right now." A single tear ran down her cheek as she spoke. "I've been watching what's been happening here today, and ye're right, there are certain things in our lives we can control and others we canna. I've blamed meself long enough for what Ian did to me, and now 'tis time to blame the one responsible. I fought the best I could, and any man canna see that is no' worth having." She broke down crying, and Dylan rested her head on his shoulder, clutching her to himself. "Now go find me brother," she added as she pulled back and blew her nose.

"You're a fine lass, Annie Foster, and any man would be lucky to have you." Tears filled Dylan's eyes. He wanted to hold her in his arms forever, protecting her from the wickedness of the world, but was he worthy of someone so pure and innocent? Such thoughts had never even occurred to him before, and for the first time in his life, it really mattered.

He was just about to give her a kiss on the forehead when Betty Foster came running toward them, so any further discussion on the subject would have to wait.

"Lovit be God," Betty cried, her hands shaking as she reached out to her daughter. Annie smiled and hugged her mother. Other family members followed in turn, each overjoyed at Annie's recovery.

Dylan stepped back, his heart close to bursting with happiness. He loved Annie—not just a passing infatuation or a desire to get under her skirts, but real love. Excited to share the revelation with Will, Annie's words echoed through his head, transforming his joy to rage. The bastards had taken Will.

Dylan had grabbed Graham by the shoulder, intent on alerting him to his son's kidnapping, when Betty began to panic.

"Will!" she shouted. "Where's me Will?"

"They've taken him," Dylan said, a lump forming in his throat as he thought of what that might mean. Annie reached over and took his hand.

"Gather together all ye can," Graham Foster shouted. "We'll leave afore the sun sets and ride with horn blaring. I want me William back unharmed, or the Armstrongs will pay a heavy price."

"'Twas a Rutherford what took him," Annie said, "and a Rutherford should pay."

"Which one was it, Annie, darlin'?" Graham asked.

Dylan knew she longed to say it was Ian, but he looked at her sternly. "You're better than that, Annie Foster."

"'Twas Fergus and Sandy Rutherford I saw carry him off . . . but Ian was there, ye can be sure of that."

"So be it!" Graham commanded. "We ride to the Rutherfords and retrieve our Will . . . or exact our revenge, whichever the case may be."

Dylan joined the men as they readied themselves once more. They would ride in hot trod, with sleuth hounds and trumpets proclaiming their lawful approach. He thought of Edward, how hard he'd tried not to interfere, but how could they avoid it?

This is my life, Edward. How can I not be a part of it?

Just before they were ready to leave, Dylan walked over to Annie. "Would you have a kiss for a brave warrior, lass?"

"I do thank ye, Dylan, for ye're a good friend to me brother. Ye're no' duty-bound to go, ye ken."

"As you say, Will's my friend, and a poor one I would be if I didn't ride to his rescue."

Annie stood on her tiptoes and kissed Dylan gently on the cheek. "More than that I canna give ye just yet, but I'm sure there's many a lass would do ye the honor."

"'Tis not many a lass I'm looking for, Annie." Dylan leaned down and kissed her gently on the forehead, for he understood what she meant.

"Get yerself home safe, Dylan Hetherington."

Dylan smiled, handing Annie his amulet. "Don't ask me how, Annie, but I know Maggie Armstrong, and that amulet belongs to her. I don't love her, not the way you might think. I can't explain it. All I can do is ask you to trust me. If anything happens to me, I want you to somehow get it to her, without putting yourself in any danger, do you understand? 'Tis not that important, but you are."

Annie hesitated for a moment, and Dylan felt the sting of fear cut through him like a razor's edge, but then she took deep breath and answered, "Aye, I understand, and I trust ye, though I'm no' sure I should."

"And why not?" Dylan grinned, relieved that his request had not caused her to turn him away.

"Many a promise I've heard ye make a lass just to have yer way with her," Annie taunted, though the twinkle in her eye told him she was teasing.

"Who's been telling you that?" Dylan replied with mock indignation. In truth, his heart was near bursting with joy to see the old Annie returned, the one he had met when he'd first arrived.

"I have ears that hear and eyes that see."

Dylan felt his cheeks flush, and he stammered as he spoke. "That was . . . they didn't mean . . . I . . . ."

"I'm no' asking ye for any promises, lad." Annie smiled. "I'll take care of yer locket. All I ask in return is that ye care for yerself so as no' to break every heart from here to Carlisle."

This time Dylan leaned over and kissed her on the lips. "I'll come back to you, Annie." With the feel of her lips still on his, he rode off toward the north in search of the Rutherfords. He would be back, with Will, for he'd never break a promise to Annie, not even if it meant breathing his last.

****

Betty stood with the other women, watching their men ride through the barmekin gate. Annie stood next to her, pressing the amulet close to her heart, and Betty could see the love in her daughter's expression.

"Ye've eyes for that one, have ye, Annie?" Betty wrapped her arm around her daughter's shoulders.

"Aye, Ma, but I'm no' fooling meself," Annie replied. "I ken the tales he tells."

"He's a rogue, our Dylan, that's sure."

"Aye, he is," Annie smiled, mischief glinting in her eyes, "but I think he's my rogue."

Betty squeezed her tighter. Dylan Hetherington had somehow brought her daughter back to her, and for that, she just might give him the benefit of the doubt.

CHAPTER 36

Maggie gasped when Fergus reached the crest of the hill and she saw the unconscious form he had thrown across the saddle. Will's head hung limp, his hair ragged as they galloped along the misty fields, his blood trickling down amongst the golden tresses and dripping occasionally to the soil below. Try as she might, she couldn't dispel the nagging doubt she had about Will's guilt. But if he were innocent, they would let him return home unharmed. Andy had promised her as much. At any rate, he would be brought to the warden and given a fair trial.

The reivers continued over the Bewcastle Wastes, dropping small bands of Armstrongs and Elliots along the way, until they were well within their own borders. Then, and only then, did the remaining party stop to refresh their horses in the crystal waters of the River Esk.

"What d'ye think, Ian?" Fergus said. He jumped from his horse with a hearty laugh, his boot crushing a batch of bluebells into the dampened ground. "A fair exchange?"

Ian glared at Maggie in disgust. "For what I got in return, I'd say 'twas more than fair. He'll bring a better price, that's certain." He spit on the ground, wiping the residue from his mouth with a swipe of his arm. "Unless of course, he meets with some tragic misfortune along the way, a bit of Jedburgh justice, perchance."

A wicked grin crossed Fergus's face. "That would be a shame now." He yanked Will's body onto the ground and began to slap his face to wake him up. "Mayhap ye'd like something to drink now, laddie?"

"What did you mean by that?" Maggie interrupted. She walked over to Ian, her arms placed on her hips.

"'Tis none of yer affair, wench," Ian said. "That is, unless ye've given yer heart to him as well as yer virtue."

"What! I never . . . How could you ever think—"

"I can see what ye've done, lassie." Ian tugged the chemise from her shoulder, but she raised her hand and pulled away, pushing the material back in place. "And was it sweet? Was his tongue warm and tantalizing as it caressed yer bare white bosom?"

Maggie reacted at once, attempting to slap Ian across his windburned cheek, but he stopped her cold, grabbing her wrist and twisting it roughly.

"Ian!" She cried out in pain. "If you keep behaving like this, my uncle might get the idea you don't want to marry me, and I certainly wouldn't contest it."

He pulled her close, rubbing his lips against her ear, clearly not wanting her uncles to think anything was amiss. "Oh, I'll marry ye, wench. Have nae fear of that. No' to do so now would put me at odds with yer family, and the Armstrongs are a force to be reckoned with."

Placing his hand on her behind, her drew her so close she could feel him hard against her leg, and bile rose in her throat.

"Besides, I'll have nae trouble handling ye, especially now yer father's out of the way, leaving yer future in Geordie's hands. Yer dowry alone is worth far too much for me to throw away. So ye see, the benefits of taking ye to me bed far outweigh any grief ye might give me. But mind this, I'll do as I please and sleep where I wish, and ye'll have noucht to say about it."

He licked her ear, and she tried to wrench herself free, but he squeezed all the tighter. "Stay still, ye wee trollop, or I'll take ye behind yon bush and lift yer skirts right here."

"I guess you want to die, then, because my uncles would kill you."

Ian yanked her behind a gorse bush and laughed. "Geordie's already given his word, and ye're to be mine. He'll no' blame a lad for being that glad to see ye again, rescued from the clutches of Will Foster. The pack of fools all think he's to blame for yer da's death."

As the realization of Ian's words sank in, Maggie began to feel much too nauseous to speak. How could she have been so blind? Will had been telling the truth. It was Ian who had murdered her father in cold blood, and now he planned to use her to gain influence with the clan. She balled her hands at her sides, quelling the pain and disgust.

"Ian, I swear if you do anything to harm that innocent man, I'll never marry you."

"Dinna swear, lass. It disna become ye." He took her face in his hand and squeezed her cheeks harshly. "And ye'll be more than willing when the time comes, aye. Ye can be sure of that. Or I'll see to it ye get a bit of what Annie Foster got."

"My uncle . . ." Maggie started to speak, but it didn't even seem to faze the brazen reiver.

"Yer uncle will ken noucht of it, lassie!" With that, he kissed her hard on the mouth and ran his hand up her bare leg.

She squirmed to free herself, but he pinned her against the rough bark of a nearby oak. Just when she thought she might upchuck into his mouth, he shoved her aside and strode over to Andy. He spoke only a few words, but she could see the anger rising in her uncle's cheeks. What was the bastard telling him?

Whatever he said, it was enough for Geordie Armstrong and Hob Rutherford to be called over, and though Maggie moved to join them, Fergus put his arm against her chest, warning her to stay clear. She clenched her fists all the tighter, not about to be dictated to by the likes of Fergus Rutherford.

"Either you move that arm, or I'll see to it my cousin Alasdair separates you from it." Without another word, she pushed him aside and continued on her way.

"What is it, lass?" Geordie barked the question, and Maggie could tell his patience was wearing thin.

"I want to know what you plan to do with Will Foster."

"'Tis none of yer concern, lassie," Geordie said, "but ken this, he'll pay dearly for what he's done to ye and yer da."

"But he's done nothing," Maggie said. "He's innocent."

Andy frowned and tightened the points over her torn chemise. "Did ye willingly allow him to do this, then, lass?"

"No, of course not, but—"

"Then noucht more need be said." Andy pressed his finger against her lips, a gentle smile on his own. "We'll handle it, lassie."

Maggie could only shake her head in desperation, for Ian and her uncle Sim had by then dragged Will to his feet and brought him to his knees before Geordie.

"Didn't any of you hear what Ian just said?" She could hear herself screaming, trying to get her uncles to listen. "Are you all blind as well as deaf? Didn't you see how rough Ian was with me?"

The reivers just looked from one to the other, shrugging and poking each other in the ribs as snide smiles crossed their faces.

"Looked like a wee bit of foreplay to me," Fergus finally said.

"What? You filthy little piece of shit. I ought to give you a good swift kick in the balls."

"That's enough, lass!" Geordie bellowed. "Ye'll learn ye place right enough once yer husband takes a good hand to ye."

Maggie turned to Andy, her mouth and eyes wide with shock, but he just shook his head.

"I'm no' sure what ye were trying to say, lass, but I'm certain it wasna something a lady should be saying. Mayhap Geordie has a point, aye? Now stand back and let us get on with it."

"Will Foster," Geordie said, his voice cold and sure, "ye've been found guilty of murder, and this act alone demands that ye pay with yer life."

"I've killed no one!" Will spoke with conviction, his words strong and steady, though Maggie's uncles paid him no mind.

"But yer heinous crimes dinna end there," Geordie went on, "for even as me brother lay cold in his grave, ye stole away his grieving daughter and, with malice of heart, forced yerself upon her."

"No!" Will groaned. He looked up at Geordie, his eyes filled with confusion. "I didna hurt the lass."

Much to Maggie's dismay, Geordie continued undaunted. "And so it is, ye shall die this day, with nae honor and nae glory. An eye for an eye, I say. Make it swift, lads."

Maggie could almost hear Will's heart pounding beneath his thick leather jack, but once more his emotions remained within. "May God forgive yer murderous souls," he yelled as they dragged him into the clear water of the nearby river. "I've done nowt of which I've been accused."

"Uncle, please!" Maggie couldn't believe her eyes or ears. She grabbed Geordie's arm, begging him to stop, but he'd have none of it, and with a firm but gentle hand, he nudged her aside.

This couldn't be happening. She looked at Ian, but her heart no long gave the slightest flutter at the sight of him. There was only a sickly numbness that permeated her entire body. Edward had been right, after all. Though Ian didn't come right out and say it, his remarks were all too clear. Not only had he raped that poor girl and brutally molested her, but with cold and calculated precision, he'd ended the life of Maggie's father, pretending all the time to comfort her. And what was more, he'd blamed it all on Will Foster. She could see through Ian now, and she hated what she saw.

As she gazed at Will, though, she saw all the virtues her father had spoken of. He was brave and daring, gallant and sturdy, a man who valued his word and kept it at all cost. She'd never really been able to hate him, and at last she understood why. Will Foster embodied all that her father was, all that she'd been taught to love, and now he was going to die. Die because she had been unable to clear his name.

The three men had by now ventured quite far out into the river, and Andy turned to await Geordie's command. Maggie looked to her eldest uncle one last time, shouting desperately and begging him once again to stop, but he simply glanced across the river and gave a firm nod.

****

On his brother's signal, Andy undid the leather bands that held Will's hands. "Make peace with yer Maker, rogue."

Will just stared straight ahead, blessing himself quietly. His heart pounded, and he felt sick inside, but he refused to give them the satisfaction of calling him a coward. He began to pray, his voice steady and calm, *"Deus meus, ex toto corde . . ."*

But it appeared Ian had heard enough. He thrust his sword hilt into Will's back and pushed him to his knees.

The cool water splashed around Will's chin, and he closed his eyes for a moment in an effort to retain his composure. Taking a deep breath, he finished his prayer. When he opened his eyes again, he looked up to Andy.

"I love her, and for all the gold in England and Scotland combined, I would do nowt to hurt her. I swear it with me dying breath, by heaven above me, by my part of paradise, and by God himself, I didna kill yer brother, nor did I violate his daughter."

Will sensed that his plea touched Andy's heart, for the man wavered slightly. "I've kent ye since ye were a wee bairn, lad, but there's too much proof against ye. If only our Maggie could be sure of what she'd seen."

Ian's fierce gaze showed no such scruples, nor did he seem inclined to allow Andy the time to develop any either.

"May ye rest in peace," he said as he grabbed Will's hair and shoved his head beneath the surface.

Though still stunned from the blow he had taken, Will struggled for all he was worth, gasping as his head momentarily broke the surface.

"Are ye with me, Andy?" Ian said. "Think of what he did to the poor wee lass and yer brother as well. Will ye no' avenge him?"

"Aye." Andy nodded, and though Will could sense the hesitation in the man's voice, he also knew it would do no good. Andy pushed hard on the back of his neck, and so his head went under the rippling water once more.

Though he refused to show any fear, Will continued to fight for his life. Almost by instinct, he reached up, clawing at Ian's face and clutching Andy's jerkin. He pressed up against their combined strength, straining to keep himself from succumbing to the watery depths, but it was to no avail. The river was winning. A blanket of warmth was enveloping his entire body, lulling him into an eternal sleep. Soft voices beckoned him, enticing him to release his tentative grip on life. He could feel his hand begin to slip down Andy's chest as the strength left his body, until there was no longer any movement at all, and a peaceful slumber descended upon him.

****

Maggie's heart sank as Will's arms began to rise lifelessly to the surface, his tawny hair floating aimlessly on the gentle current. How could she have allowed such a savage crime to be committed? But what could she do? Her words had been of no consequence, but her actions, were they drastic enough, may yet have some effect. She only prayed they had come in time.

Noticing how preoccupied Geordie had become, Maggie decided on a course of action. She rushed forward in tears and collapsed in her uncle's arms. With daughters of his own, she suspected he would react according to his fatherly instincts in spite of his clear aversion for such emotions. To her gratification, he did just as she had hoped. His powerful arms caressed her trembling body. He patted her on the back, speaking softer than Maggie had ever heard him speak, and a momentary wave of guilt washed over her, though it didn't last long.

"There now, lass," he said. "'Twill soon be done, and yer father will be avenged."

"Aye, that he will," Maggie said. She grabbed his dagger from its sheath, whirling around beside Alasdair and holding the blade to his neck. "Kneel down, Alasdair. Now, or so help me I know how to use this."

Alasdair did as he was told, though his eyes flashed with unspoken questions. They were questions Maggie had no intention of answering, for there was a more important issue at hand. She turned toward the water, shouting to her uncle.

"Now bring him out or I'll slice Alasdair's throat before you can draw your weapons, and if you've any doubt of it, just remember whose daughter I am."

"Dinna listen to her," Alasdair said in defiance. "Me life's a small price to pay for bringing that murderous scoundrel to justice."

Under ordinary circumstances, Maggie knew Geordie would have challenged such a threat, but Alasdair was his only living son, not to mention his heir, and in spite of his gruff manner, it was clear the man cared a great deal for the boy. Even now she could see the anger and grief crossing her uncle's face, battling for precedence, as he gazed into her eyes. Her only hope was that he would see her father's resolve there, that he would sense Robert's strength in her voice. Whatever disagreements the two may have had, the one thing Geordie could never deny was his brother's strength of conviction. Would he sense that same determination in her? After a moment's hesitation, she had her answer, for Geordie motioned for Andy to bring Will's waterlogged body ashore.

"'Twill do nae good, lassie," he said. "The lad's dead and gone."

Indeed, it did look that way, for Will's face was pale and his lips had a bluish tint as he lay on the moss-covered bank. Maggie's heart pounded against her ribs, for she feared her uncle was right and that she had acted too late. There was still hope, though. She thought back to the last summer she'd spent on Long Island. There was that boy who had been pulled out of the ocean half-dead. He'd survived, though, and if she could just remember her first-aid training, perhaps Will would as well.

"Lay him on his side and pound his back," she said, "between his shoulders." When no one responded, she pressed the knife firmer against her cousin's neck. "Do it now!"

"Maggie," Alasdair said, his voice desperate, but she paid him no heed. Never again would she make him choose between her and his family. If he believed she would kill him, there would be no decision to be made.

"Stay still, Alasdair!" She forced her lips together and glared at Andy. The look in his eyes told her that he noticed the small drop of blood trickling down his nephew's neck. Whether it was a belief that she truly would act on her threats that guided his subsequent actions or something inside that told him she was right, she couldn't say. Either way, he wasted no time in doing as Maggie instructed, though it seemed to make little sense to him.

A bit of water ran from Will's nose and mouth, and she continued with more resolution than she felt. "Now turn him on his back and tilt his head. When you've done that, pinch his nose closed and breathe into his mouth, four deep breaths."

"What?" Andy asked as the men all stared in puzzlement, obviously convinced she had taken leave of her senses. "Ye want me to kiss a dead man?"

"Just do it," she shouted. Her anger was rising, and she had all she could do to keep from stamping her foot like some petulant child. "If you don't breathe your life into him, I will surely take Alasdair's."

Her fist tightened on the hilt of the dagger, and once more Geordie nodded. "Do it, lad!"

Ian's eyes grew wide. "Are ye all out of yer heids?" He reached out to grab Andy's shoulder, but the older reiver cast him a withering glance, and he backed away.

"Much as I hate to admit it, the lad's gone, lass," Andy said. "Let him rest in peace."

Maggie could feel the heat rising in her face, the nerves in her fingers protesting as she gripped the hilt so hard her nails pierced the palm of her hand. "He will be if you don't get to it," she insisted.

Andy nodded, his brows furrowed as he bent over the form before him. Again and again, he blew into Will's mouth, but the young Englishman was not responding. Andy sat back on his heels and shook his head. "I'm sorry, lass. 'Tis nae use."

Her mind in turmoil, Maggie returned to that summer on Long Island and that boy on the beach. What had they done next? She stared off into the distance, transporting herself back to that day, to that moment on the sand, and the answer came to her, carried across time and distance on the ocean breeze. "Now put your hands over one another and press down on the center of his chest, hard and fast."

Andy shook his head, once more doing what he was told, but before he could even get started, Will responded. In one violent burst of foaming vomit, he coughed, sending a torrent of river water across Ian Rutherford's new suede boots.

Maggie sighed in relief, unconsciously allowing her grip on the knife to grow slack. Fortunately for her, only Ian noticed, and in his eagerness to disarm her, he made such a commotion that she was easily able to recover her advantage. Not that her renewed hold on Alasdair would have made any difference to Ian, but one word from Geordie certainly did. Ian stopped in his tracks, at least for the moment, but now what? They still needed to escape, and that was going to be easier said than done.

"Now that ye've saved him, wench," Ian said, his hand grasping the hilt of his sword, "what do ye plan on doing with him?"

"Don't even think it," Maggie said, "or Alasdair's death will be on your head." It was obvious that Ian was chomping at the bit and longed to plunge his sword through Will's heart. Only her uncle stood between them, for he had risen and placed his hand on his on sword. But how long would that last? She had to think of something fast.

"Put it away," Geordie commanded. "Dinna even think of defying me on this, wean!"

Ian's lips were pressed together so tight they had turned pale, almost disappearing completely from his face, but nevertheless he complied. As he did, his sword caught a glint of sunshine, and it gave Maggie an idea.

"No, don't sheathe it," she instructed the depraved Scotsman. "Throw it out into the river."

"What!" Ian protested. "Ye go too far, wench!"

"And throw your boots there as well," Maggie continued. "After all, they are already wet." Oddly enough, she was beginning to enjoy herself now that she knew Will would be all right.

Ian opened his mouth to object, but Alasdair interrupted.

"Da!" he said, gasping for air. "Please do as she asks. She means what she says."

"Do it, laddie!" Geordie placed a hand on his own sword, his eyes daring Ian to defy him.

Maggie shifted her head to the side to look down at her cousin. She hadn't pressed any harder on the knife. Certainly not enough to cause him to react in such a manner. But Alasdair just stared straight ahead, although she could swear she spied a twinkle in his eye as she looked back down toward Will.

Ian's jaw was set in stone, and if it were true that looks could kill, she and Will both would have expired there on the spot. Fortunately, the old saying was more literary than literal, and they both survived the Scotsman's murderous glances.

"Now, every last one of you, do the same with your weapons and your boots," Maggie said. "You as well, Uncle."

"Maggie?" Andy protested. "Think what ye're doing, lass. 'Tis March treason to be aiding such as him. Ye ken I love ye, darlin', but if ye carry this out, they'll be little even I can do to save ye."

"And will you seek to drown me too, Uncle?" she asked.

A sudden wave of guilt crossed Andy's face, and he threw his sword out deep into the Esk. "I'm only thankful yer father didna live to see this."

"My father warned me about Ian," Maggie said. "Gran did too. I didn't know what they meant at the time, but it was him they were warning me about. They knew what he was, or at least suspected it, but I was too blind to see, and now so are you."

"Ye dinna ken what ye're blethering about, lassie." Geordie's eyes flashed with sadness as he followed Andy's lead, tossing both sword and boots out across the rushing current.

"The rest of you, do the same. Now, please, before my hand slips."

Geordie nodded, albeit with understandable reluctance, the embarrassment of being bested by no more than a slip of a girl carved in his expression, and one by one each of the reivers followed suit, tossing their weapons far across the Esk.

"Now, Maggie," Andy cautioned, his eyes on the knife at his nephew's throat. "Stop and think. What has Alasdair ever done to ye?"

"No more and no less than Will has done to you," she said.

"Will ravished ye and murdered yer father," Andy said. "Have ye forgotten that?"

"No, how could I ever forget that awful day? But it wasn't Will," Maggie replied. "And less harm was done to me by his hand than Ian has done with his tongue alone, though Lord knows Will has had many a chance."

"But Ian loves ye, lass," Geordie said.

"Ian loves no one save himself, and I'll not be a part of that." Though her voice stayed strong and steady, there was a lilt of amusement to it as she realized what she was about to pull off. Never before had she acted so recklessly, and yet, firm in her conviction, she knew it was the right thing to do, regardless of the consequences. Now if she could manage their escape, they'd be home free.

CHAPTER 37

Will sat on the ground, his arms resting on his knees. Lord, he felt nauseous. Water pounded in his ears and ran from his nose, but that wasn't the worst of it. Still dizzy, he rested his head in his hands, hoping to stop the incessant throbbing that pressed against his eyes.

What on earth had happened? The last thing he remembered was Ian shoving him beneath the water. Lifting his head, he waited for the ground to stop spinning. God's teeth, he must be seeing things. Did Geordie Armstrong just throw his sword out into the middle of the Esk?

Will blinked to clear his vision. His brain must be waterlogged.

"Will. Will," a soft voice whispered his name. An angel calling him to heaven, perhaps? Maybe if he went with her, the nausea would subside. *Oh God! Too late.* He leaned over in the grass and heaved up another batch of river.

Get ahold of yerself, man, elst ye'll be in the water again, and this time Ian Rutherford may win out. Wiping his sleeve across his mouth, Will sat back up. His stomach ached, but the need to vomit had dissipated, and the thumping in his head had died down to a low rumble.

"Will! Can you hear me?" Maggie asked. "Do you think you can ride?"

Will looked up, surprised to see Alasdair kneeling with his hands on his head, a knife at his throat, and Maggie's head sticking up from behind him. He wasn't exactly sure what she was about, but it had to be better than a

397

watery grave, so he gave a tentative nod, praying he wouldn't once more set off the tabor residing in his head.

His legs were unsure, and he stumbled a bit as he rose, grabbing Andy's arm to steady himself. As he did, the Scotsman's eyes met his.

"Ye take care of our Maggie, laddie, or I'll hunt ye down like the blackguard ye are, and they'll never find a trace of ye."

Will didn't say a word, but made his way over to a nearby hobbler and grabbed on to the horse's mane. With a grunt, he put his foot in the stirrup and pulled himself up. Though a momentary wave of nausea gripped his gut as the horse pawed the ground, he patted the animal's neck, and the feeling passed.

Taking a deep breath, he settled himself in the saddle and tried to make sense out of the scene before him. What did Andy mean, take care of Maggie? He would love to, but he was fairly certain she'd sooner run him through than become his wife. Yet she must have had something to do with him finding himself on dry land and no longer gulping water. The question was why?

He swallowed yet another wave of queasiness and concentrated on his unlikely savior. What had happened to change Maggie's mind? Had his words convinced her of his innocence after all? As unlikely as it was, the thought somehow comforted him, quelling the nausea and dizziness, at least for the time being.

He watched in silence as Maggie and Alasdair inched their way toward him. Why didn't Alasdair just grab her arm and shove her away? He'd always thought the lad was made of stronger stuff, but then, what did Will care if it kept him from becoming a waterlogged corpse? Right now all he wanted to do was get as far away from the Armstrongs as possible. He'd sort the rest out later.

****

Maggie could see Will's discomfort, and, thinking it best that they be on their way, she instructed Ian to scatter the remaining horses. His eyes filled with fury, and for a moment she thought he'd refuse her, but on Geordie's command he did as he was told, albeit with more than a hint of resentment.

"Would ye leave us to walk home in shame, lass?" Geordie asked.

"For what you've tried to do here today, it's shame you deserve, Uncle."

"How could ye be so weak, man?" Ian's face was turning a deep crimson as he spat out the words. "She's just a wee lass, and ye let her—"

"Haud ye wheesht, man." Geordie's voice thundered across the river valley. "She's Rabbie Armstrong's bairn, and she's standing for what she believes, nae matter the consequences. I may fault her reasoning, for she's no' in her right mind, 'tis sure, but I'll no' fault her heart."

For an instant, Maggie understood exactly what her father had meant about Geordie. Beneath the rough exterior, beneath the harsh manners, lay a kind and noble heart. It didn't really matter which side of the border you were on. There were good and bad men on both alike. Geordie, Andy, and Will were true Border reivers. They lived by a code of honor, no matter how hard that code was for Maggie to understand. But Ian and the others like him were simply thieves and murderers, and yes, rapists. Maggie understood the difference now.

"I'm sorry, Uncle." She stared deep into Geordie's eyes, and for the first time since they'd met, she felt they understood each other, even if they would never agree.

"Ye'll no' be welcomed anywhere this side of the border," he cautioned her, though there was no anger or vengeance in his voice. "Ye ken that."

"She'll be welcome in my home," Will said, his voice firm and clear, though Maggie could see he continued to suffer the effects of being half-drowned. She feared he would fall from his horse, but he steadied himself by grabbing onto the animal's mane.

"Scotland will mourn for ye, lassie," Geordie said, a catch in his voice. "Now be on yer way."

"Will, can you take Alasdair's sword?" Maggie asked.

Will reached down without saying a word and grabbed Alasdair's weapon, holding it to her cousin's back. His hand was surprisingly steady for his condition. Maggie looked up at the Englishman, praying he wouldn't actually hurt her cousin. He must have understood, for he nodded slightly, holding the sword steady but making no attempt do anything more.

Maggie released her hold on Alasdair. Tears filled her eyes, but as he looked at her, he smiled softly, a slight bob of his head signaling his consent. There was only Andy left, and she could see the pain in his face.

"Try to understand, Uncle, sometimes what is right is not always what we'd like."

"Aye," he said, his voice gruff and stern, but the sparkle in his eye told her he recalled the day he'd spoken those very words to her. "And sometimes ye must let yer heart lead the way."

Maggie bit her lip to stifle a sob and wiped away a lone tear. She mounted behind Will, determined to give him all the support he needed, and together they galloped off to the south, to England, and, she hoped, to refuge.

****

Will rode the pony hard until they crossed the English border, then, after a short distance, he stopped at the base of a heather-covered slope set among some birch trees. His head was still spinning, and as he dismounted, he staggered, leaning up against his nagg for support. Maggie jumped down to his side, steadying him as they walked over and sat down beneath the silver trees.

"I'll get you some water," she said in an obvious attempt to be helpful.

"No, lass!" Will grabbed her by the arm, taking care not to press to hard. "Are ye daft? I think I've had enough water for one day."

"Oh, Will, I'm so sorry. I wasn't thinking."

"'Tis all right, lass, but d'ye reckon there's something a mite stronger in that saddlebag?"

"It's Ian's hobbler, so most likely there is." Her laughter sounded like the soft summer breeze, and while his head continued to throb, it didn't stop a more pleasant sensation from gripping his loins.

She smiled before she stood and hurried over to the horse, tying the animal to a nearby tree. God, she was beautiful. The setting sun glinted off her auburn hair, making it sparkle with crimson shards of light, and her skin shone radiant against the shadow of the trees. No wonder Ian wanted her as his own. Will's stomach turned sour at the thought, and he recalled how much she hated him.

"I didna kill yer father, lass, truly," he said when she returned with a skin of what he hoped was more than water.

Maggie sighed and sat down beside him. "I know. Ian practically admitted it—not in front of my family, of course." She pressed her lips together and opened the pouch, scrunching up her nose.

"Aqua vitae, lass," Will said, praying he was right. "And I wouldna mind a slug of it."

"Not until I've used it on that shoulder." Maggie reached out to undo his jack, but he stayed her hand.

"I'll be needing a bit of fortification, I reckon." He took the small leather skin and drank deeply, wiping his arm across his mouth when he finished. The potent liquid felt good going down and went some way to stopping the ache in his shoulder and the throbbing in his head.

"Your shoulder's bleeding again." Maggie yanked the pouch from his fist. "So now that you've *fortified* yourself, let me tend to it."

"Dinna fash, lass. I've survived worse. Why are ye so concerned anyway?" He shifted against the tree, repositioning himself so that his shoulder wasn't rubbing on the rough bark. "The last I mind, ye were sitting astride Andy's hobbler, watching yer kin bash me ower the heid and no' raising a finger to stop them."

"I still thought you'd murdered my father then. After all, you did ride out from behind him just as he fell, and whether you put it there or not, it was your dagger they found in his back."

"Did they now?" Will asked. "And who told them 'twas mine?" The words had no sooner left his lips than he moaned inwardly, the answer obvious.

Maggie threw him a pitying glance. "It had your crest on it, Will. And in my defense, my Uncle Andy did say they were just going to hold you for ransom and make sure you appeared at the next Day of Truce."

A sharp pain passed through his shoulder, and he winced, pressing his lips together to stifle a groan.

"That's it! I'm looking at that shoulder." She went back to unlacing his jack, and his pisle throbbed again.

"Leave it be!" His tone sounded harsh even to him.

Maggie stopped short, tears flooding her eyes. "What did you expect me to believe? Ian may be a liar, but he's a good one."

Will laughed out loud. "Finally figured that out, did ye?"

"You're one to talk. He was supposed to marry your sister. How did that happen?"

"Aye, I reckon ye're right there." Will shrugged his good shoulder. "But yer uncles should have kent me better. Geordie could have at least sat down with me da and talked it ower afore making any decisions."

The corner of Maggie's mouth quivered, causing a dimple to appear. "And I suppose you're right there, but Geordie's not one for having rational discussions. You should have heard him and my father go at it."

Will scratched his head. "Go at what, lass?"

Maggie giggled. "Things they disagreed about, which was almost everything. My da could hold his own, though." She sniffled, blinking away the tears. "Now let me look at that shoulder. I hope you don't think I alienated my whole family just to have you bleed to death."

"Aye, about that. I'm still no' sure I understand why ye risked so much to save me back at the river. Even if ye did ken the truth of it by then, sure ye would have counted that wee tussle in the barn against me."

Maggie scowled. "Hmm, perhaps it should have, but my da taught me better. No matter what you did, my family had no right to murder you in cold blood. You deserved your day in court." A smirk crossed her lips. "Besides, considering what you've been through, I think a little more of what you got in the barn might be a more appropriate sentence."

Will shifted position, debating whether he should protect his privates or take his punishment like a man. Lord knew his behavior was far from chivalrous. "Aye, well I suppose I should just be thankful ye saved me life, but what d'ye plan on doing with me now?"

Maggie barked out a laugh. "I'm not sure I know. As a matter of fact, I never thought very far beyond getting you away from there."

"Ye werena plotting yer own revenge, then?" Will rubbed his swollen lip and shifted again. "For what happened in the barn."

"What?" Maggie stood up and moved closer. "Oh, of course. I do think it would be best if you closed your eyes this time. That way you won't see it coming."

Will swallowed hard. *Holy Mother, she'll ruin me for sure.* "Would ye prefer me to stand as well?"

"No, I think it will work just as well from where we are."

"Aye, get on with it, then." He did as she asked and closed his eyes, just wanting to get it over with. *Ye deserve it, Will Foster, for ye acted nae better than Ian.*

Will's eyes popped open as the warmth of her lips caressed his own. He'd expected pain to explode in his groin, not the pleasant sensation of her mouth seeking his. Ripples of excitement caused his thighs to ache, arousing the need he'd been trying so hard to subdue. If she was going to kick him in the bollocks, this was a strange way to go about it. His lips parted of their own volition, and he closed his eyes once more, his hand rising to cup the back of her head.

Lord, if ye mean to take me, please to do it now, for I'll die happy in her arms.

All too soon, she pulled away, and Will opened his eyes to see her kneeling over him, a touch of mischief in her smile.

"So I take it ye're no' planning on wedding Ian anymore, then."

"No! And for the record, that was all my Uncle Geordie's idea anyway. I liked Ian all right, but I was certainly never in love with him. My father was ready to go to blows over it if necessary, but then he was killed, and I . . ."

Her voice trailed off, and Will dropped his arm so that it rested around her shoulders. How he longed for her, but did she really want him, or was it

403

all just a test? Only one way to find out. Either she'd return his embrace or she'd give him a right skelp in the lugs. One way or the other, he had to know.

Taking another deep breath, he began to lean forward, his heart pounding at the thought of her soft, supple lips against his once more. He was so close, moments from ecstasy, when Maggie reached out and touched his shoulder.

"You really need to let me clean that up. It won't take a minute."

Will stared at her, watching in disbelief as she ripped a bit of material from her petticoat and soaked it in some of the golden liquid from the flask.

"This would be easier if you'd take your jack off."

"Aye, I'm sure it would," he replied, having been denied the only real salve he needed. "And 'twould give me the greatest of pleasure to feel yer tender touch against me fevered flesh, but in truth I just need a wee bit of rest."

Maggie pressed her hand against Will's forehead and lifted an eyebrow. "You haven't got a fever, so stop being so dramatic."

"Then leave me to rest a bit, aye, unless ye've something better in mind."

"Are we safe now, Will?" Maggie asked abruptly.

"Safe?" Will shrugged. "As safe as a body can be, I suppose." He put his arm around her shoulder once more, pulling her down beside him and into his embrace. For once, she offered no resistance. "But dinna worry, Maggie Armstrong, for on me life I swear I'll nae let a thing harm ye."

"You once asked for a kiss, Will Foster. A kiss I could not freely offer then. I've granted your request now, though, and were you to ask, I might give another."

His smile broadened. "Would ye do me the honor, lass?"

He leaned over, covering her mouth with his own. Unlike before, Maggie offered no objection. Her fingers no longer clawed at his hair, but gently ran through it as he laid her back amongst the fragrant bluebells to kiss her slender neck.

"I want ye so, Maggie Armstrong." He could barely speak above a whisper. The mere thought of her took his breath away. While he kissed her neck, he tugged at the laces of her bodice, his fingers fumbling with each heavy cord. His persistence was rewarded when the material came loose and her kirtle fell aside.

A ripple of desire ran through him as he pushed down her chemise to caress her fair, plump bosom. He wanted to dive into the warmth of their blossoms, suck at their nectar and feel them harden as he lifted her skirts and plunged himself deep into the guarded sanctuary of her femininity. But he forced himself to move with the gentle hand of a sculptor. Here before him was a work of art, more beautiful than any he'd ever imagined, and he dared not risk harming one inch of its pristine surface. For she was a virgin—he could sense that within his very soul—and so he suckled as light as a babe at the soft pink nipples.

They responded to his tender touch, peaking beneath the moist warmth of his lips. She pressed her hands against his back, her body arching toward him. A virgin she may be, but not so much of an innocent as he suspected.

Maggie answered with a soft gasp as his hand slipped beneath her skirts, but still there was no cry of rebuke. No fear blazed in her eyes, no sickening anger, just a flicker of expectation.

Will slid his fingers up her silken thigh until they reached the apex of her sensuality. A sudden cry of pain stopped him short, and he sprang back.

"What is it, Maggie? Have I hurt ye, lass? I didna mean to, I swear by all that is holy!" Will's heart filled with anxiety as he awaited Maggie's reply, for he feared her answer, feared that he may have mistaken her reaction, or worse yet, that it was all some cruel trick designed to punish him.

"No, I'm fine, but that silly jack of yours is piercing my side." A pale pink glow brightened her cheeks, and with the hint of a smile touching her lips, she began to undo the suede ties that fastened the tough leather of his jerkin.

Will sighed in relief and removed the offending garment at once. Though a sharp, stabbing pain pierced his shoulder, he managed to wince only slightly when it slid across his wound.

"You really should let me put some fresh wrapping on that," she said.

"'Tis fine, darlin', for nae arrow causes me pain." Will brushed her hair back. "'Tis yerself that's inflicted the wound that tears at me heart, and only yer love can heal it."

Maggie started to laugh, but something in his expression must have alerted her to the insult, for she stopped abruptly. "You're serious?"

"Nae, I meant no' a word of it!" Will sat up and grabbed his jack, trying to ignore the dagger that pierced his heart anew. So it was all just a joke. Well, two could play at that game, but even as he started to speak, he couldn't be that harsh, couldn't pretend she was nowt more than another whore for him to conquer.

"I kent what ye were about all along. 'Twas a cruel trick on both our parts."

"Trick? What are you talking about?" Maggie pulled her chemise up over her breast. "You think this was all a joke?"

Will could see the color rising in Maggie's cheeks. Not the pale pink flush of innocence, but the deep hue of unbridled anger.

"You laughed at me expression of love." What was wrong with him? The words had come blurting out, like a lovesick pup. But the deepening color in Maggie's cheeks made him fear she might have some sort of apoplexy right there before him, and so he continued. "This may all have been nowt but sport to you, but 'twas real to me."

So what if she did think him a fool? He'd been called worse by far less beautiful, and in truth he would risk any amount of embarrassment just to hold her in his arms for but a moment.

"Expression of love!" Maggie's color paled to a shy pink. "Oh! I thought . . . I mean, I've never actually heard anybody . . . Why didn't you tell me, Will?"

"I did and was mocked for me troubles."

"No, I mean why didn't you just come out and say it without all the poetry?"

"What difference would it have made? Happin yer heart still belongs to Ian Rutherford, after all, for most maids long to hear sweet words."

"Well, maybe I just want to hear your true feelings. And if you were so worried about Ian, why didn't you warn me about him?"

Will clenched his fists to still his shaking hands. "If ye recall, I did try, lassie, but ye'd have none of it. Yer words cut me deeper than any sword or arrow ever could, nae matter how mighty the warrior, and I was powerless to defend meself."

He groaned as the words passed his lips. She would just laugh again. But this time Maggie didn't mock him. She stared deeply into his eyes, and his breath quickened as she unlaced his linen shirt and ran her hands across his chest.

"Then let me soothe you now, Bonnie Will," she said, her lips touching his once more.

CHAPTER 38

Maggie's hand trembled as she touched Will's warm flesh, his heart pounding against her fingertips. "Do you really care for me, Will, or is this just your way of thanking me for saving your wicked life?"

A spark of silver lit his eyes as once more he laid her back among the wildflowers. He leaned over, brushing his lips against her own, his fingers tugging at the linen chemise. With a muffled groan, he pressed his bare chest against her naked breast, and her nipples prickled with excitement.

She knotted her fingers in his hair, the color of ripe wheat and golden sunshine, and as his arms engulfed her, she melted into them, sighing with pleasure. Never before had she felt so lost in emotion.

Her father's words came to her on the breath of a gentle breeze. *I kent I loved yer ma the moment I saw her.* And now, Maggie realized why, in spite of all the accusations, she could never truly despise Will.

Her lips quivered as Will's tongue touched her own, sending fluttering waves of ecstasy surging down her spine.

He pulled back for a moment, his voice breathless and husky as he whispered in her ear, "If this be gratitude, lass, then I shall seek to thank ye for all eternity."

He fumbled with her skirts, lifting them as he ran his hand up her thigh. The cool damp leather of his breeks chilled Maggie as they brushed along her bare legs, arousing a desire for the naked flesh that lay beneath.

Trailing his lips along her neck, he kissed his way to her breasts, his tongue circling the tips until they piqued beneath its warm, moist touch. As he suckled at her hardened nipples, his hand slid deep along her trembling thighs, teasing them apart until they opened like the petals of a flower. She clutched at his coarse linen shirt, and he slid his hand deeper. His fingers brushed her entry, making her long for the feel of him, until at last he slipped his hand inside her, delicately caressing her gentle folds and releasing charges of unbridled passion.

A cry of desire caught in her throat, and she arched her body toward him. As she did, he pulled his hand away, and for a moment, disappointment surged through her. Had she done something wrong? But then she realized he was fumbling with the ties on his breeks and a new wave of excitement caused her heart to race.

His naked skin burned against her hips as he moved over her. "If ye wish me to stop, all ye need do is ask," he said before he gently slid himself within her.

She gasped slightly as he entered, instinctively running her hands down along his back and pressing him closer until their bodies moved in a rhythmic harmony. Her pulse quickened as he throbbed within her, each movement plunging him deeper, each kiss multiplying the intensity of their desire.

"Am I hurting ye, lass?" He panted the words, his lips brushing against her ear, increasing her hunger.

"A bit, but don't stop." She groaned with pleasure as she sought his lips once more, only vaguely noticing the tiny pricks of discomfort that occurred from time to time as he grew within her.

****

Will glided rhythmically above her dampened form, his body dripping wet with erotic heat, his heart hammering against her heaving breast until it seemed to become one with her own. With an urgency in his kiss, a sweet desperation, he clutched at her hair.

Maggie pressed against his buttocks, encouraging him to thrust deeper and harder, and so he did, his hunger growing with each new assault. The frantic moans of ecstasy mingled with the sounds of nature, urging him on, until finally, in one last passionate lunge, he burst forth within her, filling her with himself, and claiming her as his own.

Maggie lay with bits of heather in her hair. The most beautiful creature Will had ever seen.

His breath was still quick as he leaned over once more to touch her gentle lips, and she sighed softly.

"Will ye marry me, Maggie Armstrong, and claim me as yer husband?"

"Yes, if you'll have me after all the horrible things I've said and done."

"Ye believed in what ye said, lass. Ye canna be faulted for that." Will settled on his back, holding Maggie's head to his chest.

"But I could have gotten you killed," she said.

"And how was that? Ye told the truth, even when ye kent it might mean yer father's death went unavenged."

"I could have said you didn't do it. I could have ended it before it even started."

"Did ye ken that for sure, lass?" Will tilted his head to look into Maggie's dark honey eyes.

She huffed a sarcastic laugh. "No, I didn't see who did it. If I had, I would have castrated the bastard myself."

Will's eyes widened, a touch of laughter in his voice. "Well then, 'tis best ye didna see. They'd have burned ye for such as that."

"It's a good thing you saved me, then, isn't it? Not that I deserved it. I'm so sorry."

"Ach, for what, lassie? If ye said I didna do it, ye would have been lying. I swore me innocence, by God above me and my part of paradise, and that should have been word enough. But for Ian's protests, it would have been."

"Oh, Will, when I think how I almost—"

"Then dinna think on it, darlin'," Will said. "Think only of us and the future we'll have together."

"The future . . ." Maggie smiled sadly.

"What is it, lass? What troubles ye so?"

"Nothing, not anymore, not as long as I'm with you."

Will leaned over and wet her lips with a kiss, then he lay down upon her and filled her once more, pressing their bodies to one another so that nothing could come between them.

There was a happiness that embraced him as they lay exhausted on a blanket of wildflowers, Maggie's soft rosy cheek against the warmth of his chest. They lay there caressing each other tenderly, exploring each other's bodies, as the sweet sound of the thrush sang in the distance, until sleep finally overcame them both.

****

Will rose with a start to the sound of distant thunder. His sudden movement caused Maggie to stir as well, and she sat up with a sigh of contentment.

"It sounds like a storm's coming. We should find some cover, I guess." She stretched wearily, pulling the chemise up over her shoulders, but Will's attention was elsewhere.

"'Tis no' thunder, Maggie," he said. "Get yerself together, lass. We've got to ride."

The alarm in Will's voice made his meaning all too clear, and Maggie fumbled to put her clothing right. "My family! They've come to get me."

"I'm no' sure," Will said as he buckled on his sword, stopping cold as a flock of peewits took to the air. They were too late. The horsemen were already upon them.

God's teeth! He should have known better than to let himself be taken off guard. With nothing to do but stand his ground, he pulled Maggie to her feet, shoving her behind him before turning to face the oncoming riders. The thick morning mist obscured his vision, prompting him to react more cautiously then he might have under ordinary circumstances.

"Be ye friend or foe, sir?" he said, hoping his voice sounded steadier than his nerves felt.

"Well now, that all depends on how nice ye are to us, laddie," a harsh muffled voice answered slowly.

Will's blood turned cold as he listened to what seemed to be a coarse Scottish tongue. "We've nowt to offer ye," he said. "We were on our way home and were waylaid by some outlaws."

"Ah, right! Be the rogues Scot or be they English?" the cold voice queried.

"Neither, sir, for they spoke with a strange tongue." No sense alienating either side until he knew where he stood.

"Outlanders, then, lad?"

"Aye, sir. That they were." The knuckles on Will's hand had turned as hard and white as marble. Not for one second did he believe these were innocent travelers just passing by, and he had every intention of being ready to strike when the time came.

Will could hear snickering in the background, and his temper flared. The rogues were just taunting him, having some fun before they attacked. He'd had enough of that. If they were going to kill him, he wasn't about to be made a fool of in the bargain. He began to slip his sword from its scabbard, whispering softly to Maggie as he did.

"When I draw me weapon, lass, ye mount the hobbler and ride south as fast as ye can."

"But, Will—" Maggie began to protest, but he cut her short.

"Do as ye're told, lass!" The words came out harsh and cold, but seeing the flash of anger in Maggie's eyes, he added on a softer note, "Please, darlin'. Ye saved me once today, now let me do the same for ye."

"What's that ye say, laddie?" The mist-shrouded rider called out again, suppressed laughter flavoring his tone.

"What is it ye want of us?" Will's temper was stretched to the limits.

"A bit of what ye've had will do fine," the man said. "Waylaid indeed! Perhaps a kiss from the wee lass will cool me appetite."

"Lay a hand on her and ye'll no' have a hand left." Will drew his sword with one hand, his dagger with the other. He nudged Maggie toward the horse, but before she could take a step, another group of riders rode up and blocked her way. Instinctively, he positioned himself in front of her once more, holding his weapons out before him. His breath was quick, but his jaw was set and his eyes steady.

"What's going on here, Bonnie Will?" one of the newly arrived horseman inquired.

"Walt? Who's that with ye?" Will's voice held a curious mixture of relief, confusion, and anger.

"'Tis yer cousin Dick, playing games again, I fear," Walt said.

Will could feel the heat rising in his face. "Whoreson, I'll drag ye off that hobbler and flog ye meself."

"Oh, calm yerself, Willie lad," Dick Foster said, though he could barely stop laughing. "We were only having some fun. After all, it looks like ye've been having a bit yerself."

Will threw his weapons on the ground and charged through the heavy morning mist. Without a second thought, he yanked Dick from his horse, holding him steady while he landed a blow on his cousin's jaw. Dick responded in kind, and the two fought bitterly, matching blow for blow. Not even Maggie's pleas or Walt's attempt at restraint could separate them.

"Ye'll watch yer tongue, Dick of the Loch." Will pushed his foot against his cousin's chest after finding himself shoved to the ground.

"Since when are ye so concerned about that Scottish wench?" Dick landed a blow to Will's stomach. "Taking Ian Rutherford's leftovers now, are ye?"

"Filthy swine!" Will gasped, trying to catch his breath. "If yer own woman was as pure as me Maggie, she'd have better sense than to be with the likes of ye."

Will was just about to throw his cousin into a gorse bush when out of nowhere came a resounding bellow, and instantly both young men stopped fighting.

"What in the name of all that's holy!" his father roared. "If you two weans want to fight that sorely, there be a group of Armstrongs back aways that'd be more than happy to oblige ye. Last I seen, though, they were haring off toward home in their stocking feet."

His father chuckled before turning his attention back to the matter at hand. "Now, William, would ye mind telling me what ye're doing with that lass!"

"Can ye no' figure that one out for yerself, Graham?" Tom Foster asked with a mischievous grin.

Will moved back to Maggie's side and retrieved his sword, just in case one of the rascals should take the taunts beyond mere words.

"That's no' what I meant, Brother," his father said before turning back to Will. "An answer now, laddie, and mind, I'm in nae mood for one of yer tales."

"She saved me life. I swear on me dagger 'tis nae tale." His jack had become oddly uncomfortable, and he fidgeted with the collar. "Her kin were bound on drowning me for the murder of Rabbie Armstrong. Maggie put a stop to it right enough, but in doing so secured her own death should she ever return to Scotland."

His father took a deep breath, letting it out in such a long, slow stream Will thought he'd surely deflate before he was done. Finally, he scrubbed his hand across his face.

"Well then, what do ye propose we do with the lass?"

"I love her, Da, and we plan to wed." Will clenched his fists, awaiting the flurry of jibes and laughter that was sure to follow.

"What's that ye say, lad?" Dick taunted. He wiped a drop of blood from under his nose and spit into the dirt. "I didna quite get it."

An intense heat rose in Will's face once more. This was not the way he'd planned on informing his family of his intent. He was used to fighting battles and winning the hearts of the local lassies. Had spent many a night in the arms of a beautiful maid, yet as daylight broke, he'd be on his way to conquer another. But this was different. This morn, as the sun hovered just below the horizon, he had no desire to find another mistress, and now half his family was standing there, waiting for Bonnie Will Foster to admit it was he who had finally been conquered.

"Well, lad," Walt said, "speak up. Or shall we let Johnnie Hetherington have a go at her?"

Will put a protective arm around Maggie's waist and clutched her to himself, holding his sword out before him. "So much as try, Brother, and I'll ruin the lot of ye."

"Stand down!" Graham's voice cracked with anger. He took a deep breath, visibly calming his temper, the tips of his ears gradually paling to a deep pink.

"Now, William," he said, "ye say ye wish to wed the lass, and yet nae more than a day or two ago ye wanted nowt to do with her, nor she ye."

"Aye, Da, I do." Will took Maggie's hand and pulled her even closer.

"And what have you to say about that, lass?" Graham asked, his eyebrow lifted in curiosity. "As I recall, ye were about scratching me Will's eyes out, or have ye forgotten 'tis yer own kin we're feuding with?"

"I no longer have any family except for Will." Maggie laid her head on Will's shoulder. "And with all my heart and soul, I love him."

Will stood firm, determined to convince his father that their feelings were more than just a passing fancy, whether it be by word or the sword.

His father seemed surprised by Maggie's answer. He stroked his beard, his brows low over his eyes, until at last he nodded and heaved a weary sigh.

"Then ye have a family with us, lass. Now the two of ye make yerselves decent afore yer mother gets sight of ye."

"Aye, Da," Will straightened his clothes. Then, turning to Maggie, he whispered in her ear, "Me mother will make ye a fine new dress, darlin'. I'm sorry for ruining this one, but I'm no' sorry for what we've done."

Maggie blushed a bright shade of pink, but she gave a demure nod, a golden sparkle twinkling in her warm brown eyes.

"Ye ken if the warden hears tell of this . . ." Graham said, shaking his head wearily. "If he disna agree, Will . . ."

"I'll marry her anyway."

"And ye'll hang by yer neck, lad," Walt warned his brother. "To marry a Scotswoman without the warden's approval, and a fugitive at that, can only bring a sentence of death. Ye speak of true March treason here, Will."

"When did that ever bother ye, Walt Foster?" Will said. "Surely no' when ye bedded Davy Scott's daughter up near Redeswire. Did ye think me so young I didna hear the stories of yer misspent youth?"

Walt scratched his beard, the hint of a smile visible beneath the whispers. "Bedding is one thing, lad, wedding another."

"Aye, and both will get ye the halter just as sure," Will countered, having no intention of letting some distant threat deter him from following his heart.

"Aye, true enough." Walt laughed as he rode over and gave Will an amiable nudge. "They will that."

"We've a handfast to prepare for, then," Graham said. "Now mount up and take yer lassie home, eh?"

Will did as his father instructed, pulling Maggie up in front of him, and together they followed the ragged mass of men on their way home. There were a few amongst them who continued to grumble about letting the Armstrongs slip through their fingers, but most just seemed happy to have him back unharmed and thought it best to leave that battle for another day.

Not all news was welcome, though. As they rode along, Dylan came up beside them. Tears shone in his eyes, but he blinked them away. "I'm so sorry, Maggie. Eddie's dead."

Maggie gasped and began to sob, and though Will held her to his chest, comforting her, he couldn't help feel a bit uneasy. Eddie had acknowledged they'd known each other, but just how close was their relationship? He needed to choose his words carefully, lest he cause offense.

"Eddie mentioned ye were acquainted, but I didna realize he meant so much to ye."

Maggie nodded, but it was Dylan who answered.

"He was an uncle to Maggie, and a father to me. I'm sorry we kept it from you, Will, but with all that was going on . . ."

Will chuckled to himself. "Well, I reckoned 'twas more than a casual acquaintance when Maggie raced down the turnpike to get to ye, nearly knocking three men twice her size out of the way in the process."

"Why didn't you say anything?"

"I've been a wee bit occupied, if ye havena noticed." Will hugged Maggie all the tighter, kissing her neck and whispering soothing words. "I'm so sorry, darlin'. We'll ride out to avenge him."

At last, Maggie wiped the tears away. "No! Eddie wouldn't have wanted that. Let's end it here."

"Whatever ye wish, darlin'," Will said, though he cast a glance in Dylan's direction, knowing her wish was not likely to come true. It just wasn't the way things worked on the Borders.

CHAPTER 39

Maggie still wasn't quite comfortable with the Fosters or their kin. After all, not more than a day or two before there were those among them who'd been ready to ravish her themselves. From the look on some of their faces, there probably still were. How could she be sure they would treat her any differently now?

She'd expected Eddie to be there to guide her and advise her, but now . . . Except for Dylan, she was set afloat in a sea of strangers, not sure of their intentions or their feelings toward her, save for Will, of course. She snuggled back against his chest, resting her hand on his thigh as if just touching him could somehow protect her.

Will must have sensed her insecurities. Taking the reins in one hand, he wrapped his arm around her waist and pressed his lips against her hair. "I love ye, Maggie Armstrong, and I swear I'll die afore I let anyone harm ye, be they kin or no'."

Maggie sighed as she laid her head back upon his shoulder. Though she still missed her father terribly, and Edward's death was a loss she hadn't expected, the void she'd felt with Ian had been filled. There in Will's arms, she found a completeness she never thought possible, a serenity that embraced her very being and eased the loneliness that haunted each night. Feeling more content than she had in a very long time, she gazed out across the purple fells and dreamed of the happiness that lay ahead.

Dylan rode on ahead, a sly smile on his lips, while Walt circled around behind them, shaking his head and chuckling to himself. Will's father brought up the rear, shouting out orders and keeping them all moving. He had a quiet authority about him, unlike Geordie, who bellowed directions like a fishmonger selling his wares.

The ride went much faster than it had on her first visit, and by the time they rode up to the Foster stronghold, the mist had melted away and the sun shone bright across the barmekin wall. How different it looked in the daylight, with the warmth of Will's love embracing her heart. Not the foreboding tower she remembered, but a stately structure whose rough-hewn stones glistened like jewels in the early morning light. A small stream babbled along quietly just to the north, beckoning the gentle hills of purple heather that surrounded it in a bed of velvet.

They had barely ridden through the barmekin gate when Maggie heard a voice that made her heart stand still. Somehow she was more nervous about this encounter than any other.

"Will, me lad!" Betty Hetherington said. "Lovit be God, ye've come home to us safe and sound." She started to run toward them but stopped about three feet away, her hands on her hips. "But why have ye brought that minx with ye again? Has she no' caused us enough grief?"

"She saved me life, Ma." Will jumped down from the saddle, then reached up to help Maggie off the chestnut pony. "But more than that, I love her, and she loves me."

"Ye love her! She nearly gets ye killed, and ye say ye love her." The look on Betty's face was incredulous. She clearly didn't believe her ears. Reaching out, she pushed Will's hair out of the way to reveal the knot on his head. "Hmph! Too much beating about the heid, I say."

"Now, darlin'," Graham said, the hint of a smile tickling the corner of his mouth. "We've all seen far worse than that wee bump."

Betty whirled around. "God's with ye, Graham Foster." Though her voice was stern, the light in her eyes belied the threat in her voice. "If anything had happened to me Will, I'd have flogged ye for sure." She stood staring up at her husband, hands held akimbo on her hips and eyes mere slits in her otherwise pleasant face.

"And what would ye like to flog me with, mistress?" Graham grinned as he jumped down from his hobbler to put his arm around his wife.

"No' now, Husband." Though she swatted Graham's arm, a coy sparkle lit her eye. "There's a dress here needs fixing afore every one of ye worthless ruffians lose yer eyes. Come on, then, lass."

Maggie followed Will's mother into the large thatch-and-stone cottage that stood next to the peel. It looked warm and comfortable inside, maybe not by twentieth-century standards, but certainly as far as the sixteenth-century border was concerned.

"Me Will do this?" Betty asked, her tone sharp as she pointed to the torn chemise.

"It got torn in the foray," Maggie said as the heat rose in her cheeks once more.

"Hmm." Betty nodded, but a quick lift of her eyebrow told Maggie she didn't believe that for a moment. She seemed perfectly willing to let it go for the time being, however. "So ye saved me Will's life, did ye, and how was that?"

Maggie followed the woman up the stairs to a comfortable-looking chamber. "They'd charged him with my father's murder and my kidnapping and planned on drowning him right there. I couldn't let that happen."

"And why no'? Surely ye had enough hate for him when ye were last here." She opened a trunk at the foot of the bed and pulled out a pretty blue gown and gray kirtle.

"That was before I knew the truth," Maggie said, "and saw what Ian Rutherford really was capable of."

"Turned ye away, did he?" Betty scoffed. "Well, get those things off. I may be able to salvage something."

The temperature in Maggie's cheeks was rising steadily, but she did as the woman instructed. "Not exactly. He was more than willing to marry me, but only for my dowry and to gain influence with my family. Not a very good reason for marriage."

"As good as any, I suspect."

"Not for me!" Maggie said, forgetting herself. "I think two people should love and respect each other before they marry." She wanted to add, '*the way you and your husband do*, but refrained, thinking how terribly forward such a statement would be.

"The way ye loved Ian Rutherford, ye mean," Betty said, her voice thick with contempt at the mention of his name.

"No! I don't know what I felt for Ian, but I didn't know him well enough to call it love. Attraction, maybe," she added begrudgingly. "But what does it matter? He wasn't the person I thought he was."

"Oh, and now ye've discovered Ian's true motives, me Will's good enough for ye, is he?" Betty seemed to be deliberately trying to pick a fight, but Maggie wasn't going to let her.

"No, that's not what I meant at all. I think I've always loved Will, but I was to be betrothed to Ian—through no fault of my own, I might add— and Will was my sworn enemy. Come to think of it, that was through no fault of my own either."

"So what's changed yer mind about that, then?" Betty's eyes were narrow slits again, but this time there was no loving light behind them, only a wariness that convinced Maggie she was facing an uphill battle. A battle she had every intention of winning.

"At the water, with death at his door, Will never wavered, and I could see the truth in his eyes. I know you must hate me, but . . ."

"Will loves ye, so I'll accept ye at that, but I'll tell ye now, I dinna trust ye, no' as yet, anyway. So tread lightly."

With that, Betty handed Maggie the gray kirtle, but as she did a frown creased her forehead anew, and she sighed. "We'd best get to the handfast afore too long, I see, elst folks will be talking. Now step out of that petticoat as well. A little soaking will take care of that stain."

Maggie's cheeks were on fire. She'd never been so embarrassed in her life. The woman barely tolerated her as it was. Now she'd probably see her as nothing more than a common slut. What if she convinced her husband to forbid her marriage to Will? A sob caught in her throat and came out sounding more like a disoriented hiccup.

Betty closed the chest and sat down on it. "Did he force himself on ye, lass?"

Maggie's jaw dropped. "Will? No, it just happened."

Betty sighed again and got up. "Right then. If ye're to be part of this family, lassie, ye'll take on yer fair share of the chores as well."

"Yes, of course." Maggie followed the woman back downstairs.

"Go down to the stream, then, and fetch some water. And dinna be dawdling along the way, aye."

Maggie grabbed a large wooden bucket and started across the courtyard, glad to be out of the cottage and Betty's scrutiny. She hadn't gone more than a few yards, though, when Will jumped out and pulled her into the stable.

"Have ye a kiss for yer intended, wench?"

"Not now, Will." Maggie giggled, more than willing to give in, but she thought better of it and gave him a gentle peck on the cheek.

"And what was that supposed to be? A poor excuse for a kiss, I'd say."

"Ye'll have to wait for more," Maggie said. "I've chores to get done, and I don't think your mother will take kindly to me tarrying along the way, especially with you. She knows we've already . . . You know."

But Will wasn't listening at all. He pulled her close and kissed her as if he feared he would never have the chance again.

Maggie dropped the empty bucket on the hay-covered ground and laid her hands upon the smooth leather of his doublet. "Your mother, Will." She pushed him away for a moment, protesting halfheartedly, but Will only pulled her back and kissed her deeper and more fervently.

"There'll be time enough for that after the vows are said, Will Foster!" Betty shouted from the doorway, her arms knotted across her chest. "Now leave the lass be and let her get back to her work. She's chores need doing, and so have you, I'd wager."

"Aye, Ma!" Will grinned mischievously before stealing one more kiss to bid him on his way.

****

Betty Foster walked back to the cottage, a spring in her step and a smile of contentment on her lips. Though she was not about to admit it, she liked Maggie and was pleased that the young Scotswoman had finally seen the evil in Ian Rutherford. She was even more delighted that Maggie had fallen for her fair-haired boy. Though how could a girl not be enchanted by such a handsome young lad?

"She's no' half-bad for all that," Graham said. He was sitting at the large kitchen table, picking at a piece of stale bread, a tall tankard of ale by his side.

"And when did you sneak in here?" Betty asked.

"Since when do I need to be sneaking into me own home?"

The stocky reiver grabbed her around the waist and pulled her down on his lap. Even in his mid-sixties, he was still a handsome man. His dark hair was peppered with strands of silver now, but Betty had loved him for as long as she could remember and always would.

"Since we've both work to be doing," she said, though she knew well her harsh tone would never fool him. Instead, she kissed him long and hard before pressing her hands against his broad shoulders and wriggling out of his grasp.

Graham grinned. "Ye admit I'm right, though, eh?"

She shrugged, feigning indifference as she brushed down her rumpled skirts. "Perhaps she'll do, though the test will come when the Armstrongs ride against us." She glanced out through the barmekin gate and sighed. "Ye ken they will, Graham. She's still one of their kin, nae matter what she's done."

Graham scrubbed his hands over his handsome face—and it was still handsome, Betty thought as she refilled his tankard. She knew he realized what was to come, but there was something more on her mind.

"Perhaps we should send our Annie ower to the Hethingtons. Catte will take good care of her, and she'll be safe from Ian Rutherford, that lecherous swine. By rights, he should be dancing under the gibbet for what he did, not claiming a lass as fine as our Maggie for his own."

Graham's eyebrow shot up, his smile broadening. Betty knew exactly what he was thinking and slapped him across the shoulder with her dish cloth. "All right, I'll admit, she does seem like a fine lass. She is Rabbie Armstrong's wean after all, and from what I saw, he was still a fine specimen of a man."

Graham threw his head back and let out a hearty laugh. "D'ye think to make me jealous, wife? I may have to put ye ower me knee."

Betty's eyes crinkled in a smile. "Ye could try, I suppose, but ye'll no' win me affections that way."

"It might be fun trying, though."

"Aye, that it might," she said as she headed for the stairs.

Graham took a quick gulp of ale and followed his wife's lead.

EPILOGUE

Walt noticed Johnnie Hetherington watching from the shadows, quiet as a serpent. "Something ye need, Johnnie o' Dell?" he asked as he surprised the dark-haired rogue.

"Nae, Walt, just resting me eyes afore starting home."

"I thought ye'd be spending the night," Walt said, "seeing ye came all this way."

"Aye, 'twas me plan at first," Johnnie said. "I'd a mind to go on to Hexham for the market, but a good night's sleep and a buxom woman in me bed are more to me liking, I think."

"Well, I can offer ye a good night's rest, but I fear ye'll have to look elsewhere for the woman." Walt spoke casually, though they both knew his words held an unspoken warning. "There's no' a lass here'll give ye a turn of the head."

"Aye, such rumors they spread about me," Johnnie said, a forced laugh in his voice.

"Rumors?" Walt raised an eyebrow but stopped short of an outright insult. "Aye, well, ye'd best take care if ye're meaning to cross the Wastes while the sun's so high."

"Ach! I'll be fine." Johnnie snorted. "'Tis in me blood."

Walt nodded, and after bidding his cousin on his way, he headed off toward the peel. His eyes followed Johnnie through the barmekin gate and across the small burn, finally losing sight of the rogue as he mounted a distant knoll. There was something wicked about that one, but then that was no surprise to anyone. A nagging suspicion kept tugging at Walt's gut, though, one he couldn't quite explain. All he did know was that Johnnie Hetherington was up to something, and that didn't bode well for Walt or his family.

GLOSSARY

Afeard: afraid

Afore: before

Alnwick: headquarters of the English Middle March

Aqua vita: whisky

Bairn: babe

Bannock: unleavened, round, flat loaf made of oat or barley meal

Barmekin: defensive stone wall surrounding a peel tower along the Borders

Bastle house: fortified farmhouse

Beacon: part of a network of signal fires situated on towers and hillsides that warned of approaching raiders

Benefit of clergy: blessing of the Church

Bide: stay

Bill: charge or complaint

Blethering: incessant, foolish talk

Blood feud: a lengthy conflict between families involving a cycle of retaliatory killings or injury

Bollock dagger: a kind of dagger carried by the Border Reivers

Braw: fine, beautiful, attractive, grand, admirable

Brae: hill

Breeks: breeches

Broken man: man who was declared an outlaw and whose family would not stand surety for him

Bucking tubs: tubs used to soak clothes in lye or urine to remove stains

Burgonet: an open helmet, usually having a peak and hinged cheek pieces

Burn: stream

Cannot see the daylight till him: basically he's Betty's "blue eyed" boy and can do no wrong.

Canny – pleasant, nice, good judgment

Clype: tattletail

Dale: valley

Day of Truce: when opposing wardens met to dispense justice and resolve differences

Docking the dell: having sex with a woman

Drowning hole: cheap and quick means of execution in any river

Fash: worry

Fechting: fighting

Fell: hill

Gallowsbreid: one who deserves to hang

Garderobe: bathroom

Gibbetted: left hanging on the gallows (gibbet) for public viewing

Gob: mouth

Greeting: crying

Handfast: trial marriage or betrothal binding for one year, after which each party could decide to   stay together or part.

Happin: mayhap, perhaps, maybe

Harebell: Scottish bluebell

Haud: hold

Haud yer wheesht: be silent

Heath: an area of open uncultivated land

Heid: head

Heidsman: head of the family

Hobbler: Border horse

Hot trod: legal raid in retribution for an offense

Ideot: idiot

Jack: a sleeveless tunic worn for protection, made of thick quilted material, sometimes with pieces of metal sown between the layers of cloth.

Jedburgh axe: an axe with a distinctive round cutting edge

Keek: peek

Kye: cattle

Latch: a small, light crossbow

Lea: an open area of grassy or arable land

Lug: ear

March: Border district between England and Scotland; each district was divided into three Marches: the East, Middle, and West

Midden: dunghill

Neb: nose

Outlander: one from outside the Borders

Peel tower: fortified tower house

Pend: undercroft

Plaid: blanket

Plucking her plum tree: taking a woman's virginity

Put to the horn: declared an outlaw and could be hung on sight

Red hand: basically caught with the goods or in the act.

Sard: intercourse

Scumfishing: the practice of stacking straw against the entryway of a peel tower and setting it afire in order to smoke the inhabitants out into the open.

Shedding her shanks: having sex with a woman

Shieling: hut

Skelp: slap

Skelp in the lugs: slap across the ears

Surety: to take responsibility for someone's appearance or debts at the Day of Truce

Swive: to have sexual intercourse

Tawse: a leather strap divided at the end into two or more lashes

Trip step: an uneven step built into the turnpike intended to unbalance attackers storming the tower

Turnpike: a circular staircase used to access upper floors in a tower

Undercroft: basement or ground floor

Wagging a wand in the water: a waste of time

Wame: stomach

Wastes: the Bewcastle Wastes, a bleak, desolate area of fells and moors used by reivers as a hiding place

Wean: wee one, child

Widdie: gallows or gibbet

Yett: hinged iron gate

Made in the USA
San Bernardino, CA
05 December 2019

60944137R00263